PRAISE FOR

Trouble the Water

"... will seize readers from the first page and not let go."
—Kirkus Reviews

"With compelling characters, a charming peek into Charleston society, a heart-racing romance, rich historical detail, and an epilogue that will have you holding your breath, Friedland has written a well-crafted novel that will stay with you long after you turn the final page."
—Susie Orman Schnall, award-winning author of *The Subway Girls*, *The Balance Project*, and *On Grace*

"Friedland is a modern Bronte sister remixed with Kathleen Grissom or Leila Meacham. *Trouble the Water* is the riveting story of Abby, who travels across the sea, fleeing Liverpool, poverty, and an unsavory uncle, for Charleston, where a wealthy friend of her father, Douglas, lives. Douglas has pledged himself to the fight to end slavery, and for that, he has made the ultimate sacrifice. Abby fights inner demons and tries to find her place in Charleston high society while her brooding guardian reconciles the past and returns to his beloved cause. Lovers of Civil War-era historical fiction will rejoice at Friedland's triumphant novel of love, friendship, and the most important issues of the day."
—Bethany Ball, author of *What to do About the Solomons*

"The complicated history of the antebellum South comes alive in Friedland's debut novel and offers readers an exciting and fast-paced literary journey that explores complicated relationships, the importance of friendship, and the necessary power of love."
—Kris Radish, best-selling author of
A Dangerous Woman from Nowhere

"With a plucky heroine, a dashing hero, and the backdrop of the clandestine abolition movement in the antebellum South, Jacqueline Friedland masterfully weaves a tale full of passion and honor, duty and survival, evil and the beauty of basic human decency. *Trouble the Water* will make your heart pound and swell, and keep you reading well into the night. Highly recommended!"

—Loretta Nyhan, author of *I'll Be Seeing You, All the Good Parts,*
and *Digging In*

"In a narrative tapestry woven of brilliant threads of history and drama, Jacqueline Friedland introduces her readers to seventeen-year-old British-born Abigail Milton; her generous but reluctant benefactor, Douglas Elling; and the complex world of antebellum Charleston. The evil of slavery, the nascent abolitionist movement, and the courage of an operative of the underground railroad are explored against the background of the vanished world of debutante cotillions, social intrigue, and the slow maturity and melding of skillfully drawn protagonists. Friedland's research is impeccable, her writing fluid. *Trouble the Water* is that rare pedagogic novel that engages as it teaches."

—Gloria Goldreich, author of *The Bridal Chair*

TROUBLE

THE

WATER

TROUBLE

THE

WATER

A Novel

JACQUELINE FRIEDLAND

Published by SparkPress, a BookSparks imprint,
A division of SparkPoint Studio, LLC
Tempe, Arizona, USA, 85281
www.gosparkpress.com

Published 2018

Printed in the United States of America

ISBN: 978-1-943006-54-0 (pbk)
ISBN: 978-1-943006-55-7 (e-bk)

Library of Congress Control Number: 2017959097

Book Design by Stacey Aaronson

To Jason
For always being sure

I

∽

CHARLESTON, SOUTH CAROLINA
1842

ouglas urged his horse onward at a feverish pace, gripped
by panic that his wife might have been taken, or his
daughter. The evening's vacant streets worked in his favor as the
animal tore across the cobblestones, racing furiously toward his
estate. The horse huffed and spat, sweating into the moonlight,
as Douglas struggled to focus on speed, rather than on his
dread. Rounding the corner onto Lightbourne Street, where
candlelight emanated from the windows of quiet houses, he had
the sudden thought that it couldn't be today. Whatever that distasteful man, Wilson Bly, meant by the threat, Douglas told himself, it wouldn't be this very same day when he had only just
been alerted to the possibility of danger. He began to relax
slightly, feeling added relief now that he was so close to home.
He eased up on the horse, slowing to a trot and patting the animal's hide in recognition of its exertion.

He and the horse continued east at a lighter pace, and
Douglas inhaled deeply, trying to calm his racing heart. As the
humid air filled his lungs, he caught the scent of smoke, sudden
and sour. His alarm returned afresh, beastly in its force. Digging
his heels into the horse's sides, he urged the animal to resume its

breakneck pace. They barreled across the remainder of Light-bourne, and Douglas began to detect the din of disaster, shouts, and clamor from afar. As the horse cut onto Meeting Street, Douglas was greeted by a vision that would terrorize him the rest of his days.

The Elling estate was alight against the dark night in roaring, spitting flames. Fire was bursting forth from the east side of the house, licking its way up the walls, reaching its hands skyward, like crackling, roaring calls of prayer. There were people running every which way, bodies emerging and disappearing behind the fog of smoke in a frenzied crush as they tried to help manage the fire.

Douglas searched the crowd for his family as he rode onward, forcing the horse toward the fire. "Sarah! Cherish! They could still be inside!" He shouted into the air of the maddened crowd around him. At the perimeter of the property he jumped from his horse, still screaming as he rushed toward the flames. "Sarah! Cherish!"

"No, Mr. Elling!" The family butler ran out from the masses, from the darkness, and grabbed Douglas's coattails, trying to hold him where they stood at the edge of the drive.

"Jasper! Oh, thank God! Where are my girls?" Douglas shouted over the popping and crackling of the fire.

"Please, Mr. Elling, there is nothing we can do now. Come with me, to safety." Jasper pulled Douglas's arm, trying to move him back toward the street, toward the faceless crowd of onlookers.

"No, take me to Sarah!" Douglas shouted again. "Where are they?" His voice was eclipsed by the sound of roof crumbling into the house below it.

"Mr. Elling, I am so sorry!" Jasper leaned close and shouted into Douglas's ear to be heard over the commotion.

"The market! I was out at the market!" He shouted that again, as if his prior whereabouts were the main focus.

"I am so sorry, sir!" Jasper was repeating himself, his bursting words nearly meaningless to Douglas. Though if the man was shouting, Douglas reasoned, Sarah and Cherish must be safe. People didn't shout at times of death. There was no comfort in shouted words.

"Where are they?" Douglas pressed, his eyes searching the darkness.

"Sir, they didn't make it out."

Douglas looked blank faced at Jasper. Then with a sudden start, he began running toward the house again.

"No, Mr. Elling!" Jasper shouted, racing behind Douglas.

A male house servant appeared from out of the bedlam, catching Douglas by the arm.

"No, Mr. Elling! You can't! There ain't nothing you can do now. You'll never make it out."

"Let go of me, Demett!" Douglas bellowed. "I have to save my family!"

"Mr. Elling!" Demett shouted back, holding firm to Douglas's arm, and motioning for other bystanders to help restrain his employer. "The mistress and little miss, they went inside not long before the fire started," Demett explained as three other men, strangers, joined in detaining Douglas, their hands and arms straining against the force of his determination. "Time we saw the flames, me and the boys in the stables, we couldn't do nothing about it. I come running over, but up by Miss Cherish's bedroom was blazing the worst. They must have started the fire just underneath, probably in your study, sir."

"Demett!" Douglas roared. "Let go!" He bellowed as he struggled, pushing and twisting against the men, "Let me go!"

"They wouldn't have made it out in time anyhow," Demett

continued as though he hadn't heard Douglas, as though he was unaware of the droplets of sweat drawing lines on his own soot-covered face. "There ain't nothing you can do, sir," Demett counseled, two hands still gripping Douglas by the arm. "You go in there, you're sure to die. Nobody wants that. Not Miss Cherish nor Mistress Sarah, neither."

Douglas looked from Demett back to his smoldering home, calculating whether there was any hope. He needed to run straight inside the house and rescue Sarah and Cherish, just as he'd rescued so many others before them. He could carry his girls to safety and watch them take big, redemptive gulps of fresh air. It could still be a mistake. They might come running home from the opposite direction at any moment, letting everyone know they hadn't been inside after all.

But as he looked back at the crackling, raging flames and falling timber, he knew Demett was correct. The fire was raging precisely where Sarah and Cherish would have been that evening, the flames too violent, too fast to flee. With all his bravado and blasted ideas of his own invincibility, he had been too late. His five-year-old daughter with her bountiful blonde curls and exasperating will, his brave, sparkling wife—they were gone. They were lost, absent, consumed.

Douglas sensed the air leaving him, the despair curdling into each part of his body as he registered the significance of the words he had been told. He felt the anguish arrive, piece by searing piece, to each vein, every muscle. The agony erupted, turning every bit of him to ash, to paralysis, to nothing. He gazed at the foundering structure that had been his sanctuary, blurred before him because of the smoke, the tears, or perhaps because he would simply never see anything with clarity again. Demett released his hold on Douglas's arm, motioning for the other men to do the same. Douglas thought how Sarah would chide Demett not to give him much room at a time like this. Sarah would have reminded Demett of Douglas's tendency to be impulsive, to be reckless, hotheaded. But now he felt only defeat. He was aware of his bulky frame crumpling onto the gravel beneath them. He saw Demett look to Jasper for guidance on how to proceed with their devastated employer. Jasper simply shook his head.

Douglas absorbed the tableau before him as if observing his own poorly arranged dream. He watched from his knees, motionless in a sea of chaos. It was as if his world had gone silent, as though he was trapped outside a window, watching this impossibly horrific scene, the townspeople with their buckets, attempting to extinguish the firestorm, lest their own houses catch the flames.

Douglas looked at his old friend, Jasper, and then back up at his smoldering home. He recognized a roaring in his soul, and then the world beyond his body faded to nothingness, turned to black, and was gone.

2

∽

CHARLESTON, SOUTH CAROLINA

Three Years Later

1845

bby glanced back toward the empty steamship, her face sticky with sweat and sea dreck, and she wondered again whether this journey hadn't been a grand mistake. She despised Lancashire, but at least there, she wouldn't have been trapped in this stifling Charleston heat, not knowing a soul. It was too late though, and there wasn't any use in wishing that her foul bastard uncle hadn't ruined her, ruined her plans, ruined her England. She edged her brow with her soiled sleeve and scanned the harbor crowds once more, searching for her escort. She had been waiting nearly two hours, watching the crush of people swarming around her while her stomach grumbled for food. Her da had sworn to her—on his only good carving knife— that Douglas Elling would receive her with generosity. She should risk this journey, he had said, and accept Elling's charity, never minding that the man had returned only one of her father's letters in nearly two years.

She had been foolish to hope that life would be any better for her here. Elling had paid for her passage as a first-cabin passenger aboard the ship, but it didn't mean he was upright, just rich enough where the money was of no consequence to him. Abby adjusted the twine in her dark hair, lifted her canvas sack, and hopped off the fence where she had been perched. Best to figure something out already. Still wobbly from weeks on the water, she craved a proper bath and a hot cup of tea. Even a damp cloth to cool herself would have felt like extravagance.

Squinting through the harsh sunlight, she looked toward the storefronts at the far end of the wharf. There were crowds, crowds everywhere, and each person seemed to be hurrying about with such purpose. She made her way through the thrumming horde, consciously dodging eye contact with the men, whites and Negroes alike. She sensed herself disappearing into the sea of people, her worn gray dress rendering her nearly invisible against the women draped in vivid reds and oranges, the men with faces the color of coffee and peanuts, potatoes and milk. Her stomach growled again as she recalled her last meal, so many hours ago, as food stores ran low on the ship.

She was looking for Elling Import & Export, but the only sign she could decipher from a distance read, Auction & Negro Sales. Maneuvering through the soupy air, she ignored the hooting peach sellers calling out about sweet juice and the fancy ladies lurking in nooks, pulling at the men passing by. Abby wasn't certain what she had expected of Charleston, but it wasn't this, this pandemonium. She reached the auction office and peered inside the large picture window. The place was dark, so she straightened her spine and plodded on. She heard an excited yelp down the wharf and turned to see a dark woman running with glee toward a younger Negro man. The woman had dropped her baskets and was shouting chirpy robust words in a language Abby had never heard. As her arms reached out for the fellow, a white man kicked the woman to the ground. Abby felt a twinge, a rising of bile, but she forced the feeling down to that place inside herself where she locked all her suffering. This voyage wasn't about anything but her own survival.

She walked past two more office doors, neither of which seemed like they could belong to Douglas Elling, the man who was supposed to be her new patron saint.

"You lost, darling?" An older gentleman, wearing a bow tie and carrying a folded satchel, materialized from the crowd.

"Could you tell me where to find the office of Elling Export?" she asked, speaking for the first time since her arrival.

"That's an easy one," he answered in a gravelly drawl. "Just three doors on that way." He pointed a finger in the direction she had been walking. "A word to the wise, Miss," the lines in his face folded deeper, "you're better off doing what business you've got elsewhere." He tipped his hat and walked on.

Well, that was all well and good, but where, pray tell, could she go instead? She would not add to her parents' burdens by failing to arrive where she'd been expected. Abby walked on, finding the correct door and pushing it open cautiously. Though the door had been unlocked, the office was empty. Scattered papers and pristine mahogany desks told her that the office was still in use, just unoccupied at present. There were only a couple hours remaining until it would grow dark. Perhaps she could spend the night here and hope someone helpful appeared in the morning. The leather chair in the corner was spacious enough to accommodate her for the night. Better than being left alone outside at the port. She could at least sit and remove her boots if nobody came.

But then she heard muffled voices and sounds of movement, likely from a cellar beneath her. She knew she ought to call out, let someone know she was there. She placed her bag down on the bulky chair, careful to keep quiet, and started for the cellar. The first door she opened revealed only a closet crowded with boxes, so she moved to the door across the room, but again found only a closet, this one stocked with books and papers, inkpots and envelopes. She scanned the large room, turning in a circle until she noticed a tall bookcase askew from the wall, protruding at an inelegant angle. Peering behind the bookshelf, she saw the staircase for which she had been searching. It was like something from the books she had read as a child, when her life had allowed for luxuries like pleasure reading. This stairwell wasn't meant for the public. Abby hardly counted as the public though, did she? Houseguest or charity case that she was.

She'd already waited long enough for the hallowed Mr. Elling to remember fetching her. Elling had been a childhood friend of her father's. More like a much younger brother, her da would say. But what did they know about the man now? Only that his wife and daughter were long dead, and that he'd become something of a bear ever since. The man had made arrangements for her in response to her father's plea. But there wasn't reason to credit any of it. She would not allow herself to be hunted again, not by bear or bastard.

Down the steps she went, doing her damnedest to step lightly so she might catch a glimpse of what lay below her before she announced herself. Curse her factory boots and their clunky soles, made to withstand hours at the weaving loom, never minding how the foot inside felt about it. She managed to creep quietly, reaching the dim landing at the bottom, in time to make out several men huddled at the far side of the cellar. It was too dark to see clearly what they were doing. It looked as though one man was punching another repeatedly in the gut, but the rustling noises didn't match the jolting action. She could hear hurried, hushed conversation, bits about haste and payments.

She wondered if she was walking in on something illegal, gambling, or smuggled goods, which might make sense so near the waterfront. Wouldn't it be just her luck to traverse the entire Atlantic only to find herself with a criminal for a guardian?

She resented the word guardian, almost eighteen, as she was. She promised her parents she would endure this arrangement, though really, she was old enough to be on her own already, more weary and tattered than someone older, too. Presently, she simply wanted to determine where she would be spending her first night, and if she had to interrupt the gathering before her to do that, so be it. As she mustered her courage to call out, everything shifted abruptly before her eyes. There were suddenly only two people remaining in the cellar, as though the others had been consumed by the far wall. Left before her remained a large black man, wide as a bull, and a white man in business clothes, each with his back to her as they continued speaking in murmurs.

"Hello?" Abby finally called from where she stood on the bottom step.

Both men turned swiftly, clearly surprised they were not alone. The white man spoke first.

"My apologies, young lady. Business is generally conducted on the main floor. If you'll just return upstairs, we'll be up momentarily." He spoke professionally, in a crisp British accent, as he hastened toward her.

The fine cut of the man's clothes told her that she had found Douglas Elling. She was disheartened to note his flagrantly neglected personal hygiene, obvious even in the dim light of the cellar. He had a ragged mane of dark overgrown hair spilling to his collar and a shocking abundance of facial hair. Just the sort of beard that would capture wayward tidbits of a meal, where they might remain lost for days. How appropriately fetid.

"I'm Abby. Abby Milton?" She hated herself for sounding timid. "I imagine you are Douglas Elling."

The man stopped as he neared her, where she still stood on the lowest riser, and looked at her blankly. Then as he squinted his eyes against the dull light, Abby saw understanding dawn. "Abigail?" He sounded startled.

She nodded.

"But, you're here now? They said you were arriving on . . .," he trailed off, looking exasperated. "Oh, damn. It was today, then? Demett," he looked toward his companion, "you were to collect her from the pier. I reminded Larissa last week but forgot utterly to tell you. Well, Abigail, come up, and we will get you settled." He studied her a moment longer. "You do look like your mother then, don't you?" He asked, his voice softening.

She didn't answer.

They climbed up to the main office, and Douglas motioned for Abby to sit on a corpulent armchair. She could see now that he was younger than he had appeared in the dark basement, and that his suit, which had looked fine from afar, was rather worn, and ill fitting, too, hanging loosely as though Douglas had once been a larger man. Even so, he had a broad, commanding frame that Abby imagined would be useful in whatever illegal enterprise he was engaged. He looked at her blindly for a moment, as though he had forgotten who she was. She raised her eyebrows in challenge.

"I'm sorry," he began, moving to the larger desk in the room, shuffling papers about. "It's been a busy afternoon with too many loose ends. Regardless, welcome to Charleston, then." He was speaking quickly now. "I'm sorry we left you abandoned like that. Clever of you to find the office. Demett will carry you to the house so you can settle in. Just let him know where you've left your baggage."

"I haven't got any baggage. It's just my sack." She pointed to the canvas bag beside her.

"Oh. Right then." His speech was still hurried, and Abby was unsure whether he was embarrassed by how little she had brought or if he simply wanted to be rid of her. "Well then, hop to. Off you both go."

It shouldn't have surprised her, his disinterest. He had agreed to host her only as a favor to her father, and now here she was expecting a lady's welcome. Clearly it would be paramount for everyone if she stayed out of his way, remained invisible. Despite her parents' promises of benevolence, she saw little advantage that could come from sharing a home with a grumbling widower. Her parents had also promised that advantages would flow from her uncle's benevolence back in Wigan. They had exalted the man over and again, insisting he was so charitable, providing so much for Abby, for her whole family. Well just look how that had turned out.

She thanked Douglas for his hospitality, but he was busy stuffing papers into a large brown envelope, his focus already elsewhere. She looked to Demett, who was reaching for her withered sack.

"I've got it." She snatched the bag from under him. She might be a charity case, but it wasn't as though she was useless. She had usefulness in bloody spades.

Abby followed Demett in silence, walking through a back door of the office to a quiet alleyway where two horses were tethered in front of the waiting coach. Demett reached to help Abby into the carriage, and before she could stop herself, she recoiled from his calloused hand.

"Forgive me for intruding, Miss Abigail," Demett lowered his outstretched arm, "but ain't you never seen colored folk before?"

"Of course, I have," Abby snapped. There were free blacks in Liverpool, but very few in Wigan, where her family had been living since her da's shop flooded. None had worked at the weaving mill, where she'd been spending fourteen hours a day since she was ten years old. It was hardly Demett's color that frightened her anyway. He was actually rather pleasing to look at with his glossy skin and straight white teeth, his hair only beginning to gray at the temples, but all men had the same nasty appetites, and it wasn't possible to know which ones had cruel thoughts in their heads.

"I just don't need anyone carrying my bag for me or helping me climb a step," Abby quipped. "I can handle it just fine on my own. It's how I've always done." She climbed into the coach and fixed her eyes toward the opening of the alley, where she caught a glimpse of another horse-drawn carriage passing by, three ladies rooted inside with pastel parasols obscuring their faces.

"Oh, I see, Miss," Demett answered. "You just want us all to know you ain't nobody's burden."

Abby kept quiet, digesting Demett's perspicacity.

"Well don't you fret," Demett continued cheerfully as he climbed up to the raised bench in front of her. "If helping you around the Elling estate means staying out of your way, I'll do my best."

"Thank you," Abby answered quietly to the back of his wooly head, now contrite. She turned her gaze toward the scenery as they emerged from the alley.

As they drove into an area with fewer shops and more homes, Abby regarded the rows of residences situated neatly together and so close to the street. There were tall houses of red, lavender, alabaster, and pink, different colored shutters on them all. Some had porches wrapping around every floor, while others were protected by dark wrought-iron gates. Women came and went from the homes, perhaps to market, in the most impractical dresses. Hoop skirts double the size of what she remembered from Liverpool.

The carriage finally turned onto another, narrower, street, and Demett guided the horses into a tree-lined gravel drive. "Here we are, Miss."

Abby's breath hitched as she perceived the Elling estate. The red brick home sat at the end of the circular drive, picturesque with arched windows and thick black shutters. It was just how she had pictured homes in the American South, only much, much larger. The house was framed by manicured magnolia trees and bordered on its side by what Abby assumed were the stables. There had been many impressive homes along the short ride from the harbor, but this one dwarfed them all.

Her family's Wigan flat would have fit, in its entirety, on the front porch of this house. It was difficult to grasp that she had forsaken her pallet in the front room, the one she shared with her sister, Gwendolyn, and often Charlie too, for a home such as this. Abby thought about what might be expected of her in exchange for her new housing and fought against the acid rising in her throat. She noticed that the far side of the home had a different look, with brighter bricks, as though it had been constructed only recently, added to the existing structure. What absurdity, she thought, that people with so much space, such amplitude, could feel obliged to add more.

Demett pulled to a halt near the front entrance and jumped off the carriage, reaching out his arm to assist Abby. She hesitated but then smiled politely and placed her hand on his bulky forearm for balance, noticing the dirt beneath her own fingernails.

"You let me know if you need anything, Miss Abigail," Demett told her. "You go on over to the front door and use the big knocker. Otherwise Larissa will never hear you. Normally it'd be Jasper, the butler, who opens the door, but he had to go off on something today." Abby studied the hefty wooden door but did not move towards it.

"You'll like Larissa," Demett encouraged her. "She's been waiting on your arrival ever since your father's letter. You're giving her something fine to do with herself again." He nodded at her in farewell.

The brass knocker, with its engraved E, looked to cost more than her mum earned in a whole year of laundering. Abby felt it was a shame to use something so fine for banging on. She snorted in protest and then knocked three times. She waited but a moment before the door opened, revealing a middle-aged woman of fading beauty and a man who appeared to be the butler, despite Demett's assertions to the contrary.

"Abigail!" The woman seemed inordinately overjoyed. "You've finally arrived. You must be exhausted from your journey. I am Larissa, your governess, and this is Jasper, our butler." The older gentleman nodded at Abby, confirming his identity.

As she showed Abby into the house, Larissa continued talking with refined enthusiasm. "You can't know how thrilled we are to have you here. The house has been horribly quiet for the last few years, ever since the fire. It was coming time for me to take my leave already, until we found out about you, that is." Larissa paused, studying Abby for a moment before adding, "Mr. Elling had given us the impression that a little girl was coming from England, but you clearly are a mature young lady, not a child at all. Rather pretty, too, I suspect," Larissa squinted, "once you get past the rags and dirt you're wearing. Come, let me show you to your room."

Stepping into the front hall, Abby was overcome by the opulence of the home. Never had she seen the likes of it. Not even when they lived in Liverpool, when they spent time with upper-class folk, when they might have been considered upper-class folk themselves. There was gold, mahogany, incandescence, everywhere. In the center of the home, leading up to floors above, was the most magnificent spiral staircase. The marbled stairs appeared to keep winding upward, floating straight into the sky.

Larissa watched Abby's eyes growing wide and told her they would have a grand tour in the morning. Except, the woman added, they would not venture into the east wing, as Mr. Elling had closed off that part of the home after the fire, though he first completely refurbished it. Abby realized that the repaired wing must have been the newer construction she noticed outside a few moments earlier. She knew little about the deaths of Sarah and Cherish Elling, only that they perished by fire.

Abby's parents had insisted that she was helping Mr. Elling as much as he was assisting her. He could use youthful energy in his home they said, just as she needed a roof to sleep under and suppers that included more than broth. After her last tantrum, they declared it was the only suitable solution. She could not stay in Lancashire continuing to claw at her own skin. Never mind what percentage of the family coffers she filled, with so many mouths to feed and endless debt, it wasn't enough.

If only she could have told her parents about Uncle Matthew, but he had threatened and threatened. She had long since determined that feeding her siblings was worth more than her innocence. But then she was unable to control her actions at home after each of the afternoons she spent with him. The rage she felt in the aftermath of Matthew's attentions would come at her in violent bursts, and she had no place to stow it. Instead, her anger would seep out, soiling everything.

It was no wonder her parents wanted to be rid of her. Mr.

Elling didn't seem to want her much either. Well, so be it. She would learn from her governess until her eighteenth birthday. Then she would find a new path, perhaps become a governess herself. She would go far away and evaporate, where she would never again be a victim, nor have to think about her squalor, and the filthy memories that she would never escape.

But this house, she reflected with cautious enthusiasm, this house was an exploit in itself. Abby thought to write to Gwendolyn and tell her of all the elegant details and adornments that would have captivated her sister, except that such a list would also render the girl mad with envy. Abby worried for the girl, left behind so near Matthew's clutches, and she wished anew that her parents had sent Gwen instead. Yet it was Abby who was here, with the banister beneath her hand, as smooth as blown glass, supporting her burdens as she followed Larissa up the stairs.

3

CHARLESTON, SOUTH CAROLINA
1845

This is my room, you're certain?" Abby asked.

"Are you unhappy with it?" Larissa's brow furrowed as her hand moved to the tight bun on her head, almost as if she was checking whether the wound ball of faded tresses was still attached. Abby thought the governess looked like she was trying to hide her prettiness beneath that long tent of a skirt and shapeless blouse. Much the way her ma did in Wigan, always covering her lustrous hair beneath a kerchief before she left the flat. Her ma disliked anything that glistened, whether it was her own hair or a neighbor's shoe buckle. It rendered her sorry to recollect what she'd been.

"Um . . . uh, no." Abby stammered, looking from Larissa to the bedroom and then back to the governess. "It's just . . . well, not what I expected. Mr. Elling has already been quite kind, even paying for my passage. I'm not sure this is where he means for me to be resting my bag." Abby noticed the bursting pillows on the four-poster bed and wondered how it must feel to settle one's head down upon them. Her own head was itchy. Hot and jumbled.

"Oh," Larissa smiled, the lines outside her pale eyes crinkling like a silk fan. "Of course these are your quarters. Mr. Elling made clear you were to be treated as a member of the family."

"Even so," Abby protested, "I am not a member of the family, just the daughter of a once-dear friend. I needn't be given a room of the first order." This lavish treatment did not sit well with her. Douglas Elling had barely made eye contact with her before abruptly dismissing her from his office. Surely her care was not a priority to him, and she did not belong in this room.

Larissa's smile faltered as she seemed to understand that Abby was uncomfortable with the room, truly. Abby began chewing on her thumbnail while she waited for Larissa's response. Her skin was still salty from the sea, making her mouth fill with water. She suddenly heard her ma's voice in her head. Not her ma from Lancashire. Her ma from seven years earlier. *"Abigail. Young ladies do not gnaw on their own flesh."* Abby snapped her wet hand to her side, fighting the urge to wipe the dampness on her skirt.

"Abby, dear, all the guest rooms at this estate are equally lovely, and equally empty. Nothing you do or take will possibly be a financial burden on Mr. Elling. Take a rest, and I'll return before supper. Go on." Larissa shooed her, urging her to move beyond the threshold.

Abby felt temptation pulling at her. She chanced farther into the palatial room, reconsidering the space as something that might actually be available to her. If all the rooms were just as this one, there wasn't really a choice to be made. It would probably only create more burden, more trouble, if she refused these quarters.

Larissa prattled on about sending tea and cakes up to the room in advance of supper. Abby barely heard the woman as she absorbed the opulence of the bedroom. She was anxious to remove her stockings so she could feel her toes sink into the thick carpet, its pink and gold fibers bursting forth from the floor like fairies. She noticed that the carpet matched the gold inlay on the cascading drapes. There was also a crystal chandelier demanding attention at the center of the coffered ceiling, shooting rainbows of refracted light onto the large mahogany bureaus on either side of the room's fireplace.

Abby looked again at the plush bed piled high with decadent quilts of deep pinks and creams, and stepped closer to it. She thought of strawberries and cream, and her stomach rumbled. She hadn't dreamt of strawberries in years, and now she could almost feel the honeyed seeds wedged between her teeth. Suddenly she tasted all the weariness of her weeks of travels. The effort she had undertaken to maintain her bravery, her pretense of capability, during her journey was abruptly too much. Suddenly nothing seemed as imperative as simply lying down.

Thankful for the upholstered footstool, she climbed to the bed and sat, sinking into the endless cushion, so far from the floor that her legs dangled like a marionette's. Her crusty boots looked more degenerate now that she viewed them floating above the glistening rug, like buzzards let inside the house. There wasn't much she could do about it though, unless the governess might rather look upon her split stockings beneath.

"Very well then," Larissa finished with a note of resignation, as though she had been awaiting some response. Abby tried to think what the governess might be waiting to hear, but before she managed to formulate a reply, Larissa was quietly closing the door behind herself. Abby shrugged, unsurprised that she was disappointing people in her new life already. She began unlacing her boots, relieved by the familiar task. After each boot dropped to the floor with a satisfying *thunk*, she thought how her ma wasn't here to make sure each shoe was put neatly by the door, laces facing the wall.

She lay back, feeling sleep grab her eyelids. Back in Wigan, her brother Charlie was probably curled up beside Gwendolyn on the pallet next to the embers of the stove. Abby would have been lying on Charlie's other side, if she weren't here, one of her legs kicking across at Gwendolyn, pushing her to make room, while the other leg lay on the dirt floor. Abby jumped down from the bed deciding to straighten her boots. Confronted again by their muddy soles, she reconsidered and hid them altogether, stashing them underneath the bed, where they would stop shouting out about how she didn't belong here.

THERE WERE BIRDS, VERY RUDE BIRDS, CHIRPING. ABBY lay in bed with her eyes closed, trying to ignore the trilling. As she became aware that she did not feel the ship's rocking, she thought groggily that the vessel must have reached port. She rolled over in bed, the satin comforter twisting around her legs. Shaken by the softness of her bedding, she opened her eyes with a start. She was in Charleston now, not onboard the steamship. She was in the most wonderfully exquisite bed, and it was there for her use, only hers, for the next several months. Unless someone decided they'd made a mistake after all. Seven years she had worked in the mills, trudging home covered in cotton dust, to sleep in a damp, rodent-infested tenement. Surely, she was entitled to savor this bed for a moment. At least until she was told to evacuate these quarters.

Before Wigan, her da had owned a shop in Liverpool, the city where they once had a pink-brick home. He sold furniture, enough to keep Abby clothed in toile dresses and patent-leather shoes, and to provide tutors for her and Gwendolyn. The tutoring for her younger brothers would have begun in short order, as well. If not for the flood.

Her mind flashed to her uncle, despite herself, and she wondered if she would ever be free of him. There had been days back home when she would bloody up her arms, trying to tear her skin clean off, scratching as if to release herself from her own body. She created new wounds, scrapes and gashes that her family lacked the soap to clean, adding weight to the shoulders atop her mother's aching back.

Abby's stomach cramped with hunger, and she remembered that Larissa said supper would be at nine. The sunlight streaming through the window told her she had long since missed that meal. She rose from the bed, still clad in her frayed cotton dress from the day before. There was only one spare dress in her bag, and that one was no better. She pondered whether she might find a way to bathe today. Surely people at this fulsome estate must be blessed to have a bath whenever the mood might strike. Noticing a small bowl of water near her bedside, Abby splashed her face with the tepid water and used the cloth beside the ceramic bowl to dry off. It helped, but hardly enough. The weeks of sea travel had left a layer of muck and salt on her skin so thick that they required nothing less than full soaking to remove.

There was a mirror affixed to the wall above the washbowl, a small hexagonal piece of glass, only slightly larger than Abby's face. She could see in the mirror how the weeks at sea had changed her. Her skin was a new olive color, not the alabaster she remembered. Her cheeks were too hollow, rendering her cheekbones overly prominent. She removed the twine holding her long hair, running her fingers through the brown locks to calm them. Her hair had grown back quickly from when she'd chopped at it with a kitchen knife the year before. She saw determination in her green-gray eyes, her pupils so small they were nearly invisible in the foggy mirror. She arranged her hair into a haphazard plait and stared at herself another moment in resignation.

The hunger in her gut wouldn't have her delay any longer before leaving her quarters to search for breakfast. Poking her head out the door, she saw Larissa just rounding the corner.

"Oh, good," the governess smiled, her pale blonde bun still neatly in place, another drab outfit beneath it. "You were in such deep slumber when I brought the scones last night, it seemed cruel to disturb you. You must be famished." The governess linked her arm with Abby's and led her toward the celestial staircase. "Let's take care of breakfast and then fetch you a bath. You must be anxious to get clean again."

If Larissa knew Abby better, the woman wouldn't offer such promises. Clean. Abby nearly snorted. She would never be clean.

***

AFTER HER FIRST LEISURELY BATH IN SEVEN YEARS, Abby's skin felt flushed, abraded. She remembered how her da used to sniff her freshly washed hair when she was a young girl, his nose against the crown of her head, and she experienced a longing for home she hadn't expected. She found Larissa waiting in the second-floor parlor, just as she'd promised.

Abby settled herself on a foam-green davenport, and Larissa charged straight to business, providing her an overview of her days to come.

"During the days, you will study in the house, your primary company being only myself and Jasper. We will have to find other ways to entertain you, I suppose. As for Mr. Elling, you'll see precious little of him, as he spends every waking hour at the wharf."

Abby exhaled a slow breath, remembering again the strange scene she happened upon at Douglas's office. The less she saw of that peculiar man, the better. In fact, keeping mainly to herself in this new life sounded easier than anything she'd done in a long time.

"In the mornings," Larissa continued, "we will study more rigorous subjects, arithmetic, history, geography, and philosophy."

As she listened, Abby eyed the cucumber sandwiches and peach pastries waiting on the china dish before them, wondering how many would be polite to take. Both would muck up her dress if she tried to pocket extra.

Afternoons, Larissa continued, were reserved for instruction in feminine accomplishments—painting, quilting, music, French. "I will also instruct you at the pianoforte thrice a week," Larissa concluded.

It seemed Abby was being groomed for something. Marriage, presumably. She had long ago decided she would never marry, never submit herself to another person's whims, someone else's fate.

"I know it must seem isolating," Larissa said. "Being alone all day with only the staff for company. A young lady needs to get out, be part of society. We'll get you set with the young people of Charleston in no time, and you'll have more friends than you can corral." Larissa paused to fiddle with her hair bun again. Abby had the urge to pull out the pins, let the woman's hair fall in brazen waves. After a moment, Larissa continued, "I've been living two and a half years in this house without any worthy purpose. And finally, dear, you are here, so we must make the most of it."

"You were the governess for his child?" Abby asked, as understanding dawned.

"Yes," Larissa nodded vigorously. "Mr. Elling's deceased wife, bless her soul, hired me as governess for Cherish. She would be seven years old now." Larissa was silent for another moment, staring blindly at the pleats in her wool skirt. "Before that," she finally continued, "I had been teaching at the Hadley School for girls in Massachusetts, near where I was raised."

Now Abby understood why Larissa spoke her words with such a flat twang. Beyond the differing accents, she was not particularly knowledgeable about the differences between North and South in America, except to be aware that there was no slavery beyond Maryland or Delaware.

"Why did you not return home after they died?" Abby asked bluntly.

"Well, if you must know, my father is a disagreeable man. Living in his house as a spinster . . ." she trailed off as though searching for the correct words. Meanwhile Abby helped herself to a pastry from the platter, syrup seeping onto her fingers. "My father felt too much shame," Larissa admitted. "He could not abide my failure to marry, and he tormented me for it. After I made Mrs. Elling privy to my circumstance, she begged for my promise never to return to him."

"Well, why not go somewhere else? Why stay here?" Abby asked as she chewed. She couldn't wrap her mind around the idea that this energetic woman had chosen to remain in a Douglas Elling's house with no purpose whatsoever. She had not taken Larissa as the type to be seduced by the opulence of the estate, so what then, was the impetus for remaining? Perhaps there was something illicit between Mr. Elling and the good governess. Though the ages of it were wrong. Even under all that natty scruff, Mr. Elling was clearly closer to her own age than to Larissa's. Still, people did odd doings, didn't they?

Larissa tilted her head at Abby the same way her ma did when she thought it was charming that Abby was being dense.

"As an adult woman with no husband, I do not have a cornucopia of choices. No respectable woman can reside in a home without the protection of a man. Whether it's a father, a brother, or even a son." Then she added jokingly, "I see we have much to catch up on in our lessons in propriety."

The governess could mock Abby all she wanted, study her with those condescending eyes, but the woman's explanation seemed incoherent all the same. "But Mr. Elling is not your father, brother, or son," Abby persisted. A curtain was opening in her own mind, letting in the thought to learn from Larissa's experience what options might be available for herself in the future. Once she had mastered the skills they had discussed, she could do as Larissa had done, earn a living teaching young girls.

"No, he's not," Larissa conceded. "Ours is indeed an unorthodox arrangement, but the community has been gentle about judging this household ever since the fire. As my employer, Mr. Elling is a suitable protector. Especially for one such as myself, who no longer has any real prospects of marriage to fret about losing."

It still seemed odd to Abby, Larissa waiting in the house all day with nothing to occupy herself. Abby wanted to ask if Mr. Elling was still paying her for doing naught. But she was starting to like this diminutive woman with the oversized smiles. Abby did not aim to offend her, and so decided to cease the inquiries.

"By the by," Larissa continued with another thought, "Mr. Elling informed me about your prior circumstance. None of that matters now that you're here, where you will be treated in the manner your breeding demands. I know you must miss your family, but since I never did take with a husband, nor have children of my own, I have more than enough love in my heart to bombard upon you."

Right, thought Abby, her own inner darkness swirling again, like hateful vapor clouding her mind's eye. A cautionary plume living permanently where she used to hold her hope. I challenge you, dear governess, to love me like you've offered once you've seen inside my rotted soul.

4

CHARLESTON, SOUTH CAROLINA

Three Years Earlier

1842

ouglas escorted Sarah into the Cunninghams' ballroom, surveying the throng of gentlemen planters who milled about, joking with each other and flirting with the ladies crowding the room. There wasn't a single friendly face among them.

"Make yourself useful, dear, and fetch me a beverage," Sarah asked, likely sensing his discomfort, providing him a task. "I think I should enjoy a lemonade. Meantime, I'll go say how-do to Madeline Hart. She has known me too long to snub me in public."

Douglas entered the refreshments parlor and walked toward the pack of gentlemen surrounding the oversized bar. The beverages on display ranged from blackberry wine and peach brandy to whiskeys and imported liquors, standard fare for an evening ball in Charleston, but notable here because of the sheer abundance of bottles, each bedecked with a frivolous gold tassel at the collar. He felt a hand grip his shoulder and turned to find Ben Baylis, a friend of his deceased father-in-law. Well into his seventies, Ben was a longtime rice planter of the low country.

"Douglas," Baylis's voice was a quiet rumble. "A word?" He raised his silver eyebrows and jerked his head to indicate Douglas should follow him. After piloting them toward a secluded corner of the room, Baylis charged straight to his point.

"Listen, talk is spreading like a virus. Upright folks around town, they keep adding your name in sentences with words you want to stay away from, words like abolition, words like traitor and criminal. There were whispers months back, but now, seems I'm catching snippets every damn day. I don't know, son, what you're involved in, but I'm charged to watch out for the well-being of my friend Nat's only daughter. Folks ought to know better around here about what they'd be risking."

"Baylis," Douglas feigned a scoff, "don't tell me a tough old bug like you has started listening to old ladies' gossip."

"It's not ladies who've been saying it." People were still filing into the lounge, the crowd growing and buzzing. Douglas stepped closer to Baylis, inching them both farther into the corner.

"Well then, who exactly has been spreading these rumors?"

"It's not just one person, don't you see? It's everywhere. You want to sniff out a source, I don't know what to tell you. Maybe you start with that Wilson Bly. He may be one ill-tempered son of a bitch, but he's got a host of farmer friends who cling to his every word."

Before Baylis could say more, they were interrupted by Sarah's approach. "Why, Benjamin Baylis!" Sarah beamed at her father's friend. "Had I known you were here, I would have spent the last ten minutes combing the property for you. Save me a dance?"

"Sarah, my darling," Baylis responded with a warm smile and deepening wrinkles at his eyes, all his former gruffness gone.

"If you've got room on your dance card for an old fellow like me, I wouldn't miss it. Now," he continued as the sound of a waltz began drifting in from the ballroom, "go practice with your husband so you'll be ripe to handle my fancy footsteps."

"Yes, Douglas, let's," Sarah agreed as she pulled Douglas toward the ballroom.

"Happy to oblige, my sweet lady," Douglas nodded subtly to thank Baylis, trying to indicate he had taken their conversation to heart.

Sarah led Douglas to the parquet dance floor where they began waltzing, spinning clockwise around the room along with several others. Glancing across the floor, Douglas noticed many of Charleston's wealthiest planters in attendance with their wives and daughters. He was anxious to recount for Sarah the substance of his conversation with Ben Baylis. It was likely no one would even hear them with the music providing cover. Still, he thought the better of unveiling himself amongst the many merrymakers spinning past them. Apparently, he had grown too careless recently as it was.

As the song ended and Douglas and Sarah made their way off the floor, they were approached by a sashaying Cora Rae Cunningham, the eldest daughter of their hosts. A girl on the cusp of adulthood, she was confident in her abundant charms.

"Why, Mr. Elling, don't you look handsome," she fluttered her eyelashes up at him. "Ain't it just a shame you're a married man." She put her gloved hand to her breast in a gesture of despair.

"And nice to see you too, Sarah," Cora Rae added. "I ought to call you *Aunt* Sarah, doesn't it seem, since you grew up with Mama. All those many, many, many years ago," she finished with a satisfied smirk.

"Nice to see you too, Rae," Douglas nodded before turning

back to Sarah. "Please excuse us though. I was just taking my fetching wife for a lemonade."

Cora Rae flashed Douglas an exaggerated pout and turned on her heel.

The elderly Madeline Hart appeared beside Sarah, emitting a quiet gasp before she spoke. "It's shameless, propositioning a married man like that. Since she turned sixteen, that little miss thinks she can do what all she pleases. Just shameful," she added, outraged.

Widow Hart then leaned in closer to Sarah, the brandy rank on her breath as she whispered, "You know, dear, I don't believe a word they say about your husband. He's just too charming and polished to be involved with any outlaws. You stay by me tonight, and we'll set everyone right."

"Thank you, Mrs. Hart," Sarah whispered back with appreciation. "You needn't put yourself out. We are quite comfortable with who we are."

"Oh, nonsense and pishposh is what I have to say to that," was Mrs. Hart's retort as she took Sarah's arm firmly in her bony hand. "Douglas, dear," Mrs. Hart continued, "your wife and I are going to survey the confectionaries."

Sarah flashed Douglas a comic look of defeat as she was pulled away. Smiling, Douglas turned back to the men he had been approaching. A group of local planters congregated at the side of the bar, engaged in rowdy debate. Douglas recognized many of the men, including Grant Howard, who every year harvested fields of indigo, sending his yields to Northern factories via Douglas's shipping fleet. He also spotted Luke Barndale and Tripp Hanneford, two of the most prolific cotton producers in the county. The men seemed to be commiserating about recent proposals from Northern lawmakers, each pausing periodically to swig from glasses filled with amber-colored spirits.

"Those Jonathans up North," Grant Howard complained, "they think they can dictate our operations even though they're miles away. I don't see the Yankees producing any raw materials. It's just factory after factory up there, fields of steel. They'd best leave the planting to the planters."

Douglas saw his opportunity and interjected, "That's right, Grant." As all heads turned his way, he stepped closer. "The Yankees think they can govern the South without knowing an ounce of Southern truth. We have real issues that need addressing, like getting our railroads running, to point to only one."

"This conversation doesn't concern you, Elling," Grant responded as he began turning his broad back on Douglas.

"Sure it does," Douglas answered, pulling one of the stools out from underneath the far end of the bar, nonchalant as he made himself comfortable. "You all think I'm too young to know my arse from my earlobe, too new to this country, but even if I didn't begin here, aren't I now a Southerner anyhow? Haven't I got all my wealth tied up in South Carolina just like the rest of you?" He nodded as he looked around at the others. "If the Northerners do exactly as they please," Douglas continued, "there soon won't be money or privilege remaining for any of us, myself included. And say what you will about me, gentlemen, but you know I like luxury in my life. That's official."

The men considered Douglas, and he could see curiosity entering their faces. There was something else in their eager eyes that seemed more than just party drunkenness. Douglas silently prayed he could win them over. He refused to laud slavery, not even to maintain his cover amongst the Charlestonians, but he was prepared to criticize the federal government for its legitimate flaws if that meant preserving his image with a secure guise.

"Don't the rest of you agree?" Douglas asked. "The government can't continue treating the North like the favorite son when so much of the country's wealth is being created down South."

At a few murmurs of agreement, Douglas felt his companions warming to him. Perhaps attending this party had been a sunny idea, indeed. Dispelling suspicion was crucial if he hoped to disappear soon on another voyage in the Eastern Atlantic.

"Elling, how can you stand by us in the South when you don't support slaveholding? How can you sit there, pretend you're one of us?" That was John LeGrave, one of the younger men.

"Look, gentlemen," Douglas responded carefully, glancing around the bar to make eye contact with each of the men. "I come from Liverpool. I was not raised with slaves. It's not what I know or need. What the rest of you do, that's your business. Why should I care when it's your rice and cotton that keep my boats loaded with cargo? You people do your business, and I'll do mine. I am a Southerner now, and I stand with you all as my neighbors."

The men began nodding slowly, in what Douglas hoped was approval, even acceptance. Had he realized it would be so easy, he would have attempted months ago to recast himself in the eyes of the local aristocracy. Only, Douglas straightened as a feeling of dread crept into his veins, perhaps this was *too* easy. It didn't ring true that a few offhand remarks would be sufficient to undermine months of scorn and disapproval.

"Elling," Grant Howard spoke up, "a few of us were going to meet Thursday for a spot of gentleman's poker. Join us?"

Something wasn't right. Their brief debating was not sufficient to warrant this invitation into the fold. He would play along until he could figure just what had set his former enemies to opening their hearts so easily. He remembered his conversation with Ben Baylis and decided he would visit that farmer, Wilson Bly, as soon as possible. Bly was known for speaking his roughneck mind. Maybe he could shed some light on the question of these mercurial men.

"As long as you all don't mind being catawamptiously chewed up, it would be my pleasure," Douglas forced out a laugh and then excused himself to return to his wife.

꙳

Three Days Later

DEMETT KNOCKED TWICE ON THE OUTER DOOR OF THE deserted barn, a staccato pronouncement signaling that William Lloyd Garrison had arrived. Supporters of the Southern States Liberation Congregation, or the SSLC, had traveled surreptitiously to an abandoned property on the outskirts of town to be present for Garrison's visit. Many of those in attendance were young men seeking adventure, blessed with youthful indifference towards the risks inherent in their actions. Even so, Douglas felt the weight of their peril like sandbags on his shoulders. At least the isolated barn where they now waited was a secure location. The long-abandoned structure stood alone at the entrance to a wood, an overgrowth of thorny brush obscuring its decaying walls. The place was almost entirely camouflaged during daylight and hidden even more so behind the curtain of night.

Douglas slid the door open to reveal Garrison, along with two bulkier companions. Garrison was surprisingly diminutive, nearly dwarfed by the two men flanking him, ironic for a man with such a hefty reputation. He certainly looked much younger than his thirty-seven years, but Douglas knew better than to be deluded by appearances. Garrison was a thunder stroke, and Douglas was anxious to impress him.

"Mr. Garrison," Douglas ushered the men inside and hastily

shut the door before extending his hand, "I am Douglas Elling. I hope the journey was uneventful."

"It's long overdue we meet, Mr. Elling," Garrison responded with his Northern twang and a sturdy handshake. "Though I cannot claim it a pleasure to be here, ensconced in the mud of your Carolina swamps, hiding like a criminal." Garrison's eyes shifted from Douglas toward the other men scattered throughout the shadowy barn. "I hope everyone is aware of the acute risks we face." Garrison addressed the room, and Douglas noticed a handgun hanging at the hip of one of his beefy comrades.

"Indeed," Douglas answered, looking toward the group, "And I've reminded each fellow over and again that there will be no repercussions should anyone develop reservations. Their feet have remained planted, though. These men are committed. Mad as hatters, perhaps, but committed." There were concurring murmurs from amongst the men.

"Let me lay out who's in attendance." Douglas continued, "Twelve of these men accompanied me aboard *The Voyager*. Several of those twelve have traveled here from up North, like you. As for the others," Douglas surveyed the men, "that's Kyle Doogan," he pointed toward a tall man who was leaning against a stall divider. The cloudy gas lamp in Doogan's hand illuminated only the bottom half of his square face. "I met him only recently," Douglas explained, "but Doogan was recommended to the SSLC by Tommy Branch, who has been an SSLC member since its inception."

"You needn't bother with further endorsements then," Garrison nodded crisply at Doogan. "I'm quite familiar with Branch. He's risked hide and hair for the movement, not just with those antislavery pamphlets, but also sheltering refugees. Any friend of Tommy Branch is a friend of mine."

"Of course." Douglas felt himself beginning to sweat beneath his collar, possibly from the oppressive air in the withering barn, but more likely a product of his ambition to impress Garrison. "This fine fellow," Douglas motioned to an older man with thinning hair, "is Archibald Hutchins." An errant shaft of moonlight reflected off the man's wire-rimmed glasses, obscuring his eyes behind the glare.

"I discovered Mr. Hutchins's antislavery sentiments only recently, after his Negro coachman confided in Demett, whom you met outside. It's almost laughable, as I have been doing my banking with him for years, yet I hadn't an inkling. I trust this man, and I'm confident he would not betray us."

Archie Hutchins extended his pale hand to Garrison and explained, "Obviously a gentleman of my age cannot commandeer slave ships, but what I do have is money. I've been trying to help with buying supplies, rations, whatever it is that needs buying."

Garrison pulled a handkerchief from his breast pocket and wiped the damp night from his brow.

"Tell me, Mr. Hutchins," Garrison inquired, "the money you see, it comes through slavery, isn't that so? All the wealth in this town is generated by a slave workforce. When bondage comes to an end, so too does the flow of money. If the money from plantations dries up, what becomes of your banking business?"

Archie shrugged, "I speculated on some land in Virginia years back. Petersburg Railroad bought it from me for more than a whole hog at Christmas dinner. Haven't needed any business beyond that for years. What I care about now is not sitting idle, not averting my gaze while guiltless people spend their lives in bondage. Families getting ripped apart . . ." His voice caught in his throat, and he coughed into his hand, attempting to regain composure. "I only regret I didn't speak up when I was a younger man, that I was so involved in my own life that I didn't think to care."

"Well," Garrison bobbed his head, "it's never too late to find your personal hallelujah. Glad to have you."

Douglas pointed back toward Doogan, where three other men stood beside him. "The only other additions to the group are men you recommended, Frank and Gabriel Tompkins and John Colby. Hold the lantern higher, Frank, so everyone can see your faces."

"The Tompkins brothers!" Garrison nearly cheered. "There's no organized group for them in Columbia County, but they knew there must be Underground nearby. They came through a convoluted channel, but I thought these strapping boys would be a boon to your Blackbirder Blockade."

Douglas nodded, as Garrison had alluded to this idea in previous letter. Their written correspondence had been opaque, as it needed be, so Douglas was pleased to learn that he interpreted the letter properly. The growth of the Blockade by even two men was a tremendous benefit when the whole brigade consisted of only twelve other souls.

Motioning to the other newcomer, Garrison called, "John, come closer." As the man emerged from the shadows, Garrison explained, "John Colby, here, came down from New York. He's built relationships with local free blacks and has established new railroad stations, as we like to call them. I'm confident there are more sympathizers to be found down these ways, but I understand the difficulty of ferreting them out." He shook his head in dismay. "Bravery like the kind in this room is scarce." He paused and looked from each man to the next, sending a message of approval with his hard, dark eyes. "I expect Colby will travel between North and South frequently, hopefully escorting runaways along the way."

John Colby's shaggy dark hair fell just below his jawline, a messy, hodgepodge affair that was at odds with the sophisticated cut of his collar. He nodded soberly at the group and then reached out to shake Douglas's hand. "I'll be doing what Mr.

Garrison says, but I'd as much like to get out there on the seas with the rest of you. Scare me up some traders," he joked.

With introductions complete, Douglas cleared his throat and began, "I'd like to take this opportunity to speak about the SSLC and update everyone on some recent developments." Several of the men in the spectral room nodded and moved closer, creating a haphazard circle around Douglas in the shadowy dust and grit.

"We formed the SSLC three years ago. Sam Green over there," Douglas motioned to a squat man on the edge of the group, "he and I were the first, and we've been quietly growing our membership ever since. We have been focused on the illegal slave trade that continues to flourish, despite having been outlawed for nearly thirty-five years. Until international trafficking in slaves has ceased, there can be no meaningful abolitionist movement domestically."

"Hear, hear!" Sam Green called out. Others nodded and mumbled in agreement.

Encouraged, Douglas continued, "Slave trading is a crime punishable by death, yet only one man has ever been executed under the law, despite the numerous illegal shipments every year. By the by, there are similar smuggling problems in Britain." Douglas saw that Garrison was nodding along with the others.

"For this reason, we formed the Blackbirder Blockade. With only twelve active members, our operations are primitive, but our first mission was a great success. The ship from Britain that we seized was carrying over two hundred captives. After disenfranchising the ship's crew, we deposited them back on the coast of Ghana and then brought the Africans to Freetown in Sierra Leone. From there, the Africans were permitted to determine for themselves the manner in which they wanted to repatriate."

"And what of the traders?" one of the Tompkins brothers asked. "We leave them to die?"

"Nah," Douglas shook his head. "We left them a few days' walk from the Cape Coast Castle and told them the way. They could find passage home from there, one way or another, providing they were willing to suffer the humiliation and risk criminal arrest."

"Ha!" Garrison called out, apparently delighted anew by the mischief of it, even though he was already thoroughly familiar with this information.

Douglas continued, "Slave traders have become careless in the wake of lax enforcement. The crew we met was entirely ill-equipped to defend themselves. Given the nature of my export business," Douglas explained, "we have access to ships and supplies for scouting and pirating efforts. We have tremendous financial support, too. Certain of my merchant contacts have enlisted a few foreigners to re-situate the captives once they return to African shores, helping them to return to their former lives or find better than what they left behind. At this juncture, what we need is more manpower, so I am elated to see the new faces here tonight."

"If I may add," Garrison stepped toward the middle of the cluster, "the Blackbirder Blockade has been one of the most significant recent triumphs for the abolitionist movement. The diversion by the Blockade of that one ship may not sound like much, but it resulted in the return of more than two hundred would-be slaves to Africa. The ship was likely bound for Havana, and nearly half of those people would have died during the Middle Passage, from starvation or disease. Of those who made it to Havana, many would have been auctioned and then smuggled to other destinations, especially the American South."

"Furthermore," Garrison said, "these blackbirding slavers haven't devised any effective precautions to help themselves avoid detection, by our men, or by Britain's Royal Navy. If only the Royal Navy ever apprehended anyone," he scoffed. "In the six months since the Blockade's mission," Garrison chuckled, "I bet they've already become a legend, a cautionary tale. The deterrent effect may be even more powerful than the actual missions."

Douglas felt his chest rising in response to Garrison's praise, his entire being bolstered by the knowledge that his efforts created a source of optimism for other abolitionists.

After the meeting concluded, the men made staggered exits, some walking as far as two miles to the locations where they had left their horses and wagons. Garrison lingered with John Colby, the shaggy-haired man from New York, both waiting for a final word with Douglas.

The lanterns were now extinguished, and the room was dark but for the moonlight edging in through the fragmented roof.

"Douglas," Garrison began, putting a hand on his shoulder and guiding him slowly toward the exit, "I see great promise in our relationship. I believe you are an immediast, like me, who will settle for nothing less than immediate emancipation of all souls held in bondage. Full rights granted at once, and no compensation for former slaveholders either." He seemed as though he wanted to spit at the thought of reimbursing slaveholders for the cost of slaves who were freed.

"Some consider my approach too radical," he went on, tugging at his necktie. "They would prefer a gradual end to bondage, to avoid mutiny or what have you. And then there are the issues about whether women should be permitted to participate in our meetings. To my mind, equality is an easy concept and there can be no exceptions, whether predicated on color or sex. I know, Douglas, that we are like-minded gentleman. We will be heard!"

Spittle flew from Garrison's mouth as he shouted the last bit, and Douglas felt himself becoming nearly intoxicated on the strength of Garrison's passion. "Just tell me how I can be of service," Douglas responded, anxious to hear what Garrison had in mind.

"What I envision is you and Colby overseeing all developments in the South. You will be our eyes and ears, our outrider down this way. Sympathizers will end up at your doorstep, one way or another, and you will either enlist them in the Blockade, or assist in finding local tasks for them. We can enumerate the details at a later date. All you need to digest at this moment is that if you're willing, you and Colby will be our freedom commanders for everything south of the Mason-Dixon Line."

"Mr. Garrison," Douglas answered with a grin, "I've been hoping for years to work alongside your people. We will improve this nation for all its inhabitants, black and white alike. I would relish nothing more, sir."

Douglas reflected that his own fervor seemed to grow deeper, more urgent, with each action he took to advance freedom, like he was fueling an addiction. He was further inspired by Garrison's apparent faith in his abilities. He wondered if he ought to mention his declining reputation amongst the planters of Charleston, that their suspicion toward him as a sympathizer had been growing steadily. Perhaps the scrutiny by his neighbors would undermine his effectiveness as one of Garrison's soldiers. He thought back to the Cunningham ball, remembering the foreboding he felt after those men warmed to him. Douglas resolved to hold his tongue until he knew more. There was no need to jeopardize his position with Garrison after working so long to capture the man's attention. Whatever the situation, he would handle it.

"Well that settles it," Garrison concluded as he and Colby proceeded toward the door, Garrison's two henchmen stepping out of the shadows to follow. "You will be hearing from us, Douglas." Garrison patted Douglas on his shoulder.

As Douglas returned home, he hoped Sarah would be waiting up like she often did.

"Sarah!" Douglas called from the hall as he spotted the candlelight casting a glow from his study. "Sarah, my love!" Douglas huffed with excitement when he found her waiting peacefully on the settee beneath the windows, a needlepoint pattern poised on her lap. "Now *that* was a meeting. Nearly twenty people, new manpower for the Blockade, accolades from Garrison. I hardly know where to begin. I could feel it in my blood, the changes that are coming down the lane! Abolition is going to take hold at long last, until the whole ghastly system has been destroyed."

"I'm so pleased the meeting went well," Sarah smiled, as she stood to put her arms around his neck. "If there is anyone who can add force to Garrison's army and valor to his ideals, it is you, my darling."

"Really, I couldn't be more glad about anything than I am to have this opportunity."

"I don't know, Douglas," Sarah pondered in a wistful tone, planting a light kiss on his cheek and taking his hand in her own. "I'm sure we could find something that might just be the cherry on top of this exciting day." She ran her hand slowly down his arm to make herself clear.

Douglas raised his eyebrows at Sarah's invitation.

"What?" She blushed as he smiled down at her. "I've got to remind you that younger girls like Cora Rae Cunningham have not a single advantage over a fully ripened woman like me."

Douglas barked out a laugh. He had forgotten about Cora Rae's forward behavior at the ball.

"Here I thought you might be focused on my involvement in a criminal enterprise, but all you can think about is getting me into bed with you then? It is no wonder I adore you." He gathered Sarah into his arms and lowered his face to kiss her.

"So you haven't been pining for a certain young redhead?"

"You can't be serious, Sarah. The girl's behavior renders her utterly displeasing. And anyway, I will only ever have room in my eyes, in my heart, for you. In my hands, too." He squeezed her on the rump for emphasis and added, "So you must allow me to smother you with love and protection for always."

The thought of protecting Sarah prompted Douglas to remember his intention of visiting Wilson Bly. If that rice farmer was the source of the rumors, he would need to be given a new perspective, and soon. Douglas had attempted over the years to maintain his reputation as a foreign eccentric, rather than an outright abolition sympathizer. He thought again about the inexplicable behavior of the wealthy planters at the Cunningham ball and again, he felt a seeping dread, like black smoke, wafting over his bones.

His visit to Bly would be the first step in quelling the suspicion, as Bly was known to run off at the mouth and would certainly divulge whatever they discussed. It would be better, Douglas reflected as he ran his fingers through Sarah's curls and deposited small kisses at the base of her neck, to smooth everything over before his next Blockade journey. He could fix this, and he would. Tomorrow. In the meantime, he would take his wife upstairs to see just how much those hands of his could hold.

5

CHARLESTON, SOUTH CAROLINA
1845

Abby dismounted from Allegra, the four-year-old quarter horse that had become her favorite. She stroked the mare's abundant black mane and turned toward the stables, where Antonio and Reggie would be waiting to help the animal cool down.

"That's my girl," she whispered, reaching into her pocket for her last sugar cube.

Both Abby and the horse were winded from a hard ride around the back pasture of the estate. Abby had taken to horseback riding quickly, and she easily convinced Antonio that she should be permitted to leave the corral on occasion. Although the pasture was relatively confined for a bulky animal like Allegra, it was wide enough that they could take several swift clips, where Abby would bend low, relishing the whip of hot wind against her tearing eyes.

As she approached the barn, Reggie came out to meet her and reached for the reins.

"I like to see a rider enjoying her animal like that, Miss Abigail. It fills up a horse's soul when you savor the ride. You look full of joy perched up on her." He smiled widely at her, the expanse of his bald head reflecting the sunshine of the day.

Abby didn't think it fit to call her feelings joy. What she felt atop that horse was more akin to safety, relief. As she looked back at Reggie and took in his kind, dark eyes, his mahogany skin, she didn't feel the impulse to sass him. In fact, Abby realized, it wasn't just Reggie, but her constant need to answer back and keep everyone afar seemed to be slackening. Perhaps it was the hearty food giving her better strength to tolerate people, or that she had been in Charleston for several weeks and was beginning to believe she might actually be safe from harm. Certainly, the riding was serving as a balm.

Reggie and Antonio, both relatively young men, had turned her into a competent horsewoman over the past four weeks. Abby wasn't entirely sure how the Spanish Antonio had come to be in Mr. Elling's employ, except that after one of Douglas's journeys abroad several years earlier, Antonio had returned with him. With a piece of straw constantly dangling from his lower lip and shirtsleeves rolled always to his elbows, Abby thought the Spaniard looked more American than anyone she'd met since her arrival in this country. Unlike Antonio, who was comparatively new, Reggie had been at the Elling estate since before Douglas, back when the home was owned by Nat Henderson, Douglas's father-in-law. Reggie told her that when Mr. Henderson died, he freed his slaves as part of his last will and testament. Reggie, along with a few others, had asked Douglas to let them stay at the estate as wage earners. Abby had wanted Reggie to tell her more about what that was like, going from slave to freeman, but she didn't think it was her place to ask, and so instead they spoke of other subjects.

Each day as Reggie held Allegra's lead, coaxing horse and rider through circles in the dusty corral, he rattled off for Abby what he fancied best about South Carolina, formulating new answers each day. He listed stately mulberry trees and their tart fruit, salamanders crouching beneath warm rocks, the pungent smell of sweet Carolina grasses. He did not speak much about his personal life, but then, neither did she. He reminded her to keep her back straight or to fix the position of her feet on the saddle's stirrups, all while he munched on an endless supply of pistachios that he pulled from his pocket.

Abby felt particularly energized after today's brisk ride, and she wasn't yet disposed to return to the gilded caverns of the quiet house.

"Can I help cool her down? Just show me what I need do."

Reggie looked sheepish. "Miss Abigail, grooming down the horse, that's my duty. Besides, if Miss Larissa Prue see you cleaning the bit or sponging Allegra's belly, she'll be spitting mad. It's no task for a young lady."

As much as she was enjoying her time with the horse, Abby did not want to disappoint Larissa or make Reggie uncomfortable.

As Reggie reached out again for the reins, Abby noticed that his hand was rubbed raw on the palm, probably from carrying the burlap feed bags she had seen him lugging earlier in the day. Remembering her brother Charlie's constantly chapped hands, Abby thought she could accelerate the healing of Reggie's raw skin. After all her years caring for her siblings, she was a bit of an authority on ointments for laboring hands.

"Let me see that," she said, taking his fist.

Reggie pulled back immediately, as though scorched by the touch, just as a loud voice called, "Abigail!"

Abby dropped her still-outstretched hand and turned to find Douglas Elling emerging from the darkness of the stables, storming toward her with anger so palpable she could almost see steam seeping from his skin, rising out from beneath his dreadful, unruly beard. It was early for him to be home from his office, and she wished she could have hidden away in her room like she usually did when he returned to the property.

"Are you insane?" he demanded. "Grabbing hold of a black man's hand like that. He doesn't want you touching him." He stepped toward Abby as he bellowed, and she could see a vein bulging beneath the scruff on his neck. There was a look of bitterness on Douglas's face, an expression of disgust that prompted Abby to inch closer to Reggie, but this only seemed to anger Douglas more.

"Do you not realize this house is not an enclave? We are not so private here that you can go cavorting with the Negroes." He was getting louder as he stared Abby down, never sparing a look in Reggie's direction. "This is not bloody England, you know. There are rules here. Your white skin mustn't touch black skin. You are not to act as though they are the same as you. Not ever!" He stepped even closer to Abby, so that their bodies were nearly touching as he lowered his head, forcing her to meet his icy eyes before he continued.

"I am duty bound to your parents to allow you to remain here, but I am not obliged to abide your stupidity." The quietness of these words was even worse than the shouting.

Abby's many weeks of fear had finally been realized. This man was indeed wicked, and cruel. She wanted to defend Reggie, but she was frightened. As she looked at the enraged monster before her with his shaggy hair flying in every direction and spittle forming in the corner of his mouth, she saw danger and potential for anguish. She watched his menacing hands clench into fists at his sides and then unclench, and she wanted only to escape. She suddenly pivoted and ran back toward the house, covering her ears with her hands the whole way. She wouldn't listen to his horrid yelling if he started again, she wouldn't. She would hide in her room and not come out, not until he was gone again.

THAT NIGHT AT SUPPER, LARISSA DIDN'T MENTION THE incident with Douglas, and neither did Abby. Perhaps Larissa hadn't heard about their row, or she thought it unimportant. Maybe Douglas treated people this way regularly, and so it hardly bore mentioning. Abby had watched from her window before the evening meal as Douglas mounted his horse in the circular drive and departed again. She hoped he would be absent for hours and she could continue avoiding him as she had done perfectly well before today. Her face was freshly washed, and now she was trying to focus on the roast ham before her.

Larissa had been using each meal as an opportunity to provide Abby with instruction in proper manners. She had stated at the outset that social etiquette was different in the States than in England, and so the rules for dining in South Carolina would, of course, be unknown to Abby. Abby was fairly certain that proper table manners must be the same on both continents, but that Larissa was graciously trying to help her avoid feeling unrefined. Abby tried to listen with sharp attention as Larissa explained that women must remove their gloves upon sitting and spread their napkins across their laps. It was important to avoid noises when chewing, Larissa often reminded her, and one must never stare if another's table manners were lacking. After a bit of coaching at the beginning of each meal, Larissa would generally turn the discussion to topics Abby found more engaging, such as Charleston's history or local vegetation. But tonight, Abby was distracted by the effort of trying not to remember her afternoon.

"Well, if I cannot garner your attention for etiquette, perhaps my other news will interest you." Larissa dabbed at the corner of her mouth with the white napkin, a knowing smile twisting her lips, as Abby waited for her to continue.

"You've been invited to attend Gracie Cunningham's debut."

Abby looked at her blankly. She had not an inkling who Gracie Cunningham was or what she might be debuting.

"It's a ball, darling. You're going to your first evening ball."

"Oh! That sounds lovely," Abby perked up, but then felt immediately deflated. "But I'm sure Mr. Elling would never approve it." Besides, Abby realized after her brief flash of excitement, what would she want with a ball anyway? She wouldn't know anyone there, wouldn't know how to behave, wouldn't be regarded as a suitable companion. She was only the destitute girl siphoning off riches from an asocial curmudgeon, one who apparently used to be more important than he was now. She wondered why she had been invited.

"Nonsense. I spoke with him just before he left, and we have his full endorsement on the matter. He did mention that he himself would abhor such an event, but he has no intention of standing in our way. He agrees it is appropriate for you to be introduced to society. As a member of Mr. Elling's household, you will be an honored guest with all the proper pedigree supporting you, I assure you."

Abby was caught off guard by the oddity of it all. As of this afternoon, Abby was sure that Douglas Elling found her to be a supreme nuisance, a draining blight upon his property, and a brainless one at that. When he'd barked at her about his duty to continue housing her, Abby had been near equal in her sensations of relief and disappointment. Just as she'd begun to grow comfortable at his estate, he'd materialized to set her straight. If he had set her loose, she would not have returned to Wigan, not for a million pounds. She was reaching the conclusion that it would be wise to hatch a plan, on the chance that he did decide to rescind his generosity, whether now or in a few months. She would not be at the mercy of that man, no matter the consequences.

How foul he'd been to poor, gentle Reggie, who'd never done anything off target. She could allow that perhaps she had behaved inappropriately, reaching out to touch a man as she had. His color was irrelevant to the propriety of the gesture. How Reggie must have felt listening to Douglas rant that he was inferior to Abby. Especially when Douglas clearly thought Abby was pretty low herself.

In any case, she couldn't fathom that Douglas would want her parading about at a social event where she would surely be associated with him.

"You're certain?" she asked. "Won't they all handle me as though I am beneath them? They know all the dirty linen about why I've come to stay, I'm sure."

"Hardly," Larissa patted Abby's hand. "You are the esteemed ward of one of the wealthiest men in Charleston. You'll see, that is one of the attractive peculiarities of America. It matters not where you've come from, only where you end up. It will all be arranged to your satisfaction."

An evening ball. Abby speared a piece of ham onto her fork and watched the amber juices drip to her plate as she considered the prospect. After only five weeks in Charleston, she would attend a bona fide Southern ball, the kind she and Gwendolyn had imagined when they played at waltzing as children. Douglas's approval of her attendance made little sense to her, but there was no reason to spit in the face of opportunity. There had to be a way she could use this chance, take measures to establish her own future. She would have to grow acquainted with people in the community if she hoped to find suitable reason to remain in the States after her patronage expired.

Larissa explained that since Abby had neither the wealth nor upbringing to host her own coming-out ball, she would make her first foray into society at someone else's ball. Larissa spoke gently, as though she understood how difficult it must be for Abby to be deprived of her own ball. Abby hardly needing consoling. She was fairly enthused about witnessing the regalia of Southern society while escaping the attention of her own coming-out ball, which sounded quite horrid, in fact, all that staring and fuss.

She had a transient thought that this event might result in meeting a few friends, provided she could find any young women who would do more than laugh at her lack of suitable heritage, her primitive dance steps, her confusion with cutlery. In Wigan, she had worked too many hours and spewed too many insults to allow for friends, but even when she was wretched, she at least had Gwendolyn. Now, since arriving in Charleston, she lacked any contemporary companions at all and was surprising herself by bemoaning the isolation she thought she craved.

It was becoming a repeating pattern since alighting in Charleston that again, Abby was feeling overwhelmed. Even with the many privileges she had received since her arrival, she was still emerging from a stupor of poverty, still grieving the years of hardship. For so long, she thought she would never again experience indulgences like thorough personal grooming or frivolous leisure. Yet at present, she could envision herself in an elegant gown, her hair arranged in some complicated fashion, perhaps laced with flowers, or even looped into braids.

Abby knew girls generally went to balls aspiring to attract husbands, but marrying was not her intention, she declared to herself for the umpteenth time. And besides, she was too busy planning her new life, the life she would have when she found a position as tutor, or governess. She would be permanently free of indigence and defenselessness, of Douglas Elling and insults, of England and agony.

"It all sounds splendid," Abby responded, her thoughts dashing onward, bustling with possibilities.

6

CHARLESTON, SOUTH CAROLINA

1845

Abby gazed down at herself in disbelief. It was hard to fathom that only a few months ago, she had been plucking dirt from beneath her fingernails at a factory table in Wigan, and now here she was. Lavishly bedecked in yet another new gown, she felt splendid enough to pass an evening with Queen Victoria herself. If they kept decorating her like this, with the crinolines and the satins, the hoops and the head-dresses, perhaps eventually she would be so magnificent on the outside as to forget who she was within.

Ida, a recently hired lady's maid, was finishing arranging Abby's hair. At Larissa's urging, Mr. Elling had approved the enlistment of a few additional staff members to render the es-tate more hospitable for a proper young lady. Ida was a member of Charleston's ever-growing population of free blacks, and she had previously been employed as a laundress at an elegant hotel on Broad Street. Abby hadn't told Ida that her own mother also did washing at a hotel back in England, thinking that if she knew, Ida might resent attending to her.

"Well, fancy that," Larissa smiled as she handed Abby the

silver-framed looking glass. "You look like more of a fine young lady than seventeen other Charleston belles put together." Ida had fastened Abby's dark hair into a small chignon, curling wispy pieces around her face into cascading tendrils.

How Larissa had gone on and on readying her for this evening. When Larissa attempted to outline the rules for ballroom dancing, Abby had interrupted that she was not interested in dancing. How quickly Larissa had corrected her with pursed lips and a declaration that only the worst of all hosts would allow an unmarried young woman to remain idle at his event. The master of the house would actively recruit gentlemen guests to entertain any lady who seemed to be lacking attention, she'd clarified.

As if she knew that Abby's thoughts had now traveled back to the dancing ahead of her, Larissa returned to the subject, as well. "I'm certain you will have plenty of young gentlemen vying for space on your dance card, so best to get in the spirit for that."

At Abby's horrified expression, Larissa laughed.

"Oh, don't be such a crepehanger." She swatted Abby's shoulder playfully. "You won't spend much time with any which one of them. You'll have the same banal conversation with each gentleman who leads you onto the dance floor. You'll agree it has been unseasonably warm, that the host has chosen lovely flowers, that Charleston is so festive this time of year. And then the dance will be over, and your partner will be on his merry way." She paused to glance at her own reflection in the small mirror, pulling at a lock to let it escape from her bun, softening her face. Turning back to Abby, she continued, "All the other young ladies will be vying for undivided attention from the gentlemen in attendance. So if you prefer to be left alone, you most likely will be. Perhaps that will help your quest for spinsterhood. Although I am not giving up on you yet." She patted Abby's shoulder again.

"All finished, Miss Abigail," Ida stood back and admired her handiwork, a proud smile on her thin lips.

"Thank you, Ida." Abby touched the twist of her hair gingerly. "I'd never have known how to do this."

"You enjoy yourself now," Ida told her, placing her hands on her wide hips. The woman nodded, as though satisfied with her creation and added, "Just your shoes now. I'll be back to tidy up after you get going." She nodded to Larissa before leaving the room.

"One more thing to make you all the more fetching," Larissa said as though she has just remembered.

Abby watched Larissa rummage through the cluttered mass of cosmetics on the vanity table and willed herself not to snap at the woman for prodding her toward courtship. Larissa finally pushed aside some vials of perfume and seized the item for which she had been searching. It was a yellow winter jessamine flower, just like those blooming on the vines outside Abby's bedroom window.

"I know how you love the smell of these," Larissa smiled as she fastened the bud in Abby's hair. "May this bloom bring you luck tonight. Perhaps a husband, as well," she winked.

"Larissa," Abby warned. She was nervous enough about the ball as it was. She had already resolved to make the most of this evening, to acquaint herself with women who might one day be mothers of young girls she could teach. That was the goal of it all now, wasn't it, to position herself for successful spinsterhood? Despite her misgivings about the men, the dancing with its touching and handling, the perusing and gaping, she instructed her nerves to stand down. She should feel comforted, assured of safety by this town's extensive rules of propriety and the presence of Larissa as her chaperone.

"You really must come off that notion, Larissa," Abby told

her, trying not to be exceedingly gruff. "I shan't ever be interested in marrying."

"Come now," Larissa cocked her head, undeterred. "It's just a matter of finding the right boy. And besides," Larissa took one of Abby's hands in both of hers, squeezing gently, "I'm just trying to keep you near me as long as possible. If you don't find a suitable caller here, your parents will eventually find someone for you in Lancashire, I'm sure. Then you'd leave us for good. There are plenty of charming gentlemen here in Charleston." Larissa laughed and added, "Perhaps you could save us all a heap of trouble and allow one of them to pick you."

"Nobody will be picking anything from me, thank you very much!" Abby snapped, pulling her hand away, her anger boiling over at the faceless men she imagined, grabbing and clutching her, harassing and repelling her. As injury and bewilderment flashed across Larissa's face, Abby quickly readjusted herself.

"Wait, don't get cross with me," she pleaded as she reached out, reattaching herself to Larissa's hand. "I don't know why I am so sharp sometimes."

"Don't think of it another minute," Larissa answered, the briefest flicker of a shadow crossing her face again as she glanced out the window into the darkening sky. "Let's just be on our way." Larissa lifted her pastel cape from where it rested on the bedpost. "I'm sure the Cunninghams' residence will be resplendent tonight, bedecked from the roof to drive, every last fountain. Don't forget your shawl, dear. We have to protect all of you from the chill, even your lovely bosom."

And just like that, Abby felt it again, that raging anger that she couldn't control. She didn't know where it came from or what to do with it. The feelings didn't seem true to her. Or rather, they were true, but they weren't truly a part of her. Of course she knew where they came from. They came from the poison that was Uncle Matthew. But she couldn't let it go, couldn't get past it, felt the rage at the strangest times, from a bland reference to her bosom. She used to know who she was inside, who she had been until that horrid man wrenched it all away. And now Larissa saw good in her, and for some reason, it only made Abby angrier, uglier. If the woman could stop talking about suitors and bosoms, maybe Abby could focus on something other than the searing hatred in her gut, the nastiness she simply couldn't quash.

~~e

As THEY ARRIVED AT THE CUNNINGHAMS' GRAND ESTATE, Abby surveyed the large group of people mingling on the sweeping verandah. It was just as Larissa had described, everyone in their greatest finery, the light from surrounding lanterns lending the evening a whispering, ethereal glow. Gentlemen in tails and white gloves. Each young woman glistening more brightly than the next.

"Keep your head up, Abby," Larissa instructed on a quiet breath. "Shoulders back. You are more entitled to this evening of indulgence than anyone. Now come along and try to smile."

Larissa led her up wide brick steps toward the front door. She was grateful that her connection to Douglas Elling and her status as a foreigner had excused her from the need for her own formal presentation. Still, it seemed there would be many introductions for her to suffer through before the evening could be tucked away.

"Well you must be Abigail Milton," a mature red-haired woman looked her over from head to toe before meeting her eyes with a smile. The stately woman was waiting just inside the door, first in a line of official receivers that appeared to run at least ten bodies deep. Taking in the woman's dazzling chartreuse gown, her regal posture, and self-assured movements, Abby understood that she was meeting the lady of the house.

"I'm Regina Cunningham," the woman confirmed, as she reached to take Abby's hand into her chartreuse glove. "I'm so pleased you accepted our invitation. We are all so fond of Mr. Elling," Regina continued, her light eyes studying Abby's face. "We were just delighted when we heard he finally added some life back to his empty house. And hello, Larissa. So nice to see you again," Regina continued, sounding genuine as she nodded to the governess. Observing Regina's pink cheeks and arched brows, Abby wondered if she had ever seen such a lovely redhead.

She followed Larissa forward, next meeting Regina's aging parents. Abby was pleased by the benign elderly man, who was evidently nearly deaf, but smiling and nodding in an enthusiastic effort to keep pace, his wife, gentle and bland beside him. Just as Abby began constructing an internal dash of calm, she discovered Cora Rae, Regina's eldest daughter. Cora Rae stood fourth in the receiving line, her arresting beauty immediately eclipsing Abby's appreciation of Regina's physical appearance. She was taller than her mother, willowy, and magnificent in her youthful vibrancy. Her lustrous red hair was curled in long ringlets, falling around her shoulders in an artful cascade. The red was so vivid, it appeared almost as though the woman was surrounded by red-hot flames. Abby saw a strength inherent in Cora Rae's fierce beauty, and she found herself envious.

Abby felt a light touch on her shoulder and pivoted to see that Regina had stepped out of her own place in line. "I have to bring something to my daughter upstairs, but let me introduce you; this is my oldest daughter, Cora Rae."

"It's just Cora now, Ma. How many times do I have to say it?" Cora Rae looked at her mother in exasperation and then glanced toward Abby. "Cora." She repeated and held out her hand with a stiff smile.

As Abby answered, stating her own name, the porcelain features of Cora Rae's face transformed from indifference to something else entirely, something hungry. "You're the one staying with Douglas Elling." An accusation. Abby wondered if this was the first assault, if Cora Rae was already mocking her. Still, Abby kept her feet in place beneath the armor of her long dress and nodded lightly. Cora Rae studied her a moment, her eyes leisurely perusing Abby's person, while a complicated smile twisted at her lips. "Oh dear, we *do* need to talk." She laughed breezily and then looked beyond Abby and Larissa to the next guests, implicitly dismissing them both.

Larissa ushered Abby through the remainder of the line, offering brief and polite greetings as they passed. The receivers consisted of relatives of the Cunninghams, aunts and cousins, rather than other members of the immediate family. All the while Abby pondered Cora, shaken by their encounter, bracing for other discomforts of the evening. From Larissa's description of the Cunningham family, Abby now remembered that the oldest daughter was only one or two years her senior, but that statuesque woman on the receiving line seemed too sophisticated for a person still reaching for twenty years.

Abby followed Larissa deeper into the house and caught her breath as they entered the glittering ballroom. The crowds of people milling about on the parquet floor did not diminish the staggering effect of the room's lavish decorations. Every corner of the ballroom seemed to be overflowing with fragrant flowers and sparkling threaded beads, looped like vines from surface to surface. The room's multiple fireplaces had been festooned with garlands of dark greens, red berries, and yellow flowers so large that their blooms looked to have burst forth in an explosion of life. There were ladies in cascading dresses of every imaginable hue. The brightness of the ladies' wide gowns was tempered by the soft lighting of countless crystal wall sconces. Overhead there were several crystal chandeliers, filled with flickering candles, adding to the room's elegant glow. It was no wonder these genteel planters enjoyed their social season. Abby was so overcome by the thrilling ballroom that she nearly forgot her own insecurities.

As the women circulated about in their cumbersome hoops and shining evening gloves, Abby realized they were queuing to receive their dancing cards. Larissa finally spoke from beside her, resuming her litany of instructions. The governess explained that the refreshments and the ladies' changing room were both just down the hall. She assured Abby that one gentleman or another would offer to bring her a lemonade at any moment, and that a proper lady would do no nothing other than accept graciously.

Before Abby could even decide where to situate herself, she was disheartened by the prompt approach of a young man. The plain-looking gentleman requested Larissa's permission to introduce himself to Abby.

"Please forgive my unorthodox approach, Miss Milton, rushing you as I have, but I was concerned I might miss my chance. This is a town that adores new faces when they are as bewitching as yours."

The man, who identified himself as James Winters, appeared close to her own age, svelte and simple to look at. He asked Abby to save him a dance. The governess was clearly nervous as she watched for Abby's reaction, but Abby answered that she would be pleased to add him to her dance card, just as soon as she secured it from the committee. He smiled sheepishly and declared, "My friends call me Lanky." With that, Lanky

James offered her a sideways smile and departed, his gangly arms getting in his way at every turn.

Abby smiled in relief. This part of it all, at least, was apparently easy. Merely accepting verbal invitations and adding people's names to her dance card, well, it was little more than a harmless list. The actual dancing, she was not prepared to focus on yet. As she watched James Winters approach another young lady, she was further appeased. She needn't fret and could focus instead on projecting the right kind of image, just the sort that would cast her as a respectable and refined young woman, perfect for teaching young girls.

Abby's dance card was full within only a few minutes of their arrival. Perhaps the local gentlemen had been advised to treat the charity case kindly, or maybe like that James Winters said, she was appealing simply because she was new blood in an old town. With her card closed out, Abby's focus returned to her surroundings, which she was now free to savor until the dancing began. In contrast to the refined opulence of Douglas Elling's estate, Abby felt the Cunninghams' home was rather ostentatious, as though each decoration had been placed to maximize the impression of wealth. Even so, it was hard to resist ogling every lustrous thing before her. She felt like a wide-eyed infant, transfixed by any shiny object.

As she wondered whether all plantation owners maintained second homes that were equally well-appointed, there was a stir in the ballroom. Larissa leaned over and whispered that it was time for Gracie Cunningham to be presented. This was her official "coming out," as they called it.

Guests meandered toward the foyer, waiting at the base of the split staircase, as notes from flutes and violins commenced floating through the air. Gracie's father, Court Cunningham, appeared on the balcony, walking to the top stair to await his daughter. He was a square-shaped man with a handsome weather-worn face and closely cut, ash-colored hair. As Gracie emerged in a sparkling dress of soft white tulle, there were collective sighs and murmurs of approval. Gracie's dark hair was pulled into a mass of carefully arranged curls, held in place by a pearl-covered tiara. The girl's hair, black as a beetle back, was so different from her sister Cora's deep russet locks, but Abby saw that the sisters had the same perfectly milky complexions. There were glittering jewels sewn into Gracie's dress that might well have been real diamonds. She approached her father with a cautious smile, her eyes darting rapidly over the guests from her vantage above them all, and Abby could see even from afar that the girl lacked Cora's self-confidence. Court extended his arm and led Gracie slowly down the stairwell, a self-congratulatory smile resting on his face. Gracie, on the other hand, seemed to be holding fast to her own precarious smile, grasping it with all her might.

"This is a very grand introduction," Larissa tilted her head to whisper in Abby's ear as they gazed up at the stairs. "Recently, more parents have been presenting their daughters in groups at cotillions, rather than individually. But the truly high families, like the Cunninghams, they still have the luxury of presenting girls independently." Larissa's eyes traveled back to Gracie and Court Cunningham as they reached the bottom of the flared staircase. Without looking away from the girl on debut, Larissa added rhetorically, "Isn't it just lovely?"

Abby nearly shuddered. Perhaps the presentation was lovely, but it appeared rather more like torture for the poor girl on view. She supposed there were other young ladies who would feast heartily on the attention, like that Cora Rae for starters. Gracie's older sister must have relished her own coming out, Abby reflected, which likely occurred a couple of years prior to this night. Gracie, however, seemed reluctant at best.

Abby's thoughts were interrupted by a change in the music. It was time for the formal dancing to commence. Abby turned back toward the ballroom and saw Lanky James Winters making his way toward her. It was perfectly obvious why everyone called him "Lanky," with his long skinny limbs and his awkward lumbering gait.

"My lady," he extended his hand to her with an unexpected grace. "If I may still have the honor of a dance?"

Abby flinched away from him, opposed to the gratuitous physical contact. She then felt Larissa's hand on her shoulder as a gentle reminder.

"Excuse me, Mr. Winters," Abby attempted a modest smile, "of course."

"Please, really, call me Lanky," he told her, and he led her off toward the dance floor.

As Larissa had foretold, the dance consisted mainly of spins and turns with a few offhand comments about the weather and such. And then the dance was over. Abby passed three or four equally ephemeral dances with other young gentlemen whom had reserved space on her dance card. Each dance required little more than brief, prosaic conversation, only the most proper and impersonal touching, and so much delightful spinning and twirling. As the evening wore on, Abby grew eager to inform Larissa that she found the dancing to be great fun. She did love to exhaust herself physically, and the endless twirls felt nearly as satisfying as running outdoors or riding Allegra. If only they could spin a bit faster instead of having to be so terribly civilized about it all.

Eventually, there was a recess to the dancing, and several women began seeking escorts to the refreshments area. Abby thought she would ask Larissa to take her, as well. A lemonade was just what her arid throat needed. As she scanned the group of chaperones standing near the wall, a firm hand clasped her forearm.

"There you are," Cora Rae declared with delight. "Come, let me take you for some victuals so we can get to know each other, don't you think?" Honey oozed from every thick Southern word she uttered. The skin of Abby's neck prickled, noting something amiss with Cora Rae's enthusiastic effort to commandeer her.

"Um . . ." Abby began, searching nervously for Larissa, then catching sight of the woman's blonde bun far across the ballroom, her head bobbing as she talked with a matronly woman near the violinists.

"Oh, shush, darling. Your governess won't mind if I take you off myself. I am one of the hostesses here, aren't I? I've just been waiting with such anticipation to make your acquaintance." She led Abby out of the ballroom, so much friendlier now, too friendly. "You know, my mama and daddy were very special friends with Douglas Elling before that tragedy that happened over in his house."

They entered the refreshments lounge, where a large circular table laden with decadent pastries occupied the center of the room. The setup reminded Abby of the fountain in the courtyard outside, the ladies here swooping like rock doves as they plucked sweet treats from the tiered display of cakes and tarts. There was also a bar, like the kind in the pub room of the hotel where her mother worked, with gentlemen crowded around, calling out for the beverages they were after. Abby too began to make her way toward the bar, but Cora Rae put a hand on her arm, halting her by the room's entryway and instead directing her toward a line of serving slaves waiting by the wall.

"Get us two sweet teas, Crispin, and hurry now," Cora Rae quipped, her attention still on Abby. An elderly black man stepped out of the shadows and scurried away with a quiet "Yes'm." Until that moment, Abby had failed to notice the many house slaves in attendance at this event, so wrapped up had she been in her own discomfort. Looking around the room, she became aware of several other slaves hovering in the background, awaiting instructions from guests or the hosts. They wore dark pants or simple black dresses, standing quietly at attention, ready to serve. She was ashamed at her blindness, her selfish preoccupation. It was still unfathomable to her that all these people were made to work for no wages at all. At least the pittance she earned in Wigan had been something to bring home at the end of the day.

Cora Rae pulled Abby toward a burgundy settee and patted it in invitation. She then continued, "I'm outright dying to hear, how is our poor, dear Mr. Elling doing these days? We're aware that he goes to his shipping office each day. But none of us knows, I mean *really* knows, how it is that he's doing." Cora Rae leaned forward and Abby could smell a flowery cologne on her, thick and spicy.

"Well, I'm sure I don't know the answer . . ." Abby began, glancing toward the table of confections in search of an exit from this encounter.

"Oh, you mustn't be shy with me," Cora Rae explained. "Douglas and I, well we had a close relationship, if you know what I mean." She smiled knowingly at Abby.

Cora Rae opened her mouth to continue, but she was interrupted by the arrival of Gracie and another girl, who looked like a younger, rougher version of Cora Rae.

"Rae, is this Miss Milton?" The younger girl asked while looking at Abby. Before Cora Rae could answer, the girl added hastily, "You're prettier than I expected. Older though."

"Wini!" Gracie swatted the girl's arm and turned to Abby, "Please excuse my baby sister, as she has a way of always saying exactly what's on her mind."

"It's lovely to meet you," Abby answered, standing to extend her hand, relieved to reclaim some breadth between herself and Cora Rae. "I am Abigail, Abby, Milton."

"We know all about you," Wini told her excitedly. "And I'm hardly a baby, Gracie, now that I'm fifteen." The girl shot a sideways glance at her sister. Abby noticed Wini's full bosom above her tiny waist and thought how jealous her own sister, Gwendolyn, would be, always lamenting her late-blooming body. Wini already had a figure like Cora Rae, each curve in perfect proportion. Gracie, on the other hand, was thicker than her sisters, shaped more like a butter biscuit. "We were so glad you were coming tonight, Miss Milton. After Douglas lost Sarah and Cherish, he stopped coming around," Wini continued, and Abby observed that the girl's skin was grainier than both her older sisters', her features less precise. "For a long while they were the youngest friends our parents had, the only ones we found amusing, even though we are sort of relations with them. Now that we're older, it's better, since the folks they invite to come calling are nearer to our age."

Abby wondered whether the poor girl was pausing to breathe with all the circuitous chatter occupying her airways.

"Anyhow," Wini continued, "we thought maybe Douglas would be gladdened up when you came, but it seems like nothing has changed. It's just a shame is all, after how he and Sarah used to be so adored by Charleston. That was before that nastiness rose up about Douglas. Remember that, Gracie?" Without missing a beat, Wini rambled on. "We didn't give up on him because the Ellings were like family. Except for Rae didn't think Douglas was family. She still thinks he's bounty she's going to claim, even though he never had the least bit of interest in her, now you know that's true, Rae."

"It's Cora, for mercy's sake." Cora Rae growled in frustration.

"Our new friend is not interested in listening to this prattle. Abby and I were talking privately, weren't we, Abby?" Cora Rae tried to shoo away her sisters.

Before Wini could launch into another diatribe, Gracie stepped forward and addressed her sisters with a firmness Abby would not have expected.

"Girls." Gracie looked from Cora Rae to Wini, transmitting some sort of chiding with her eyes, a silent message to each. She took Abby's gloved hand into her own and continued, "We've all been interested to meet Abby, but this is my night, and I am choosing her as my escort back to the ballroom." After the assumptions Abby had formed about the girl just a few minutes prior, she was surprised that Gracie had the ability to be so firm.

As Gracie whisked her away, Abby felt an unfamiliar sense of relief replace her physical thirst.

"Pay no mind to my sisters," Gracie told her apologetically. "Rae has always had an infatuation with Douglas Elling, she can't help herself. But I wanted, well, I've so looked forward to meeting you, someone who's seen different parts of the world, lived a different life than, than all this." She motioned as if to indicate the house, the ball, Charleston. "I didn't want them corrupting you, I suppose."

They walked through the open hall, slowing their pace as they approached the ballroom. Abby tried to stay focused on Gracie's words, rather than the glistening gems along the waistline of her iridescent dress, stones that were even brighter from this close vantage point. She wondered what would happen were she to pluck a stone for herself. She realized Gracie was still speaking and forced herself to remain fixed on the girl as they reentered the main party.

"If you ask me," she was saying, "Douglas is the reason that Rae isn't yet affianced. She *is* almost nineteen years old," Gracie explained. "None of us can figure out why she's holding out for

him. Douglas never did give Rae the slightest bit of encourage-
ment." Grace shrugged her petite shoulders.

"I can hardly imagine Mr. Elling encouraging anyone at
all," Abby scoffed. "He's too busy brooding and yelling to think
about women. But oh!" Abby clapped her gloved hand over her
mouth in regret. Realizing her lapse in etiquette, she hastened to
add, "Not that I don't think he's a lovely man. I certainly appreciate all he's done for me."

"Don't worry," Gracie patted her hand, "anything you say
to me is just between us. Keeping secrets is something at which I
excel, I promise."

Abby nodded, finding that she did want to trust Gracie, at
least to try trusting, like dipping a single toe into the pond.
Maybe the girl reminded Abby of her sister, Gwendolyn, in her
easy kindness, though she seemed more serious than Gwen, less
impish. "Still," Abby answered, "it's unfair to criticize him after
the way he's taken me in."

"He used to be quite a different sort of gentleman. You
know, he moved to Charleston all the way from Liverpool just to
be with Sarah, and they married so young."

Abby nodded. She did know. She had heard from Larissa
what a whirlwind the courtship between Douglas and Sarah had
been. "Apparently, Douglas was smitten something awful with
Sarah. I imagine it was just too much for one man to lose." Gracie looked a moment longer at Abby. The music was resuming,
and the time for serious conversation was drawing to a close.

"It is a shame though," Gracie added, as she raised her
hand to signal a passing house slave. The young Negro woman
was carrying a tray full of goblets of lemonade. Gracie removed
two glasses and handed one to Abby before continuing. "Douglas Elling used to inspire us all, such chivalry and charm. Maybe
if you spent time with him, you could help him rediscover those

aspects of himself." Then she shook her head as if she were discounting someone else's bad idea. "But how can you force a bag to billow again after it's already burst?"

As people made their way back toward the dance floor, two by two, like animals boarding Noah's ark, Gracie concluded, "I'm just so glad to have made your acquaintance. Perhaps you would come calling next week for tea?"

"I would like that." Abby felt herself smile, a bit too widely. Here was something unrolling properly, at last. A friendship with Gracie Cunningham would legitimize her in the eyes of local women, and it might actually bring her some measure of fulfillment, too. She drank greedily from her glass as she followed Gracie back toward the ballroom.

7

CHARLESTON, SOUTH CAROLINA

Three Years Earlier

1842

As Douglas rode toward Wilson Bly's ramshackle farm-house, the glare from the setting sun did little to conceal the dismal state of the man's property. With its sagging roof and faded paint, Bly's home appeared to be in only marginally better condition than the long-abandoned barn that Douglas had visited the night before. The squat two-storied building might once have been charming, with its deep second-floor balcony, outlined in curling wrought iron and running the length of the house. If only the windows weren't slathered with mud, the brambles overgrown, crowding the porch and walls, seemingly unaware of where the house was meant to begin. The dwelling's ashen pallor was only heightened by the dry, half-barren fields surrounding it, with yellow grasses and dusty patches overtaking anemic sprouts of rice. Douglas was hardly an expert on farming, but even he knew that Bly's property was too far from the river for a rice crop to thrive.

Douglas rarely came out this way to where the small farmers

lived. He was aware that Bly owned only about ten slaves to work this scant farm, a sorrowful pittance of human labor for most Charlestonians. Even so, he'd never realized quite how pitiful, or how dilapidated, Bly's holdings were. It made sense to Douglas now why Bly would be tramping about, angry and slanderous, when he was taunted by all the wealth and opulence of the grand plantation owners. The number of slaves a person owned was often determinative of that person's social status. Bly's ten slaves were inconsequential when compared to the hundred and fifty owned by someone like Court Cunningham. If the Southern slaves were freed, struggling farmers like Bly would be forced to compete with the free blacks for paltry earnings, for sales, for sustenance. With slavery intact, at least there was one class of people at whom individuals like Bly could thumb their noses. It was no wonder Bly would be so vocal about Douglas's suspicious activities. *Alleged* activities, he reminded himself.

Douglas reached the coarse wooden door and pounded his fist against its panels.

"Hello there," Douglas addressed the elderly black man who answered the door. "I am Douglas Elling, here to see Mr. Bly."

The slave showed Douglas to a bench in the entryway, and hobbled off to inform Bly of his visitor. Douglas opted to remain standing as he scanned the dark hallway and digested the decrepit insides of Bly's abode. The guts of the Bly residence were in no better state than its outer body.

"What are you doing here?" Douglas heard Bly before he saw him emerge from a shadowy doorway.

Douglas had forgotten just how unpleasant Bly was to look at. His personal grooming apparently mirrored his landscape care. He was overgrown in all the wrong ways, with tobacco stains on his jagged teeth and mysterious discolorations throughout his wrinkled shirt. Although he appeared to have large and sturdy biceps, their significance was entirely eclipsed by his oversized belly and extra chin.

"Hello, Mr. Bly," Douglas held his hat in his hand and nodded, attempting respect. He was, after all, trying to win over this hardheaded, disagreeable fellow. "I was hoping we could spend a few moments in your sitting room to discuss something."

"I don't know why you've come, Elling, but I'm a busy man. Whatever you got needs saying, just say it and move on. I got more important things to deal with." Bly crossed his arms over his chest, his rolled shirtsleeves showcasing the impressive quantity of hair on his arms.

"All right then," Douglas smiled, determined to turn Bly. "I've come because I wanted to quell your fears about my political affiliations. I am neither your enemy nor your adversary."

Bly snorted as his stomach bounced beneath his arms. "You sure as hell are my enemy doing all your nigger-loving hoo-ha. I ain't rich like you, Elling. I need my slaves to make my living."

"Hold on, Bly," Douglas held up his hand. "That's the thing. I've come to explain that I am not the political foe you think I am. True, I don't hold slaves of my own, but that's only me. What the rest of you Americans do is neither my business nor my concern." Douglas lied with ease, knowing that his mistruths had a higher purpose. "Now, I too have a living to make, and these rumors you've been spreading are bad for business. I can't have you alienating my best exporters."

"Wait," Bly responded with a look of surprise on his ruddy face. "You think that *I'm* the source of all the blathering about you?"

Douglas raised his eyebrows and asked, "Well aren't you?"

"Hell, no," Bly proclaimed, curling his lip and preparing to dismiss Douglas. "You got bigger problems to worry about than me. Glancing toward a rattletrap grandfather clock in the corner of the room, Bly continued, "It's about sundown now. If I was you, Elling, I'd get on back to my own property and make sure to keep my family safe after dark sets in." Bly started toward the door to show Douglas out.

"My family?" Douglas asked in alarm. "What has my family got to do with any of this?"

"A lot of people don't like your principles, Elling, think you've been kicking up dust about the Southern way of life. Lots of 'em is bigger people around here than me. People want you gone, and I don't hardly blame 'em. You ought to go on back where you came from, rather than coming into our houses and looking under our bedcovers. But they been talking about doing you harm to send their message. That ain't never been my way." Bly opened the door and continued, "Go on home, Elling. It ain't me you need be carrying on about."

Wasting no time in reaching Bly, Douglas grabbed him by his collar. Leaning low into Bly's face and speaking with barely controlled rage, Douglas warned, "Now you open up your filthy ears, Bly. First, you're going to tell me who is threatening my family, and in what way. After that, you're going to make sure to spread word that if anyone in this town so much as glances at my wife or daughter sideways, there's going to be hell to pay." Bringing his face even closer to Bly's, Douglas repeated, "Hell to pay." He stared at Bly a moment longer before pushing him away in disgust.

"For Christ's sake, Elling," Bly bleated, smoothing down his hopeless shirt. "I ain't the type for mob violence. Especially not when there's women and children. I don't know who it is, but there's a hum out there about you getting your reprisal. It ain't my doing. I'm busy enough." He looked toward the front door. "The farm," he added. "The whispers people been passing, it's supposed to go down soon. I don't know the day, but you better go on, get off my land, and make sure your people is still in fine feather at that big house of yours."

8

CHARLESTON, SOUTH CAROLINA
1845

bby climbed the steps to the Cunningham home for
the second time since arriving in Charleston and tried
to remain unruffled. When Gracie sent the note inviting her for
tea, mere days after they were introduced at the ball, Abby envisioned a modest gathering of two, something simple, befitting a
budding friendship. But when Mr. Elling's servant deposited her
outside the Cunninghams' home that afternoon, it was obvious
that events would not be as she had anticipated. Two female
house slaves awaited her arrival, standing at attention in starched
black uniforms on the gravel drive beneath the spacious porch.
Both attendants led her into the foyer, where they presented her
with a cool towel for her hands and a glass of water, with actual
ice in it. After inquiring whether she was sufficiently refreshed
to join her hostesses, as though a simple carriage ride might
have taken so much out of her, one of the slaves led Abby to a
large drawing room. As soon as she glanced through the room's
doorway, Regina, Cora Rae, and Wini rushed at her, eager to
greet her. Too eager, ravenous even. Gracie followed quietly
behind them.

"Abigail!" Regina burst forth, ahead of her daughters, radiant in her yellow silk day dress. Abby again took note of the woman's arresting complexion, a face as though it had been crafted from smooth, rich oils.

"Darling, do come in," she reached for Abby's gloved hand. "Please, you must forgive us. I understand this afternoon was intended for you and Gracie, but we couldn't resist. You don't mind if we stay and have a little hen session, do you? No of course you don't, dear."

Abby looked toward Cora Rae and Wini, who trailed so closely behind their mother they were nearly standing on her skirts. "Come, settle in with us," Cora Rae stepped forward and pulled at Abby's arm, directing her toward a wide settee that was covered in tufted rose-colored fabric.

"Abigail," Wini piped up as she followed behind them, "you have the shiniest dark hair I think I've ever laid eyes on. Do you do that egg wash? I've been wanting to try it."

Abby put a hand to the loose ringlets Ida had set for her that morning and thought of her mother's glossy hair.

"Wini," Regina scolded, "if I see you take a single egg near that hair of yours . . ." She tugged playfully on one of Wini's russet curls and raised her eyebrows at her daughter, letting the threat of her unspoken words hang purposefully.

"Come girls," Regina looked at her daughters as she patted the sofa, "sit and let us properly familiarize ourselves with each other." Gracie still hadn't spoken, hadn't met Abby's eyes.

Abby folded her skirt neatly beneath her as Larissa always instructed and lowered herself onto the settee, where Cora Rae instantly fluttered down beside her. Regina and Wini seated themselves on the creamy divan opposite, leaving no room for Gracie, who moved to an upholstered chair beside them.

As Wini and Cora Rae fixed their eyes on Abby, Regina

lifted a silver bell from an end table and wobbled it three times, creating a surprisingly shrill jangle, like pebbles falling into a kettle. Abby waited for whatever action was meant to commence in relation to the bell, but nothing happened. As the Cunningham women sat in the sunlit room, each with her back straighter than the next, Abby sucked in a breath and pushed her shoulders back. And then the staring began. They sat in silence as Cora Rae, Wini, and even Regina silently explored her person, their eyes roving over her from head to toe and settling expectantly on her face.

Abby wondered what exactly was expected of her, what they were searching for. Larissa had geared the preparatory work for today's visit toward a meeting between Abby and Gracie alone. For this, this viewing, this displaying of herself before prying eyes, Abby was utterly unprepared. The unbridled eagerness of their expressions as they ogled her told Abby that, clearly, they thought there was something most thrilling lurking beneath her quiet exterior. Was it a prurient interest in her destitute past that intrigued these Cunninghams, a hankering for details about her mum, the tenement laundress? Or was it the fact that she, a former street urchin, was now comfortably installed in the home of Douglas Elling?

"Gracie," Regina puffed out her middle daughter's name before any conversation had begun, "do see if you can hurry Clover along with the tea. Ever since that creature became pregnant, she's next to useless." She hastened her daughter out of the room with a hand motion.

Abby began to stand, reluctant to remain in this lion's den with its silent pervading stares. "I could go and help," she began.

"Nonsense," Regina shushed her. "Sit down and let us unwrap you. Gracie will handle it."

Unwrap! Abby had to bite her tongue to refrain from spitting back at Regina that she was not an object to be unfolded for anyone's greedy pleasure. Not anymore. She felt the familiar urge to strike at something. She fisted her hands against the velvet of the settee and reminded herself of the importance of staying composed, of impressing the Cunninghams to lay a foundation for her future.

And so she swallowed her violence, her bile, and tried to distract herself by evaluating the drawing room as she waited for Gracie to return. She hadn't noticed when she arrived the sheer quantity of fittings in the room. There were several other sofas, bookcases, wing-backed chairs, console tables, and even multiple upright clocks, items plugging nearly every free space. It was like Da's old furniture shop, only without the justification.

Abby looked back toward the red-haired women opposite her, forcing herself to meet their gazes, to show strength, when Regina finally, at last, began conversing.

"I do hope I haven't offended you, Abigail," Regina began, and Abby realized she had been too transparent. She wanted to dig her fingernail across her forearm for her stupidity, but she would not make another mistake, not here.

"Of course not," Abby responded. "I am delighted by your gracious invitation. But please, call me Abby." To her relief, her voice held steady.

Regina seemed intent on explaining herself further.

"You must understand, dear, we were all so intertwined with Douglas and Sarah before the atrocious conflagration, our families were like braided bread," she made a quick plaiting motion with her hands. "And then he cut himself off from us so completely, well from everybody. But from *us!*" Regina looked as surprised as if she had just that minute learned of Douglas's behavior. "Oh good, the tea," Regina stated when a slave woman appeared at the door. "Just set it right there and leave it be,

Clover. If I wait for you to pour, I'll miss church on Sunday. Let's hope that our guest here can forgive the barbarity of her hostess doing the serving." As Regina swiped a plate of pastries from the tray and held it out toward Abby, she continued. "My apologies for our abominable help."

"Enough, Mama," Cora Rae scolded, a loaded impatience creeping into her tone. Abby stole a glance at Clover, whose eyes were trained on the floor as she exited the room.

Abby felt herself swirling with resentment at the glaring effortlessness of the woman's existence, that she should feel put out to have to lift her hand to pour tea. Gracie finally reappeared in the drawing room entryway and made her way back to her seat.

"What was I saying?" Regina looked at Wini for help, but then remembered. "Oh yes, my mama was half-sister to Sarah's uncle. It was the wrong half, so we didn't share blood, but it always felt as though we did. I still remember the spring Sunday when she was born. I was nearly twelve years old, and I thought her parents had created her as a present, specially for me." Regina assumed a faraway look in her eye, a crease deepening between her eyebrows, and Abby realized that Sarah's passing might have been a difficult experience for Regina, too. The woman let out a breath of resignation and continued, "Anyway, it's no leap to Holy Mary that I considered Douglas like my very own brother-in-law. They were so much younger, full of optimism, it always made me feel responsible for them, for their well-being." She exhaled pointedly. "Now we can hardly get Douglas to acknowledge us. We do worry about him in that house all by his lonesome. Not that you aren't there, so I suppose he's not actually all alone, but you understand."

Abby nodded as Regina finally reached for the teapot and began pouring. A pleasing scent of lavender wafted toward her.

She accepted the cup and saucer from Regina, hoping that her hostess would soon cease this meandering and reveal her purpose.

"I'm not sure if Gracie told you, Mrs. Cunningham," Abby began.

"Oh please, darling, you must call me Regina. Otherwise I feel about ninety-seven years old."

"All right, Regina." Abby tried to smile in response, but was sure she'd offered the woman a grimace, at best. "I told Gracie when we met that I hardly see Mr. Elling. I'm uncertain what I can tell you that you wouldn't already know." Abby looked to Gracie, who was focused on spooning a cube of sugar.

"Oh, no dear." Regina shook her head. "We aren't trying to collect information from you about Douglas. No," she put a hand to her chest in horrification and looked pointedly at Cora Rae. "I was simply hoping to enlist your help."

"My help?" Abby asked, surprised.

"Why, yes!" Regina exclaimed, excited anew. "I was thinking," she paused to sip her tea, wrinkled her nose at it, and replaced her cup in its saucer. "It really would be best if Douglas started getting out more, socializing, just mingling with civilized folk. The only people he speaks to on a daily basis are Negroes and sailors. That simply can't sustain a person. I'm not quite sure what we need to do, but we'll come up with something, won't we girls?"

Regina looked briefly at her daughters, who chanted a chorus of "Yes, Mama."

"And you, Abby, dear," Regina smiled sweetly, "are in the best position to help us. So what do you say?" Regina asked expectantly. "Are you onboard?"

Abby tried her tea and burned her tongue. Regina, Cora Rae, and Wini were watching her intently. Abby was trying to build her reputation, lay groundwork for her future. Disappointing

Regina Cunningham would clearly be ill-advised. Yet, she couldn't jeopardize her position in Mr. Elling's home by colluding with these people, if that was what they were after. Well done, she thought to herself. After only one bout of socializing, she'd managed to get herself into an impossible situation. As she set her cup on the table, she resolved that she better agree. She could play the weasel later if necessary, back out or fail in her responsibilities.

"You just let me know when there is something I can do," Abby nodded.

"Wonderful, darling!" Regina exclaimed. She then easily redirected the conversation to the menu at her upcoming luncheon, sparking a brief debate over cherry varieties between Wini and Cora Rae. After only a few moments of banal chatter, Regina directed Cora Rae and Wini, "Come girls. Let's give Gracie the private teatime with Abby she intended."

"Wait, no," Cora Rae protested. "You may not want to extract information from Abby about Douglas, but *I* do! I want every last detail she can tell us."

"Now, Rae," Regina began, as she stood.

"It's Cora!" Cora Rae snapped.

"Cora." Regina acquiesced. "I won't have you busy-bodying with Abby. It's one thing to scheme when the overall goal is charity. I've told you girls dozens of times that charity is a lady's best way of giving thanks to God for her good luck. But nosiness, Rae—I mean Cora," Regina looked down at her daughter, "that's just bad breeding. Come." Regina motioned again for the girls to stand and then ushered them from the room, leaving Gracie to entertain her guest.

As the footsteps receded, Gracie finally looked at Abby. "I'm so sorry about, well about . . . that." She spoke quietly, contritely. "When those three get an idea between them, there's just no stopping them. Oh goodness, Abby. I'm mortified by the way they bombarded you. You must be fuming."

"I am not cross with you," Abby replied gently, "just confused, to tell truth, about what that was." She had, at the start of tea, been angry, brilliantly angry, with Gracie, for subjecting her to that examination by her family. When she had been greeted by Gracie's mother and her sisters, she had determined Gracie's overtures of friendship a trick of some sort to lure her to this meeting. But as she watched Gracie retreat further into herself in the presence of her sisters and mother, like a fading shadow, she realized that Gracie too had been ambushed.

"It's just, well," Gracie stole a glance at the empty doorway and leaned closer to Abby. "They *are* plotting and scheming, regardless of what Mama says. Mama might only be involved for Rae's sake, so I suppose her intentions are benevolent, but they're catching you up in the middle of something that is not your dilemma. Especially when your welfare is dependent on staying in Douglas's good graces. They're my family, and I reckon I love them, but Heaven knows, I don't share a common trait with any of those three, not even the red hair." Gracie's breath caught at something, and suddenly her eyes began to pool.

"Gracie, what is it?"

Gracie shook her head as she tried to compose herself. Abby wondered again if the girl was sincere, or if she was putting on theatrics, kicking up a fuss for Abby's benefit, but instinct told her Gracie's distress was genuine.

Gracie looked again at the door and then began to explain. "It's Rae," she wiped a hand under her eye. "It's always Rae, refusing to let me have anything of my own. She gets everyone into trouble and always manages to extricate herself from blame. And this time, well," after one more glance at the door, she explained, "all this mess is because she's still in love with Douglas."

"In love with Mr. Elling!" Abby blurted, incredulous. She remembered Gracie mentioning Cora Rae's affection for Mr. Elling at the ball, but Abby hadn't imagined it was anything as serious as this. "But she's so beautiful. And young. And he's, well he's, well," Abby stammered, flabbergasted as she pictured the man she knew, the fellow she had seen brooding and growling around the estate. "He's Douglas Elling." Abby looked at Gracie in disbelief.

"Abby, please, keep your voice down." Abby nodded and Gracie continued, "Yes, she is very much in love with Douglas. Has been for years, for as long as I can remember. He wasn't always such a lout. And he isn't even that old, only twenty-six, despite the way he behaves. I suppose all the youth went out of him after the accident."

Gracie lifted her teacup and looked at Abby, "After Sarah died, Rae decided it was her chance to finally become Mrs. Elling. As you can tell, it's hardly panned out. She has refused proposals from four other men, and Daddy's near apoplectic. I suppose Mama is trying to help Rae catch Douglas because she simply won't accept any other gentleman in his stead."

"So what good am I?" Abby asked, still unclear as to why they had toadied over her so.

"Oh, who knows what they've cooked up." Gracie's shoulders slumped. "But you mustn't do it, Abby. Douglas simply wouldn't stand for this scheming. Not the Douglas I knew. Especially not by someone living under his roof. I couldn't bear it if he sent you back home on account of my family's nonsense."

"Don't trouble yourself over this, Gracie," Abby told her calmly, as she tried her tea again and found it finally cool enough. "I've battled forces much worse than a lovesick girl and her mother. It will be fine. For all of us, I'm sure."

Abby was genuinely growing less perturbed. Rather, she felt

relieved that their odd behavior had nothing to do with her in-auspicious upbringing and current status as a charity ward. Abby was sure she'd be able to appease the Cunningham brood without having to do much at all. There wasn't much that one *could* do to infatuate a man like Douglas Elling.

"If you say so," Gracie conceded tentatively. "But ughh! I just find them so infuriating! It's like I don't matter at all, and they just do as they please regardless of what I say."

"Well, how is it if we focus on something cheerier?" Abby waved her hand dismissively. "Why don't you tell me more about you, instead of your sisters?"

Gracie dabbed at her eyes with a napkin and nodded. The young women passed another hour, enjoying their tea and biscuits, and getting better acquainted. Abby told Gracie snippets about her family, small easy details about her siblings, how she missed them, even Joseph and Christopher. Gracie asked questions about her studies with Larissa and then abruptly shifted the topic again, declaring that she was so relieved to have met Abby, as she was bursting to confide a secret in someone, a secret her other friends would certainly reveal if they knew. She proceeded to confess that she was smitten with a young man named Harrison Blount, a longtime acquaintance, whose parents owned the plantation neighboring her own family's Cherry Lane Plantation on the outskirts of Charleston.

"He hasn't any notion I exist," Gracie complained. "I can't compete with Rae's dazzling appearance. But he's dashing like you couldn't imagine. I just want to talk about him all the time, everything about him, even his hair, you should see his hair," she smiled thinking about it, "like spun gold. I hadn't seen him while he was studying in France. He was gone a year, maybe two, I don't even know. And then he visited a few days before the ball to see my Daddy. I was done for." She laughed happily at her fate but then quickly sobered. "Though I'm sure he's be-sotted with Rae, like everyone else." She put her small fist to her mouth and almost whimpered.

"Come now," Abby chided, "give yourself more due. Why, you're beautiful, and sweet. You have those big dark eyes, lashes enough for three women. And kindness is the most important, isn't it? Any gentleman who'd choose your sister over you would be a fool."

"I'm not sure I believe that," Gracie responded skeptically, "but I still appreciate your saying it." Her shoulders dipped again as she regarded Abby. "You're very sweet. I'm so glad we've met."

Abby stood, realizing now that Demett had likely been out-side for some time, waiting to carry her back to the Elling estate. She looked at the tea and fixings strewn about the low table and fought her urge to help tidy up.

"I'm glad we had this chance to talk," she told Gracie, and realized only after she said it that she meant every word.

"Thank you for coming and putting up with my foolish fam-ily. Oh, Daddy would be just mortified if he knew what they were up to!"

9

CHARLESTON, SOUTH CAROLINA
1845

"Ah, there you are." Regina Cunningham appeared at the entrance to the drawing room, where Gracie had been sitting with a book of poetry since Abby's departure. Gracie had hardly looked at the sonnets, ruminating instead on Harrison, on her sisters, on the kinship she felt with Abby.

When they met at the ball, Gracie had taken a swift liking to Abby, perhaps because she imagined Abby so similar to herself, an empathetic soul stifled by her surroundings. Gracie wasn't certain what had given her that impression, perhaps the invisible armor Abby seemed to wear at the ball, her cautiousness, the distance she appeared to crave from Cora Rae. And then today, when they were alone, Abby had quickly put Gracie at ease, forgiving her mother's conspiring, focusing on Gracie instead. Abby seemed uninterested in the trivialities that consumed Gracie's other friends, less likely to discount a friend for failing to measure up. What a relief it had been to finally breathe normally in the presence of another young lady. She hadn't worried whether Abby would judge her manners, her hair, her waistline. Even with her stays pulled taught, she could always hear her mother's voice reminding her to "suck it in, Gracie, pull in that navel." She never could maintain a figure like her sisters', and it was tiresome trying.

"I was wondering where you'd got to." Her mother smiled at her, not unkindly. Regina glanced to the other side of the drawing room and noticed the tea service that still sat in disarray on the table. "Would you believe that after all this time, Clover has not yet returned to collect the trays?" Regina shook her head. "It's like that girl is asking for it, dropping ashes on her duties. She should count her lucky voodoo feathers, or whatever they're into these days, that we don't operate like that. How am I to run a household with this shirking?" Regina glanced at a tall wood-encased clock in the corner of the room and added, "It's near time to dress for supper. Why don't you collect yourself and come change now anyway?"

"I'll find Clover, Mama. You go ahead and change your own dress." Gracie hated to think of Regina laying into meek Clover, especially while the woman was so large with child. Regina had been particularly hard on the young slave since her pregnancy began to show. "I promise I will be strict as a wasp with her," she lied.

Regina regarded her daughter dubiously, but she then ran an exploratory hand over the twist at the back of her head, where strands were slipping loose from a white silk ribbon.

"I suppose I could use the time to have Ebony fix this. But don't go easy on Clover. Pretend you are Cora Rae, let her know her place."

"Yes, Mama." Gracie stood and tried discreetly to pull her crinoline underskirt away from where it had begun to cling to her perspiring legs.

As she walked toward the kitchen in search of Clover, Gracie considered the latter parts of her afternoon with Abby, and now this small success of convincing her Mama to let her take charge, even with something so small. When she neared the kitchen, she called for Clover. Receiving no response other than the continued tapping of her own feet against the marble floor, Gracie poked her head tentatively through the swinging door.

"Clover?" She called again, this time more gently. Regina was adamant that her children not mingle too closely with the slaves, that it would only lead to vexation. Even their favorite house slaves would seize the first opportunity to take advantage, Regina warned. Plus, it just didn't look nice. And Regina simply would not have it, she had declared repeatedly, not in her house. The slaves seemed reluctant to spend much time in the proximity of the master and his family anyway. She looked about the large kitchen now and became concerned. Not only was Clover absent, but Cook was missing, as well.

"Cook?" Gracie called as she stepped into the kitchen. Gracie couldn't remember Cook's real name. Maybe Thelma. Daddy had bought Cook when Gracie was just a toddler. Cook was large and exuberant, and she seemed to have a soft spot for Gracie, perhaps sensitive to her Mama's criticisms of Gracie "running to fat." Gracie wasn't all that big, just misshapen, too much of herself in the middle, not quite enough up top. And she was much bulkier than her sisters. Cook always saved little treats for Gracie nonetheless, inordinately pleased when a spare cookie allowed her to catch a smile from the girl.

Gracie stepped farther into the long, rectangular kitchen, past the large copper pots lining the counter, the bags of flour, grains, and rice resting neatly in the corner, when she noticed that the back door was ajar. Perhaps the women were at the smokehouse out back. As she walked toward the door, Cook suddenly came bounding back into the kitchen in a burst of patchwork linen and mismatched scarves.

"Miss Gracie!" She nearly bellowed. "What you doing in this kitchen? There something I can get for you? You best not let your mama catch you. She'll chide you double. Once for being too near the slaves, and the other for being too near the sugar." The dark, rotund woman smiled broadly, revealing the missing tooth on the upper-right side of her mouth.

"Um, no . . ." Gracie responded as she tried to peer around Cook's large frame to look for Clover outside the door. Cook stepped to the side, moving her kerchief-covered head directly in front of Gracie, obscuring her view entirely. It was almost as though she had blocked Gracie intentionally.

"I was searching for Clover," Gracie explained. "Have you seen her?"

"Sure, I did!" Cook responded with her characteristic gusto, as if her every sentence were announcement of a triumph. "She went around back to get more water in case y'all wanted a little finish before coming up from the tea with your guest. Thought the Missus might be wanting some nice cool water, and all," she repeated. "Wash down them sweets. She just yonder," Cook began to point and then interrupted herself. "Here she is now."

As Clover stepped through the door, Gracie noticed again how heavy she was getting with child, round like she'd hidden a fat goose beneath her smock. It was supposedly only a few months into the pregnancy, but Clover was growing at a rampant pace. It was no wonder she seemed short of breath.

"Miss Gracie here just wondering what was holding you up, girl," Cook told Clover with a pointed look. "You best be getting them desserts cleared from the parlor, now. You don't want the Missus wondering where you got off to."

"Miss Gracie," Clover looked flustered, a droplet of sweat slipping down her smooth, tawny face. She was near Gracie's own age, perhaps a few years older, and so lovely to look at, her long braids and wide eyes giving her an ethereal aspect, even in her pregnant state. "So sorry, Miss. I gone have them desserts and tea out in no time," Clover said softly as she picked up an empty tray and waddled toward the swinging door that led to the rest of the house.

Gracie thought the tray alone looked too heavy for the young woman to carry, never mind the weight it would bear when it was loaded with the trappings of afternoon tea. She was tempted to offer help, but her mother would have her hide for it. The only way she could assist Clover was to hold the door open and let her pass through.

As Gracie made her way back to the drawing room, Clover following several steps behind, Regina appeared in the corridor, lustrous in her lilac dinner gown. "Well it seems our Gracie has saved the day, hasn't she?" Gracie was struck by the acerbic tone of her mother's voice. Turning to Clover, Regina added, "Just get it cleared away. And do expect we'll be speaking later."

"Yes'm," Clover replied meekly, eyes to the ground as she nodded at her mistress. Gracie hadn't protected Clover from her mother, after all. Just delayed their confrontation.

Gracie and Regina watched Clover as she disappeared down the hallway into the drawing room, mother and daughter each wrapped up in their own thoughts. As Gracie tried to shake off her aggravation at being discounted yet again, she noticed her mother wiping furiously beneath her eyes, as though erasing evidence of tears.

10

∽

CHARLESTON, SOUTH CAROLINA

1846

*I*n the Elling Import & Export office overlooking Charleston Harbor, Douglas cracked the knuckles of his fingers one by one, finding no gratification in the loud popping noises. He could not focus on the shipping ledgers today, and it was a waste of his time to try. Ever since the governess had taken Samuel's daughter to the Cunningham ball the week before, he'd been horribly distracted. And now he understood that the girl had returned today for tea with Regina and her daughters, as well.

He had worked so purposefully, ever since losing Sarah and Cherish, trying to isolate himself from Charleston society, blaming the wealthy planters, all of them, for his family's annihilation. He had long been too sad, too defeated to seek revenge, had it even been possible to determine which bandits had been the murderers. He thought only to create this artificial distance from people, his neighbors, friends, and acquaintances alike, to close himself off and indulge in his suffering.

When Abby departed from the Elling property for the ball

the prior week, Douglas had caught but a glimpse of her shimmering skirts as she walked out the door of the house with Larissa. He knew Demett was waiting in the drive for her, perched atop the Growler, the same coach he had ridden in with Sarah the last time they attended a ball together. It was all the same—the ritual of it, the soft evening light, the pervasive smell of jasmine drifting up from beneath the windows, the sense of possibility, and the nagging feeling of foreboding. As he'd stood in the hallway of his nearly empty estate, Douglas had the feeling his eyes had been pasted open, that he couldn't look away from the stagnancy of his grief.

How could it be that more than two whole years had passed and nothing had changed, except perhaps that he felt worse? All this time that he had existed in the world without them already, and he hadn't done a damn thing with that time. Here he sat, still luxuriating in his despair, the deaths of his family not yet avenged, and his own life a hollow shadow of his former reality.

Douglas's gaze floated to his window, where he could see amber rings from the late-day sun reflecting on the harbor. He watched a paddle-wheel tugboat as it churned through the water. His thoughts meandered back to his own days at sea, the rush of the Blockade mission, rescuing all those people. After only one mission, he had lost his family, and Southern slavery was as rampant, as insidious as ever. Sarah would tell him that by retreating, by abandoning his abolitionist work, he was rendering her death meaningless. Even so, he simply could not participate in something that had brought such misery upon them. His only involvement now was to allow Demett access to his cellar tunnel for the odd group of refugees. It hardly made him a hero.

And then there was this business with the Milton girl. Ever since he had found her in the pasture with Reggie, grabbing onto his hand like they were about to say grace, Douglas's reaction had been nagging at his conscience. When he first arrived home that afternoon, he had watched the girl from afar, taking advantage of the moment to study her, her poise with the horse she rode, her easy smile with Reggie. He had noticed that she looked healthier than when she first arrived from Wigan, with a flush to her cheeks and more meat on her slender frame. He could see that she had Samuel's high forehead and his nimble grace. Her crisp jawline and shining hair were all her mother's though. She looked older to him than she appeared at first. Not so much a girl now, but an attractive young woman. Her dark hair had grown longer, and it was arranged in an upsweep of wavy tendrils, a flattering compliment to the disappointingly plain riding habit she wore.

He recalled while he watched her that Larissa had described the girl's tastes as simple. The governess had reported Abigail's reluctance to improve upon the meager wardrobe with which she'd arrived. He hadn't focused closely on what Larissa relayed about her, registering simply that the girl was getting on fine, that he was doing his duty for his old friend, Samuel. But as he had watched Samuel's daughter in that moment, flourishing in the sunlight like catmint flowers, he was disgusted at himself, the way he had received her, or more aptly, had neglected her, as a guest in his home. Samuel had been nearly an older brother to him for so many years, sheltering him from torment when others would not. Yet Douglas hadn't taken the slightest bit of interest in his daughter. For Christ's sake, he barely knew a thing about her. Other than that she was becoming a capable horsewoman. To say that he was doing his duty to his old friend was laughable, an utter farce.

He had still been watching her when he resolved to do better. But as he had begun walking toward the barn to greet the girl, that was when she had reached out and taken Reggie's dark hand. He hadn't stopped to wonder at her purpose, as it wouldn't have mattered anyhow. Instead, he felt his knees nearly buckle with panic. It was all he could do to shout out from where he stood, to make her understand, remove herself from risk. He had been struck, as if by physical force, with the magnitude of danger the girl could be in, simply from residing in his home. He thought of Cherish then and was moved to act with decisive and immediate action. And so he bellowed. He opened his lungs like gates to the fires of Hell, showering his wrath down upon her. He had raged at her with everything he had, each whooping jab helping to ease his own panic. The invectives erupting from his mouth did not even make sense, like that nonsense he had spewed about white skin never touching black skin. One had only to consider the many slaves who assisted their mistresses with bathing to know he had ranted absurdities, that black skin came into contact with white as a matter of course, many times throughout a Southern lady's day.

When he retreated to his study after the incident, a new panic had arisen. What kind of a person had he become? That the only way he could show kindness was by barking reprimands, inciting fear, and roaring in the face of a lady?

Weeks had passed since that day, and still, he'd done nothing to remedy the situation. Douglas looked back at the ledgers on his oak desk, the numbers scrawled in so many columns. He didn't need to finish the calculations to know the shipping company was as profitable as ever. He was frivoling away too many minutes trying to focus on one thing while his mind was set to brooding on another. At the present moment, Douglas felt fit only to growl at the moon.

He found his manservant, Jovian, arranging spools of rope in the store room, and requested to be carried home.

AS THEY PULLED INTO THE DRIVE, DOUGLAS DECIDED
to look in on his horses, an attempt to calm his nerves before
heading to his study for a hefty tumbler of whiskey. He meandered toward the outer door of the barn and noticed a slim figure standing at one of the stalls inside. She appeared only as a
dark silhouette at the far end of the long stable, but he knew it
must be Abigail. She was offering some hidden treat toward the
newest stallion in his retinue. He would have expected that skit-
tish thoroughbred to buck or jump, at least to whiny unhappily,
in rebuke of the lady's advances. That was how the charger had
been reacting to everyone else. What an impressive waste of
money that beast was proving.

To Douglas's surprise, the horse nibbled quietly from Abigail's
hand, even nestling its nose against her wrist while she leaned
over the stall door. As he watched her operating so evenly with the
horse, he decided that this moment could be a superb opportunity
to start afresh with her, to begin acquainting themselves in earnest. It was the principled way to behave as her host. Startling
himself with the direction of his thoughts, he realized that attending to the girl's well-being might also provide him a purpose,
a direction beyond grief. It wasn't much, just a nudge against a
steel gasket perhaps. Sarah would be furious if she knew how un-
congenial he had been to his unfortunate houseguest. Man alive!
He almost laughed as he imagined her tearing into him with the
brand of outrage that only a good Southern upbringing could
engender. Douglas pushed his hands into his pockets and walked
purposefully toward the stable, ready to make amends with Abigail.

As he entered the dark corridor, he heard her murmuring
indistinctly to the horse. She was fiddling with the divider, un-
fastening the door. He realized too late that she meant to go

inside with the untamed beast, the animal that Reggie had warned Douglas was unpredictable and highly excitable.

"Abigail, no!" He called out to her, but she was already entering, his yelling only pushing her farther into the stall in surprise or in terror. Between the sudden noise and the unexpected visitor in his space, the animal commenced an awful commotion, rearing up twice in quick succession, huffing and whinnying. Douglas reached the open stall door as the chestnut steed came rushing out. He jumped out of its way and called for Jovian, hoping that one of his men would catch the animal. When he looked inside, dust high around his face, he saw that he hadn't moved fast enough to avert disaster.

There was Abby, lying unconscious on a slick pile of hay against the wall. He could see from twelve feet away that her left shoulder was out of place. The horse must have knocked her down instantly.

"Jovian!" He shouted. "Demett! We need help!"

He bent next to Abby, attempting to assess her injuries. He could see the rise and fall of her chest at least. It appeared she had only been knocked into, rather than trampled, but he didn't dare move her on his own, lest he exacerbate her injuries. If only he hadn't come upon the girl so suddenly, hadn't reacted so abruptly. Please, God, she should be okay, Douglas prayed as he thought of his friend Samuel. The man would probably be asleep in bed now, miles away, and already finished with this infernal day. Yet here lay his daughter, unconscious in a barn halfway across the world. Douglas wouldn't wish the death of a daughter on even his lowest enemy.

At the sound of hammering footsteps, he called out, "We're in here! She's hurt!"

"Oh, Lordy!" Demett blurted as he poked his head into the stall. "Sir?" he looked to Douglas for instruction.

"We've got to get her inside without disrupting her position. She's a wisp of a thing, but I think it might take three of us to keep her steady." Douglas looked at the other stable hands who had arrived, their faces heavy with concern for the crumpled girl. "Reggie, Jovian, help me carry her," Douglas commanded. "Demett, fetch Dr. Markinson and beg him to hurry."

As the three men lifted her, Douglas realized this was the first physical contact he'd had with a woman in years. Or a girl. Whatever she was. He hadn't quite settled the question, but it didn't matter at the moment. "Easy," Douglas cautioned as they walked into the afternoon light with Abby supine between. There were too many of them holding her, he realized. It was another error in judgment, another mistake he'd made today. She was lightweight enough, and they were fat, clumsy bulls surrounding her. It might do more harm to rearrange now though. Douglas noticed Abby's limp wrist resting against Jovian's dark forearm as he held her, skin to skin.

He tried to remember what his father had taught him about head injuries. Was it to wake the patient or let them rest? He decided to talk to her as they walked, "Abigail, we've got you. We're almost to the house." He felt Abby shudder in his arms. "Hush now," he spoke gently to her closed eyes. "Hush, and let us get you well."

When he looked up, he noticed Jovian and Reggie exchanging surprised glances. Well, let them puzzle, he figured. All that mattered was keeping this young woman alive. He knew the minute he laid hands on her, he couldn't say why, that his new mission was to rescue her, not only from the immediate incident, but from whatever it was that had pushed her from her British home, ragged and defeated, to him. She was under his protection, and there was a reason Samuel had sent her. Maybe at last he could save just one person who was actually relevant to the story of his own life.

DOUGLAS WAITED ON THE LANDING OUTSIDE ABBY'S room, grimacing at the closed door, wondering when in Heaven's name Doc Markinson would emerge. It felt like the man had been in there with her for decades already. He needed to know she was going to be all right, that she wasn't suffering terribly, that she wouldn't be paralyzed or permanently addled in her brain.

He cursed himself again for his dimwitted behavior. Of course she had been frightened by his approach, Douglas shook his head in revolt. He had barely uttered a word to her since her arrival months ago, except to terrorize her for her kindness to Reggie, and today suddenly he materialized, barreling down upon her in a dark stable. He should have realized the atrocious folly of it all. But because of his obtuseness, here they were.

At the sound of the door creaking open, Douglas threw his hands into the air.

"Finally!" he exclaimed into the empty corridor.

Dr. Markinson emerged, stuffing supplies into a black leather carryall. Douglas waited silently as the white-haired doctor shut the door with painstaking care.

As the latch clicked, he launched into the man. "Well? What's the prognosis?"

"Please, Mr. Elling," Dr. Markinson held up his hand and moved a few steps toward the stairwell before answering. "The guardianship arrangement makes it troublesome, no doubt, but her parents will forgive this." He smiled at Douglas, as if that were the whole story, as if they were in cahoots.

"But what of her condition?" Douglas barked.

Dr. Markinson sighed, making great effort to show he was indulging Douglas.

"Miss Milton had a nasty tumble, son, but she'll recover in

time. She dislocated her left shoulder, and she's a bit concussed from the bump to the head. Likely she'll suffer a good deal from the arm for the next few days. Heck, maybe a week. But I finished setting it, and she should heal quickly enough." He looked back at the bedroom door and pushed his round eyeglasses higher on his nose. "Y'all just need to manage the pain. I left the laudanum with the governess. It's to administer as needed, and certainly enough to keep the young lady senseless for the first days. You'll want to switch to willow bark when the pain begins to subside." Dr. Markinson put his hand on Douglas's arm in a gesture of comfort, as if he'd only just noticed that Douglas was genuinely concerned.

"We've been through heavier trials in the past, you and I," Dr. Markinson told him, referring to the night Cherish was born. Douglas stepped back, unprepared for memories of that night, forcing his focus to remain on Abby. Dr. Markinson charged on, oblivious to the jarring effect of his words. "Dislocating a joint like that, it can smart, but it repairs. As for the concussion, bear with the girl. She mightn't seem right about the head for a few days, but that'll just be pain and bruises talking."

Douglas nodded, relieved. "And there's nothing else, no lasting damage?"

"Rest easy, son," Dr. Markinson smiled, "it's just the shoulder, and it's hardly a permanent injury. She's fortunate. With a steed like that, it could have been much worse."

Douglas watched the doctor shuffle off and then turned back to Abby's quarters. The governess was inside with the girl, and Larissa would certainly report accurately on the girl's condition, but he did want to see her for himself. He was the one with actual responsibility for her welfare, wasn't he? He suddenly felt very weary. He ran his hand over his eyes, as if trying to clear the dust off them, and then rapped lightly on the door.

"May I see her?" he asked Larissa in a hushed voice.

"Please," she motioned for him to enter. Abby was sleeping, her dark hair loose, arrayed neatly around her head, and her bandaged arm held tightly in a sling.

"Can you stay with her while I go to the kitchen to work out her meals?" Larissa walked toward Abby and retrieved a wool wrap from the chair beside the bed. "She's going to need mostly broth the next few days. Doc said we should keep her sedated while her arm mends, that we'll need to feed her while she's only fractionally conscious." Larissa straightened her blonde bun absentmindedly.

"I'll leave the door wide," she added as she left the room, and Douglas knew she was thinking of Abby's reputation, even in the girl's incapacitated state.

He looked uncertainly about Abby's bedroom and walked toward the oversized bed. It occurred to him that he'd never been inside this room, as it had been unoccupied for the duration of his residency in the home. He looked to Abby, motionless in the center of her downy sheets, her head settled on a plump, white pillow with her face turned politely to one side. Her dark lashes rested against her cheek, just grazing her smooth skin. As he stood awkwardly next to the bed and looked down at her, he thought that no one would guess from her appearance what an ordeal she had been through.

He walked to the bedside chair and sank down, wondering how long Larissa would be. Glancing to the filigreed clock on the nightstand, he realized that Abby would normally have been readying for her supper now, instead of being confined to her bed in this unconscious position. If only he'd acted more thoughtfully. As he watched her, she began to stir in the bed, adjusting her position. First one leg moved beneath the comforter, and then the other, then the first again. She seemed to be gaining momentum with every shift of her frame, becoming increasingly agitated. She began to moan quietly, and then she was thrashing her head from side to side.

Douglas stood, wondering how to calm her. As he leaned over her, she began to scream, piercing shrieks of alarm, as though she was being hunted by demons.

"Abigail!" Douglas shouted in alarm. He reached down and tried to steady her, worried most of all that she would damage her arm. He held her in place by the other shoulder, which barely did an ounce of good as her screeching persisted. He needed more leverage and thought to hold her down more forcefully, but it wouldn't be right to have his hands all over her while they were alone.

"Abigail!" He leaned closer to the bed and yelled into her closed eyes, trying to reach her through the opiated haze, the raucousness of her cries. "Abigail!" he yelled again. "Abigail, stop this, it's all right." She persevered in her screaming and the vigorous writhing, twisting the bed coverings and worrying Douglas. Dr. Markinson had warned about unsettling behavior, but Douglas couldn't just let her thrash about, else her shoulder might become dislocated all over again.

He'd never paid much heed to the rules of propriety anyhow. He sat on the bed and took her face in his hands, trying to steady her, as she continued in her fit. "Abigail, can you hear me? You must be still so you don't injure yourself!" She opened her eyes and looked at him, but it was patently obvious she didn't see him at all. Her mind was occupied somewhere very far away. She closed her eyes again and continued to flail about, her undamaged arm swatting at him as her voice began to grow hoarse from the screaming.

"Abigail," Douglas said again, keeping his own voice steady. "Can you hear me? It's Douglas."

She rolled fitfully out of his grasp, toward the far edge of the bed, and Douglas quickly pulled her back toward himself to prevent her tumbling to the floor.

"Whoa. You mustn't move so, Abigail. You've injured your shoulder, and you must try to keep still." He pushed at her gently, trying to encourage her back to the position in which he had found her. As he adjusted her, Abby's agitation intensified.

"You!" She screamed through her sleep, as if she had just noticed a presence in her dreams, her eyes open again, blank and frightening. "You!" She roared again, her tone loaded with hatred. "Again! How dare you lay your palms on me! You! You've had the last of me. No more!"

"Abigail!" Douglas shouted at her again, trying to wake her from her hysteria.

"To the Tower of London!" she screamed into the room.

"Just relax, Abigail! You are in Charleston. You were hurt. You're all right, but you must calm down." They were going to have to rethink the laudanum if this was her reaction to it.

She began to laugh in her sleep. "You won't have me again." She laughed more as her lips twisted into a distorted smile. "Matthew to the guillotine! Huzzah, Uncle!"

Dear God! Douglas hurried to the console table at the side of the room and poured a hasty glass of brandy for her, thinking he could use one himself. He rushed back to the bed, splashy bits falling onto the pristine rug.

"Drink this, Abigail. It will make you feel better." He took hold of her good hand and tried to wrap her fingers around the glass.

"Get away from me!" Abby screamed and pushed in every direction, sending the glass of brandy soaring through the air and crashing into the vanity table. At the sound of the glass shattering, she let out another piercing scream.

It was obvious to Douglas that his presence in her chamber was only aggravating her. He moved toward the door to call for the governess, who was already running back up the stairwell.

"What's happened?" Larissa demanded as she ran toward the bedroom.

"I don't know." Douglas shouted over the wails. "One minute she was resting peacefully and the next she was out of control. I think I am only upsetting her. Perhaps you will do better."

"Yes, yes, let me. Doc said this might happen. All the pain and then the drugs, just too much. I'll call if I need help." Larissa disappeared into the room and shut the door quickly behind her. Douglas waited outside, too concerned to retreat further. Within only a few moments, the commotion subsided.

Douglas put his ear to the door and heard only the indistinct murmurings of the governess. He waited, wondering if there was something he should do. After several minutes of feeling useless, he began to make his way down the stairwell, pausing every few steps to listen for disturbances from above. When he reached his study, he took care to light the extra lanterns, one on his desk, and a matching pair on either side of the sofa. Although Jasper had left the usual sconces alight and waiting for him, Douglas felt he lacked the tolerance for any shadows tonight. He sank down into the leather swivel chair and rested his palms flat on his large desk, a strange restlessness making his fingers dance. What in God's name had Matthew Milton done now?

11

CHARLESTON, SOUTH CAROLINA
1846

Gracie sat in the upstairs parlor, along with her mother
and sisters, entertaining Lorraine Blount and her
dull but beautiful fifteen-year-old daughter, Millicent. Lorraine
had once been a comely woman, but she now appeared ridiculous in her overt pursuit to maintain her vanishing youth. She
and her daughter wore their blonde hair in matching styles of
upswept ringlets. While Millicent appeared rather darling with
the buoyant curls topping off her frothy pink dress, Lorraine
only looked drabber for the comparison to her blooming daughter right beside her.

Regina always made sure to invite the Blounts, who owned
the neighboring property to the Cunninghams' Cherry Lane
Plantation, to come calling at the King Street residence during
the winter months. If they didn't extend invitations while they
were on retreat from the plantation, Regina told her daughters,
there was no telling what life might be like or who would come
calling when they returned.

Gracie had never minded the long days without callers on
the plantation, glad to wander the orchards or read on the porch

swing, enjoying her own company. Not like Rae and Wini, who would bicker and cry boredom until sunset. Even so, she was heartened by any logic that would lead to her spending time in the company of the dashing young Harrison. Gracie glanced at the tall grandfather clock in the corner and wondered how long it would be until the boys returned for supper.

Court Cunningham had invited Lorraine's husband, Preston, as well as their sons, Harrison and young Brody, to hunt pheasant for the afternoon. Regina and her daughters were to entertain Lorraine and Millicent until the hunting party returned and they could all sup together. Sitting now on the pink settee, wedged between Cora Rae and Wini, Gracie tried to stay focused on the conversation, even though it seemed like Lorraine and her mother had been cycling repeatedly through different variations of the same few topics. Someone had closed the door to the verandah earlier, and the air in the room had taken on a stagnant, husky quality. Returning her attention to the conversation before her, she heard her mother complaining, yet again, about the declining demeanor of her house slaves.

"It's just been so trying for us, wouldn't you say?" She looked toward her daughters for validation. "Ever since the Hopwoods' boy ran off last winter and never got returned, it's like they all think it's only a matter of time, like they can cease putting forth any effort." She pursed her full lips. "We've always prided ourselves on the fair treatment of our people, but if this keeps up, I'm fixing to speak with Court."

Lorraine offered Regina a knowing smile. "Indeed, my dear. We have the same troubles with ours. We've got our work cut out for us, trying to run our homes properly in the wake of constant unpredictability, when you can't trust a one of them. This one is stealing food again or that one is trying to seduce the overseer. If you want to know what I really think," she leaned toward Regina with an air of collaboration, her childish curls moving along with her, "I hope South Carolina does secede from the Union, just like Robert Rhett keeps pressing the legislature. Settle the Negroes right back into place. Preston believes Rhett will make senator soon. Oh but all this discussion of politics does make my head ache." She slumped back in her chair and placed the back of her palm against her forehead in a theatrical motion.

Gracie knew that she should try to contribute to the discussion, as ladies' conversation was a skill she had been working on with her mother. Then again, Cora Rae hadn't had much to say either, apparently just as bored by this monotonous prattle as she. She looked over at her older sister and saw her reaching for the teapot.

"No, Rae, not today," Regina admonished her, swatting away her daughter's hand. "Clover and I had words, and I won't have us changing our personal customs, pouring our own tea each time we entertain."

"Must you always be so hard on Clover?" Cora Rae snapped as she lowered her hand. "Besides, everyone pours their own tea," Cora Rae argued.

"Not the Cunninghams." Her mother's voice was stern as she glanced again toward the room's doorway just as Clover appeared with two other slaves following behind her.

"And here she is anyhow," Regina told her daughter before turning to Clover and reprimanding her in a harsh whisper that was audible to all. "Too slow." Regina glanced dismissively at Ginny and Saul, the two other slaves who had appeared with the refreshments, but her gaze returned swiftly to Clover. As the contrite house slave began pouring the tea, Regina's eyes lingered on the young woman's growing belly.

Gracie considered her mother's perspective. She supposed it

was accurate that Clover had been slower lately, less attentive. Gracie had never been able to get into the spirit of punishing the slaves though, demeaning them like animals when they failed to execute their duties with the requisite precision. She did believe wholeheartedly in the necessity of slavery, of course she did, but she abhorred certain aspects of the system. She agreed that each person had their station in life, and it seemed clear enough that the calling of the Negroes was to serve their white masters. But the brutality with which some masters treated their slaves, torturing them, shackling them nightly, whipping them beyond repair, well, Gracie just couldn't see the humanity in that.

It was an ongoing problem she supposed, but at the moment, she was most preoccupied with which dress to wear to supper after the men returned from their hunt. This was the first time since Gracie's coming out that she and Harrison would be together. If she failed to impress Harrison tonight, upon his first occasion with her as an eligible young lady, he might never think of her again. Harrison Blount was the most handsome young man on whom Gracie had ever set her eyes. His flaxen hair and dark-brown eyes were only the beginning. At six foot three inches, he was one of the tallest boys in the county, and his shoulders were broad, his neck thick and strong. He was energetic and clever, too. She felt a freefall in her belly when she thought of the cleft in his chin.

Gracie sobered at the thought that Harrison would likely be assigned a seat between herself and her overbearing sister. Her parents would be concerned only with maximizing the odds of the Blounts and Cunninghams having a match between them; any daughter would do. He would likely turn to Cora Rae, victim to her pull at the table, before he even had a moment to notice Gracie. That was how occasions always unraveled with Cora

Rae—Gracie fading into the background, Cora Rae shining all the brighter.

Gracie was roused from her musings at the sound of Regina asking her daughters, "Don't you agree, girls?"

She dutifully joined the refrains of "yes, Mama," though she couldn't begin to guess at what trite statement she had agreed to this time.

Regina announced it was time to freshen up for dinner, and the ladies began to rise. Gracie watched as Millicent took her white gloves from her lap and placed them onto her hands. She thought to invite the girl to dress along with her in her room. Although Millicent was a bore, she seemed kind enough, and perhaps if they bonded, the girl might say something flattering to her brother about Gracie.

Wini, who was already walking out from the parlor, called over her shoulder, "Come on to my room, Millicent, and we can ready ourselves together."

Gracie cursed herself for her burden of hesitation and the lost opportunity, as she watched Millicent follow after her sister. As Gracie made her way dejectedly to her own quarters, she realized Cora Rae was following purposefully behind her. Weary from the tedious ladies' afternoon, Gracie lacked the energy for whatever insipid confrontation was looming. Cora Rae entered the room right behind her, closing the door after herself.

"Is there something you need from me, Rae?" Gracie asked, trying for politeness. "Cora, I mean." Gracie forced her lips into a smile as she added, "It takes a while to break such a long-standing habit," referring to how long she had called her older sister "Rae."

Cora Rae walked farther into the bedroom, turning her back to Gracie and gazing at her reflection in the large framed mirror above the room's fireplace. She straightened the vermeil necklace that hung above the neckline of her dress, studying its garnet jewels in the mirror before turning to Gracie.

"We need to talk about Harrison," she declared, and Gracie felt herself stiffen, as though she had suddenly become a stone, dropping to the bottom of a pond.

"What, why ever, why?" she stumbled.

"Well, you do fancy him, don't you?"

"What business is that of yours?" Gracie felt heat spreading from her neck to eyebrows. For what earthly reason did Cora Rae need to know about this?

"Well, I've been thinking," Cora Rae began, as she paced toward the window in that feline style of hers. "I've decided I shall take him for myself." Cora Rae pivoted back toward her sister with a wicked smile.

"For yourself?" Gracie cried, failing to keep her voice steady. "Why? You haven't the slightest bit of interest in Harrison."

"Well, the way I see it," Cora Rae explained as she seated herself on the edge of Gracie's four-poster bed and ran her hand over the floral comforter, "if you won't help me beguile Douglas Elling, despite your advantageous position as the confidante of that stray who's staying at his house, well, you deserve what you get. I'll have to find some gentleman or other for myself, won't I? And Harrison Blount *is* the second-most handsome man in Charleston."

"Cora Rae!" Gracie scolded in shock. "You wouldn't. Not even you would do such a spiteful thing. You haven't the slightest bit of concern or affection for Harrison. You'd only be enchanting him to abuse me. I know it!" Gracie looked at her sister in disbelief, stifling the urge to spit at her. "What do you want me to do? Rae! Are there no limits to your selfishness?" Gracie held up her hands in despair, her large eyes grown wider in surprise at her sister's cunning.

"You know what I want you to do," Cora Rae drawled sweetly. "Procure for me one specific man, and I will keep away from yours. I don't much care how you do it, but Douglas Elling has been mourning his dead wife for long enough now, don't you agree?" Cora Rae rose from the bed. "It's been over two years, and I'm ready to have my turn with that man. I'm not getting any younger, Gracie. Get in there and do it."

"I'm sorry, I don't know what I can do to help your cause, noble though it may be," Gracie added with a snort.

"Well then, it's a mighty good thing I've got Harrison Blount waiting to become infatuated with me, isn't it just?"

"All right, all right, Rae. Cora." Gracie acquiesced with a huff. "I cannot believe you would do something so low. What do you need me to do?" Gracie felt her stomach tighten as she waited for Cora Rae's response.

"Now that's the spirit," Cora Rae approached her sister and began fiddling with the girl's dark hair. Gracie shook her off, but Cora Rae seemed unfazed. "First, you mustn't breathe a word of this to your friend Abigail. I need you to get into that house, get yourself back into Douglas's world. Let him see you regularly. He should warm up to you sooner or later, since he was always keen on our family. Well, before the fire." Cora Rae sneered as she added sarcastically, "What a tragedy *that* was."

"Cora Rae, shame on you!" Gracie reproached her. "I will help you if I must, but you best respect the dead. If you don't pray for the dead, the dead won't pray for you," Gracie warned. "And Lord knows, you need it!"

"If you say so," Cora Rae responded dismissively. "I think it shan't take much more than your continued presence to remind Douglas of how highly he regarded us. After a few weeks, you will invite him to tea with our family. In the interim, you will listen to any and all conversations that occur at the Elling estate while you are there, and you will inform me of what all you hear. Now that isn't so arduous, is it?"

Without allowing Gracie opportunity to respond, Cora Rae added, "If you do this favor for me, I will do you the favor of avoiding your precious Harrison like he's carrying the pox. I do believe that's the only way I can prevent him from falling for me. And frankly, I'm not even sure that will work, but I'll do what I can." Cora Rae walked toward the door and then added, "I'm so glad we had this talk. It's something, being sisters."

12

CHARLESTON, SOUTH CAROLINA
1846

*A*lone in his bedchamber, Douglas lay awake for the third straight hour, taut and heated. The three drams of scotch he'd drunk before settling into his bed had worn off, and he was as alert as ever. Sleepless nights were hardly unfamiliar to him, but something about tonight was different. Instead of enduring the endless, lightless hours focused on his own losses, he was thinking about Abby. Larissa informed him earlier in the day that the girl had wakened, lucid, but the governess was adamant that he must wait at least one more day before visiting her again, lest he rattle her as he had done during her delirium. He thought about her now, Abby, resting in her bandages and tangled bedsheets at the opposite end of the house. He longed to see with his own eyes that she was recuperating, that she felt calm again, intact and secure. He couldn't say what had come over him to suddenly feel so fixated, but ever since her accident the day before, he had been unable to expel her from his disordered mind.

He simply couldn't figure what to make of her, her history, her contradictory actions, her evolving presence in his home. There were other curiosities, as well—her fear, which was so pervasive, yet erratic. He thought of her overfamiliarity with Reggie, where she was slick with recklessness. There was no inkling of fear then, not until Douglas arrived. There was also the girl's changing appearance, her lack of wants, her grace and independence. He remembered his impression when he first beheld her upon her arrival so many months ago, a dusty obligation with withered clothing and barren eyes.

Had she any idea what she stumbled upon in the cellar to his office that day, as he and Demett shepherded refugees to the Underground tunnel? He wondered how she would react, if she would think to expose him. Perhaps she had kept quiet only from fear of losing her lodging. Or maybe she had heard the rumors about him and despised him for his lawlessness, his failure to support the Southern way of life. He didn't think so. He remembered how comfortable she'd seemed with Reggie that day with the handholding. Even based on their limited encounters, he had the sense that Abby was too committed to self-reliance, to independence, to think highly of American slavery.

She had seemed like a stray orphan that day of her arrival, reeking of sea travel, of sweat, resentment, and uncertainty. But the few times he had laid eyes on her more recently, he was surprised to notice that she had developed a refined loveliness. Perhaps it had been there underneath the dirt and the misshapen haircut all along. And once she had a few weeks of proper meals behind her, he could see that she was curved and hewed, not so young after all.

Then there was this business about her uncle. What had Abby been remembering when she conjured Matthew in her delirium earlier? It was not challenging to conjecture, but he found himself desperate to think of an alternative explanation for her agitated shouts. Douglas had known Matthew Milton since they were children, and had always found the fellow distasteful, at best. When Samuel had taken Douglas under his protective counsel so many years ago, Matthew had already been a parasite. Samuel shielded Douglas from the boys whose families disapproved of his father, fending off beatings, teaching him to fight, to practice and hone his physical skills. Matthew, who had been closer in age to Douglas, had been too busy worrying over his own social status to ever consider Douglas anything but a nuisance. Matthew had been a nasty, lying, slippery sort. But he wouldn't have imagined that Matthew could stoop so low as to abuse a young girl. His own niece. Douglas squeezed his eyes shut, as if to clear himself of the vile images coursing through his mind.

Douglas sat up and lit the lantern beside his bed. He ached for his friend, Samuel, who had lost so much, his shop, his livelihood, his ability to protect his own child from ruin. Douglas imagined what Matthew must look like as a grown man now, surely with the same hanging belly and pockmarked skin he had in his adolescence, and it was almost too much for his mind to clutch. Douglas wondered if he should write and tell Samuel what he had discovered about Matthew. No, it would suffocate Samuel if he knew what had occurred just beyond his reach. Douglas realized now that it was the unwanted attentions of her uncle, the man supporting her family, that must have engendered Abigail's discontent in Wigan, the melancholy Samuel had referenced in his letter.

Glancing toward the windows at the far side of his chamber, Douglas saw faint light beginning to stalk the dark sky. As the light outside grew more robust, he rose and approached his wardrobe, relieved to begin his day and finally escape the crush of his musings. At the sound of sudden tapping on the door, Douglas pulled on his dressing gown.

"Yes, come in," he called, surprised to have a visitor to his bedchamber at this hour. At any hour.

The door opened slowly, and Demett peeped his head around the corner.

"Sir, sorry to be coming up here like this. It's just I wanted to catch you before you left, and you're always saying we shouldn't be so formal when it's just you."

"It's fine, Demett. What is it?" Douglas was weary from lack of sleep, from the sobering thoughts Demett had interrupted.

"Well, sir," Demett stepped awkwardly into the room and closed the door, taking care to do it quietly. "This all right?" he asked, gesturing to the closed door.

"Yes, yes, it's fine. Let's have at it."

"I wouldn't have come asking nothing of you, not when you're always so troubled. But with the way you've been acting lately, I can't say, but it seems something about you is different. For whatever reason, I don't know, sir, but it's like you're stirring a little, I don't know why. But there's some things been happening, and well, I thought you should know about them is all." Demett looked down at his feet and placed his palms almost in a prayer position, except that his fingertips pointed toward the floor.

"Why don't you sit, Demett," Douglas said, motioning to a barrel chair beside his florid sofa.

"I'd rather stand, sir." He seemed to wince as he said it.

"What do you mean about how I've been acting?" Douglas asked.

"I can't really say, sir. It's just something I see. Like you're noticing things, like you're curious or something. Like I said, I can't really say."

"Never mind about that," Douglas waved his hand and walked back toward his bed. He pulled his bed covering up toward the pillow and sat down.

"What is it you want to discuss? What's happening?"

"Well, you ever know Clover? The house slave over at Massa

Cunningham's? She's expecting in a few months." Demett hesitated, and Douglas nodded encouragingly. "Well, she been telling some folk, some colored folk, about how she don't want to be bringing a child up in bondage. She been talking about escape. That's what those of us who talk have been hearing, and I just thought that since you used to be able to help with this sort of thing. . . ."

"No." Douglas stood up abruptly, suddenly back to the sour version of himself. "You know where I stand. I made myself clear long ago, Demett. I'm finished with it all. I won't turn people away if they show up at the dock, looking to use my tunnel, but that's it. That is it." He walked over to the wardrobe and began removing clothing for the day. "I'm sorry to seem harsh, but you know as well as anyone that my efforts have done nothing for this country. They have only brought pain down upon me. I won't go back down that road." Douglas looked hard at Demett and then nodded dismissively. "I will see you downstairs, Demett. That is all, yes?"

"It's just that, Clover, sir," Demett swallowed but didn't move toward the door. "Well see, sir, I don't think she stands much chance, trying to run off with a baby almost half out her belly. She look to be almost six months along already. If you could just . . ." He tapered off again and waited.

Douglas pictured the pregnant Clover, and his resolve became like water, trickling away from him. Ever since losing Sarah and Cherish, he had been rejecting pleas for help from abolitionists, over and again. But those had been requests for leadership, not appeals on behalf of someone specific. He looked up at the coffered ceiling and huffed out an exasperated breath. He did not want to get involved in this. But he knew too well what could happen to a runaway who didn't have the support of the Underground.

"I'm sorry for Clover, Demett. Truly. Can't you find some-body else to help? Or at least convince her to wait until the babe is out?" But Douglas already knew the answers to those questions. It had been a long time since Douglas had been to the Cunning-hams' or seen any of their slaves. In truth, he barely remembered Clover. But a pregnant woman should have every right to seek a better life for her unborn child, a life of freedom. He couldn't condemn her for wanting that. Without the help of the Under-ground, she might never make it out of the Carolinas alive. Or if she did, she would undoubtedly be recaptured by slave hunt-ers, who kidnapped slaves and free blacks alike in hopes of hefty rewards. He thought of the punishment Clover would sustain after being caught. Perhaps significant flogging, strong enough to kill the unborn child. Maybe she would be tarred and feath-ered before even being returned to her master.

"Damnit!" Douglas slammed his fist into the table where he'd been laying his clothes, disrupting his neat pile. "This isn't even my own damn country. It's not my concern if it's all botched up. I feel like my bloody head is going to explode!"

Demett showed no response to Douglas's outburst, and sim-ply continued to wait, his eyes focused on the air behind his em-polyer. Douglas did not want to get drawn back in. But he couldn't sit idly by while an innocent woman exposed herself so foolishly. As much as Douglas wanted to turn a blind eye, it was simply against his nature. Why did Demett have to come in here shak-ing out this news, just as he was starting to feel slightly human again? Douglas's head was aching with all the conflicting emo-tions and ideas that were battling their way through his mind.

"Let me think about it," Douglas finally answered. "Get word to Clover that she should wait. I need a few days to figure this out."

As soon as Demett had gone, Douglas slumped back onto

the bed and hung his head in his hands, closing his eyes, searching for stillness. He thought, again, about leaving this godforsaken South Carolina, better yet, the whole blasted country. But Douglas had promised his father-in-law, Nat, so many years ago, that he'd stay in Charleston to oversee Henderson Shipping, make it his own, after the man's death. He imagined too that the spirits of Sarah and Cherish still hovered somewhere over Charleston. If he left, he would feel as though he had left them behind. No, like it or not, Douglas was bonded to South Carolina.

He wondered if there was some way he could help Clover from a distance, without truly involving himself. He had sworn not to get tethered to abolition again. That path had brought him too much suffering. He wouldn't decide yet. A few hours, a day, he needed to consider what was being asked of him. He felt a frantic urge to get out of doors before the splitting headache radiating between his eyes grew worse.

Heading to the wharf, Douglas gazed out from the coach into the waking day, watching the morning's first merchants push carts toward the market. He worked aggressively to think of anything but Clover, and it wasn't long before his musings landed back on Abigail. She was a perfectly real victim of circumstance whom he could help without having to touch anything relating to abolition. He could begin with charity within his home. It would be what Sarah would want, wouldn't it? He would have to tread lightly, but he could get to know her, show her that there were still kind, trustworthy people she could rely on in the world. He could shore up her confidence, her comfort in her own skin.

He wouldn't be fighting to change history, like he had been when he was so caught up in abolition. But at least he would be helping to make Abigail's world a little better, and maybe his own, too. As for Clover, if only the decision were so easy.

13

CHARLESTON, SOUTH CAROLINA
1846

At the sound of knocking against the open door, Abby lowered her arm from where she had been holding it out to Larissa and turned to find Gracie standing in the doorway with a nosegay bouquet.

"How's the patient?" Gracie asked, a wide smile illuminating her ivory complexion.

"Gracie! Come in," Abby beamed. "Larissa was just fastening my sling. Come in and sit with us."

"There you are. Snug as a bug in a rug," Larissa announced as she finished adjusting the dressing. "I'll leave you girls to yourselves, but you stay in bed, Abby. I won't have you tiring yourself out. Not even for someone as agreeable as Gracie."

"Don't worry, Larissa," Gracie laughed. "I will be a very strict guardian." She pulled a wingback chair closer to Abby's bedside, smoothing her rose-colored skirts into submission before sitting.

"You best not get out of line with me, young lady," Gracie played.

"Yes ma'am," Abby responded with amusement.

Larissa smiled at the girls' easy banter. "Hand me those buds, Gracie, and I'll set them in water for the bedside." She reached out to Gracie for the bouquet.

As soon as the door closed behind Larissa, Gracie turned eagerly back to Abby. "So, is it true? Did Douglas really pull you out from under a savage horse just seconds before it trampled you?"

"What? No." Abby started, without thinking to hide her irritation. "Is that what people think? That's not what happened at all," she snapped. "I was visiting with a new stallion, and Douglas came in shouting about something, spooking me and the horse both. All I could see was this broad figure moving towards me."

"Goodness!" Gracie exclaimed. "How frightening. For all you knew, it could have been one of the coloreds coming to attack you." Gracie sounded horrified.

Abby ignored the ignorant comment and continued, "I was just walking into the horse's stall when it happened. That's the last thing I remember. Larissa thinks Mr. Elling acted the hero, finding me after the horse throttled me." Abby shook her head. "If you want my opinion, it's clear the whole thing was entirely his fault."

"Oh." Gracie looked blank-faced at Abby.

"Look, it's no major concern," Abby hedged. "Mr. Elling has been incredibly solicitous since the accident. It's obvious that he feels badly about what happened. So, no need to worry. Now tell me what's been happening outside. I've been cooped up almost a full week in here. Distract me." Abby forced out a laugh as she tried to lighten the mood.

"All right," Gracie agreed easily. "Truth be told, I'm near bursting to talk to someone about the affair Mama hosted for the Blounts last week. You're the only one I can trust, the only one Cora Rae hasn't got to. If I lay it all out, you'll keep everything just to yourself, won't you?"

"Oh, the dinner! With all the commotion, I'd nearly forgotten," Abby answered. "Yes, no, I won't say a thing. Whom would I tell?" She sat up straighter in the downy bed and readjusted the position of her bandaged arm.

"Well, Mama placed me at the table right next to Harrison." Gracie was speaking quietly, as though there might be someone with an ear to the door. "I don't think Mama and Daddy know how I feel about him. I would just die from embarrassment." She flushed, and Abby found herself wondering what Gracie's life had been like up until this point. Was there more to her new friend than crystallized evening gowns and a flattering glow? She hoped so, as that had been her impression when they had tea the week before.

"The whole family knows perfectly well that Harrison and I would be an advantageous match. With Cherry Lane situated right next to Blount's Bluff, that's the name of their place, well, just think what we could do if our families united. Forgive my immodesty, but I dare say we'd have the largest plantation in all of South Carolina."

Abby nodded, her eyes large, as she tried to wrap her mind around the amount of wealth Gracie was describing, a growing feeling of irritation in her chest at the shallowness of it all. But then she berated herself again. It was not as if she wasn't enjoying a lavish lifestyle herself lately. Not everyone had to be a martyr.

"Mama and Daddy are just hoping that he chooses one of their girls. They probably don't care much which. That's why they put Rae right on his other side at the table."

"They didn't!" Abby gasped, trying to get into the spirit of the conversation. "So what happened? Did Cora Rae monopolize him all night?"

Gracie smiled appreciatively at Abby, the smattering of light freckles on her cheeks climbing closer to her eyes. "Well, thank the fine Lord, she was as mean as could be to Harrison, right from the get-go. She actually asked to move her seat at the table when we arrived in the dining room, said she wanted to be closer to Harrison's sister. Mama was horrified. But it didn't take long before Harrison was focusing all his attentions right on me. I guess he didn't have much choice." She finished with a sudden look of defeat, as if there were no chance she would draw in a handsome young man all on her own. Abby felt a stab of shame at her harsh thoughts about the girl a moment before. She hated to see anyone feeling worthless, primarily because it reminded her of the worst parts of herself.

"You are deranged," Abby told her with a smile. "I'm sure Cora Rae could have sat down in his lap, and he still would have had eyes just for you. You're magnificent."

"That's nice of you to say, but I think we both know better."

"Not likely," Abby said in dismissal. "Regardless, didn't you tell me Cora Rae fawns all over anyone in britches? I'm surprised, especially with someone as handsome as your marvelous Harrison. Why was she so hateful to him?"

"Oh," Gracie shifted in her seat, looking suddenly uncomfortable. "I can't say that I know. Whoever knows what's what with Rae. But the point is," Gracie said, moving on, "I think it went well. I think he might call on me!"

Larissa tapped lightly on the door and entered with a tray bearing biscuits and Abby's medicated tea.

"All right, you chatterboxes," Larissa visually inspected Abby. "I think that's enough visiting for the day. Gracie, you have been Abby's first outside visitor since the accident, and I'd like to make sure she takes everything very slowly." Larissa placed the painted porcelain tray on Abby's bedside table and began straightening the bed coverings. "I can see that Abby's tiring, and I have Mr. Elling waiting for a quick visit with her, as well."

"Ugh. Again?" Abby groaned.

"Abby!" Larissa admonished her.

"He's waiting now?" Gracie asked with palpable enthusiasm. Abby marveled that the Cunningham family really did perceive Douglas Elling as an attraction of the first order.

"I just don't see why he must persist in visiting me so relentlessly," Abby looked at Larissa. "This is his third day in a row. It isn't like his sudden notice of me will heal my shoulder faster."

"Come now, Abby," Gracie responded. "Isn't that the sweetest? He must feel just awful. And really, even though he's been a curmudgeon, don't you think you owe him even a bit? I mean, with all his generosity." Abby felt herself bristle at Gracie's phrasing. She didn't like to think of herself as indebted to anyone, especially not a volatile, incomprehensible man like Douglas Elling. "And," Gracie added, "maybe his visits could help you pass your time on bed rest more pleasantly."

"But I don't even need to be in bed anymore." Abby knew she was whining like a child. "It's just out of respect for Larissa that I am even remaining in this bedchamber," she said, glancing pointedly at the governess, "but I really feel more than adequate to be up and about."

"Abby," Larissa spoke quietly but deliberately, "Mr. Elling has seemed a bit more jovial these last few days, more so than I've seen him in a long time. If the visits with you are contributing to his own healing process, well, doesn't that just make your spirit soar?"

Abby rolled her eyes. *No, it did not make her spirit soar.* Abby was fairly certain that whatever spirit she had, it would never be in the business of soaring anywhere. Although Abby had grown fond of her governess, sometimes she found Larissa's flowery musings so tiresome. Part of the issue, of course, was that Abby was really too old to be under the care of a governess at all, but like it or not, she had made a promise to her parents, and she would stick with it, as was her way.

Abby looked at Gracie and Larissa, both of whom were waiting expectantly for her response.

"All right," Abby acquiesced. "It's not like I have much choice, do I? I shall try to seem cheerful."

"That's my girl," Larissa nodded and turned to Gracie. "Follow me, dear, and I will see you out."

As the door closed behind them, Abby's stomach lurched. She tried to prepare herself for another visit with Mr. Elling, to take the truer part of herself and ball it up, scurry it away behind the harder bits of herself, her filth and mettle. Was it going to be today? Would he demand that she repay him for hosting her these many months, make good on the debt that Gracie was so quick to mention?

He had actually been somewhat lovely since Abby had gotten hurt. Not that she remembered much from the first day, when she had been drugged into deliriousness. But Larissa made sure Abby was fully informed about the manner of Mr. Elling's doting. And once she regained full lucidity, Abby sometimes found herself surprisingly engrossed in Douglas's company. She hated to admit it, but he was, in fact, rather charming. Even beneath that ratty beard.

But just as she felt herself getting roped in by his magnetism, she always remembered her own vulnerability. When she caught a glimmer of the potency in his blue eyes, or when she studied the thick expanse of his shoulders, the overpowering strength that must lie beneath his timeworn waistcoat. If she failed to stay on full alert with herself in his company, she could begin to feel Matthew's fat hands on her body again. Bruising her breasts and leaving her skin crawling with filth.

Although Mr. Elling had recently begun to display a gentle

side, she knew what a scourge he could be, badgering his servants, treating people as though their very existence was only a matter of opinion. Her sick visits from Mr. Elling had so far been pleasant, but she wasn't about to start trusting this mercurial man, simply to have him pounce on her as soon as she became complacent.

Abby leaned back against her pillow and turned toward the bright windows with a heavy sigh. If she feigned exhaustion, perhaps he wouldn't stay. She asked herself what more a girl with empty pockets and an injured arm could do besides wait to see what fate doled out.

The door opened, and Abby's fists clenched.

"Abby?"

At the sound of Mr. Elling's voice, Abby felt a surprising surge of relief. This was not Uncle Matthew creeping into her bedroom. She reminded herself to breathe.

"Yes, come in, Mr. Elling," she responded as she turned toward the door. He smiled at her, unperturbed by her tepid manner, as he entered the room and announced, "I've brought a different bit of reading, a play." He held up the small book in his hand, and Abby was intrigued in spite of herself.

"And for the umpteenth time, please call me Douglas. I'm not even a full decade your senior, and we've been sharing this house for months already. Certainly it's appropriate by now to use first names, yes?"

As Abby continued to look at him blankly, he wiggled the book and added, "It's Shakespeare."

Had he known of her affinity for Shakespeare?

"*Twelfth Night*." Douglas seated himself in the chair Gracie had been using. "Do you know it?" he asked lightly.

"I do," Abby began, as she watched him closely, carefully.

"Oh." Douglas gave a quick apologetic nod. "Here I was,

keyed up to entertain you with some new material. But," he continued, slipping the small folio into his breast pocket, "I shan't bore you with diversions that you've already exhausted."

"No, no," Abby sputtered, immediately regretful of her unenthusiastic display for the play which, in fact, she had never read. She raised her pillow behind her back and continued, "It's just, I was saying that I've heard of it." She was wretchedly bored waiting out her recovery period, an arbitrary imposition from Larissa, no less. If she were still in Wigan, she'd have already been back at the dusty factory table, working double time with her one good arm, frantic to keep her job, her eleven shillings per week. Her fingers twitched at being so sedentary now, so useless. Shakespeare would certainly help pass the time, if only he'd leave the book and just let her read to herself.

"This is the play with Viola as heroine? I've never actually read any of the verse. You needn't trouble yourself though. I am well enough to read on my own." She reached out for the text.

"Nonsense. The doctor was clear that you were to do no reading for at least seven days. Now tell me, Abby, have seven days passed since our adventure in the stables?"

"Is that what you're calling it now, an adventure?" Abby snapped. "More like attempted murder." Abby flinched as soon as the words escaped, worried she had gone too far. She looked up at Douglas, who barked out a laugh and opened the play, flipping to the first page.

If music be the food of love, play on;
Give me excess of it, that, surfeiting,
The appetite may sicken, and so die.

Abby barely had time to reflect on how easily, how amicably, Douglas had accepted her declaration of his blame for the accident before she was thoroughly engulfed in the riotous love triangle of Olivia, Viola, and Duke Orsino. She relaxed on her pillow, absorbed in the story of lovers foiled.

"You're beginning to look thoroughly fatigued." Douglas announced after they finished the first act. "With the condition you were in only a few days ago, it's best we not push. I'm hardly your first visitor today either. You rest, and we can pick up again tomorrow." Abby wanted to tell him that no, she really did not feel tired, that she could listen to him read for hours yet. But she was also glad to have him withdraw, leave her in peace so she could put her fear back into that other part of her heart, where she could fold it up and pretend it did not exist.

Except as she looked at Douglas, she noticed that again, she did not feel the fear she expected. She felt alert, coiled, but not in a negative way. She couldn't quite name the emotion, but he was correct that she didn't feel restful with him there.

"Only a few days ago," he told her, as he stood, "you were so feverish and confused. I was terribly worried. As you know, your father is one of my dearest friends, but he'd rip my tongue out with his bare hands if I let anything happen to you."

"That would be awful. I'd have no one to read me the rest of the play. You're right, you should go. For both our sakes." Abby wasn't sure who was more surprised by her sudden playfulness. Douglas raised his brows, but otherwise didn't let on.

"Right, then. I'll be back tomorrow." Douglas studied Abby a moment longer, a lock of his unshorn brown hair falling onto his forehead as he looked down at her in the bed. With a brief bow, he turned and strode confidently from the room.

Alone again, Abby huffed out a pent-up breath. She looked toward the closed door and wrinkled her brow. By her count, Douglas had visited her no fewer than five times since the accident, and she'd be damned if he didn't seem like he cared about her well-being, at least a smidge. In all his visits, he hadn't come close to laying a finger on her inappropriately. Was it possible that Douglas was actually a decent sort of fellow? Otherwise, he was putting forth quite a lot of calculated action to manipulate her, and she was hardly worth such effort.

Abby nestled more deeply in the bed. The sling on her arm made sleeping at night difficult, so she was actually a bit tired. Her head was beginning to pulse a little as well, likely from trying to decipher Douglas's intentions. The man she met upon her arrival, the one who shouted at her weeks later for helping Reggie with his blisters, seemed so different from the one who had been visiting with her each day since her injury.

Well, it was no matter whether he was a genuine sort or crooked, Abby decided. If he would just have done with all this visiting, so much the better. She couldn't say if it was guilt over the accident or licentiousness that sent Douglas repeatedly to her door, maybe a surprising clandestine grace, but it would be the easiest thing if he just left her alone. Though she wondered at the tiny part of her, the part huddled beneath her guardedness and constant vigilance, that was quietly looking forward to his next visit.

14

~

CHARLESTON, SOUTH CAROLINA
1846

racie sat on the back verandah, wilting slightly in the glare of the late-day Charleston sun and squinting at her needlepoint. She was distracted from her task, thinking alternately about Harrison Blount and Abby Milton. It had been unusually warm this month, and again the air was sticky with the scents of tree sap and soil fermenting in the unseasonable heat. Still, Gracie preferred this mugginess to the company of her sisters, and there was no avoiding them unless she was out of doors, where they so rarely cared to venture. She inhaled deeply, trying to refocus herself, savoring the scent of the crape myrtle shrubs beside the house.

"Gracie, there you are." Cora Rae smiled in triumph as she emerged from the adjacent parlor. "I've been looking everywhere," she added as she stepped through the French doors from the house. Cora Rae always knew precisely which colors to wear to flatter her appearance, and today's emerald riding dress was no exception, as it highlighted her brilliant green eyes and contrasted starkly with her amber hair. Cora Rae's beauty continually stunned Gracie, not least of all because it concealed such a distasteful character.

"Well here I am, aren't I?" As she looked up, making no effort to hide her annoyance at Cora Rae's de trop arrival. "What is it?"

"You know what I want. Mama told me hours ago that you went over to visit Abigail.   Well, let's have it." Cora Rae sat delicately on the wicker rocker beside Gracie's. "I just couldn't wait a minute longer. Tell me everything." Cora Rae was developing a lovely pink glow upon her smooth cheeks; whether it was from the heat of the warm day or her excitement about Douglas Elling, Gracie couldn't say.

"Did you see Douglas? You've wheedled your way in at least a bit by now, haven't you? Tell me that much, or I might just have to reconsider our recent bargain." Cora Rae removed a paper fan from the band where it hung on her wrist and began waving it at herself with furious refinement.

"I'm sorry if I just don't have much to tell yet." Gracie replied defensively and turned back to her needlepoint as she spoke. "I told you that Douglas and Abby barely have any relationship at all, so for me to have contact with Douglas through his houseguest, well it's attenuated, at best."

Cora Rae's eyes flashed in burgeoning anger, and Gracie quickly backpedaled, cautious not to violate the terms of their accord about Harrison.

"As despicable as I think this whole thing is," Gracie continued, "I actually did manage to get a brief audience with Douglas during my visit. Nothing significant occurred mind you, but it was something, I suppose, so I thought you'd be pleased. I had to fairly beg Abby to stomach a visit from him." Gracie hated the idea of being dishonest with Abby about her purpose in the Elling home, but perhaps she might contrive an approach that would appease Rae without hurting anyone. Gracie justified her thoughts by reminding herself that she would have visited Abby today regardless of Rae's demands. The girl had suffered an awful ordeal with that horse, and Gracie had simply done the Christian thing, visiting her friend while she convalesced. Maybe it would be better for Abby if she and Douglas were on closer terms anyway. After all, it was rather odd the way she was staying in his house but wanted nothing to do with him.

As she failed to extinguish her lingering guilt, Gracie studied Cora Rae. How she and this creature could have been spawned by the same source was a mystery to her.

"Really though, how could you have me do this, Cora?" Gracie's distaste for her sister could be heard plainly as she pronounced her sister's name with cutting sarcasm. "Abby is my friend. Not that you have any understanding what that means." Cora Rae's friends seemed to change on a weekly basis.

"Abby is soft-hearted and merciful." Gracie continued, with building bravado. "How could you make me use her like this? It won't do any good anyway." Gracie shook her head, her mahogany curls dancing frenetically around her face as she continued. "Douglas is clearly not interested in finding another wife, especially not one who handles everyone around her just to suit her own purpose."

"Oh, puh . . . lease!" Cora Rae snorted as she stood. "You're as much of a user as I am, sugar. Ready to turn on your little friend as soon as it suits you. You didn't think twice about deceiving her when it came to your own interests. And who's acting uppity anyway?" Cora Rae released a vicious laugh. "That girl is nothing but a beggar. She's a project to you. We all know how you are. Sweet little Gracie, always seeking out strays and orphans. Well you might as well use this particular mission of yours to help your older sister." Cora Rae paused and then added with a sneer, "Unless of course, you've changed your mind about Harrison." Cora Rae glared at Gracie spitefully.

"Rae!" Gracie snapped in frustration. "I already said that I would help. Why do you have to go on about it? It's only been a couple of days yet. I'm not going to make striking progress in less time than it takes to squash a mosquito. Now I told you, I had an audience with him. It was just a first step. If I persist, I may eventually be in a position to invite him over for something. But it will take time, and I would appreciate you not browbeating me each day in the meanwhile. Now if you don't mind, I was trying to finish this pattern." Gracie picked up her needlepoint and began to turn away from her sister.

"Oh no, Grace Cunningham," Cora Rae scathed. "Don't you go turning your back on me. I hold your whole future in the palm of my hand. I can snatch Harrison's interest off you so fast you wouldn't know what hit you. I think it's best you start showing me some respect." Cora Rae stopped and looked at Gracie for a moment before adding, "You know, you're actually not a useless person, even though you act all meek, such a victim. I know you've got grit in there." Cora Rae twirled an amber lock gracefully around her finger. Sighing, she concluded, "If you could manage to be helpful with this, this one thing, we might actually start to be friends again, you and I." Cora Rae raised her eyebrows at Gracie before flouncing back into the house. As she was about to disappear from view, she called back over her shoulder, suddenly sounding cheery, "Just make it happen, and we can be finished with this ugliness, *tout de suite.*"

Gracie wanted to scream. Finished with this ugliness? Cora Rae would never be finished bringing ugliness into people's lives. Wasn't Gracie the good one, the ethical, well-behaved, and loving daughter? But somehow Cora Rae, shrewd, crafty, Cora Rae, was the apple of her parents' eye.

It made her fingers itch the way Cora Rae always got exactly what she wanted. And now she was forcing Gracie to betray a friend. For what, really? To ensnare a man who cared nothing for her. Gracie wondered if she should simply inform Cora Rae that she would not participate in the scheme. That Cora Rae could seduce Harrison Blount however she chose, and it wouldn't matter to Gracie. But, oh it *would* matter. She felt ill every time she imagined Harrison mooning over Cora Rae. She couldn't let that happen. So instead she would continue to act as her sister's agent. She would just have to do her best to prevent Abby from getting hurt in the process.

⁓℮

AT THE SOUND OF RAISED VOICES ON THE VERANDAH above them, Clover immediately ceased her whispering and looked at Thelma, the family cook, in alarm.

"Ain't nothing," Thelma assured Clover in a whisper. "Just them girls fighting again. We'll wait them out."

Clover nodded at Thelma, feeling a tug at her heart. Clover had been relying on Thelma for as long as she could remember, following her instruction, attaching to her. But here she was now, figuring out how to leave the woman behind. They were meeting for the second time this month, plotting behind the lattice underneath the back verandah, like their own little army, a brigade of the discontented.

The oldest in the group was Abel, who'd been working the house alongside Clover since she was a pickaninny. He was always running his toothless mouth about rushing north, but never acting. Clover figured he was too old or just too scared, and she didn't blame him either. Not after the way slave folk were always hearing about recaptured runaways, the ones who got covered in tar or beaten so badly they never woke up. Even Massa Cunningham, who didn't do beatings, made clear that an attempted escape would be punished in the harshest ways possible. Abel was living by proxy through her, Clover figured, trying to help her achieve something he had concluded would never be possible for himself.

And then there was Dicky, only sixteen and raised up on the Cunninghams' plantation since birth. He planned to escort her partway as her guardian, he said. He kept promising he'd get back to the Cunninghams' before anyone noticed him missing. Now Dicky wasn't the father of that baby growing in Clover's belly, and Clover hadn't told anyone who was, but everybody knew just the same. None of the slave men ever came calling on Clover because she belonged to the massa specially, since before she was old enough to understand. That was why she needed to get away so desperately. Otherwise her child would be sold off, right away, before the missus might discern the resemblance of the babe to her husband.

Thelma kept telling her it was a rattlebrained idea, trying to get North, that most runaways never made it. They just got brought home, Thelma said, where they got beaten, where they got dead. But Clover said she and Dicky were going, whether Thelma liked it or not. So here they were, organizing behind the balustrade. They knew these meetings must be sharp and infrequent. Otherwise someone would begin to suspect. Other slaves were the worst risk of all. All so eager to gain favor with the massa or missus, they'd squeal on one another just as soon as there was reason to raise an eyebrow. Some slave folk took a wicked pleasure from watching a runaway writhe and scream at the whipping post. She begged the Lord not to let that happen to her, nor to that babe who was kicking so much in her belly. She hadn't any idea where her own mother was now, but she was going to find a place to be with her baby, where they would not be separated.

Clover aimed to leave as soon as possible. She and Dicky

planned to steal down to Charleston Harbor, where Clover would burrow aboard a northbound boat. They were trying to collect the money for her journey, without any sense of how much she needed. They figured maybe the time would come when she had to pay for part of her passage, rather than sneaking aboard, skulking below decks and such. Or she likely might need to buy some victuals along the channels. Abel suggested that she secrete extra notes, too, to bribe any troublemakers. The money was hard to come by, but Clover and Thelma had been using the little spare time they found, staying up nights making baskets to bring to town when Thelma was out on pass doing the marketing for the big house. She sold what she could, but they still counted only a few coins between them. They would keep at it, trying to gather enough money to carry Clover all the way to Canada.

It wasn't much of a plan, Clover knew, foolhardy even, but better than staying put, losing her baby, and ending up with the massa right back on top of her. Thelma was still talking about finding some Underground in South Carolina to help, telling Clover to wait a little longer. But that babe inside her wasn't going to wait forever, and so she would have to get moving soon.

Clover had long ago heard tell about a code. There was a system local slave folk used to help runaways get on along to where they were going. Signals, like if there was a yellow quilt on the clothesline, it meant "go this way," or if there was a gourd near the door, it meant "not now; come back later." Something like that. When Clover started planning her escape, Thelma had begun asking around quietly, carefully, about the code and any people who could help. As it was, she knew that word of her inquiries would spread among certain black folk, like the oozing of too-old jam. What Thelma found was that most people knew nothing. And everybody was too afraid to talk anyway, averting their dark eyes and shushing her. Until she thought to ask Delilah, who was courting with that freeman, Demmet. He was a comely fellow with a ready smile, quiet, but like he was always thinking on something. Delilah said Demett might know something of the Underground. It would be difficult finding a person to dip a hand in with them, she warned Thelma. Still, she pledged that her man would try for Clover, and they would send word soon.

At the sudden quiet on the above verandah, Dicky made as if to start speaking, but Clover held up her hand. She was certain she had heard only one pair of slippered feet leave the porch. By the sound of it, that had been Miss Cora, losing her patience with Miss Gracie again, fed up with her younger sister always being miserable. Clover couldn't fathom why Thelma favored Miss Gracie so, not when it was the oldest sister who defended the slaves to her mama, who passed old dresses to Clover now and again for fabric.

As they waited for the second Miss Cunningham to take her leave, Clover looked from Thelma to Abel and Dicky. Lordy, Lordy. They were a motley bunch of black folk. Unless they got themselves joined to the right people, well, she could hardly bear to finish the thought. After a few more moments, they heard a groan full of aggravation from above, and then a second set of troubled feet scampering off.

"Now then," Thelma whispered as she took up the purpose of the meeting again, "before y'all go running off to get snared and killed, I'm telling you, you best wait a few more weeks. Three weeks at the most. My girl Delilah gone come through for us on this. Meantime, you just stay put and keep to planning and working so y'all are ready when the Underground come calling. Dicky, you figure yet which path you plan on taking down to the river?"

"Well, I was gone scout it out some when I get my next pass, but then I thought it was reckless. If we be doing practice runs, it only be more opportunity for the massa to discover us. And then maybe this Underground, they be telling Clover to do it different anyway. . . ." Dicky trailed off as he looked from Clover to Thelma for guidance.

"You out of your mind, boy?" Thelma scolded. "You ain't even gone make it as far as that property line if you don't get yourself a better plan. Just because white folks around here is mean, it don't mean they stupid. You can't go running off on hope alone, nothing but ragweed and wind. Why you think more folks don't make it North? They all think they can just start moving their feet and God gone take them the rest the way. Well let me tell you, child, it's man that brought us into bondage, and only man gone get anyone out."

"Thelma, watch your voice now," Abel warned as she grew louder in her passion. Abel's words drew Thelma up short, and she paused in her tirade. She looked about at her compatriots, swatted at a spider's web that hung on the underside of the verandah, not far from her head, and squinted her eyes like she was trying to think where to begin again. Clover felt a stinging behind her own eyes, so she inhaled deeply through her nose, the way Thelma always told her. Never show him you're crying, Thelma would tell her about the massa. Just breathe in hard through your nose. But she couldn't stop herself today, first with the sniffling and then quietly rocking in grief, in dread, silently weeping.

"Oh no, honey. What's this?" Thelma asked, still pulling the stubborn web from her hand.

"I'm just so scared. What if we get snatched? What'll they do to my baby?" Clover raised her dark eyes to Thelma and shuddered. "How do you want me to wait three more weeks when this babe is near out my belly already? If I don't go soon, I ain't never gone make it."

"Tsk, tsk." Thelma put her thick arm around Clover's shoulders, squeezing too tightly, as if to smother her own foreboding.

"Come, child. You got to pull yourself together. There ain't no crying on the path to freedom, now. We're gone find them Underground people, and they gone get you out of here. You and the babe both. Just have patience. Three weeks ain't too much more. When you spent your whole life in bondage, why three weeks ain't nothing but a day of picking cotton when it rain. You just wait, and we gone get the help you need." Thelma used her starched apron to wipe Clover's tears.

"We best be getting back afore we be missed." Thelma directed. "Not like the other day when Miss Gracie come right into the kitchen and none of us is there." Thelma shook her head. "We'll find a way to meet again in a few days' time. In the meanwhile, Dicky, I expect you to scout out your route. It ain't never gone work otherwise. And I'll have to report you to the Missus just to save your fool hide."

"Yes'm," Dicky nodded, not meeting Thelma's eyes.

Dicky and the others knew that Thelma would never betray them to the Missus, but they also knew better than to say so. "Now remember," Thelma repeated in a low whisper as she looked into the eyes of each member of the group, "not a word to anyone. No matter how much they seem to be your friend."

They each exited the hiding place individually, hastily scurrying back to their daily tasks—Abel to the shed where he had been repairing a carriage, Dicky around back to the horses, Thelma returned to the kitchen, where she had been glazing a ham. Clover stopped into the smokehouse, hoping to invent a feasible reason why she had been gone from the house. She stepped back out from the smokehouse with a side of beef in her hand and raised her eyes skyward. "Please, Lord," she whispered, "let us find the Underground."

15

CHARLESTON, SOUTH CAROLINA
1846

Douglas climbed the grand staircase two risers at a time, charging upward as though he was being pushed by an invisible force. He had left his harborside offices after less than half a day's work, something he seemed to be doing with surprising frequency these days. Ever since deciding a few days earlier that he would devote himself to Abby's healing, mitigating whatever damage had been done to her in Lancashire, he'd felt an astounding change begin to bleed into him, altering the colors of his moods. Abby's presence in his home was now affecting him like fresh paint spilled, seeping boldly across a tired canvas. He turned left down the wide corridor and knocked tentatively on Abby's bedroom door.

"Come in!" she called brightly from within. This was a surprise, as she generally needed some handling before warming up. Even then, it seemed any kindness he elicited from her was nearly involuntary.

As Douglas nudged the door open, he saw Abby sitting cross-legged in the center of the bed. She was covered by a modest dressing gown and had her hair plaited into a long rope at the base of her neck. It was not the first time she had received him in bedclothes. Following her accident, standard rules of propriety seemed to matter even less than usual in this household. At the sight of her braid, he noticed again the luster of her hair, something that surely hadn't been present when she first arrived in Charleston.

Abby looked up and grinned back at Douglas so broadly that he almost gasped in surprise at the marked change in her behavior. She held up a piece of paper like a hard-won prize, punching it into the air.

"I've had a letter from my da!"

Ah. So it was her da, not he, who was the cause of her elation. He was startled to feel bereft at the realization. He wondered whether this was the first letter she had received since her arrival. He hadn't noticed any posts coming or going, but then, he'd not thought to look.

"Splendid." He tried to answer with equal cheer, but he couldn't stop himself before asking, "Is it the first you've heard from him?"

"Oh," Abby's smile faltered as she refolded the paper in her hand. "I suppose you don't know how it is for them." She spoke kindly, gently almost, perhaps softened by thoughts of her family. "Even sheets of paper are so dear. And they are strained always, my parents." She then added more quietly, "I haven't written myself, which I suppose has been unfair of me."

Douglas didn't answer but walked into the room and seated himself in the chair near her bed. The room smelled of flowers and fresh tea. As he contemplated his best response, Abby seemed anxious to fill the silence.

"He's gotten a promotion at the mill. A spinner. That's near the highest job you can want at a mill, apart from foreman. He'll be doing twisting, or warping I suppose; he didn't say."

She looked down at the folded letter and made a quiet sound, somewhere between a chirp and a sigh. "Da thought he'd be a piecer forever. Picking up yarn and doing a child's job. Carrying cans of yarn slivers from the carder to the drawing frame, naught much else. But it's really happening for him. Maybe there will finally be some money to save, to put toward getting out, back to Liverpool."

She glanced back up at him and suddenly flushed red in her cheeks.

"I'm sorry," she blurted, as she began hastily stuffing the letter back into its torn envelope, her fingers suddenly clumsy. "I'm, well . . ." she struggled to recover from her lapse in restraint.

Douglas hadn't realized before this conversation quite how far Samuel had fallen, though he couldn't say he was astonished. To have sent off his daughter, surely circumstances had been dire. Even so, he was pleased that Abby finally saw fit to tell him anything at all about herself, or her family. Prior to this moment, she'd not confessed so much as a favorite food, keeping everything always contained, as though sharing information about herself would somehow weaken her. Douglas could not help her overcome the damage of her past if she wouldn't let him get to know her. He would need to encourage her, show her that she had been right to offer him a glimmer of her memories.

"You know, when I was a young boy, your father looked after me almost every afternoon. His father and mine were always so busy teaching and doing their research. Perhaps your father told you, my father was a professor at Oxford alongside your grandfather." He watched Abby, trying to gauge her response, determine if this was an acceptable direction for their conversation. They'd never spoken of their families before. She held tightly to the letter in her hands, a flush still upon her cheeks as she regarded him. Douglas could only assume she was waiting for him to say more.

"Your granddad took my father under his wing and was, I'm most certain, the driving force behind my father's many professional successes. My father was quite young, compared to your granddad, and he had some rather unpopular views, especially for a man at Oxford."

Abby ran her hand absentmindedly over the edge of the envelope in her lap, watching Douglas with an ambiguous look in her eyes.

"Your granddad was a brilliant physician. I always thought that at least one of his sons would follow in his footsteps." Douglas shrugged. "It was a curiosity that both sons thought to pursue livelihoods in business rather than medicine."

"You think my da made a bad choice?" Abby's chin rose. "All this mess with the weaving mills and the impossible wages could have been avoided if he'd gone on to Oxford instead of chasing his art?"

"No, no, that's not what I'm saying at all," Douglas hedged. "It's just that often a son will follow in his father's footsteps. Your father is more skilled with woodworking than any man I've met. How could he have chosen anything other than opening a furniture shop? And besides, it's not as though I became a doctor either, to my father's great chagrin, I might add."

Abby's shoulders relaxed, and then after a pause, she laughed.

"What?" Douglas smiled, glancing around self-consciously.

"No, nothing," she shook her head with a grin.

"I don't think so, Miss Abigail. You can't laugh in my presence and then refuse to admit the reason. Have you any idea what that does to a man's pride?"

"I'm just thinking of you as a physician. You have the most terrible bedside manner."

"I, what?" Douglas stood, trying to reign in his feeling of offense. Here he had been running his mind ragged trying to be the perfect damn caregiver to her.

"It's a joke! I'm kidding. Yeesh. You can sit back down." Her tone was laced with suppressed laughter as she smiled at him. He lowered himself into his chair and felt himself smiling back as he took in the way her eyes tilted up when she smiled. He couldn't get a handle on her. He would have imagined her too timid for such jibes. He was quickly learning that timid she was not. He realized he was regarding her for a beat too long and looked down at his hands so he could reorganize his thoughts.

"Do you mind if I open the window?" he asked. Suddenly the room felt too warm.

"It's your house."

"But your room," he answered over his shoulder as he pushed the window frame to make way for the fresh air. It was a cool day, finally appropriate for the season. The scent of evergreens wafted gently into the room.

"If I am to be in charge in my own room, then may I demand that you tell me more about your relationship with my da? I like hearing about him before I knew him, when he was still an optimist with an exciting future ahead of him."

So, this was positive. Headway that she wanted to talk more.

"It's not much of a demand, dear Abigail, if you ask permission first, but I am happy to oblige."

Abby picked up a decorative pillow from beside her. "Don't give the sick girl a hard time," she reprimanded him as she threw the pillow at his head.

He dodged to the left and the pillow flew past him as he laughed. He barely had time to register his surprise at her sudden boldness before she continued teasing, "You're lucky my good arm is incapacitated or that absolutely would have knocked into you."

"Well then, I better get back to my story, shouldn't I?"

Abby raised her eyebrows and waited for him to start talking.

"Well," he began, his voice turning more serious as he returned to his chair. "My mother passed away when I was five years old. Pneumonia." He told her with the calm detachment that he had mastered over the years, though he was sorry to sober up the lively atmosphere of a moment before. "After that, my father threw himself into his work, professing to his students and advocating reform for medical education, against the wishes of his colleagues. I still needed looking after, so he often deposited me up the road in the care of your father, who was happy to accept a shilling to do as my father asked. Despite our age difference, your da and I grew attached at a swift rate. Soon my father was leaving me off regularly without the least bit of guilt over it. And he was right, as I relished the time spent in your father's company. He knew so much about the world. He'd already figured out tobacco and girls. Fighting, too." Douglas smiled at Abby and admitted, "I was a rather puny child, and many of the other boys took umbrage at my facility with letters and numbers in school. Add to that my father's work," he shrugged. "Suffice it to say that if it weren't for your da, I would have been pummeled rather flat on more than one occasion."

Abby sat quietly listening. The breeze from the open window rustled the papers on the bed. When he remained silent, she asked, "What won't you say? What was the problem with your father? What was his work that made you a pariah?"

"Ah. Nothing more than a gentlemen's dispute turned ugly amongst their children. He was part of a movement to train physicians through clinical work, rather than teaching from books alone. He felt it was the more responsible method of practicing medicine."

"It seems reasonable," Abby agreed. "So, it was just your charming personality that led the other boys to despise you?" She smiled, making clear she was joking, that her mood was still in this new, lighthearted place.

Douglas felt himself grinning back, disarmed by her unpredictability. "Hardly," he scoffed. "My father's peers didn't care for the idea of soiling their hands. Manual labor they called it, and they complained bitterly to anyone who would listen. Not so different from the gentlemen in Charleston if you think about it—keeping their hands clean at the expense of their consciences." He was getting off topic, and he knew better. Even so, he realized that he hadn't spoken so openly about any part of his past since before the fire, even his childhood.

"Well," Douglas said lightly, "here we are some twenty years later, and progress has been made, at least at many of the hospitals. My esteemed father continues to advocate for his ideals back in London, even at his advanced age." He reached into his jacket pocket, "I've brought *Twelfth Night*. Should we get back to it?"

"Yes, please," Abby responded affably. "I was beginning to worry you'd blabber on all day and never get to it. Perhaps the other boys were annoyed by your constant chatter, not your father's work, did you ever consider that?" She spoke with a smile in her voice, obviously teasing.

"Oh, is that how it is then? I see." He deadpanned as he opened the book.

Well, well, well. Perhaps they'd had a breakthrough today, Douglas dared to hope, as Abby's behavior was markedly different toward him today, friendlier and so much less cautious. Douglas began reading aloud, and Abby lay back onto the pillows behind her, closing her eyes to listen.

As he read about the saga of Viola and Orsino, Abby laughed at the descriptions of Viola's cross-dressing. She sat up during the telling of sword fights, rapt, and she sighed as she listened to the poetry of unrequited love.

At some point, Douglas glanced up from the play and saw Abby studying him. He smiled at her lightly and turned back to the text. He felt charged by the fact that Abby seemed to be looking at him, seeing him truly, maybe, for the first time.

He hadn't yet determined exactly how he would help her, or precisely what she had endured, but Douglas knew that he had to create a deeper connection with Abby. And truth be told, he wanted it. He was enjoying her company more each day, and they could both use more friends in their lives, if naught else. He could be a loyal friend, whom she could depend on and trust.

As Douglas neared the end of the scene he was reading, he reminded himself that the paramount way to bring Abby around was to proceed with great care. If he pushed her too hard or too fast, she would only shove back. He had seen again today how quickly she could become defensive. If he failed to tread lightly, she would run in the opposite direction. The superior choice would be to leave their meeting today while she was still enjoying herself. The sooner Douglas could persuade Abby to initiate their visits, the better. Especially since her time on bed rest was quickly coming to an end, which would deprive him of justification for seeking her out so regularly.

"All right then," Douglas announced as he stood. "That's the end of the scene and my cue to let you continue resting." He bent to retrieve the pillow she had thrown earlier and tossed it lightly to the bed.

Abby looked up at Douglas surprised. "But . . . oh," She appeared unsure quite what to say. A few days earlier, she had seemed so offended by Douglas's mere presence that she would have rejoiced at his departure. Not today though, Douglas fought the urge to smile at his progress.

"Well," she told Douglas tentatively, "thank you for reading to me again." She reached beside her for her father's letter again, perhaps planning to respond upon Douglas's departure.

"It is always a delight, my lady," Douglas told her with a bow, as he turned to exit the room.

When he was halfway to the door, Abby burst out, "Wait!"

"Yes?" Douglas turned and flashed her a solicitous grin.

"You will come back, won't you? I mean, to finish the play," she asked.

"Of course. You have only to invite me. Good day." As he closed the door behind himself, he felt a growing sense of victory. He had made his move, as though his relationship with Abby was an elaborate game of chess, and he could not help feeling that he had arranged his pieces on the board into a stunning display. Those dark protracted days of wallowing in his own emptiness were finally going to be replaced by something constructive. He was going to get through to this girl and do something decent with himself for the first time in too long.

─❧─

AS DOUGLAS DESCENDED THE SPIRAL STAIRCASE IN self-satisfied thought, he noticed Jasper standing in the foyer, staring up at him and holding a rag motionless in midair.
"Is something amiss, Jasper?"

"Pardon? Uh, no, sir," Jasper stammered, righting himself. "It was just your whistling that caught me by surprise. Please excuse me." Jasper turned his back and began wiping at the large mirror on the east wall, polishing away invisible streaks.

Douglas hadn't realized he was whistling. He felt a quick pang of guilt, regret at the lighthearted mood he had landed in. But then he checked himself. Ever since the fire, he had lived inside the protection of his despair, as though he deserved no other emotion. But as he walked through the foyer, opening the door to the cool January sunshine, he sensed a new pathway expanding in his mind. There was a place somewhere outside of hopelessness, pulling at him. Allowing aspiration in his life was not the same as leaving Sarah and Cherish behind. He would have to stop feeling that he betrayed them each time he felt the urge to smile.

Shoving his hands in his pockets to stave off the cold, he turned toward his stable, the gravel drive crunching beneath his feet. It was time he called on Midnight, the steed that had injured Abby. Douglas had bought the horse on the supposition that it could be tamed. Reggie, in particular, had a spectacular ability with horses. Had he broken the horse, the animal would have proven a lucrative investment. He was unsure what to do with the beast now, other than examine the animal and decide whether it should be put down or sold. Probably he should sell the horse into the Deep South, Douglas quipped to himself, thinking of the standard punishment for unmanageable slaves.

The turn in his thoughts was riling him up. Years ago, he'd been unable to refrain from joining the fight, incapable of restraining himself, of remaining inert in the face of the many injustices he witnessed. He had been passionate about the righteousness of his actions, convinced that he should join the battle because freedom was a God-given right. But he had not thought enough about what it could cost him. Young and stupid he'd been. Focusing only on his sanctimonious ideals. When he was a child, his father had often complained that Douglas was too eager to act, impulsive, hotheaded. Reflecting on his reaction to American slavery, he could appreciate that his father had always been correct. As soon as Douglas had achieved a basic understanding of the slavery system, he'd gone running off with cloaks and daggers to squelch it, and look where that got him. Even so, his thoughts returned to Clover. How could he ignore her plight? He knew he must reach a decision and respond to Demett because time was running out.

A loud whinnying sprung forth from the stables. Douglas reached the door and peered into the dark corridor, where a group of men congregated at Midnight's stall. Demett and Antonio were watching Reggie and two of the younger stable boys at work. The boys were working a shard of wood out from Midnight's hoof, and the horse was allowing their ministrations. He was complaining something awful, with whinnies and snorts aplenty, but he was submitting. Other horses in the barn were responding to the animal's distress with whinnies of their own.

"What happened?" Douglas shouted over the din the horses were creating.

"Ain't nothing too much, sir," Reggie called back. "This fellow stepped himself onto a fallen branch outside, and a bit broke off in the hoof. We have it almost out," Reggie assured Douglas, looking up at him quickly and then returning his attention to the horse.

Douglas shook his head. "We won't be keeping this beast. Not after the way he treated Miss Abigail last week. I'm relieved to see him behaving though. He may actually fetch a decent price. Demett, after he's healed, let it be known that he's back on the market, and let's see how we do."

"Yes, sir. That all?" Demett held Douglas's gaze, waiting. It was obvious that Demett was still thinking of Clover, waiting for Douglas's answer. Douglas wasn't ready yet. He knew which way his heart was heading, but what would it cost him this time? His head was beginning to pound with the weight of the decision he was creeping towards.

Douglas nodded back and retreated to the opposite end of the stable, where he stopped outside Pawnee's stall. She was the sandy-colored Shetland pony that he and Sarah had presented to Cherish on her fourth birthday. She was standing quietly in the stall, as if she had been waiting for him. Generally, Douglas was unable to greet Pawnee without a vice tightening on his heart. Today the pain was not so terrible. In fact, Douglas noticed an odd sense of calm as he stood with her.

As he ran his hand over the pony's head, letting her nuzzle into his arm, he thought of Abby. It was easier to focus on her than on Clover, as he had already committed to assisting Abby. Even putting aside what might have happened with her uncle, the girl was alone in a foreign land. She was defensive and closed off, keeping herself at a distance from others. Surely, he could do something more to ease the burdens that shadowed her. She deserved a second chance at life.

At the notion of second chances, Douglas realized that perhaps he should be thinking about himself, too. There might actually be room in his life for something other than obsessive grief. He was not ready to relinquish his sorrow, but maybe, maybe there could be more. He was not doing Sarah and Cherish any service by torturing himself. Whether it was Abigail's influence or simply the passage of time, something had pushed him into an unfamiliar place. He rubbed his hand over his chin as he considered his evolving outlook. Feeling the unruly hair of his beard, an idea occurred to him. He would start by shaving his beard. He'd not brought a razor to his face in all the time they'd been gone. He had relished his ugliness, an outward reminder to all who gazed on him of the anguish he'd endured. But now it seemed wrong, indulgent to persist as he had. It was time he cleaned himself up. He reached into the feed bag beside him and removed a few pellets, holding them out for the pony. She nibbled them from his palm, her downy lips curving up and tickling his hand. Perhaps if he demonstrated to Abby that he, the most miserable of characters, was granting life a second chance, despite everything, well maybe she could be inspired to do the same.

His own second chance would start by looking better, and acting better. The beginning of a new beginning. Douglas surprised himself with the vain thought of wondering whether he was still handsome underneath all that fur on his face. He smiled and walked toward the house. The beginning of a new beginning. He liked the sound of that. And Lord almighty, he was looking forward to a good shave.

16

CHARLESTON, SOUTH CAROLINA
1846

*I*t felt grand to be back in the fresh air. Now that Abby was comfortably seated on the stone bench in the corner of the rose garden, she sensed an eternity had passed since she'd last been outdoors. Though it had been less than two weeks, it seemed like so much had changed during her confinement. There was a new chill in the air, and really, that was the least of it. Abby pulled her wool wrap closer to her body, taking care not to jostle her injured arm. She had been careful, fastidious, trying to keep herself immune to the people in her new life so that none would have power to hurt or control her, to devastate her. Now it seemed she was slipping. She had noticed that her outlook toward Larissa was softening, and more shockingly, her attitude toward Douglas, too. And there was the letter from home, stirring up so many emotions that she would have preferred to ignore.

The bare rose bushes swayed in the breeze, a few stray leaves still intact alongside an abundance of thorns. Abby wondered whether this had been Sarah's garden, a place where she too came for solitude, fortitude. She questioned briefly whether the cold bench beneath her was meant for sitting, rather than only adorning the garden, akin to the sculpted frogs placed strategically along the path back to the house. It irked her that there was still occasion for confusion every day in her new life. She opened her writing journal to peruse what she'd composed the day before. If Larissa found her hard at work, it would bolster Abby's argument that she was strong enough to resume most activity.

Larissa surely had the best intentions when she demanded that Abby remain in bed so many days following the accident with Midnight. But Abby, and probably Larissa too, knew that she had been well enough to go about ordinary business for several days already. Mercifully, Doc Markinson had been back yesterday evening, and he declared there was no reason why Abby should resist returning to a more typical daily schedule. Nothing too taxing, certainly no calisthenics, but customary activities for a young lady would be fine, he'd granted, provided she took added care with her shoulder.

Abby had never been fussed over so much, and the coddling did not sit well with her. She had never before had the luxury for feebleness, and it was unsettling to dabble in fragility now. Perhaps she should realize that it was pleasant, agreeable, to be cared for and doted on, but she was much more comfortable standing on her own two feet. She looked down at the open pages of her folio, attempting to review the introductory portion of her essay on French philosophers.

As many times as she tried to push Douglas from her mind, she failed. She could not stand the fact that he had altered, changed himself, forcing her to reconsider her own judgments. Her inability to understand him, his actions, it made everything else in her current life feel more tenuous. At least in Wigan, she had known what she was up against. When she had judged

Douglas as cruel, that had been clear-cut, easier to understand. And yet . . . Douglas wasn't wicked. He seemed to care genuinely about her well-being after the accident. Perhaps because her injury was all his fault, Abby sniffed. No, she was certain that Douglas had come to see her out of concern, instead of guilt. And truth be told, she had enjoyed his company, especially listening to him read *Twelfth Night*. That was, of course, until he simply stopped showing up.

It wasn't as if she had ever considered him anything more than a nuisance anyway, she tried to convince herself. She could very well get her own copy of *Twelfth Night*, couldn't she just? Maybe not yet, but after she became a teacher, as she planned, she would have enough money to do as she pleased. At least to buy her own damned books. She wouldn't need Douglas, or anyone else, to read with her.

Abby stared down at the writing on her lap without seeing the words. What was it about Douglas Elling that she was incapable of shaking from her mind? Since the date of her first arrival, he'd vacillated between rudeness and benign neglect, shifting from rage to unexplained kindness. And then, just as she had begun dallying with the idea of Douglas as a friend, he'd deserted her, mysteriously quitting their regular visits.

Well, why should she care anyway. She wasn't some pet to be trifled with, there for his amusement only when it suited him. But she worried despite herself, perhaps she had offended him in some way. She could seek him out, instead of acting like a damned mouse, and ask outright why, suddenly, days had been passing without an appearance from him. Maybe she was being insensitive, she wondered, trying to adjust her perspective. Certainly, he must still suffer enormously from the great tragedy in his life, losing his entire family in one fell swoop. She couldn't know how such heartrending grief would affect a person. Maybe it was she who was being selfish, waiting around for Douglas to materialize. Or perhaps she was simply too self-centered, assuming that his absence had anything to do with her at all.

As she thought about his losses, her sense of exasperation began to dissipate. Her equilibrium shifted as a different understanding dawned. Based on what Larissa had told her, Abby must have been the first person with whom Douglas had forged any connection in years. Maybe he felt some sort of kinship with her because of his closeness to her father. And what had she done? Pushed and shoved, rebuking him until he had surrendered. How could she have been so obtuse? She had thought their last visit had gone rather well, but perhaps by then he'd already had enough of her recalcitrance.

She would have to make this right. She would not add decency to the long list of amenities that Matthew had taken from her. She was going to find Douglas tonight, and she was going to be kind to him, come what may.

⁓℮

IT WAS THE FIRST EVENING ALL WEEK THAT DOUGLAS had returned home from the wharf at a reasonable hour. Abby decided to seize the opportunity and attempt a visit with him prior to her supper with Larissa. It hadn't been but five days since Douglas's abrupt absenting of himself, but Abby had become more convinced by the hour that seeking him out was the proper way for her to behave. The last thing this unfortunate man needed was to be rejected by the first individual whose social company he had sought since the deaths of his wife and child. Her father had been very clear that an express purpose of her journey was to help this man.

As Abby neared the study, she was surprised to hear Douglas already involved in a discussion with someone. It had been only a few minutes since he returned home. The door was closed, but she recognized Demett's voice coming from within. She raised her fist to knock, but hesitated. Her meeting with Douglas might be more effective if they did not have an audience.

"Thank you, sir," Demett was saying. "I really want to help, much as you let me."

"All right," Douglas answered. Abby could hear a clinking from within, and she imagined Douglas was pouring himself a drink.

"It's taken much planning, but the hours I've put in over the past few days seem to have paid off. You're confident you can get a message back to Clover and be discreet?"

Abby realized that something of substance was being discussed between the men, that she should either leave or make her presence known, but her curiosity overtook her senses, and she leaned in closer toward the door.

"Yes, sir," Demett answered with conviction.

"Jethro Lions and Wyatt Holder will go to the Cunninghams' property in four days. You know who they are, yes?"

"Yes, sir," Demett answered again. "Free blacks. Both live out near the Quakenbush farm."

"Right," Douglas continued. "Lions and Holder will collect Clover from her cabin after midnight. She is to leave a washbasin left of the cabin door so they know which shack is hers."

Abby knew she should not be eavesdropping, but she couldn't tear herself away.

"A washbasin," Demett repeated, as if he was reminding himself already.

There was silence for a moment, and Abby held her breath to listen for footsteps coming toward her. But then Douglas continued.

"The men will help Clover off the property and guide her through the woods to the Ashley. They've agreed to take only her. No one else can accompany her. Make sure she knows."

"Yes, sir," Demett answered one more time.

"Other men will be waiting at the riverbank with a raft to carry her to Sullivan's Island."

Abby struggled to comprehend what she was overhearing. From the sound of it, Douglas was planning a slave's escape. It couldn't be. This man who had seemed so self-involved, so reclusive, she could not have imagined it. She was simply unable to fold her mind around the idea of it. Douglas an abolitionist! She thought back, conducting a quick mental catalog of her few months at the Elling estate. No, he hadn't acted in any way that would suggest he had been conducting unlawful activities. Perhaps there was more to it, something she was failing to understand. But then, she remembered with a start, there was that secret passageway in his office at the peer. And the long hours that he remained out from the house. She supposed it was possible—how really, could she know for sure? And a Cunningham slave, at that. She remembered Clover from her teatime with Gracie. Abby recalled the slave girl's caramel complexion, her long dark braids, and her swollen belly.

"I've arranged for her passage with a Northern exporter of pig iron, a ship's captain sympathetic to the cause," Douglas continued. "She will have to board during the dead of night and then be secreted in a wardrobe in the captain's quarters for the entirety of the voyage. Once she reaches New York, she will be guided to an abolitionist community that will orchestrate the remainder of her journey."

"Meanwhile, we will stage a diversion in Charleston. When Clover is missed by the Cunninghams the morning after her escape, we'll send a local boy to report that she's been spotted traveling west. He will deliver the news that a pregnant Negro woman has been parading herself about in parts of North Carolina, professing to be a fugitive, escaped from the Cunninghams of Charleston. Court Cunningham will surely be offering a large reward for Clover's return, so while the slave catchers are in hot pursuit of the fabricated Clover, the real Clover will be shepherded to safety."

Abby was stunned. Who was this man she had been living with these past months? Only recently had she ceased viewing him as a monster, and now it seemed he was quite the opposite. It felt as though there were a million questions coursing through her mind. How had he managed to make all these arrangements? How did he know so well what needed to be done? Abby was suddenly near bursting with pride for him. All this time she'd thought such horrible things about him, harbored unfair notions of his character. Meanwhile, he had somehow been connected to all sorts of people, revolutionaries risking their own safety, all for the benefit of others. Well good on him! She almost wished she could open the door and tell him so herself.

"I'll explain to Clover," Demett was saying.

"Right," Douglas agreed. "I imagine once she reaches New York, she'll want to continue straight to Canada."

Abby knew that in Canada, like England, slavery was no longer legal. She heard one of the chairs scrape against the wood floor, maybe Douglas pushing back, readying to stand. She started to back away, bending her body nearly in half to keep an ear near the door.

"I believe this is going to work, but she is taking an enormous risk, and she must be made to understand," he added.

"She will be so grateful, sir. With that babe in her, she needs every chance she can find, risks and all. We all recognize the need to be careful, that there ain't no one can protect us if any of us get found out. It ain't all on you, sir. Never was, you know."

"I don't know about that," he answered, and Abby detected a sudden bristling in his voice. She'd heard enough to know that she had best quit her position before she was caught listening. Clearly their plans required the utmost secrecy, and they wouldn't take kindly to her nosiness. She scampered quickly and quietly from the dark hallway, dizzy from the bright light of her reeling thoughts.

As she reemerged in the main foyer, she paused for a moment beside the gilded mirror. Her cheeks were flushed, and her gray eyes were too wide, as if they had been pasted into a state of surprise. She needed to pause for a steadying breath before joining Larissa, or surely the governess would recognize that something was amiss. The grandfather clock in the hall's corner began to chime seven, prodding Abby to move along. She straightened her shoulders and made her way to the dining room.

As usual, Larissa was already seated at the far end of the mahogany table when Abby arrived for supper, patiently sipping water from a crystal goblet. Candelabras flickered at both ends of the table, creating a tranquil glow so at odds with the frenzied thoughts careening through Abby's mind.

"Ah, darling," Larissa smiled at Abby, "I was wondering if you'd forgotten supper." She spoke gently, but Abby knew it was a chiding. Punctuality, of course, was one of the hallmarks of a proper young lady. Normally, Larissa's correction would have ignited something inside Abby, the fury that always seemed too ready to take hold of her. But tonight, she felt something different, a pull toward Larissa and wonder that she wanted to confide in the woman, report what she had heard.

"Good evening, Larissa," Abby smiled politely instead.

"I hope you won't mind, dear. Jasper had something to take

care of this evening, so he's left the food for us to serve ourselves." She gestured at the silver serving platters, each covered with its own silver dome.

As Abby took her seat, kitty-corner to Larissa, the governess removed the dome from the largest platter, revealing slices of steaming roast beef surrounded by oversized potatoes and bright spheres of carrot. As usual, there was significantly more food than Abby and Larissa could finish on their own, but tonight Abby was too distracted to feel outraged about the waste.

Larissa reached for Abby's plate. "May I serve you?"

"Pardon?" Abby looked at Larissa's outstretched hand in confusion. What did Larissa want her to do?

"Your supper, may I serve you?"

"Oh, yes, yes. Thank you," Abby picked up her own water glass and tried to take a calming sip. She saw that her hand was trembling and quickly reset the glass before Larissa would notice. She had better start conversing, else Larissa would certainly become suspicious.

"I had a lovely afternoon studying in the rose garden," she began as soon as Larissa had finished serving herself. "And I can report yet another day with my shoulder feeling quite fit."

"I'm pleased to hear it. On both counts. It may still be several days before you are ready to return to riding horses though. What would you like to do with this newfound time? Perhaps shopping trips to town or we could invite some young ladies to come calling?"

Abby had little interest in additional clothing purchases or social visits with strangers. "A trip into town does appeal, considering how many days have passed since I've left this house. Or do you think, could we go walking along the Battery? There is still so much of this city I haven't seen." Abby congratulated herself on keeping her concentration fastened to the topic at hand.

Larissa pursed her lips, and Abby worried that she had again, exposed some ignorance, some lack of refinement.

"Is something the matter, dear?" Larissa asked, peering into her face.

Abby quickly looked away, fixing her eyes down on her plate. The juices from her roast beef had spread around the rim of her dish, creating a ring around its border, like a halo. She couldn't let on. Surely Larissa was not aware of Douglas's activities. Or perhaps she was aware, but Abby certainly was not meant to be. With a shock, Abby wondered if that was really a possibility, that Larissa was fully cognizant of Douglas's secret work.

"No, nothing," she sputtered. "I'm sorry to have given you that impression." She sat up straighter and began working at her food.

Larissa studied her a moment longer and seemed to be formulating another question.

Before Larissa spoke, Abby asked, "What about the Ashley River? Is that somewhere you have spent time for diversion?" Douglas had mentioned the Ashley in his conversation with Demett. Maybe Larissa would say something revealing if Abby kept her on the topic.

"No, I can't say that it is," Larissa shrugged prettily and then continued. "But we could try it. We could go to the promenade at White Point Gardens, where the Ashley meets the Cooper before the rivers head out to the sea."

Abby nodded as she speared a piece of meat. She imagined the park must be somewhere near Douglas's office if it was so close to the quayside. She was bewildered by her reaction to the information she learned earlier. None of this was her business, and she shouldn't care. But she felt desperate to learn more about the abolitionist work Douglas was doing, about him. She had never known a person who stretched to such lengths to help others, took such risks. Suddenly the entire Elling estate seemed like a bustling mystery, full of activities she knew nothing about. She thought of the other staff, Jovian, Reggie. Jasper's absence this evening. It was as though she was suddenly living inside a labyrinth of possibilities. She was struck too, by an overwhelming sense of shame at her own failure to take more notice of slavery since her arrival in Charleston. She had assumed the cruelty and suffering as a given, an immutable fact of life in America, but others were taking action. She had so drastically misjudged Douglas and ignored her surroundings. Her entire world now felt cockeyed, exposed. Nothing seemed more important than discovering more, about this place, about Douglas.

"Sounds nice," she answered absently as she wondered if they could visit Douglas at his place of business.

"It might be courteous for us to visit Mr. Elling at his office too, no?" She startled herself by voicing her thought aloud. "It's just that I've noticed he's returned to the long hours he kept at the docks prior to my injury."

Larissa paused with her fork halfway to her mouth, tilting her head quizzically as she gazed back at Abby. Her tight bun listed along with her, and Abby had the desire to turn the bun like a nob, fixing Larissa's head back into proper place. Had she given herself away?

"Oh, has he?" Larissa asked, as she lowered her fork. Abby noticed a slight smile playing at Larissa's pale lips.

"What is it?" Abby asked.

Larissa only raised her eyebrows and shook her head, belying her denial with a faint smirk.

"No, I just thought it might be nice for him to receive a visit is all. He was kind to me when I was hurt. What?" Abby asked again, a little more forcefully this time.

"No, I think it's splendid," Larissa answered with a satisfied smile. "You were so opposed to everything related to Mr. Elling, but it seems he's worn you down. I'm glad of it. He's a kind man, who could use good will from someone as lovely as you. It's nice to see you giving him a chance."

So she hadn't let on. Maybe she could use this, Larissa's hope for her to connect in some way with Douglas. But still, she shouldn't sound too eager.

"Oh, right. I suppose I've been considering it. Maybe you could tell me more about him, what it is that you find so estimable? I've noticed he can be rather mercurial."

Larissa released a small puff of air in apparent agreement. "Better for you to get more acquainted with him and see for yourself. Why don't you ask him to finish reading you that play? He could read it to us both." She reached down for her pocket watch and opened the silver cover with a practiced flick of her thumb. "Perhaps tomorrow. You should ask him tonight. I'm sure he's still toiling away in his study. You can stop in on your way upstairs."

Abby had the distinct impression that Larissa would have liked to push her straight out of her chair and down the hall without delay, if only decorum allowed.

"Um . . . all right," Abby answered cautiously. She wasn't sure what Larissa was playing at, prodding her toward Douglas like this, but she was satisfied by the proposed plan. With all the new information she had ingested tonight, her interest in that wonderful play had faded to a whisper. At the same time, her motivation to pursue Douglas's friendship had increased exponentially, seeming to saturate every recess of her mind. How fortuitous that she had the play as an excuse, as a reason for suspense, a way to study him. So much had changed since this morning. Everything was exactly the same really, and yet, Abby wondered whether, when she came upon Douglas next, if she would even recognize him at all.

17

CHARLESTON, SOUTH CAROLINA

1846

*A*s Abby approached Douglas's study for the second time in one evening, she paused and pushed her palm against her chest, as if the force of her touch could calm the staccato flickering of her heart. Listening for a moment at the door, she concluded he was alone and finally chanced a knock.

After some sounds of movement, Douglas called out good-naturedly from inside, "Come in!"

Abby opened the door and caught her breath. The man standing behind the desk was Douglas but was also not Douglas. He looked so drastically different from when she had seen him only a few days before, so different that it seemed almost preposterous. Gone was the ragged beard that had sprouted in all directions, giving him the air of a careless eccentric. Gone were the haphazard threadbare garments that he'd so thoughtlessly worn. Here now was a man who was freshly shaven, who had given care to himself as he dressed. The effect was staggering. Had his hair been trimmed too? His entire posture, his presence, had transformed along with his wardrobe. The alteration in the person before her was so complete that it seemed impossible to have occurred in a matter of days, to be the result of simple changes in style, clothes, and hair. It was as if the man she'd been expecting to find in the study had only ever existed in a dream, or perhaps this, now, was the dream.

As Abby stared, dumbfounded at Douglas, she felt her entire rehearsed monologue slipping from her brain. It was too much. First the conversation with Demett that she'd overheard, and now this, this confusing apparition. It was like learning that her linen writing journal was actually made from emeralds or that her hairbrush once belonged to the queen. Nothing in this place was as it seemed.

As she continued to scrutinize this new Douglas, Abby suddenly began to feel as though her skin was sizzling. She had to remove herself from the situation at once. This was not the meeting for which she had prepared, not the person, the hapless beast in need of her acceptance and compassion. No, this fellow here was like a fine-spun embodiment of sufficiency and possibility. He looked like he didn't need anything at all. Had he been laughing at her all this time? Pretending to be some sort of repugnant, grotesque misfit when all along, he'd been this, this other man, so very, very other. Looking him up and down, Abby swallowed, tried to clear her throat. She glanced over her shoulder, evaluating the location of the door. No, there was no way for her to exit gracefully at this point. She had to say something or she would appear even more the half-witted clod than she must already, after all her protracted bumble-headed goggling at Douglas.

Douglas walked around toward the front of his hefty desk and sat on its outer corner. He seemed relaxed and leisurely as he cocked his brow at her. He was clearly waiting for Abby to say whatever it was that had brought her to the study. When she hesitated, he spoke up to fill the silence.

"I shaved."

She nodded.

"Thought it time I cleaned up a bit."

Abby gave herself a mental kick in the head. *Speak, you imbecile!*

"I just came to say . . . well no, I was coming to say, if you wanted to finish the play, well I just hope I haven't offended . . . I mean, if you wanted . . ." she trailed off, disgusted with herself for allowing her brain to turn into fried eggs.

"Ugggghhhhh," she groaned aloud at her own discomfiture. "Larissa and I had an idea. But, never mind then," she mumbled and turned to leave.

"Are you feeling well?" Douglas asked as Abby neared the door.

"Yes, thank you," she answered without pausing her step. "Just a long day, I reckon. Sorry to have troubled you."

"Wait, would you?"

She turned, reluctant to look back upon his new likeness, struggling to corral her thoughts about this man whom was no longer recognizable in body or spirit. He searched for something on his cluttered desk as Abby watched him and tried to drown out the words catapulting through her mind. *Abolitionist, warrior, pretender, defender.* He seized on an item and held up *Twelfth Night.*

"Aha. What about the play then?" Before she could respond, he continued, "It was taking so long for you to recover, I did not want my visits to your sickroom to hinder your convalescence. But now that you are up and about again, I see no reason why we shouldn't pick up where we left off. I hope I wasn't being fanciful to imagine you were enjoying the play." Douglas smiled faintly.

At the hesitancy of Douglas's smile, his question, Abby remembered her original intentions, as though she'd been lifted out of a maze and set back on a straight path. Perhaps this shinier new version of Douglas was not as self-sustained as his altered appearance made him seem.

"Actually," Abby responded regaining a bit of composure, "it was Larissa's idea, we were thinking the same thing. She suggested that you might read to us both tomorrow evening following supper. If that suits," she hedged.

"Splendid," Douglas answered, sounding genuinely pleased, and Abby thought that yes, her original ideas about his waning desire for isolation may have been on point.

"It would be lovely for Miss Prue to listen as well, though I trust you'll catch her up on all she's missed." He thumbed through the pages in his hand, as though searching for the place they left off. "It's settled then," Douglas concluded. "We'll meet in the drawing room after you've finished dining. You'll tell Miss Prue?" He looked at her for an answer, his light eyes holding hers for a beat. She felt her world begin to tilt again and wished she were standing closer to the doorknob, a railing, something to steady her. The word "abolitionist," caught like celery between her teeth, was running a loop over and again through her thoughts. *Abolitionist, abolitionist, abolitionist.*

"Yes, yes, of course," she finally answered before she turned to go.

As Abby exited the study, she heard Douglas settling back down at his desk. She shut the door behind herself and emitted a tempestuous sigh. Leaning against the cool wall, she tried to sort out what had just happened. She would have struggled to face Douglas with composure after overhearing his plans for Clover if he'd still appeared as his former rumpled, slipshod self. On top of that stunning information though, the man she had just encountered looked so strikingly different from what she'd grown accustomed to, it was a wonder she hadn't fainted outright from the shock of it all. The fact that he was bitingly handsome beneath all his shorn scruff, well that was beside the point. It must have been the surprise that was so unnerving. All this time, Abby had considered Douglas an unsightly man. Not ugly, exactly, but disheveled and straggly. To discover that underneath the unruly beard and worn suits, he was actually dazzling, it would unnerve anyone. His bedraggled whiskers had been concealing smooth, bright skin and a chiseled, Roman jaw. His shorn face was youthful, befitting a man of Douglas's twenty-six years, despite Abby's prior impression of him as much older. She suddenly understood all the talk about how Douglas had been such an eligible young man before his marriage. Apparently, it wasn't just his money that made hearts flutter. Not that he made *her* heart flutter. Abby pushed her chin up, willing herself together, and walked toward the piano room.

So she had made a fool of herself in front of Douglas, Abby shrugged as she walked. It was not the first time, and she'd guess it wouldn't be the last. Could she still offer him friendship despite his prepossessing good looks? Well, of course she could. What difference did it make? Just because he was objectively attractive didn't mean that he was attractive to *her*. Abby wasn't attracted to anyone, she reminded herself. Wasn't attracted to anyone—ever.

And anyway, hadn't she, just hours before, chastised herself for making everything about herself? If Douglas needed a friend, that need would not change simply because of his improved appearance. Clearly he had more human connections in his life than she'd realized though, if he'd been contacting so many people about Clover's escape. Were there other escapees too? It could be that Douglas was helping a myriad of Southern slaves all at once, and she'd only happened to hear about one. Her chest swelled at the idea of such admirable work, and then she had another feeling, almost like jealousy. How lucky Douglas was, to be of use, to lighten the loads of others. To be needed.

She directed her focus to the following evening. She and Larissa would sit with this man, this enigma, chameleon, defender, shepherd, savior. Certainly, by tomorrow she would have grabbed hold of herself, she concluded, more by way of command than prediction. She would behave as a proper young lady and a friend.

It would be lovely to listen to Shakespeare's play again, especially with Larissa for added company. As Abby approached the piano room, she heard Larissa humming softly and practicing notes from Bach's "Minuet in G." Abruptly, Abby was able to laugh at her own foolishness. She would not become enamored with this man, whether because of his bold courageousness or his horribly superior appearance. It hardly mattered whether he was the most remarkable man in all the New World. She would never be romantically interested in any man. She was going to be a spinster and a school teacher. Abby had made her mind to that end months ago, and no man was going to distract her from her course. Least of all Douglas Elling.

~⊙

AS ABBY DRESSED FOR SUPPER, SHE TRIED TO CALM her nerves. Her lady's maid, Ida, was stooped behind her, fastening the buttons on the back of her lavender silk gown and chattering away about different remedies to ameliorate Abby's penchant for biting her nails. Her favorite approach, Ida was saying, was to use the juice from a bitter gourd.

"You make a paste by crushing the gourd. It looks something like okra inside. You just put the gourd on a sieve to get the juice out. Miss Abigail, you hearing me?" She looked up from the button she'd been working on and fixed Abby with a pointed stare in the mirror.

"I'm sorry, Ida. I didn't sleep well last night, I suppose. Please, continue."

Abby tried to listen, as the nail biting really was a coarse habit, one that had become worse since just yesterday, but she was so besieged by her own cogitation that it was hard to hear Ida's words. Since the night before, she'd been able to think of nothing but Douglas. She was not surprised at herself for her interest in his abolitionist activities, as she'd always had a penchant for rebellion, especially in the name of justice. The trouble really, was that each time she thought about his subversive work, she felt a glimmer of something else besides admiration, a feeling that she couldn't name, but which she felt compelled to resist.

She found herself rehashing her previous interactions with Douglas, all now infused with new subtlety in the wake of her enlightenment. That day he yelled at her for touching Reggie was not about bigotry, as she had thought, but about protecting them all from suspicion, from discovery. His visits to her sickroom even, had perhaps come at the expense of time he could have devoted to his insurgent endeavors. Realizing that Douglas might have been somewhere, anywhere, other than his lonely office if he had not been with her, she wondered why he had chosen to spend so much time with her. She felt another flicker of something, a swirling in her belly, but she quickly tamped it down, choosing to focus on his actions, nothing else. Even the long hours allegedly passed at his office began to seem suspect, infused with possibilities. She found she wanted to know every last detail about Douglas's involvement in abolition, not that it was any of her business.

Two dogs barked outside in the courtyard, jolting Abby from her contemplation. She stepped away from Ida and glanced out the window in time to see Gracie Cunningham hustling herself toward the door of the Elling residence in an obvious dither. A young male slave followed quickly behind her, a stoic expression on his face.

"Whatever in the world?" Abby wondered as she hastily grabbed her shawl from the vanity stool.

"I'm sorry, Ida, it looks like we have unannounced guests. I must go and see what the trouble is." A spontaneous visit was certainly unusual for young ladies with formal Southern rearing like Gracie's.

Abby reached the front entryway just in time to hear Gracie apologizing profusely to Larissa.

"Miss Prue, I would never go visiting unannounced like this, and surely not at mealtime. Oh but I am sorry! It's just that the carriage wheel came dislodged not more than two feet from your drive. I am simply mortified!"

Gracie was standing just inside the closed doorway, her porcelain cheeks flushed, her white gloves showing traces of dust from the street. Several tendrils of her dark hair had fallen loose from the intricately plaited bun behind her head. It was the first time Abby had seen the girl looking anything less than flawlessly assembled.

"Gracie, what's happened?" Abby asked, concerned for her friend.

"Abby, please forgive this awful intrusion." Gracie looked relieved to see Abby and embarrassed all at once. "You must think I'm downright crude, appearing before supper without an invitation. Our carriage broke down, and we weren't more than a hop away from this house. I thought I'd send Jono back to King Street on foot. But, well, if it wouldn't inconvenience you all something terrible, I was hoping I could wait here until he fetches another carriage. It does look like it's fixing to storm out there." Gracie glanced behind herself as though she was assessing the weather through the closed door.

"Gracie, you mustn't be ridiculous." Abby took Gracie by the arm and led her farther into the house. "I'm sure Larissa would agree that you must stay here with us, and you must stop worrying about your manners around us. True friends should feel comfortable taking certain liberties with each other. Isn't that so, Larissa?" Abby spoke bravely, despite her worry that perhaps Larissa would disagree.

"Abigail is correct," Larissa added. "Join us for supper, and we will prepare one of the bedrooms so you may spend the night. There's no need to venture out again in the rain."

"Oh, that's an impeccable idea." Abby concurred, pleased to have the diversion and the additional buffer between herself and Douglas during the evening's impending reading. "Run and catch Jono," she added. "He can eat supper here with the other servants, and then Jovian or Demett can drive him back to King Street afterwards in one of Mr. Elling's carriages. He needn't walk so far in the cold. He can return for you tomorrow."

"Darling," Gracie turned to her with a dismissive laugh, "his kind are built for physical challenges far greater than walking through a storm. And anyway, Papa would have my hide if I let him sup with a group of free niggers."

Abby winced at Gracie's words but realized she best hold her tongue.

After Gracie retired for a moment to freshen herself from her ordeal in the street, the women took their seats in the dining room. Jasper was waiting nearby, along with an elderly footman, who began serving the women boiled mutton and corn pudding. "By the by," Larissa placed her napkin daintily in her lap and looked at Gracie, "you've picked an auspicious evening to get stranded with us."

Gracie looked puzzled by Larissa's comment. She glanced quizzically at Abby sitting across from her and caught the end of a tortured grimace on Abby's face. "I can't imagine why," Gracie giggled. "Whatever it is though, the thought has put the oddest expression on Abby. Please, Larissa, do explain."

"Whatever you saw on my face," Abby interjected with too much acidity, "had nothing to do with your conversation, as my mind had drifted to something else." She paused while she dabbed at her mouth with her napkin, as though trying to wipe away whatever Gracie had noticed. "Do forgive my poor attention." She spoke more gently now, remembering herself. "What was it you and Larissa were discussing?"

Abby detested that she wore her emotions like a banner about her face, calling out her private thoughts through a subconscious scrunching of her nose or narrowing of her eyes. She was like a weathervane, her mother had chanted time and again when she was younger, foretelling the tidings from the way her mouth curled or her shoulder twisted. As she grew older and circumstances changed, her parents lost the ability to translate what they saw on her face, misinterpreting everything. Hopefully Gracie too would simply misinterpret whatever she saw as some unexplained part of Abby's contrarian nature. She did not want Larissa or Gracie to gather any inkling about the disturbing effect Douglas was having on her. There was also the subject of Clover, a slave in Gracie's home. If Gracie connected Abby's expression to thoughts about Douglas, even if it was a far leap to the rest, well, she couldn't risk exposing anything about him.

Abby smiled at Gracie in an effort to move the conversation along.

"Forgive me for making such an uncharitable comment then, Abby," Gracie pleaded. "I would hate for you to think I was mocking you in any way." Gracie's hand flew to her chest as she spoke, her pale fingers stark against the shadowy gray of her dress.

"Gracie, you needn't be so proper all the time. What were you two talking about?" Abby looked from Gracie to Larissa.

Larissa placed her fork and knife on the side of her plate, angling them just so, before she spoke. "I was about to inform Gracie that she's had the good fortune of arriving on an evening of entertainment." Turning to Gracie she continued, "Mr. Elling will be providing us with a reading of Shakespeare following supper."

"Oh, how delightful," Gracie clapped her hands together like a child. Abruptly pausing, she wrinkled her nose and asked, "Nothing too melancholy, I hope, knowing the dishumour he's been suffering and all. I feel so disheartened by plays like *Romeo and Juliet*."

"I often feel that way from Shakespeare's tragedies, as well," Larissa sipped from her wineglass. "But tonight, we will be hearing a comedy, *Twelfth Night*."

Gracie nodded and patted her mouth with her napkin. "Well then, my arrival on this night does feel fortuitous. I am heartened to learn that Douglas is engaged in such an upbeat activity." She seemed to be gazing at some faraway object as she concluded, "My family will be thrilled to hear of it."

18

∽

CHARLESTON, SOUTH CAROLINA
1846

During the ride back to her family's King Street home, Gracie tugged nervously at a lock of her dark hair, twirling the strands around her index finger and then watching them unfurl. As she braced to confront Cora Rae about the past evening's events, she fought conflicting emotions. She'd been livid yesterday when Cora Rae burst into her bedchamber, demanding out of nowhere that Gracie visit the Elling estate forthwith. Gracie knew better than to arrive for an unannounced evening visit. But Cora Rae had persisted until she overcame her sister's resistance. In fact, when Gracie declared that she wouldn't intrude on Douglas Elling's household, Cora Rae had gone so far as to begin penning an actual love note to Harrison Blount. Gracie wondered now, how long had it been since she and Rae shared a genuinely amicable moment? Perhaps she should feel regretful that the kinship they shared as children had long since evaporated, but she was too anxious about her sister's behavior to feel anything other than frothing anger.

Every time Gracie found something new to treasure, anything she considered her own, Rae appeared, threatening to snatch it away. It wasn't just about Harrison, who had come calling on Gracie in earnest just the day before. Gracie was certain that Rae's meddling would soon destroy her relationship with Abby, the one friend Gracie had cultivated outside of her family's designs, the only one who seemed indifferent to her father's wealth and status. Gracie rested her head back against the leather seat and drew in a deep breath, wrinkling her nose at the stench of brine that permeated the Charleston air on these raw days.

Now that she and Harrison had started courting, she could attest that he was even more engaging than she had imagined. During his visit, the pair had spent an enchanting afternoon playing whist in the parlor, with her mother as chaperone. He had given her every impression that she meant something special to him. Perhaps she should take more pride in herself, declare that if Harrison would be so fickle, would succumb to a letter from her brazen sister, she did not want him anyway. But oh, she just couldn't risk it, even if Rae's demands did mean jeopardizing her friendship with Abby. So she had agreed to scuttle off to the Elling residence without invitation in order to prevent her nasty sister from sending that letter.

Gracie had reasoned that she could call briefly at the Elling residence to ask after Abby's health, and if she managed to limit her stay to an hour's time, perhaps the social blunder wouldn't be so glaring. She still wanted to yank at every strand of Cora Rae's fiery hair for putting her up to the intrusion, all because Cora Rae had a sudden hankering for an update on the fabulous, fallen Douglas Elling. Or maybe she just couldn't stand to watch Gracie getting the man she wanted while her own prized stud was nowhere to be seen.

Unfortunately, Gracie's mortification had only intensified when the carriage began to fall apart. At the sound of wood splintering, she had uttered a silent oath, cursing her father's stinginess. Court Cunningham had endless funds available for entertaining guests and making himself appear important, but when it came to something as practical as maintaining his carriages, he clenched his coins. He was the same with his slaves, always ready to purchase another human for status and investment, but those darkies had to be well-nigh on their deathbeds before Court would fetch them a doctor. Pretension without preservation. That about summed up her pa.

Thanks to the faulty wheel, a visit that was intended as only a brief affront to propriety had lasted so much longer. Thank heavens Larissa and Abby had been so welcoming. She shuddered to think of the reaction her performance would have engendered at the home of other friends. Of course, they would have invited her for dinner just as Abby and Larissa had done, her compatriots of the South being known for nothing if not their generous hospitality. But then she would have been maligned for weeks at ladies' teas and sewing circles for her unseemly behavior. Abby, however, had clearly been nonplussed by her audacious arrival. At least the slave boy, Jono, had the good graces to arrive early this morning with a repaired carriage. Gracie listened now to the steady rolling of the wheels beneath her, carrying her back to her home, and she wondered if Rae didn't have something to do with that damaged wheel.

Gracie gazed out the carriage window into the Charleston morning, the streets just coming to life with people, the cobblestones still slick from the rainstorm during the night. As they passed the large homes on Ann Street, slaves opened shutters at one brightly colored home after another. Gracie watched Negroes pushing at puddles with brooms, driving water toward the street, working to restore order to lawns and porches that had been drenched with the winter rain. She thought about Abby, conceding to herself that her new friend did have a rather distinctive way about her. Even the manner in which she had behaved toward Douglas the night before was unusual. When Douglas had arrived at the drawing room to read to the women, Gracie had been astounded to see him looking dashing and fresh, so much like he had appeared years earlier.

Douglas had seemed surprised to find Gracie in the drawing room, but he was congenial nonetheless. As he walked toward the room's hefty sideboard and began pouring himself a brandy, Gracie had noticed that he was not only clean-shaven, but energetic and jovial. The change in his demeanor had been so obvious that she could sense it just from the way he put down the crystal decanter. Until last night, Gracie had forgotten just how disarming Douglas could be. His improved disposition, the warm greeting, and his arresting appearance gave Gracie the disquieting sensation that she had stepped back in time. Here was the old Douglas, the one who had been dapper and charming, lively and magnetic.

She had felt an unexpected softening toward her sister as she watched him in the parlor, a flash of understanding. It made sense that Cora Rae would pine after a man like that, that she'd be unable to relinquish her dream of beguiling someone so extraordinary. Or, Gracie thought, her hackles rising back up as she took her seat beside Abby, perhaps it was just Douglas's outrageous wealth that held her sister's interest all these years. It was so hard to know with Cora Rae. Gracie had sat beside Abby thinking of the many times since Sarah's death that she had advised Cora Rae to forsake her obsession with Douglas, to realize that the man she'd adored was as dead as his late wife, that he was gone forever and for good. Except as she sat in the glittering parlor in his home, Gracie realized that for all she could glean, Douglas Elling had now returned.

Even in the clarifying light of morning, Gracie was still reeling from the shock of seeing Douglas so much like his former self. Equally striking had been the puzzling dynamics between Douglas and Abby during the past evening. From the moment the ladies sat down, Gracie sensed that something had changed between them. Abby no longer appeared to chafe at Douglas's presence. If anything, she seemed distracted by something else entirely. More notable had been Douglas, the way his eyes kept floating back to Abby as he read. He watched her as though his attention was tethered to her by an invisible rope, pulled by her every action. He was clearly quite familiar with the text of *Twelfth Night,* as he recited so many of the lines while his eyes roved over Abby's face, barely flitting to the pages in his hands.

Gracie wondered why she hadn't considered sooner the possibility of her friend bewitching Douglas. After all, they were not so far apart in age and living under the same roof. Abby was nearly eighteen, and Douglas couldn't be more than twenty-six years old. Moreover, Abby was actually quite fetching, with her frosty eyes and swollen lips. She had a figure that most young ladies would go mad over, if they ever bothered to notice the seething curves she kept hidden beneath those modest dresses. And she was actually charming too, once you got past all her bluster. Gracie had spent the evening thinking of Cora Rae with panic.

Now in the carriage, Gracie ran her hand along her wool skirt, trying in vain to smooth out the inevitable wrinkles in a fine dress worn for a second day. She huffed out a sigh and told herself that at least Abby had appeared indifferent to Douglas. She had been so busy staring into her own lap that she seemed entirely oblivious to his repeated glances. What a drastic difference from Cora Rae. Her tart of a sister would have thrown herself across Douglas's lap after his first overly long gaze.

Abby clearly had something trapping her thoughts the entire

evening, but since she chose to keep it to herself, Gracie would try to respect that. Though now, as Jono pulled the carriage into her parents' semicircular drive, Gracie found her curiosity getting the better of her. She wondered again what had happened to make Abby so preoccupied the whole evening. What if, contrary to Gracie's prior assumptions, it actually did have something to do with Douglas? Gracie worried over what to tell her sister. What would it mean for Rae if Douglas emerged from his mourning only to forsake her yet again? What would it mean for Gracie?

19

CHARLESTON, SOUTH CAROLINA
1846

As Larissa explained the procedures for solving another equation, Abby yawned again. She and Larissa were seated in the same drawing room where Douglas had read to them the previous evening, though they were now at the mahogany card table, along the far end of the room. Larissa had proposed this spot rather than the upstairs parlor where they usually met, suggesting they might take advantage of the late-morning light, the crisp January sunshine that would be charging through the arched windows. Abby had been pleased by Larissa's uncharacteristic spontaneity, and she did mean to focus on what the governess was explicating, but her mind kept drifting. She noticed a few crumbs resting on her wool skirt, remnants of the cranberry scones they had finished with their morning meal. She swatted at them with her hand, and Larissa let out a loud sigh.

"This is just what I was afraid of," Larissa complained as she closed the mathematics textbook they had been examining. "It's been too much flurry and activity for you, too soon into your recovery. Now look how distracted you are. It's exhaustion. You have shadows beneath your eyes, nearly violet, and you're doing an abominable job of stifling those yawns."

"No, I'm sorry, Larissa," Abby reached for the book and began opening back to the page they had been reviewing. "I just didn't sleep well last night. Maybe the meat at dinner didn't agree with me." She could hardly admit that she'd been stewing all night, thinking alternately about Douglas and her uncle. She was still overwhelmed to realize she had been oblivious to so much during the months since her arrival. Though she applauded Douglas's actions, respected him all the better for his clandestine endeavors, something about the secrecy, the double-dealing, had released memories of her uncle Matthew. Through the night, horrid images had arisen from the far crevices of her mind, like black smoke, suffocating her anew. One minute she would think of Douglas, his aristocratic face and surprising ideals, and just as quickly, she would be assaulted with the specter of her uncle, his bloated features and hot breath, the duplicity that none detected. She had lain awake most of the night, greeting the morning shaken and wounded once more.

"Well, either way, these studies are not in your best interest today." Larissa pulled the textbook back from Abby and closed it again, this time keeping her hand atop the cover. "Here," she reached in her bag and handed Abby a book stamped in flowery script. "This is the next novel we'll be studying. Make yourself comfortable on the settee and read. It's the best way to make you rest, I think."

Larissa packed up the other books, piling them into the burgundy satchel that she brought to all their lessons, and then left Abby to herself in the spacious drawing room. Abby moved over to the plush settee, curling her knees beneath her. Upon closer inspection, she saw that Larissa had given her a copy of *Robinson Crusoe*, a story she'd never had the opportunity to read. She placed the volume on her lap, thinking to close her eyes for a few minutes first, as she was indeed, quite tired. As she began to doze, she thought about how it had gotten easier, since coming to Charleston, to squeeze the past into a tight hold. But today, her grip was off, and she was failing. Perhaps it was her sleepless night, or the realization that she had so misunderstood her world in Charleston. Suddenly everything felt as fresh as the day her da told her she'd be going to America.

It was as though she was still sitting there on the front stoop of her family's flat in Wigan, spreading a salve onto Charlie's blistered hands, watching her da emerge from the flat with the news. She could remember when her da opened the door, how Charlie had been complaining.

He had asked in his child's voice, "How come my hands don't get calloused like the other men? You'd think by now they'd have grown tougher, yeah?"

Abby's father, Samuel, had squatted down next to Charlie and answered before Abby. "Even handling all that twine at the canal, you're still only a green cub compared to the others. Your hands will beef up soon enough. Meantime, be thankful Wigan is failing to make its mark on you." He turned to Abby, adding, "I need a word with you, Ab."

Abby stood abruptly, "I was actually just heading to the water pump, Da. Can't it wait? Come on, Charlie," she held out her hand to her brother.

"No," Samuel answered firmly, causing Abby to look up in surprise. "It's important, and I need to speak with you now. Charlie, go help your mum with supper."

Abby stood opposite her father and waited impatiently for him to speak his piece. "Come," he said, as he sat in what had formerly been Charlie's spot on the stoop. "Have yourself a seat."

"I'd rather stand," Abby quipped. "What is it, then?"

"All right, if that's how you want it." Samuel shrugged and stood again, dusting his faded pants. "Your mum and I have decided," he began and then started over. "We know how hard it's been on you, this life we've been living since the shop closed. You weren't meant to be a weaver, and we all know it. So we've gotten you your ticket out of here. You're going to America."

Abby looked at her father, stunned.

"What? What do you mean?" she demanded.

"Abby," Samuel began. He stepped toward her and then halted abruptly, probably remembering how she generally shrank from his presence. "Come and sit."

She looked uncertainly at the stoop and then slowly started toward it. Samuel sat down again, and continued. "We've watched how you struggle here, Abby. Your mum and I, we've done all we can for you, but it simply isn't sufficient. Look at you. Wearing rags, your beautiful hair chopped to bits, crying all the time. It's not right the way you've been, and I don't know what else we can do for you here." He ran his hand through his sandy curls and released a defeated breath. "I don't know what's changed in you over the past year, but we can't keep up with your temper, Ab, and it seems that we can't fix it either. So we thought that maybe this opportunity . . ." he trailed off and looked at her.

After a moment's silence, he continued, "Well, I don't know. Is it, well, would you like to go?"

Abby looked at Samuel in the deepening gray of the evening. She noticed the new creases in her father's forehead and the dark grime beneath his fingernails. Time was not being kind to Samuel Milton.

"I contacted my old friend Douglas Elling," he continued. "He's agreed to host you at his estate. You'll have a governess to teach you the proper subjects, train you to be a young lady, instead of working you straight to your skin, as you've gotten with us. He's agreed to host you a full year."

"Isn't he the one whose family was murdered?" Abby asked. "You want to send me off thousands of miles from here to live with a wrecked widower? I've really been that dreadful, that you just want to be rid of me, is it?"

"Oh, Ab, of course you've been dreadful," Samuel laughed halfheartedly. "But look what you've been dealing with. Working sometimes eighteen hours a day, weaving and cleaning, cleaning and weaving. Then you come home to us, where you've got your chores and the other children to help look after. Top that off with playing serving girl to your rich old uncle, not a moment leftover for you to simply be who you are. Just hard work and cotton dust. Who wouldn't be dreadful in your shoes?" Kicking Abby's foot lightly, he added, "And right ratty shoes at that." She remembered feeling a rush of warmth toward him in that moment, maybe even smiling back at him.

"Douglas did lose his family, and he has been grieving hard. But he's got a grand home with plenty of empty rooms. You'll want for nothing while you're under his roof. Your mum and I, well we were hoping that having you around the house might cheer him a bit, too. It's a bit of a trade, as I see it."

Escaping Wigan, Matthew's slimy hands, how could she say no? She had worried then that Douglas Elling would be a fate even worse than Matthew. Matthew never forced her all the way, never made her have actual intercourse, only touched and fondled her while he gratified himself. There was certainly greater harm that an old, angry widower could do to a young girl sharing his home. But if he turned out a rough and filthy man, at least in America, she could run away without risking the security of her family. Unlike Matthew, Douglas Elling wasn't providing her parents with any sort of stipend that he could lord over her and use as leverage to force vulgarities upon her.

"Do I have a choice?" Abby had asked her father.

Samuel looked at his feet as he answered. "Not really, my girl, no." He reached for her hand, but as usual, she snatched it away before they made contact. "Your mum and I, we know this is the best thing for you. Arrangements have been made. You'll be sailing from Liverpool next week." He stood and walked back into the flat, leaving Abby to stare at the empty stoop.

She was dumbfounded that they were sending her away. Even though she was older than her brothers, the boys earned better wages. After all, she was only a girl, a pathetic parasite, she concluded. And now she was being shipped off, to a foreign country no less. Well, fine. She thought of her parents and siblings with growing rage, irate that she had been enduring Matthew's sexual depravity for their well-being. It would be good riddance to them all.

But what would Uncle Matthew do, she worried. She wasn't so angry at her parents that she wanted them to starve. Would he withhold his money if they sent her away? Without that monthly supplement from Uncle Matthew, there was no way the family could survive. Even with one less mouth to feed, there were too many debts remaining from the flood at the furniture shop years before, those usurious loans, payments looming always. Reminded of the magnitude of her family's financial struggle, the stubborn, disastrous debts, Abby softened.

And the thought of America *was* somewhat exciting. America! How cosmopolitan she could be after traveling across the Atlantic Ocean. She began to let her imagination carry her away. She envisioned riding horses through beautiful American pastures, practicing needlework beside delicate stained-glass lamps. She surprised herself by growing eager as she pictured fresh, clean gowns, lavish meals, and other fineries she had heard of existing in America.

Maybe if Uncle Matthew knew it was not her decision to

leave Wigan, he wouldn't withdraw his support from the family. She would have to explain it to him. As much as she abhorred being in his presence, she would have to speak with him to justify everything.

And then she had gone over there, one last time, the following Sunday after church. She remembered that to her own great surprise, she had served each course of the midday meal to her aunt and uncle's guests without a single flaw. No dropped platters or spilled soups, her tendency to clumsiness generally exacerbated in Matthew's presence, but not that day. Aware that this was the last time she would be forced to endure Matthew's leering gaze and her aunt Bianca's haughty remarks, Abby thought she had discovered a newfound strength. She would serve them their meal, but when Matthew tried to take her out back for his usual fondling, she would tell him she was leaving.

She washed dishes in the kitchen following the meal, awaiting his approach.

"Abigail, my dear."

Her insides curdled at the sound of Matthew's call. She turned to see his bovine frame closing in on her, his fingers already twitching in apparent anticipation.

"Come," he said, motioning to the back door. "Let's brave a walk outside."

Abby set down the dish she had been drying and followed Matthew around the back of the house.

Thinking back on that moment now, Abby shook her head to force her mind away from the rest. She wouldn't relive any more of it, not now, when she was resting so comfortably on a velvet settee in Charleston, South Carolina, thousands of miles away from that monstrous man. All of it thanks to Douglas Elling. How wrong she had been to think that Douglas might be anything like her horrid uncle. Douglas was complicated, but he had integrity, a certain kind of grace. She rested her head on the arm of the settee with weariness. Closing her heavy eyelids, she let sleep envelop her.

$$\sim\!\!\mathscr{C}$$

DOUGLAS WAS THERE, SHAKING HER GENTLY AND URGING her awake. Abby opened her eyes, noticing first that she was still on the settee in the drawing room and then that the skies outside had turned to the lavender of evening. Douglas was studying her with apparent caution, and she blinked in confusion.

"You were dreaming," he told her, his voice weightless, barely above a whisper. "You seemed distressed, like it was a nightmare. I hope I did the right thing waking you."

She sat up sharply, lowering her legs to the floor and hastily attempting to smooth her hair and her skirts. Her skin felt damp with sweat, her camisole clinging beneath her dress. In her grogginess, she couldn't recall the substance of her dreams, but she did have a sense of relief, as though by waking, she'd been granted a reprieve.

"No, no." She looked again toward the shadowy sky beyond the window and then back at Douglas. In her disorientation, she was struck afresh by Douglas's altered appearance, his startlingly sculpted face. She noticed that his lips, which had previously been obscured by overgrown beard, were shiny and full. The bottom one especially. She took a steadying breath, unintentionally inhaling Douglas's scent from where he crouched next to her. There was a mixture of spice and salt, a lingering scent of soap.

"I must have been sleeping for hours. You've done me a service. As it is, I'm sure I'll be awake all night after sleeping the day away."

She ran her hand over her hair again, forcing a few stray tendrils behind her ear. Watching her, Douglas rose abruptly and stepped backwards, as though only just realizing that he might be overcrowding her.

"Larissa's already taken an early supper on the assumption that you would perhaps sleep through until morning," he told her. "She mightn't be pleased that I've interrupted you, but it sounds to me like you've had plenty of time for convalescing today."

"Oh, right, yes." Abby nodded, unsure what to do with herself under Douglas's watchful eye. "I suppose I'll retire to my quarters. I can get ahead on my reading." She reached to the floor where *Robinson Crusoe* had fallen and held it up to Douglas. "I was a slouch with my studies today, and it wouldn't hurt to make up for it. Larissa's all a dither, convinced I'm still too weak to handle much activity." She rose from her seat as Douglas took another step backwards, away from her, clearing her path from the room.

Although Douglas facilitated her exit, Abby found herself reluctant to cut short her time with him. She remembered her resolution to make herself more available to him, but when she was actually confronted with his presence like this, she just couldn't manage to interact properly.

"Well then. Thank you for the rescue."

He raised his eyebrows in response.

"From whatever chased me in my dreams," she clarified.

He smiled, revealing a playful dimple in his left cheek that she'd never seen before. She surprised herself by admiring its effect, the way the small divot softened his veneer of perfection.

"Ah. Well consider it the first installment in my recompense."

"Recompense? What for?"

Douglas placed his hand in his pockets and shrugged good-naturedly. "Haven't you heard? I've about won the award for being Charleston's most hideous host, or the prize for most grim manners to a houseguest. They're still debating the official title of the award down at Society Hall."

When Abby didn't respond to his jest, Douglas's continued in a soberer tone.

"Since the beginning of your stay, my actions have been deplorable, culminating in the debacle where I essentially pushed you into that stall with a barbarous horse. If not with my own hands, at least with my unforgivable behavior. What was it you called the event, attempted murder?" Abby opened her mouth to protest, now sorry for her earlier remark, but he held up his hand to silence her.

"In all seriousness, I do consider the blame for the accident mine, and I'm disheartened to see you are still suffering the repercussions, unable to complete your daily schedule as you had before."

"Oh no, that's not, that's just because I didn't sleep last night, that's . . ." she trailed off, unable to explain to him what had kept her awake during the night. "Never mind. You don't owe me anything. I mean, look at all you have given me already. A home, an education, even the clothes I wear while we converse here. I am the one in debt to you. Though you should know I plan to repay it, all of it, down to the last halfpence."

Douglas blinked in surprise. "You plan to repay me? Nothing in this arrangement has been intended as a loan. It's all given outright, with no expectations."

"Right, but that doesn't mean I am comfortable leeching off your charity." Abby answered, adding quickly, "As much as I appreciate it, mind. Still, I will pay it all back."

"Abby, it is my supreme pleasure to be of service to you. If I'm honest, it's a relief to put my assets to good use. I do applaud your sense of independence, but maybe there is another way. Perhaps instead of returning to me that which I assuredly do not need, you spread the good fortune. Focus on something you have in excess and share that with others."

Abby tried to think what she might possibly possess in excess. Disquiet, mistrust, disappointment, nothing that others would wish to share. Douglas seemed aware of her skepticism and clarified.

"Find a way to help people is what I'm saying. It turns out, it's surprisingly gratifying. If you use your newfound good fortune to assist another person in need, then any of my alleged generosity toward you will have more far-flung effects. It would be the best repayment you could give me. There are people everywhere who could use help in one way or another. You have simply to look about, and you will be overcome with possibility."

Abby's thoughts immediately flew to slavery. Is that what Douglas was nudging at? Perhaps he was trying to gauge her attitude, determine how she felt about the captivity and forced labor pervading this city. She wanted to tell him that she overheard his conversation with Demett, that she was awestruck by his actions. When she thought of people who could use help, as he said, it seemed the thousands of souls enslaved in the American South ought to be first in line. Or, equally likely, he didn't mean that at all. He mightn't be pleased to learn of her eavesdropping, her nosing in his business. Abby chided herself that Douglas could just as easily be suggesting that she help an elderly woman retrieve a fallen handkerchief.

"I would like nothing better than to help others, but I'm afraid I wouldn't know where to begin. I barely even know anyone in this city, save for Gracie Cunningham, who certainly doesn't need help from me." She paused for a moment to collect her words. "Maybe there are others in the city, people who you know, who are trapped in an unfortunate situation. . . ." She was unsure how to say more without giving herself away.

Douglas leaned against the wall beside him, chewing on his lip as he appeared to consider something.

"Larissa did mention that you're interested in teaching. Perhaps that is the ticket, and then you needn't do anything immediate. For the present, just concentrate on your lessons and gain the requisite knowledge to pass on to others. Perhaps at some point, you will have the opportunity to teach someone who is less fortunate than you, some of the children who work in the factories back home and haven't time for proper schooling, even."

No, no, this wasn't what she meant at all. First off, it didn't seem the time to mention that she would never be returning to England. More importantly, he seemed to have missed her point entirely. She would have to think of a way to show him that she could help with his abolitionist activities. Conversing about it in code wasn't working at all.

"By the by," Abby thought to change the subject, provide herself time to ruminate on a better course with Douglas, "Larissa and I were thinking of an outing later in the week, perhaps visiting the wharf. We thought to call at your office and bring your midday meal if that suits."

Douglas cocked his head at her.

"I've always liked that Larissa," he smiled teasingly and pushed off the wall. "Meantime, I best leave you to your reading. If you aim for Larissa to allow this excursion to the harbor, you'll have to prove that her dithering is all for naught." He nodded and took his leave.

Abby looked down at the book in her hand. Yes, after her display of feebleness today, she would have to demonstrate a countenance twice as strong if she hoped Larissa would still condone the visit to Douglas's office. She thought again of the day she first arrived in Charleston and discovered Douglas in the cellar. If only she could have seen more clearly in that dim space. Her dusky memory of Douglas hitting a man repeatedly was now so obviously the product of her own preconceptions, rather than reality. More likely, he had been stuffing the man's coveralls with hay or some such to change the person's physical shape, create a disguise.

If she could view that space in the cellar again, if she had more specific information, perhaps the next time they broached the topic of helping people, she would know how to speak the proper words, the phrases that might persuade him to open up. With each passing moment, her blood itched more; she felt increasingly desperate to help with abolition. She couldn't explain exactly why it was so important to her, except that suddenly it was everything. She couldn't continue sitting idle in the face of egregious wrongs. In fact, if she did nothing, maybe then it was she who was guilty of egregious wrongs.

20

CHARLESTON, SOUTH CAROLINA
1846

"No!" Cora Rae gasped in shocked delight.

"It's true," Gracie declared, nodding for emphasis as the sisters whispered to each other in the upstairs parlor. Huddled together on the love seat, tittering as they were, any passerby would have mistaken them for the dearest of friends. Their porcelain teacups sat untouched upon a silver tray as Gracie reported all she had recently seen at the Elling estate. As much as Gracie always complained about gossips, she found that possessing information of this nature was actually intoxicating.

"I'd swear on my hope chest," Gracie grinned, "I saw him with my very own eyes. He was shaved, and handsome, and civilized as he ever was. I would go so far as to say that he was charming again. Truly charming." Gracie swallowed, remembering that he had directed the aggregate of that rediscovered charm toward Abby. She tried again to convince herself she'd imagined Douglas's mooning. Certainly, it would do no one a service to mention that small detail to Cora Rae.

"I knew Douglas would come back to himself." Cora Rae slapped her gloved hand against her knee in a gesture of triumph and then wiggled her hips in her seat, unable to contain her excitement. "You've made me so glad, I could almost hug you. What happened do you think? What caused his former self to reemerge?"

Gracie only shook her head. "I surely couldn't say, but I thought you would be pleased to hear of it, regardless."

"I knew he wouldn't grieve forever. He's too much a man to stay idle forever. He must be in a sore kind of need after keeping so long to himself, and I will be there waiting when he's ready for that certain type of soothing."

"Rae!" Gracie gasped, scandalized.

"You know you think the same. You're just too much of a prissy Mae to say it." Cora Rae opened a painted fan and began waving it at herself. "This fire is too high for so early in the day. I should call for Abel," she complained. "Or maybe it's just thinking about Douglas, getting me all warm and agitated." She ran a hand seductively down her own side, smirking at her sister. Abruptly, all the tenderness that Gracie had been feeling for her sister just moments before dissolved.

"Rae, you stop taunting me." Gracie snapped. "If you want me to keep coming with ladles full of news, then I suggest you treat me kindly."

"Don't mouth off to me, girl," Cora Rae snarled. "Don't you forget that I hold your own precious beau at my mercy. I can make Harrison Blount *my* beau, not yours, with nothing more than a toss of my hair. But come now, we were having such a cheerful time. Let's get thinking about our next move, shall we?"

Gracie knew her sister was more determined than ever to catch Douglas's heart, especially before another Charleston belle snatched him out from under her. Rae would never consider Abby part of that competition, so, Gracie concluded, maybe she needn't dwell on the thought either.

"The Montrose Ball!" Cora Rae exclaimed.

"I'm sorry?" Gracie asked, perplexed.

"It's perfect, don't you see? It's not even three weeks away. I'm sure Douglas was invited. He's invited to everything, not that he ever goes. If I can get Papa to persuade him to attend . . . But what excuse could we conjure for Papa to proposition him?" Cora Rae puckered her lips into a perfect pink tulip as she thought. Gracie waited in dismay for whatever wicked scheme her sister was devising.

"I've got it," Cora Rae declared as she stood. "Papa will have to invent a reason that he cannot attend the ball. He can implore Douglas to take me in his absence, as my escort."

"He'll never agree to that," Gracie sighed in exasperation, realizing it was unclear whether she had been speaking about Douglas or her father. Under either circumstance, the statement would hold true.

"He will, if I do things right." Cora Rae smiled cunningly. She walked toward the French doors, glancing outside and then back toward the hallway, as if someone might be listening in on their conversation. "If I promise Papa that I'll quit thinking of Douglas should this last attempt at catching him fail, I think he'd be willing, just to get me married off to someone else before I get crinkled and saggy all over. As for Douglas," Cora Rae paused for effect, "if I know one thing about him, he's not likely to turn away a friend in need. Papa will come up with something. Some reason Douglas simply must escort me. Anyway," she dropped back onto the sofa with a bit of resignation, "I really do care for Douglas. So what if I'm scheming a bit, if it lands up making the man happier in the end?"

The mettle that had risen in Gracie at Cora Rae's saucy jibes began untangling again as she considered that Cora Rae might truly be acting from genuine affection. She thought of

Harrison and the trials she'd willingly endure to preserve their nascent relationship. By participating in Cora Rae's craftiness, she really wasn't so different from her sister. For each of them, it came down to just one thing, securing that certain fellow.

"Matter of fact," Cora Rae perked up, "I'm going to speak to Pa about it this instant." Just as quickly as she'd dropped her guard a moment before, she was back on target. With a flurry of her skirts, Cora Rae disappeared from the parlor, leaving Gracie to the warm fire and the winter afternoon.

If Abby were to find out that she was constantly reporting the happenings at the Elling estate, sleuthing and gossiping, their friendship would surely be over, shattered like a crystal orb, irreparable. Even so, Gracie could not bring herself to risk Rae filching Harrison from her. He was the only gentleman she'd ever coveted, and amazingly, he returned her favor.

Before five minutes had passed, Cora Rae returned to the parlor in an obvious mood.

"What is it?" Gracie asked with trepidation.

"I spoke to Papa about the ball." Cora Rae pouted dramatically.

"And?" Gracie asked. "Is Papa going to convince him to take you?"

Cora Rae fixed Gracie with a look of defeat. "He said my idea was ridiculous, that there would be no reason for Douglas to escort me. And," she added with a look of puzzled distress, "he said he heard that Douglas already accepted the invitation to the ball anyway. With a guest of his own."

21

∽

Charleston, South Carolina
1846

*C*lover's eyes drifted over the cramped space she had been sharing with Thelma for the past seven years. With two straw pallets pushed together in the center of the floor, there was just enough foot room for a person to scuttle past on either side. There was a crooked table in one corner that someone had built for Thelma before Clover's arrival and two wooden pegs poking out from the wall that they used for hanging damp clothes. It was fitting that white folks called these shacks the slave "quarters," Clover sneered, each cabin being fat enough for only one quarter of a person, it felt like. And then they would go shoving two, three, sometimes even four folks in just one hut. The massa also gave them each a patch of dirt outside their cabins and told them they could tend a garden of vegetables. There weren't no tending on the dried-up land by the cabins though. If there were, the massa would have planted his own crops there, not tossed it all like a gimcrack to his niggers. In the dim candlelight, she could hardly see the weeds growing in the corners of the dirt floor or the cobwebs that she brushed from the ceiling nightly, only to find them restored to order each morning. No, Clover wouldn't miss it here. Save for Thelma.

The sound of pebbles splattering against the cabin door signaled that a man had arrived, and it was time for her to get moving. Thelma raised herself off Clover's cot.

"Seems it's gotten to the twinkling hour. You best get on," Thelma told her as she bent to retrieve Clover's small sack of clothes. "If you gone make it, you've got to hurry on your way." She handed the bag to Clover and then blew out the candle on the side table, just as she did each night before they went to sleep. "I'm gone lay me down here to pretend some sleep now. I'll be praying for you from the moment you walk out that door." Thelma gave Clover a quick, strong hug in the dark cabin and turned away.

"Now go on. Before this old lady gets too weepy and spoils your whole clearing out. And don't you let that baby come to life until you get where you going."

"Thank you, Thelma. Thank you and God bless." Clover said nothing more, else she might have erupted into tears at leaving the only person who had ever mothered her. If she made it to freedom, she would never see Thelma again. Thelma was too aged, too seasoned to ever run from slavery. And anyhow, fugitives had to lay low even after they made it to free states, unless they wanted one of the slave catchers to sell them back to their jilted owners. Lord, but Clover knew there were slave chasers aplenty out there. She was going to be peering over her shoulder for the rest of her days if she aimed to stay out of bondage for keeps. Neither Thelma, nor anyone else in Charleston, would ever know where she landed. Not if she did this right.

Clover stepped cautiously outside, scanning in every direction to ensure she was alone. She had repeated the instructions so many times with Thelma, reviewing, reviewing. They'd been told that she'd hear tapping on her door when the coast was clear. She was to wait three minutes and then hurry herself, alone, to the property's eastern edge. After that, the sounds of the owl would tell her which way to march. So long as she continued to hear an owl hooting, that meant it was safe to slog on. Otherwise, she was to hustle back to her cabin and wait for another day and new instructions.

The night's waning moon left little light by which to navigate, but Clover was glad for the cover of darkness. She could make out the other slave quarters, everything still and hushed, all the occupants surely abed at this late hour. She glanced regretfully toward Dicky's cabin at the end of the little lane, hoping he'd find the courage one day to run off, too. Not that she was fool enough to think they'd find each other again if he did. Meantime, he'd have to choose another house slave to banter with behind the kitchen, another girl to stare at like maybe she carried stardust in her pockets.

Clover started toward the eastern property line, crouching down as low as her belly would allow, the bulge of the baby kissing against her shaking thighs with every step. She listened for the owl sounds, wishing her thumping heart would settle down and allow her to hear better. Although she tried to watch for branches on the ground, anything that might produce a loud snap, the darkness was too strong. She could only step gingerly and hope. Suddenly she heard a dog's sharp bark, and she froze. Only a few steps into the night, and the end had come already? A moment later, the dog barked again, and she realized it was far off, somewhere else in the Charleston night.

She let out her breath in a shaky torrent of relief and tried to steady herself. In the cool night air, the droplets of sweat along her brow felt like her fear coming to life, telling her to turn around and clean forget it. Swabbing her face with her sleeve, she steeled herself to continue on. She had the baby to think of now. She began creeping forward again, every step taking her baby farther away from a life of bondage.

Clover had been directed to pass through several shadow-filled properties before risking herself on the open street, to follow the owl through the proper yards. Now she heard only the rustling of leaves in the wind, then the silence of the night. She paused her steps, praying for patience, for God's grace, and she waited. And then a faint hoot. She continued towards the owl's ghostly call, worrying that the soft hooting she followed wasn't actually coming from the men who'd been sent to help her. What if it was just a damn owl? Either way, she knew she was heading east, in the direction of the Ashley. There was no turning back now.

She reached the property line and gingerly opened the wrought-iron gate that separated the Cunninghams' parcel from the Wentworths' land, so far removed from the big house. She uttered a silent thank you to Abel for oiling those hinges a few days earlier and closed the gate behind herself to avoid leaving clues about which way she had gone. Keeping flush to the shrubbery surrounding the property line, she continued east, wondering how that owl would know if she was following. She couldn't say what she would do when she reached the street if no one was waiting, but now that she had left the Cunningham land, the biggest risk would be slowing down.

If her eyes were serving her right, there was an opening toward the dark street, not too much farther along from where she lurked. She listened again for the owl, fighting back the tears of her panic. In the silence that greeted her, she made the decision to continue forward, owl or no. She wouldn't wait like cowering prey to have a net thrown over her again. As she stepped onward, moving faster now in her resolve, she heard a rustling and then a whisper.

"Pssst!"

Clover spun around in the darkness, searching for the noise.

"Pssst," it called again. Then she could make out movement behind a shrub a few feet ahead of her, and she hurried over.

"Get down lower," a man instructed. Clover recognized him as one of the older free blacks who sometimes made deliveries to the Cunninghams' home. He was small, like a child almost, but even in the dark, she could make out the sinewy muscles in his neck. "You ain't gone be able to bring the bag," he whispered, nodding toward her gunnysack. "Put any money you've got inside your clothes, and the rest you've got to leave behind." When Clover hesitated, he added, "Child, there'll be people to get you what you need along the way." Clover reluctantly relinquished her bag, thinking of her spare dress, the thimble she kept for luck tucked at bottom, the two potatoes, nearly all her worldly possessions. The man dug a hasty hole with his hands and buried the sack beneath the lush shrubbery.

At the sound of a horse clipping against cobblestone not far from where they were hiding, Clover gasped and tried in vain to somehow make herself smaller.

"No, girl," the man told her. "He right on time. This is just right."

The horse reached almost to the spot where they were huddled and then came to a quiet stop.

"Come now," her companion looked about and then started toward the street, motioning with his hand that she should follow.

As Clover crept around the tall shrubs she saw that one man was waiting, sitting on the driver's bench of an old-fashioned covered wagon. He turned his head in her direction, and she lost all the air in her lungs. The man was white.

"Hurry now," her companion whispered. "Climb up in back." This couldn't be, that a white man would be saving her from bondage. She didn't want to get into his wagon, for whatever he might want with her couldn't be good, but she couldn't tarry in the street either. She would have to surrender herself now, knowing her fate was in God's hands. So she scurried around back, where her dark companion helped support her as she thrust her cumbersome frame into the nebulous interior.

She was barely inside before the wagon started moving. She hastily sank to the wagon floor to avoid toppling over and peeked out the back opening to see her first chaperone retreating into the darkness. She had thought he'd be coming with them. Now she was alone with the white man. No one had warned her of a white man as part of her plans, and she worried it might be a trap. She wondered if she should jump, try her luck on her own.

She shimmied deeper into the buggy, up near the front, and pushed her eye against the wagon's canvas cover, stealing a fast glimpse out from the sliver of space where the fabric met the wood. As best she could tell from her limited trips around Charleston, it did seem they were still heading east, toward the river, a lone wagon in the viscous night. She put her hand on her tight belly. She couldn't go jumping anywhere if she didn't want to hurt her child, and so she would have to trust that man up front. She wondered what he would say, how he would explain their late-night drive, if somebody thought to stop them.

Crawling around in the dark, she felt several large barrels in the wagon, the kind meant to carry whiskey. She crawled behind the cluster of cylinders, figuring that in any scenario, she should snatch the advantage of being hidden from sight. As Clover situated herself, they drove on at a leisurely pace. She estimated that the slow pace was meant to avoid suspicion, but she wished the driver would hurry her out of Charleston faster, if that was even what he was doing.

Finally, the wagon stopped, and Clover's breath caught in her throat as she tried to keep calm, wondering what was coming next. She heard the driver hop from his seat, and then he was standing there at the wagon's back opening.

"Come on out now." He spoke gruffly, and Clover wondered at her options. She peeked through the chasm of two barrels and saw that he was waiting with his hand extended, in a kind gesture it seemed. Still, she faltered. He stepped closer in and told her, "Speed is of the essence, young lady. People live or die by the swiftness of their strides hereabouts. Come now, you're at the next stop."

With no choice but to comply, Clover hurried off the wagon into a dark, forested area. She hoped the dense foliage and large weeds meant they were near the marsh, as they were meant to be. The man tethered his horse to a nearby tree and began walking deeper into the thicket.

"This way," he spoke quietly, but didn't whisper.

As they proceeded deeper into the woodland, Clover's panic grew.

"You sure this the right way, sir?" She continued to follow him at a brisk pace.

"Sure it is," the man told her. "You feel the ground getting softer under your feet, swampier? That's the river coming. Now you just stay calm and keep hushed up. We're getting closer to where you need to be. Chin up, girl. You're on the road to freedom now."

Surprised by his familiar way with her, she failed to contain her growing curiosity.

"Begging your pardon, but why you helping me, sir? What's a white man gone get from helping a slave girl like me, except for a heap of trouble?"

The man stopped and turned back to Clover.

"I ain't white." She could hear the conspiratorial smile in his voice. "My grandmamma was black as wrought iron. Just all the other white blood I got in me is enough so I can pass. Comes in handy sometimes it does." He turned and started walking again. "Watch those low branches now."

Clover wanted to ask him more questions. Was he free then, and living in Charleston? Or did he come down from somewhere else just to help her out? But remembering herself, the peril for both of them, she followed in silence. They labored through the brush, their steps growing louder as the ground heaved with water and muck beneath their feet. Clover could feel herself tiring, but she didn't dare stop. Finally, she could see the riverbank.

"This is it for me now," the man told her. "Godspeed, girl." Without another glance at her, he began retreating, falling back to the path they had just finished tracking.

"Wait, that's it? You just gone leave me here?"

"You'll be fine," he told her. "Take a minute, and you'll see." He waited not another breath before disappearing into the darkness.

Clover balked at having been abandoned. Wasn't there supposed to be someone helping her the whole way? She'd never make it herself. Not now, when she'd been relying on getting the help. There was only going to be one chance, and this was it. She had to figure something out before she got discovered. She wanted her freedom badly enough to outrun Satan himself if she had to. Suddenly, she heard another owl calling out nearer the river. She walked toward the sound and nearly toppled over the next man who was waiting for her.

"You late," whispered an elderly black man. Clover could see another younger fellow crouching by his side. She felt her heart pounding so hard that she wondered if her chest might explode.

"He just left me, that man. I didn't know where to go." She whispered through her shock.

"That's the way of the Underground," the younger man said. "Everybody's safer if people only know the one role they got to play. When your leg of the journey's over, you get out before you meet the next fellow. When nobody knows nothing, there ain't nobody to rat out."

"This way," the older man directed her.

Clover hurried behind them to a spot on the riverbank. The weeds and brush remained thick despite their position on the shoreline, as though the river had invaded the space of a forest that wouldn't recoil. She looked toward the water, where a sliver of moonlight reflected just enough to prove the river's existence before the water blended into the dark sky, all the way to oblivion, as far as Clover could see. Both men started clearing overgrowth and weeds until they revealed a hidden raft, not much larger than the wagon in which she had been riding. It was a rickety looking thing, but it was Clover's only hope. They all three climbed aboard. As they pushed off into the murky river, steam rising off the water into the cool air around them, the younger man handed Clover a coarse wool blanket.

"Best you be keeping that babe warm."

She covered herself with the blanket and settled into the raft. She didn't know where they were taking her from here, or why it made sense that they were floating south down the river. She knew only that these two men must have a plan, like those she'd met before them. Collectively, the group had gotten her this far, after all. She had to stay strong now, for the baby, and for Thelma and Dicky, who were counting on her to get to safety. As she pulled the blanket tighter around herself, around her swelling middle and her child's future, she watched the Carolina shore passing by in the moonlight, and she wept.

22

CHARLESTON, SOUTH CAROLINA
1846

Douglas opened the door separating his shipping office from the familiar pandemonium at the wharf and scanned the scene before him. Despite the solitude he'd enjoyed at his desk, the atmosphere outside was dominated by the usual flurry of raucous activity. The harbor was crowded with ships of every shape and size, many readying for new journeys, even if they had only just arrived a mere day earlier to deposit their cargo or passengers. Douglas watched the frenzy of stevedores and porters, mostly free blacks, hauling sacks and barrels to and from sailing vessels. So many men engaged in repetitive tasks. It made him think of Samuel Milton, standing hours at a weaving mill, engaged in much the same type of repetitive, endless labor. He began to make his way toward the market, navigating around pushcarts and stepping aside for oscillating men stacking bales of cotton. Abby also, he reflected, had spent too many years secreted in a dark factory, sentenced to a life of prepping and spinning fibers. It was mindless drudgery, for which she was entirely too fine. He and Samuel had agreed that Abby would remain in Charleston a year, but then what? He didn't want her to go back.

All morning, he had stayed focused on shipping business, rather than allowing himself to puzzle over the many recent distractions in his life. After the hours he'd just spent arranging sailing schedules and reviewing export revenues, he was rewarding himself with this stroll toward the market, glad for a break to purchase some refreshment. Now that he offered his mind the freedom to roam, his thoughts drifted back to the Montrose ball and the invitation he'd accepted the day before.

Poor Lisbeth and Charles Montrose probably had not the slightest idea what to make of his response to their invitation. He had chosen it almost at random from amongst the stack of neglected mail on his desk, where surely another thirty invitations, all nearly indistinguishable from each other, had lain beneath it. The very same people who shunned him for nearly a year preceding the fire now invited him to events with a fervor bordering on compulsion, as though he had become the city's most sought-after social guest. It was as though his neighbors were offering him a collective apology through excessive invitation.

Douglas had failed, deliberately, to respond to a single solicitation since the accident. He was amazed that the cards continued to pour in, but he supposed that was typical for Charleston. None wanted to be first to disregard the wealthy eccentric recluse. And what was the harm, they must have figured, since everyone knew Douglas never actually attended these events. He tried to imagine the stunned faces of old Charles and his fusty wife when they opened his reply card and found a positive response.

His decision to attend the Montrose ball was a definitive departure from his earlier approach toward Abby, but he was growing weary of the waiting game he had begun with her. The ball presented a perfect opportunity for Douglas to spend another evening in her company and provide her with a new Charleston experience. The honest truth was that he just liked being near her, that the air felt sharper to him when he was in her presence. He worried his invitation might overwhelm her, but he would offer to escort her as though it was his duty, his responsibility as her caretaker, to parade her about and show-case a bit of the city life. These outings could further her posi-tion with Charleston society, he'd remind her, in case she might extend her stay.

He approached the market on Adgers Wharf, where shop-pers crowded the aisles and shouted requests as they strove to be heard above the din. The shoppers at Adgers included foreign sailors hungry for a meal, frazzled merchants, and slaves out on passes to do the masters' marketing. With the growing number of free blacks living in Charleston, it was becoming increasingly difficult to ascertain who was free and who was owned, and Douglas was glad of it. As more Negroes roamed freely, it would be easier for fugitive slaves to blend in and disappear, one way or another. Douglas maneuvered through the crowds toward a pastry seller. He thought to purchase fresh bread and then ven-ture farther into the market for whey butter from the Irishman at the dairy cart.

As he approached the baker's table and perused the various cakes and sweet rolls laid out before him, he concluded that he must speak with Abby forthwith about the invitation, not least of all so she could purchase a dress. His marriage to Sarah had been sufficient to teach him that securing a ball gown could take months. Finding something suitable in less than two weeks would be no small feat. Even so, he was sure that sufficient financial incentive could inspire a dressmaker to sew with staggering speed. There was also the possibility that Abby would simply re-fuse him, either because of the odd nature of attending with her benefactor, or because she was still wary of him. He thought again of her reaction to his revitalized appearance a few nights earlier, and smiled. At least he knew that she didn't find him repugnant. Her stumbling words and flushed cheeks had told a story all their own.

His eye settled on a thick loaf of rye, and he raised an arm to attract the baker's attention, but then lowered it when bits of a nearby conversation reached his ear.

"Even a sloop would do fine. Obviously, Mr. Cunningham would be willing to remit any reasonable payment."

He couldn't place the voice speaking, though he was sure he'd heard it before. Turning about slowly, as if scanning the market for other purchases, Douglas found Marcus Petty, personal assistant to Court Cunningham, standing at the next stall. He was in conversation with James Irwin, one of the smaller dry goods carriers on the harbor.

"Anything seafaring, really," Petty seemed to be pleading. Pushing his spectacles higher on his nose in a frenetic motion, the older man was obviously addled.

Douglas looked back to the breads, stepping aside for a Negro woman who had approached the table with an empty basket. Motioning that she should take her turn and not wait behind him, he tried to listen for more information.

The only reason Court would arrange a hasty journey in a small sloop would be to pursue Clover. To his delight, he heard Irwin refusing Petty's proposition.

"Sorry, but we've been having a good run the past few months," Irwin responded in a booming voice, as if he meant to alert the entire market to his financial success. "I've got not a vessel to spare, even for the small fortune you offer. If any voyage returns early, I'll make sure to let you know." He turned as if to leave and caught sight of Douglas.

"Oh, but hey," he said turning his large frame back toward Petty, "why don't you ask Elling, there. Maybe he's got something extra." Irwin started out of the marketplace, and as he passed Douglas, he added, "That gives you opportunity to prove your allegiances. If you gave them a boat, it would tell everybody something."

Douglas knew there were people in Charleston who still could not abide him, those who harbored lingering suspicion about his connection to abolition, an activity tolerated no better by the local exporters than by the planters. Each group was equally committed to the economic structure in the South, with slavery at its core. Despite the current fashion of dismissing all the prior conjecture about Douglas and inviting him back into the Charleston fold, there were clearly still some in town who were unprepared to do that, Irwin included.

Douglas forced himself to ignore the challenge in Irwin's voice, to instead focus on Petty, on remaining casual. As Irwin dissolved into the crowd of shoppers, Douglas looked over at Petty, who was nervously shifting his weight from one foot to the other. Clearly, he was uncomfortable with Irwin's suggestion and too socially inept to know how to handle himself.

Douglas stepped closer to the man and spoke with a forced smile. "Don't worry, Petty, you're saved from even having to ask. The two sloops I've got now are in no shape for travel. I've just this morning finished arranging to have those vessels repaired. Their wear and tear is rather extensive, and it will take a couple of months before they can be restored to an acceptable condition," Douglas lied with ease. It would be easy enough for Petty to find a sloop from someone else, but Douglas wouldn't be the one to provide it. Even better would be if he could figure a way to convince them to search for Clover inland.

Marcus Petty nodded, and Douglas imagined the man was both relieved and frustrated, as he had still failed to satisfy Court Cunningham's needs. Petty cocked his head to the side and seemed to be contemplating where to search next for the rental he sought. The pier would not be a usual destination for a man like Petty, so despite the straightforward nature of his errand, he seemed somewhat befuddled. Douglas decided against squandering this opportunity for information.

Stepping closer to the little man, he told him, "I would of course like to assist Mr. Cunningham however I can. Perhaps if you told me why the boats were needed precisely, I might be able to hazard an alternate suggestion."

"Oh, well." Petty looked Douglas up and down, as if confirming his identity. He glanced down at a ledger he held and then back at Douglas, his discomfort palpable.

"Well, actually, Mr. Cunningham is looking to take a posse north, in search of a slave girl that ran a couple days back."

"I see," Douglas nodded slowly, surprised by Petty's forthrightness. "They know where she's gone, then?"

"Oh, absolutely. The girl's been spotted moving up the coast of North Carolina, big with child, claiming herself to be a free black. The stupidity of these niggers astounds me. They think they can outsmart us, outrun us, and this one carrying a near fully cooked nigger baby."

Douglas turned his gaze out beyond the market stalls toward the harbor, willing himself to withhold his response, clenching his jaw to keep the words inside. He shoved his fists in his pockets and waited, wondering if his silence would lead Petty to say more.

"Mr. Cunningham thought the sloop would be the quickest way to pick up her trail, rather than traveling inland. He's sending Polk Dawson along." Petty blinked, as though he'd mentioned that last piece by accident.

Douglas nodded in recognition at the name of the renowned slave catcher. People said the reason Dawson was so effective at

his profession was because he understood the mind of the Negroes. Douglas was fairly certain that the only reason Dawson
managed to continue catching slaves was because he paid off
law enforcement and clergymen at every town along the freedom road. It was also common knowledge that after Dawson
apprehended a runaway, he tortured the poor soul for the entire
journey south, just never in such a way that would leave lasting
physical damage sufficient to depress the master's investment.
He might urinate in the prisoner's food or pull out a fingernail
from the little finger. He also liked to use the women in bizarre
and profane ways. Well, let Dawson be tied up chasing the
phony, imaginary Clover in North Carolina while the real es-
capee was heading farther north on the Atlantic.

"Well, anyhoo," Petty seemed anxious to conclude their
conversation, "don't suppose it'll be that difficult to find the trail
of this twit either way, but I best be making the arrangements."

"Right," Douglas tried to force a sympathetic sigh. "I'm
sorry I'm unable to help. If I hear of any unoccupied sloops, I'll
send word."

Petty cast a defeated glance around the market and then
made a quick mark on the ledger in his hand. He thanked
Douglas and departed, melting back into the market crowds as
Irwin had before him.

Douglas turned back to the bread stall in an effort to seem
impassive, even though his pulse raced. He was suddenly glad-
der than ever that he had agreed to help Clover, astonished that
he ever could have faltered in his fight against slaveholding. By
now, Clover was probably off the coast of Virginia, or maybe
even Delaware, several hundred miles ahead of where the Cunninghams' gang would be searching, and traveling farther north
all the time. To think that in less than a month, she might make
it all the way to Vermont, where she would be able to hold a

paying job and birth her baby in freedom. Although he resisted the urge to congratulate himself too early, his heart swelled at the thought that Clover might live the remainder of her life as a free woman.

Suddenly memories washed over him. He remembered all the reasons why he had been so committed to fighting slavery in the first place. It was the substance of what he was able to achieve. It was the fact that fighting slavery was right. He had been idle and self-indulgent for long enough. He thought of Abby and worried that he would endanger another innocent, and just as she was coming to mean something to him. Larissa, Jasper, Demett, and all the others in his employ, they all stood to lose, if Douglas was reckless. But he had gained wisdom from his past mistakes, and this time would be different.

Douglas noticed the bread seller looking at him expectantly, so he pointed toward the rye loaf. As he watched the man slice the loaf down the middle and wrap it in paper, a feeling of heat spread throughout Douglas's body, embers of satisfaction flowing from his center to his every extremity. He felt charged with determination, like he might once again become someone he was proud of, someone Sarah and Cherish would have been proud of, too.

⟿

"PRETTY PLEASE, PAPA," WINI BEGGED. "ALL THE OTHER girls will be there, and if I miss the garden party, I'm sure I won't find an escort to the county dance at the end of the month. Really, Pa, Sally Ann Werther, Lucy Adams, and Daphne Dupree, they'll all be there. Surely you don't want them all being asked before your own daughter. Pleeease," she whined.

Court continued pacing the foyer. He had been marching to

and fro like this since he returned home and found Wini sitting on the steps of the center staircase, waiting for him.

"Winifred," Court stopped and looked down at his daughter, "I don't give a horse's hair what you stand to lose by missing this particular affair. You should have thought about it before you went boring your nose into the business of slaves. You should have thought . . . about anything at all, for heaven's sake. I still can't fathom what possessed you to go riding off like a wild cowboy to look for Clover on your own. Did you give even a second's thought to what people would say?"

"But Papa," Wini looked up through her eyelashes, "I was just trying to help."

"That may be," Court waved his hand in the air and resumed pacing, "but the last thing I needed was to have my own child run off after we discovered a slave gone missing. I should have been focusing on locating my property, but instead your mama and I were busy worrying after you. What'd you think, that you'd drag her back here all by your little lonesome?" He demanded, rehashing the same reprimands he'd spouted at her when she'd finally come home the evening before.

"I told you, Pa," she whined again, "I just wanted to get Clover back here before you punished her something awful."

"Well, now instead it's you being punished!" he snapped. "I don't care *why* you went after her. It's just the mere fact that you were messing in business where you had no place. If I hadn't been so focused on you and your childish antics, Clover never would have gotten so far. But now that Negress has gotten all the head start she needed to make finding her such a damn headache." Court stilled and rubbed his hands over his face.

"But, Pa, she hasn't even been gone three days. I'm sure the men will find her," Wini tried to reassure her father, "just like they did when old Isaiah ran from the Duprees."

"Wini," Court sighed and sat down beside her on the third step, "always an idealist. For all we know, the wench could have gotten as far as the Appalachians by now. I wouldn't have imagined she had the brains to get as far as South Battery. Even if my slave catchers bring her back, we've still got wreckage to deal with. I'll have to punish her insubordination severely, lest the other slaves consider following her example. Probably the whipping will be strong enough to kill that brat she's carrying. So there goes four hundred dollars I could have gotten selling the child. Not to mention money wasted on extra food she's had these past several months." Court rubbed his eyes again, looking weary. "Destroying that baby will squash any remaining goodwill between us, so it'll be best if we get rid of Clover, too. She won't fetch the same price once she's got scarring across her back. Nobody wants to spend good money on a troublemaker, even a young, fertile one. It really is a predicament."

Court turned to look at Wini and then added, "But why am I unloading all this on a young thing like you?" He reached over and tried to tousle her red hair.

"Pa, my curls," Wini leaned away and readjusted the jeweled comb in her hair.

"Before we know it, you'll have a husband and slaves of your own. He'll deal with this business, and you'll never have to worry your little head, or the curls on it either."

Wini seized on Court's comment, "But if you want me to get a husband, Pa, keeping me from the Westons' party isn't going to help."

"Oh fiddlesticks!" Cora Rae scoffed as she arrived on the landing at the top of the stairs. "We are the Cunninghams of Charleston, for land sakes. There is no gentleman in his right mind who wouldn't want to join our family. Even Gracie has an eligible gentleman interested in her." Cora Rae looked from her

father to Wini as she began floating down the stairs toward
them. "Now what were you two arguing about?"

"Pa won't let me go to the Westons' garden party," Wini
informed her oldest sister with an exaggerated pout.

Both Wini and her father stood up from the steps in order to
clear Cora Rae's path.

"Well I reckon you should have thought about that before
you started poking into slave business, right, Pa?" She linked her
arm through her father's, resting her gloved hand on his arm
and looking up at him before turning back to Wini.

"Women in our family don't give chase after niggers, Wini.
You mightn't give a hoot about your reputation, but I do care
about mine. I can't have your antics interfering with my own
chances."

Wini rolled her eyes. "Cora Rae, you're nearly twenty years
old. Don't you think it's time you hopped down from that high
horse of yours? Nobody cares about your reputation anymore."

Cora Rae gasped in outrage and looked at her father. "Pa!
You're going to let her speak to me like that?"

Court sighed again and removed Cora Rae's hand from his
arm, giving it a conciliatory squeeze before stepping back from
her.

"Truthfully, ladies, I can't get involved in this bickering.
Rae, you're long overdue in finding a husband. If only you'd
stop wasting time thinking about Douglas Elling. Not that he's
much of a match anyway. Even if those old allegations were
false, you belong with a landowner, someone who could add to
our empire through acreage, slaves, indigo."

Cora Rae opened her mouth to speak, and Court help up
his hand, silencing her.

"It's the same conversation every time. Let me save us the
trouble, as talk of your relationship with Douglas Elling is, as

always, utterly moot." He looked at Cora Rae, his wintry eyes exploring her as if assessing her for the first time. "Between your face and my holdings, I suppose you might squeeze out another year before your suitability totally expires. It seems a real shame to waste the time you have left pining for a man who has never indicated an iota of interest in you, forgive me for saying." Court stopped, perhaps worried he might set Cora Rae off on one of her rages.

"I'll have you know, Pa," she smiled serenely as she adjusted one of the gloves on her hand, "that I have a plan. It seems that Douglas Elling is rising from the dead. You told me yourself about the invitation he accepted to the Montroses'."

"Attending a ball does not mean he is searching for a wife, and even if he were, you have no reason to expect it will be you!" Court's rising voice echoed against the marbled floor of the foyer. "When will you face reality? When will you finally move on?" Softening his tone, he added, "Of course the man is a fool for failing to notice you, but all the more reason to focus on another. What about Whitney Hawke? His card is still resting on the console in the drawing room."

"Could we not?" Cora Rae retorted. "He's older than you, Pa," she shot back.

"But he has thirty-five acres in Georgetown and more than three hundred slaves. You would want for nothing. You'd have babies, and dresses, and our family would be part of a budding empire."

"She'll never go for it, Pa," Wini offered from where she was leaning against the banister. "She's in loooooovve." She drew out the last word, taunting her sister.

"I'll have you both know," Cora Rae spat, "things are happening. Things you know nothing about. There's only so long a person can grieve, even the most devoted mourner. He is going to notice me this time around, I am making sure of it. I will not settle for some haggard artifact of a man, someone for whom I feel nothing, just because you two are getting impatient."

Court was reaching into his pocket for his stopwatch, clearly losing interest in this conversation that they'd had so many times already.

"Yes, Pa, it's time for supper," she told him before he opened the watch, her voice dripping with frustration.

"Then let's not keep your mother waiting," Court answered impatiently.

As they began walking together toward the grand dining room, Cora Rae added, "You'll see, both of you, biding my time these years may have been just the thing." She looked from Wini, who was trailing a few steps behind, back to her father, and nearly growled in determination as she declared, "I *will* be the next Mrs. Elling."

23

CHARLESTON, SOUTH CAROLINA
1846

*A*bby and Larissa had just finished their stroll through White Point Gardens. It had taken Abby two days of flawless, attentive behavior to convince Larissa that she was restored sufficiently, fit for the task of leaving the house. As they meandered along the pathways bisecting the garden, the view had been astounding. Standing next to the dormant azalea bushes, Abby was able to look out past the tip of the peninsula where the Ashley and Cooper Rivers greeted each other. The gardens, irreverently green for the tail end of winter, abutted a gleaming seawall. Below, she could see the seashore, white sand littered with piles of iridescent oyster shells, purple, ebony, pink, and green, glittering in even the feeble February sunlight. Confronted by the bountiful landscape of Charleston, she could remember her old life only in various shades of gray.

Abby would have preferred to continue walking, but Larissa seemed convinced that even ten more minutes might mean sudden death for pale, fragile Abigail. If only the woman knew the trials Abby had endured in her life. Cruising at their slow pace through this manicured oasis was significant to Abby only for the ease of it. As it was, she fought the urge to break into a run, to light up her muscles, let herself fly. It had been so many weeks since she'd been able to exert herself physically, and she itched to feel that strain, the combustion in her blood, the sanitizing power of exhaustion. She sighed as she followed Larissa back toward the park's exit, straightening her shoulders and remembering her lady's posture.

They made their way toward Demett, who was waiting for them in the carriage, settled in behind two similar coaches. The next point on their excursion would be a visit to Douglas at his shipping office, just as Larissa and she had discussed. It was a short ride from White Point to the wharf, but there was still sufficient time for Abby's nerves to unravel. Despite perseverating on the issue for hours the day before, she hadn't concocted any reasonable plan for acquiring information about Douglas's Underground operation, stealing a glance at the secret staircase, or whatever. She would just have to improvise, scurry for opportunity.

It seemed she'd barely had time to swallow before Demett was helping them back out of the carriage at the wharf. Abby held a basket with Douglas's lunch, making sure to keep it level as she stepped down so as not to upset the rhubarb tart.

"Please, Miss Abigail, let me," Demett reached for the basket as Abby stepped onto the wooden boardwalk.

"Thank you, Demett, but I've got it," Abby answered, unwilling to burden him with something she could so easily handle herself.

"Stay close," Larissa advised, as her eyes tracked the hordes of people bustling around them. "It's easy to get separated in these crowds."

Abby had not been to the pier since the day of her arrival in Charleston, and she was struck again by the staggering commotion of the place. As the primary point of entry into South Carolina, a functional gateway to the entire New World, the area was teeming with people, sales, dust, and sweat. Surveying the wharf now, memories rushed at Abby. How hungry she had been when she arrived, caked with muck nearly three months thick. She had nearly forgotten in the months since arriving how her stomach had roiled throughout the journey, a victim of the seas as much as doubt. It seemed now that she was a different person entirely from that infuriated castoff, as though that girl was merely someone she had read about once in a sad story.

When they finally pushed open the door to Elling Import & Export, they found Douglas seated at his desk, an air of intense focus about him, so incongruous with the ruckus outside, as he scratched away at the pages of a daybook. He looked up as they entered, his eyes flashing from Larissa to Demett, then settling on Abby. He held her gaze a moment, his cerulean eyes seeming to search hers, and then falling to the covered basket in her hand.

"Ha. Demett, she wouldn't let you carry the food?" He glanced at Demett with a blithe chuckle before settling his focus on Abby. "You're going to give poor Demett an ulcer if you don't let him help you with something soon."

Demett smiled and held up his hands in defeat. "She been refusing help since she stepped foot in this town. Don't seem there's nothing I can do about it."

Abby felt her cheeks warm as they joked at her expense.

"Here," she thrust the basket at Demett. "There, you see? Now you are carrying it. He's carrying it," she repeated to Douglas, who was rising from his desk with amusement pulling at his mouth.

Before he could say anything to exacerbate her discomfort, they were interrupted as a group of laborers entered the office. They were white men, dressed in work clothes, rough trousers and heavy gloves for hauling goods. Abby guessed them to be stevedores.

"Apologies for interrupting," the man in front spoke, looking briefly at Abby and Larissa. "We just wanted to let you know we finished the inventory. Ready to start loading." He held out a stack of papers for Douglas, tally marks showing on the top page.

"Not at all, Walt. I was just having a quick call from home. May I present Abigail Milton, who has been visiting with me since the fall, and her governess, Larissa Prue."

"Ladies," the man removed his hat and nodded his blonde head at them. The four workers behind him then did the same.

Douglas took the papers, and Abby watched his eyes quickly rove over the figures.

"Good." He handed the stack back to the man. "Walt, go ahead."

"Ladies," Walt nodded at them again, and then the little posse was gone.

Abby suddenly wished they hadn't come. How foolish she'd been to think that they should visit him at his place of business, to think she wasn't imposing on him, his time. They were nothing but an interruption here. It seemed especially outrageous now to scour his office for signs of abolition activity, what, while he was munching on chicken legs, not ten feet away.

"Well, we just wanted to give you a quick greeting, drop your meal." She felt herself backing up, sidestepping toward the door.

"Larissa," Douglas turned toward the governess, "I have a suggestion to discuss with your pupil. If you wouldn't mind allowing us a minute to negotiate, I would be much obliged."

"Oh," Larissa's eyes widened slightly, "of course. As long as you are not up to anything that will corrupt my star student," she smiled, and Abby mentally pronounced the woman a toady, an apple-polishing traitor. Abby didn't know what Douglas wanted to discuss, but hadn't she just made it clear that she no longer wanted to be there?

"Ha. I'm sure she is beyond corruption," Douglas answered as his eyes darted back to Abby with a flicker of something mischievous and playful. "Though I must confess that my scheme will require another trip into town tomorrow."

Douglas cryptic comments were doing little to encourage Abby. She'd already determined their visit a blunder, clear misjudgment. Now she just wanted to leave.

"We can likely find the time," Larissa answered cautiously and then motioned for Demett to follow her outside.

In the seconds it took Demett and Larissa to walk out the door, Abby's mind raced through possibilities. Perhaps Douglas had discovered that she'd eavesdropped on his conversation with Demett and would expel her from his house. Or maybe he planned to discuss her return to England, simply as a matter of course. Though she hadn't even been in the States five months yet. Well in either figuration, she wouldn't be sent back. He could say what he liked, but she would never go back to Wigan, not for rubies or miracles.

As he walked toward the front of his desk and leaned against its edge, Abby fought the urge to shift from foot to foot. Fidgeting was a sign of weakness, she knew. Douglas rubbed his hand over his smooth chin, and Abby sensed he was having trouble with how to begin.

"I have accepted an invitation to the Montrose ball in ten days' time," Douglas told her. "I thought it would be worthwhile for you to accompany me."

She blinked, at a loss.

"Pardon?"

"A ball. I'd like to escort you."

"A ball?" She repeated, dumbfounded. "This isn't about returning me to my parents, then?"

"Leaving?" Now Douglas seemed surprised. "I was thinking

quite the opposite," he explained. "If you truly might extend your stay here, it's time you begin interacting with your fellow Charlestonians more regularly. You haven't been to a party since Gracie's coming out, ages ago already. I think it's time. Don't you? It might do us both good, to pass a festive evening in company with the other."

Abby tried to determine what exactly he was suggesting. He might mean to escort her almost as a surrogate for her father, but something in his gaze told her he wasn't feeling fatherly. It was exhilarating to imagine spending an evening in his company, whatever his reasons. But, she realized, she wouldn't have the first idea how to behave with him at such an event. Better to say no than to let him see her a fool. Even with all the etiquette training over the past months, Abby was certain she would make a proper imbecile of herself minutes after stepping through the Montroses' doors. And she did not have a dress for this event, as she surely couldn't wear the same dress from the Cunningham party. For her to be Douglas Elling's companion at a ball! It was laughable.

"Which means," Douglas continued, "that you will need to enlist Larissa to help you find a new gown. I'd recommend Louis Marseille's shop. I'm told he stitches faster than the other dressmakers of choice. Given the late start, we're going to need expeditiousness, or perhaps even to commandeer a gown on which he has already begun work." Douglas's tone was light and pragmatic, as if he was rattling instructions off to a secretary. "I would suggest you make the purchase tomorrow, first thing."

Abby felt her breath catch for reasons she couldn't determine. She was feeling too many emotions to put a name to them, and her heart racing underneath it all. She looked toward the back of the room behind Douglas, studying a bronze wall sconce as she struggled to organize her thoughts.

"Abby, you will do me the honor of accompanying me,

won't you?" Suddenly he seemed concerned, as if it hadn't previously occurred to him that she might decline his invitation. "It
will be almost bearable, this tedious social function, if I have
you for company. I made the mistake of accepting the invitation
before I had your assurance, but now I am fleeced, as even a
misfit such as I knows better than to default on an acceptance."

Abby wanted to say yes, that she would go with him. Not
knowing how he meant to take her, as his ward or something
more, she wanted him to reiterate his invitation and coax out
her acceptance.

"You do realize that I am hardly a debutante," Abby warned.
She crossed her arms over her charcoal dress.

"Of course," Douglas smiled back from his perch against
the cluttered desk, "which is why I think we might have a passable time together." He crossed his own arms, mimicking her
pose. "And don't you agree that it'd be wise to acquaint yourself
with local society, if you expect our neighbors to entrust their
daughters to you as a schoolmarm one day, if that's something
you're interested in truly?"

Abby cocked her head slightly and nodded, "You do have a fair
point. But if it will be so awful there, why must we go at all?"

Douglas stepped forward, closing the gap between them so
that there was barely a shaving of space remaining as he looked
down at her. He was standing so close that she could feel the
heat coming off his body. He flooded her senses, the fierce scent
of him charging into her lungs, his size an additional affront as
she tilted her head back to keep track of his eyes.

"Abby." His voice had gone quieter.

She could feel a shadow of his breath across her cheek, a
whisper of an idea. She had to check herself from leaning forward.

"The evening will be a great success, as far as I am concerned, if you simply come to be with me."

Abby felt herself nod, and it was perhaps all the answer he needed. He stepped back from her quickly, as though he had forgotten himself, looking quickly toward the door, then back at his desk.

"Right. Good then. If you'll excuse me now," he continued lightly, clearing his throat, "I'd like to say a proper farewell to Demett and Larissa, thank them for participating in the delivery of this most appreciated meal." He patted the picnic basket as though it were a greyhound and began walking out the office door, leaving Abby to herself. "I need just a quick word with Demett on another matter. We won't be but a moment."

She was still reeling from his nearness but quickly realized that this was her moment, her opportunity to explore the office. She had to rouse herself from her shameless stupor and see if she could find that stairwell again. She spun in a circle trying to remember which bookshelf she had walked behind all those months ago. Everything in her memory was blurred. She had to act swiftly if she wanted to see anything before Douglas returned. Just as she settled on a bookcase and started walking toward it, she heard shouts coming from outside. Something was clearly unraveling outside, and her sleuthing would have to wait.

The shouts and whooping grew louder as she pushed open the door, the cacophony greeting her like an assault. Larissa and Demett were just beyond the building, watching Douglas, who stood a few feet closer to the water, his back to all of them.

It sounded to Abby like a cavalcade was approaching. She tried to see past the expanding crowd, but then Douglas was standing next to her, barking commands at them.

"Go back inside, all of you. Larissa," he was shouting to be heard above the din, "take her." And without a backward glance, he was walking deeper into the crowd, away from them.

Larissa reached her arm out, but Abby shook out of her

grasp and took off after Douglas, damning the consequences as she went. She was not some crystal butterfly to be displayed on a vanity. She wanted to know what was going on.

"Abby wait, don't!" Larissa shouted, but Abby kept moving.

She had to shove at other bodies as she tried to keep sight of Douglas, who was marching at a breakneck pace toward the other end of the wharf, where it connected with the street. As they reached Broad Street, Abby saw crowds of bystanders congregating on both sides of the street. The boisterous whooping was directed toward a carriage that was meandering slowly through the street, like part of a processional. As the carriage drew closer, Abby glimpsed the source of the mob's entertainment and nearly retched. The rig was being pulled by a Negro with a yoke around his neck. The man, who wore only a loin cloth, was bleeding from his head and back. His bare feet were caked with a combination of blood and dirt. A white man stood preening aboard the carriage, his waistcoat pristine, his chest puffed out, his whip raised. The man sliced the switch through the air, eliciting new cheers, roars. As the whip connected with the man's back, he faltered, nearly toppling forward. Walking behind the carriage, there were two other Negroes, who were tethered by their necks to the rig, as if being towed. They followed the vehicle with their heads down while onlookers pelted them with rocks and bits of refuse, broad smiles on the faces of the spectators. Abby saw children in the crowd sucking lollies, bored, women with their faces painted.

She looked to Douglas beside her, whose sculpted face had gone ashen.

"What is this? Why are they using them so brutally?" she asked.

"Abby!" he demanded, startled by her presence. "You shouldn't be here." He stepped in front of her, blocking her view. "It's only a matter of time before a riot erupts from one of these displays,"

Douglas warned. "These people relish the punishment of run-aways. Like leaving a half-eaten carcass for a lion, it turns every man to a savage. You need to get back inside." Douglas motioned toward the wharf and waited for Abby to heed his advice.

"Then hadn't you better accompany me for your own sake? This is a crowd that might not look fondly on you. Isn't that so?"

"Trust me, Abby, these ruffians pose no threat to me." Abby was uncertain whether Douglas was communicating a foolish overconfidence or if he was implying a lack of anything left to lose. "That said," he added, "there is no reason for me to stand here watching this nastiness." He sneered in disgust as he looked once more at the howling crowd. "I'll escort you back."

When they reached Douglas's office, Larissa and Demett were gone. The crowds at this end of the wharf had noticeably thinned, everyone apparently gone to watch the display on Broad Street. "They must be waiting for you at the carriage," Douglas told her. "Come, I'll walk you."

She studied him, not moving to follow.

"Come," he repeated, motioning with his hand.

"I know, Douglas," she suddenly burst out. "I know about you. I heard you the other day with Demett, talking about Clover." She clamped her hand over her mouth, immediately regretful, wishing she could retract what she'd said.

"Confound it, Abby!" Douglas hissed. "Keep your voice down. Do you want to get the both of us killed?"

He took hold of her wrist and led her quickly back into the office, shutting and locking the door behind them with haste.

"Now tell me what you think you know," he demanded, his hands on his hips.

"I heard you," said Abby, "planning Clover's escape. The whole thing. It's no use for you trying to tell me I didn't or it's not true."

"And so . . . what?" Douglas asked defensively. "Whom have you told? Larissa? Gracie Cunningham?"

"For goodness sakes, no!" She retorted. "I will not betray you by revealing your participation. I think what you've done is," she searched for the proper words, "admirable, courageous, no, better than that. In fact, I'm only sorry there was no way I could help."

"Help?" Douglas stepped back at the suggestion. "The only thing for you to do is to forget what you heard. There is too much here for you to understand."

How could she convince him it was safe to discuss this with her? She was awed and inspired by his actions.

"Douglas," Abby began, "I'm like you!" She struggled to explain herself. "English, with no allegiance to the people here. You know I was not reared on slavery the way your neighbors have been. You can be comfortable discussing your views with me."

"No, no I cannot. My concern is not for myself, Abigail." He closed his eyes and inhaled deeply before adding, "The last white person I conversed with openly about slavery ended up dead." He paused and assessed Abby with a doleful gaze. "I will not put another extraordinary young woman at risk."

Abby felt the color in her face rise at his compliment.

"You will not distract me with flattery, Douglas," she told him, simultaneously trying to convince herself of the same. "I am not as foolish as I may sometimes appear," *especially in your presence*, she thought to herself. "I could help if you would let me. And, I may add, I know how to handle myself in dodgy situations. I've hardly lived a charmed life."

"Abby," Douglas groaned. "This is a dangerous game," he shook his head. "You're at enough risk simply living in my house. And you already know more than you should. We mustn't speak of this. Never again."

When Abby hesitated, he stepped closer to her. "Promise me," he beseeched her. She looked up at him, unsure whether she should continue arguing.

"Please," he placed his hand on her cheek as he told her, "I beg it of you." His hand against her skin was a revelation, a feast of warmth. How she wanted to lean into it. No, she wanted to step back, remove herself from its force. She stood motionless.

"If you were hurt by any of this, Abby, I couldn't bear it," he told her.

She wanted to protest further, to convince him, but she couldn't find the words, not while he stood so close, his hand still cradling her face. Abby finally nodded in reluctant agreement, and relief washed over Douglas's features.

There was a soft knock on the door, and Douglas's hand disappeared in a flash, leaving an abyss in its wake.

"Come," Douglas said again. "That'll be Larissa."

24

⌒

CHARLESTON, SOUTH CAROLINA
1846

$\mathcal{T}$en days later, as Larissa and Ida flitted about, helping Abby dress for the Montrose ball, she still felt beleaguered by questions. Following Douglas's directive, Larissa had taken Abby to Louis Marseille's shop on Cumberland Street, where it stood out proudly, bedecked by a large awning, between Durand's Pattiserie and Bernard Laurent's cobbling. The entirety of Cumberland Street was occupied by French merchants, from Pierre Etienne, whose ornate signage advertised silversmithing, all the way to the much grittier sign for LeRoue's pawn shop down the end of the lane. Feeling as though she had magically hopped across the sea to Paris, Abby had entered Marseille's shop with an unexpected burst of excitement.

She had noted briefly that she was more comfortable standing amidst the endless ribbons, hoops, and trims than she had been the first time Larissa had her outfitted. She sorted through fabric samples with enthusiasm, running her hand along silks and velvets, considering the depths of the colors, the way the light played across different threads. She settled on a deep-purple silk with velvet trim in the same hue. Marseille grumbled that he would never be able to create an acceptable garment by the date required, but as Douglas had predicted, the frenzied tailor managed to deliver.

And now Ida was yanking on the laces of Abby's corset. Larissa had spent the prior week reminding Abby of proper ballroom etiquette, when to curtsey and smile, when to keep quiet, and when to offer a polite laugh. The endless conventions of the Southern ruling class struck Abby as painfully trivial. Still, she forced herself to listen, to remember, so she might use this evening as Douglas had suggested—to impress the local gentry. If it happened that she managed to impress Douglas, as well, so much the better.

She scoffed at herself for acting like the type of smitten young lady she generally scorned. Ever since Douglas invited her to the ball, she found herself sleepless at night, fidgety and impatient as she anticipated the evening in his company. She was displeased by the fluttery feeling his presence now produced in her midriff. She swore to herself that she was not smitten, that she would not care to attach herself to a man, to imprison herself in that way. Yet her thoughts kept straying in the opposite direction, bothering about the ball, as though nothing was of greater imperative than delighting the man.

She had not seen him since the day he issued the invitation, and she had so many questions about how the night would unfold.

"All finished," Ida announced as she closed the final eye hook on the back of Abby's gown. Larissa looked up from where she had been searching through a drawer in the vanity table and considered Abby, her pale lips giving purchase to a broad smile.

"Ravishing is how you look," the governess assured her with glee. She handed Abby a pair of opera-length gloves.

"The other young ladies won't hold a candle to the beauty

that blazes from you tonight," Larissa told her as she turned to open the chamber door and motioned for Abby to follow. "Come, Mr. Elling and Demett are ready with the coach."

Abby followed Larissa down the spiral staircase, one hand on the banister to avoid tumbling. The gown she wore was by far the finest piece of clothing she'd ever owned, but also the heaviest. As she struggled to remain graceful on the staircase, Abby heard a gasp from the foyer down below.

"Miss Abigail," Jasper declared from the base of the stairwell, an obvious look of pride about him as he studied her. "What a pleasure to see you appearing in finery worthy of your character. Now you can shine on the outside, as well as from within."

"Oh, Jasper," Abby waved away his words as she reached the bottom of the stairwell, "you needn't gain my favor with flattery. It's just a silly costume."

"Excuse me for saying so, Miss, but there is nothing silly about it. I think you will see that you are the shining star at the affair tonight. But let us not delay," Jasper motioned toward the main entry. "Mr. Elling awaits in the courtyard."

Abby stepped outside and was pleased to discover that the evening was quite warm for February, with the promise of an early springtime whispering through the mild air. Her eyes had not adjusted to the fading light of dusk before she heard Douglas approaching from her left, his presence belied by a faint, appreciative whistle. She turned to face him, ready to playfully admonish him for his commoner's salute to her appearance. How would she ever learn to behave like a Southern belle if her escort carried on like a street cart pusher?

Her joking intentions disappeared as she turned and saw him stalking towards her on the gravel drive. His eyes sailed over her, from her upswept hair to her silk-covered toes, taking in her

appearance. She stood and let him consider her, feeling child-
ishly hopeful as he looked back to her face, then her hair, and to
her dress again. His eyes lingered on her bosom, which was
spilling over the gown's violet trim. Abby had told Larissa repeatedly that she thought the dress was cut too low in the bod-
ice, though Larissa insisted that the style was conservative in
comparison to current fashions. As his eyes returned to meet
hers, Abby saw appreciation, and something else, something like
longing.

Pretending a calm she did not feel, she raised her eyebrows,
waiting for him to speak. The silence allowed her a moment to
take in his appearance, too, his fine waistcoat, cut low to expose
a shirt front crisp as pressed paper. Dressed in his evening wear,
his appearance was extraordinary, almost too striking, an arresting assault to her senses.

"Forgive me," Douglas cleared his throat as he stepped
closer to her in the twilight. "I've not seen you dressed in formal
attire before, and I must say that I find the result most becoming. I am at a bit of a loss to . . ." he hesitated and shook his
head as if to clear it before he let his eyes glide over her again.
Waiting for him to finish, Abby struggled to maintain her posture, despite the sensation that her legs were turning to pastry
dough.

"Never mind then," he finally concluded. "Suffice it to say,
you look most enchanting, and I am honored to escort you tonight." He held out his arm for her as they walked to the carriage.

Once they were seated, Abby shimmied to the far end of the
velvet bench in an effort to expand the meager distance between
them. Douglas, suddenly businesslike, turned toward her and
began a near lecture.

"Right, so let's go over who you can expect to meet tonight.
Obviously, the Montroses. Be polite, but you'll fare better focus-

ing on guests with young children who might be in need of your services in the future. There are the Wilmots and the Hansons, all of whom were reproducing at a feverish pace a few years back. They are neighbors of the Montroses, so I'd wager they will be in attendance. If I recall correctly, Dotty Wilmot loves to discuss Roman art, or at least she did when I suffered through dinner parties with her. It might be worth showing off some of your classical knowledge, if you can work it into conversation."

As Abby tried to focus on Douglas's words, she was horribly distracted by the memory of his gaze on her just minutes before, the effects of his attention exacerbated now that he was sitting so close. She caught hints of soap and spice emanating in the air around him. She was appalled that he was able to shift into this practical mode so quickly, yet here she was bumbling about with her brain all addled by his presence. Perhaps if she'd had any experience with courting, or with any man other than her vile uncle, she might feel better equipped to handle this situation. As it was, she was still reveling in relief over the fact that Douglas no longer frightened her. It wouldn't do though for her to swoon over every man who failed to frighten her. She should follow Douglas's example and focus on the business of the evening. She had plenty of work ahead of her if she planned to erect a future for herself in South Carolina.

The Cunninghams, the Andersons, the Ardsleys, Douglas was rattling off one family name after another. She forced herself to listen, learning mainly that everyone was very wealthy, each family seeming to own a larger plantation than the next.

"I imagine I am supposed to act impressed by the enormity of everyone's holdings?" Abby asked. "If they worked their many acres themselves, then perhaps they would deserve esteem."

"Abby . . ." Douglas warned, "this won't be the place to give voice to anything you're thinking right now. You gave me your word that we wouldn't discuss . . . the things that are on your mind."

"I don't understand why you will not trust me, at least to discuss it with you," Abby argued.

"I've explained to you that this has nothing to do with trust and everything to do with your safety. Now shall I have Demett reverse this carriage and take us home, or can I rely on you to keep your views to yourself?"

Abby hesitated a moment, wondering how she went from ogling Douglas to needling him so quickly. He was right, she had promised to refrain from the topic, and certainly this was the wrong moment to be mentioning anything scandalous about slavery.

"I'm sorry. I was in error. Can we please forget I said anything?"

"Well, we'd better, since we've arrived." Douglas studied Abby for a moment longer. "Understand that you clasp our lives in your hands," he told her quietly. He took hold of her fingers and brought them slowly to his lips, holding her gaze as he placed a gentle kiss against her glove, as if sealing some sort of deal. "Now come," he declared with a new energy, giving her a gentle tug as he exited the carriage.

And just like that, they were walking into the party, Abby's hand on Douglas's arm and her heart in her throat for more reasons than she cared to count. As they stepped through the wide entryway into the Montroses' city manor, she felt herself transported. The foyer was awash in a golden glow as enticing as it was disorienting. She momentarily forgot the torrential current flowing from Douglas's arm straight to her hand, nearly forgot he was even standing beside her, as she took in the elaborate adornment and bustle surrounding her. The ballroom lay just beyond the foyer, with all its glory to be seen from one's first entry into the home. The opulence steeping from floor to ceiling was no less arresting than when she had encountered such excess at the Cunninghams' party. She heard Douglas speaking and forced her eyes away from the gilded party room.

"Lisbeth, Charles," Douglas greeted their hosts, who were waiting at a fixed post in the entrance hall. "A pleasure to see you again. May I present to you Miss Abigail Milton?"

Abby regarded the older couple, each with the same shade of biscuit-colored hair and hooked noses. They looked more like aging siblings than spouses, the effect bolstered as they studied her with equally unabashed delight.

"Welcome," Charles told her cordially before turning quickly back toward Douglas and continuing, "we were most gladdened you chose to attend our event after all this time of . . ." Charles trailed off and regarded Douglas eagerly, apparently waiting for Douglas to offer some information. Abby imagined that the Montroses were feeling quite proud that Douglas had graced their party with his presence, after rejecting so many.

"Ah," Douglas seemed to stifle a chuckle, "some things are worth the effort, are they not?"

Abby watched Charles's chest puff out with pride before she realized that Douglas had been looking at her while he spoke, and was in fact, still fixing her with a pointed look.

"Shall we go in?" Abby asked, her voice nearly smothered by violin notes that began wafting through the air.

As they entered the main party, Abby inhaled the viscous scent of calla lilies and hyacinths, blooms erupting from every crevice and basin in the hall. Gold candlesticks swelled outward from the walls, casting a gilt shimmer on everything within their sweep. As she scanned the room, Abby saw precarious towers of champagne flutes being filled by a tuxedoed slave and a raised platform in the back of the room, where the string orchestra was arranged with their violins and cellos. Douglas led Abby toward the dance cards, and she noticed innumerable heads turning in their direction. Women and men were looking first at Douglas and then at her, no subtlety to their actions. Clearly, everyone was as curious as she why Douglas had brought her to this affair.

When they reached the table where three matronly women presided over young ladies' dance cards, Abby eyed the hand-painted cards with trepidation.

"Not to worry," Douglas told her quietly as he picked up an empty card. "It's just the same as Miss Cunningham's affair." Douglas wrote Abby's name at the top of the card using a miniature pencil that was attached to the card by a cord. He scanned the listed songs on the card and then wrote his own name on one of the lines.

"I hope you don't mind I've reserved a dance for myself. Now I best get out of the way and give the other bachelors a chance to meet you." As Douglas excused himself, Abby studied the dance card and saw that there were spaces for twenty-two dances. Douglas's name was in the eleventh spot. A waltz. Abby couldn't imagine how she was supposed to tolerate dancing with other gentlemen at the ball. She had been so fixated on her evening with Douglas that she neglected to prepare herself for any other men.

Abby examined the crowd, and she considered escaping to the verandah until it was time for her dance with Douglas. But Douglas had wanted to introduce her to society, and she would not embarrass him by skulking off. She swallowed hard as she saw three young men approaching her. Objectively speaking, all three were probably quite handsome. One was dark and lithe, while his two friends were shorter but broad shouldered, both with flaxen hair.

When they reached her, the tall one spoke.

"Miss Milton, my name is Shaw Anderson. It's a pleasure to finally make your acquaintance." He reached for her hand as he smiled at her. Abby was not surprised that he already knew her name, given that gossip seemed to spread through Charleston faster than head lice in Wigan. Surely everyone in the room knew she was the English girl living off Douglas Elling's charity, finally brought out to mingle with decent folk. Abby reluctantly submitted her hand, as Shaw brought it to his lips for a flirtatious kiss. She cringed internally and wondered briefly if this was why women wore gloves to parties.

"And let me introduce my friends," Shaw continued. "This here is Charlie Meyers," he pointed to the man on his left. "And his kid brother, Stu," he gestured toward the other. Abby nodded at them both, hoping they would not follow their friend's lead in reaching for her hand. Thankfully, Shaw deprived the brothers of any such opportunity, as he continued to monopolize the conversation.

"Forgive us for approaching without proper introduction, but we three have been watching you and your purple dress since you arrived, and we've agreed that you are the comeliest young lady at this affair. Maybe in all of Charleston, or even all the world," he laughed, delighted with himself. "And the trouble is we couldn't settle on who deserved to put his name down on your card first, so we were hoping you could offer some advice on how we should resolve our conflict," he finished off with a wink.

Perhaps she should have been flattered to have three vigorous young men competing for her, but standing under their scrutiny like this, with Shaw hovering over her, the dance card committee beside her, she was feeling averse to dancing with any of them, bombarded and affronted. She hadn't minded the dancing at Gracie's party, but the way these lads were looking at her was different. Perhaps her arrival with Douglas had given the impression that she was a woman of loose morals, ready to trade her favors too easily. She felt panic taking hold and stumbled to concoct a response.

"I . . . I . . ."

As she reached for her words, Shaw was suddenly looking over her head, behind her.

"Sorry boys," Abby heard, as she turned to see Douglas standing with poorly concealed rage on his face. He continued tightly, "If you could excuse Miss Milton for but a moment."

He extended his arm to Abby and began pulling her toward the French doors at the side of the ballroom. She worried she had already done something wrong.

Once they were alone on the stone terrace outside the ballroom, Douglas turned toward Abby and a torrent rushed from him.

"I'm sorry, I'm sorry." He bent at the waist and pushed his hands against his thighs, as though struggling to catch his breath.

Righting himself, he continued, "I know I brought you here to introduce you, to let you meet the people of Charleston." He shook his head, clearly agitated. "I didn't expect to react like this. But I just couldn't let those men in there have at you. Watching Anderson and those others crowding you, breathing on you, something came over me, like I had lye in my veins. And then he winked at you. I'm sorry. I couldn't do it, couldn't . . . couldn't breathe the air while I watched you slipping through my grasp." He laughed out loud and looked up into the night sky, shaking his head good-naturedly. When he looked back down at her, his face was serious.

Abby looked back at Douglas in the moonlight, unsure what he was trying to tell her. She could still hear the music and muffled laughter coming from inside the ballroom, but she couldn't piece together what Douglas was saying right in front of her. Nothing she hoped for ever came true, and certainly this moment, this confusing, rushed moment that had crept up on her from embers of doubt, seemed unfathomable.

He took hold of Abby's hand and guided her a few steps farther from the house before continuing.

"I think we have to submit to this, this pull between us. I know it's complicated with our living arrangements, but we will figure it out. That will be the easy part. I haven't felt, not anything, not since before, but then there you were."

Abby could sense the hope growing in her chest, spreading its fingers like the light of a rising sun and expanding throughout her body.

"Abby—" He paused as he scanned her face. They were standing so close she could smell the mint on his breath. "I cannot wait any longer. I thought . . . I thought I could, but then one yearning look from another man showed me how wrong I was." He gazed down at her and moved a stray tendril of her hair from her face. "I am transfixed."

Abby grabbed the iron rail framing the patio to steady herself and give herself a moment to parse through his words before responding. She wanted to accept his declaration, to swoon in his arms and embark on some sort of fairy tale, but that was not the kind of luck she had. He'd only just begun to know her, he couldn't have any concept of the darkness in her soul, how she had already been befouled. The American Abigail was just a mirage, waiting to return to vapor.

She paused, searching for the right words and trying to temper her own response. "I think perhaps you are confused," she began cautiously, "and fancy yourself besotted, when really you are only starved for companionship. You barely leave your home—you consort with such a limited population. It is no wonder you enjoy my company when you so rarely keep company with anyone at all."

"No, Abby," Douglas said firmly. "I know my own mind, and my heart. They both belong to you. That is, if you will have them. We are not so many years apart in age and really, there is nothing that should stand in our way." He looked at her expectantly.

Abby returned Douglas's gaze for a long moment without responding. She was struggling between hopefulness and cynicism, thrilled by Douglas's words, yet petrified that his affection was directed at a false girl, someone she had invented.

"But you don't even know me!" she nearly shouted. "And once you do, everything that drew you to me will be revealed as counterfeit. I am not the sophisticated young lady you see before you. Do you forget why I am in the States at all? I am an indigent, a parasitic factory girl, smothered by filth, inside and out."

"I do know you, Abby, more than you think. We have both been polluted in the past, by forces beyond our control. But I know who you are. I see it in the way you carry yourself, wearing your lady's posture like a costume over arms that would rather swing carefree, in constant motion. I see who you are in your impulse to attend to every last bugger in need, whether it's Reggie's hands or that god-awful horse you couldn't resist. I see you, each time your lip twitches before you smile, the way you run your finger along the outer spine of a book that piques your interest. I see your loyalty to your family, and maybe, if I'm lucky, to me. I understand your trust is hard to earn, and I am aware you've been dealt great blows, that you've suffered in the past. I wish only to see you contented, and to keep your company for as long as you will bestow such graciousness upon me. I will respect your wishes if I have misjudged the situation, but please, let me know if you are with me. That you might one day perhaps be mine." He moved his face down so their noses were nearly touching. Abby felt the warmth of his breath against her cheeks.

"Are you, Abigail Milton? Are you with me?" he whispered.

Suddenly nothing mattered beyond keeping his gaze on her, feeling the warmth of his recognition, the flood of his ubiquity. She found herself nodding. She had the fleeting thought that the person he described was the woman she wanted to be.

"You are then? With me?" He prodded for definitiveness as he brushed the back of his fingers along her face.

"I confess," she answered, surprising herself with the force of her emotions, feelings that previously she had refused to wholly acknowledge, even within herself. "I am with you." They stood so close that only moonlight could pass between them. Douglas stared down at her with intensity, his light eyes having turned a deep, stormier blue. Abruptly he stepped back from her and cleared his throat.

"I think it's best I give you some space before I am tempted to ask for things I do not yet deserve."

The air felt suddenly cool without the shroud of him around her.

"Yes, perhaps we should return," Abby responded regretfully. "People will wonder what has transpired between us out here."

Douglas glanced toward the open doors, the ballroom's yellow light bleeding onto the patio stones.

"I believe you owe those rogues a couple of dances to boot." He shrugged resignedly. "Now that I am sure of you, I suppose I can bear it. I did bring you here under the guise of introducing you to society. I assume I need to take my lumps and watch you glide around in the arms of other men."

"Oh, but I'd really rather not, to tell the truth," Abby admitted. "You wouldn't subject me to those men, would you? The way they looked at me. I think, I think that our living arrangement, and then coming here together tonight, it has given people ideas about me."

Douglas was silent for a moment as he considered her words.

"Let us compromise. In the interest of limiting ladies' gossip, I think it is incumbent upon us to sacrifice a bit of your time to dances with the local gentlemen. If you can survive three waltzes or polkas or what have you, I will come and rescue you under some excuse."

"Three dances and no more?"

"And no more," Douglas agreed. "But first," Douglas smiled mischievously as he removed Abby's dance card from where it hung on her wrist, "let me add my name for another dance or two." He leaned on the railing and wrote his name with great flourish, working on the card for too long.

When he handed the card back to her, she scanned it quickly and laughed.

"I may lack experience with proper etiquette, but I'm fairly certain that you are not supposed to put your name next to eighteen of the twenty-two available dances!"

"Twenty-one," Douglas corrected her. "We've missed the first dance while we've been out here. Now get on with those other dances so that I might enjoy your company again sooner."

"When people see my card, they'll talk," Abby warned. "What happened to avoiding ladies' gossip?"

"Abigail, my darling," Douglas smiled carelessly, "they're talking already. Let's at least make it interesting."

"But you brought me here to help with my reputation, not to tarnish it."

"Oh fine," Douglas gently tugged at the card so that it tore off the string on Abby's wrist. "We'll tell the card committee that I spilled my drink and you need a replacement. But," he perked up as he placed the ravaged card inside his coat, "I intend to collect on these eighteen dances in the future." He extended his elbow for her hand. "We'd better return you to your suitors before we incite a riot."

When they reached the men, who were still waiting by the wall, Douglas bowed gallantly.

"My apologies. Miss Milton is available now." He smiled pointedly at Abby and added, "Well, she's available for the next few dances at least. Get your chance while you can, boys."

Abby was vaguely aware of herself being escorted to the dance floor by Shaw Anderson, but she was in a near trance, trying to digest what had just happened. As Shaw spun her this way and that, she replayed Douglas's words in her mind. Images of his darkened eyes swirled through her mind, memories of his warm fingers on her face. Abby felt herself grinning and hoped that Shaw would not think himself the cause of her delight. She allowed herself a quick glance in Douglas's direction, and her heart fluttered as she saw that he was watching her from where he stood amongst a small crowd of bystanders, at the outer edge of the ballroom. Abby offered a silent thank you to Shaw, a skilled dancer who was allowing her to appear graceful under Douglas's gaze.

The song ended, and Abby was handed off to one of the Meyers brothers. She couldn't say which. The song was a polka. As with the waltz, Larissa had trained Abby so thoroughly in the proper steps that she hardly had to concentrate on her form at all. She looked back toward Douglas in anticipation, but she saw that he was no longer looking at her.

He was, instead, kissing the hand of Cora Rae Cunningham.

25

CHARLESTON, SOUTH CAROLINA
1846

*R*ain pelted against the bedroom windows, persisting until Abby was thoroughly awake. She had shared a carriage home the night before with Fiona and Lemeny Weaver, sisters who lived with their parents on the other side of Meeting Street. Like Douglas, their elder brother, Amos, had stayed behind at the Montroses' for card playing after the conclusion of the dancing. Douglas had advised Abby that if she wished to preserve her reputation against his blatant display of favor at the ball, he must refrain from accompanying her home. Abby winced remembering the way Fiona and Lemeny had riddled her with questions about Douglas. They were fifteen and seventeen years old, respectively, and they had not seen Douglas since before his late wife's passing. They explained that Douglas, and his transformation back to some version of his former self, was all anyone in Charleston was talking about. Surely everyone was gossiping about her now, as well.

Glancing now toward the stormy morning sky, Abby wondered what would become of their plan to meet for a midday picnic. After returning to Abby for their promised dance the evening before, Douglas had asked permission to court her formally, beginning with a picnic in the gardens behind the house.

At a knock on the door, Abby sat up in bed, pulling the comforter up with her. She wanted to lie languid for longer, reveling in the memories of moonlight with Douglas the night before. As the knock was repeated, Abby wondered if she must answer.

"Abby," Larissa called gently, "are you up, dear?" The governess opened the door a crack and peeped in, smiling when she saw Abby half risen. "I was hoping to get in at least an hour of studying this morning. I did let you sleep in you know, though it hardly looks like late morning with the sky so brown. Oh, and there's this, too." Reaching into the pocket of her colorless wool dress, Larissa pulled out a folded note. "Mr. Elling has informed me of your plan to enjoy your midday meal together today." She raised her pale eyebrows at Abby as she placed the note back into the front pocket of her skirt.

Abby remained silent. She saw no reason to explain herself to Larissa when it felt as though she hardly understood the situation herself.

"Take heed, Abby," Larissa warned, "Douglas Elling is this city's mysterious tragic hero. All the bitterness that was hurled at him prior to the fire was replaced afterwards by sympathy and an awfully powerful curiosity. If you become involved with him, everything you do, down to lacing your boots, will become fodder for the tattlers. I happen to think it's a fine idea, regardless," Larissa added as she walked deeper into the room and began arranging Abby's textbooks on the writing desk, "but I warn you so that you will know what you risk."

Odd, thought Abby, that of the many risks she felt herself taking lately, being talked about was the hazard that made Larissa take notice. Abby's mind was consumed with other questions as she thought of Douglas. Whether to trust him, whether he might hurt her, use her, forsake her for the likes of Cora Rae Cunningham—those were Abby's real concerns. There was also the question of why she should care so much. She'd learned long ago not to let anything become too important, lest it might become lost to her.

Now Larissa was at the wardrobe sorting through Abby's dresses.

"This one," she declared, holding up Abby's hunter-green day dress. "I think it's your most flattering. I don't know why you insisted on all these stark frocks the last time we visited the seamstress. Still, this one brings out some bit of brightness in your eyes."

"Larissa, what are you doing?"

"I'm helping," Larissa smiled as she hung the dress on the door to the wardrobe. "I've been waiting for you and Mr. Elling to catch onto each other for months. Both of you so stubborn, but idealists just the same. Come, no time to waste."

GRACIE WAS STILL BASKING IN HER OWN ROMANCE OF the night before as she dressed for her Sunday morning visit to church. It had been her first ball since obtaining a real beau. To have spent the evening in the company of Harrison Blount had been as sweet as summer lemonade. Harrison had been the perfect gentleman, attending to Gracie's every need throughout the party. At evening's end, he had tried to steal a kiss, but Gracie played coy. It was incumbent upon a proper belle to be the moral compass of any relationship with a man. If she continued playing her cards right, they might be affianced by summertime.

Gracie's rumination was interrupted by the sound of Cora Rae shrieking in anger.

"No!" Cora Rae shouted from the next bedroom, "not this one, you stupid ape!"

Gracie hurried into the hallway to see what had so agitated her sister just as a shoe came flying out of Cora Rae's bedchamber. She peered cautiously through Cora Rae's door to find her sister slumped on the floor, surrounded by at least ten rumpled Sunday dresses and three frantic house slaves. The dress Cora Rae was wearing was buttoned only halfway up the back, her ivory shoulders bare between the gaping swathes of powder-blue fabric.

"Rae," Gracie scolded, "what has come over you?"

"These creatures can't find me one decent dress to wear!" Cora Rae snapped. "Is it so much to ask to hope to look passable for a trip to church?" She seethed. "Clover would have known how to find the right dress. I hope when they catch her they beat the daylights out of her." Raising herself off the floral carpet, she looked at the three frightened black women standing in her bedroom. "Get out of my sight, all of you."

The women each glanced back toward the heap of dresses, likely reluctant to leave behind the mess, but then trained their eyes to the floor and soundlessly exited the bedroom.

Gracie leaned against the doorframe and looked at Cora Rae. "Now what is it, really?" she asked.

"It's just the incompetence of the people surrounding me." Cora Rae groaned as she sat down at her vanity table, identical to Gracie's except for the mess of cosmetics and perfumes strewn across the top.

"And what else?" Gracie pressed.

Cora Rae turned back from the mirror to Gracie and sighed dramatically.

"If I must tell you," Cora Rae began, "it's your little friend, Abigail Milton." Cora Rae pivoted toward the mirror to adjust her hair, her dress still unfastened halfway down the back. "It seems you've underestimated her." She continued as she fiddled with clips in her hair. "While you were toadying up to Harrison last night, I had to watch that tramp mesmerize the man I've been waiting on for years. You should have seen how she had him looking at her. It was all he could do not to have her in the middle of the ballroom floor."

Cora Rae dabbed at her eyes with a cloth and rose to view the dresses remaining in her armoire. "And now I have to undo all the damage that *you* were supposed to prevent. I should never have entrusted you to act as my emissary." She began pulling more dresses from the wardrobe and dropping them on the bed. "This is just so typical of you, Gracie. Let me remind you that if I cannot have my heart's desire, then neither shall you have yours. I don't even think I'd take Harrison for myself, I'd just turn him off you." She looked back to Gracie with an injured expression. "I wouldn't have to resort to these ugly threats if not for your own capriciousness. Now how about you get out of my room and think on that?"

"I'm sure that Douglas is not as besotted as you imagine," Gracie answered cautiously. "I was visiting with Abby less than two weeks ago, and she did not mention a word to me about any romance between them. Anything that has passed between them must have been incredibly recent, and can therefore be un-done." She stepped farther into the bedroom and seated herself on Cora Rae's plush canopy bed, noticing that the bed coverings were still drawn back in significant disarray.

"Abby doesn't have the slightest enthusiasm for marriage, so I'm sure she cannot be all that interested in him. So any passing attraction that Douglas might harbor will probably soon wane. She doesn't suit him anyway. They are incredibly different types. You, on the other hand, have been born and bred in the same social circles as Douglas, and you have the proper upbringing of a true Southern lady."

Gracie's words seemed to have the intended effect, as Cora Rae visibly relaxed. "Well, yes, I suppose a poor girl from British slums is not likely to maintain Douglas's notice for long. That little bit of pretty she's got, it's not enough to hold a man like Douglas Elling." Cora Rae gazed approvingly at her own smooth face in her mirror and then turned back to Gracie. "Even so, I don't like leaving anything to chance. You're going to help me one more time."

Gracie rolled her eyes under closed lids. "What is it you're proposing, dear sister?" Gracie asked without attempting to hide her sarcasm.

"It's masterfully simple, actually," Cora Rae turned to face her sister and lowered her voice. "We must convince Abby that Douglas Elling is a scoundrel. Unrefined girls like your precious Abby all want the same thing from a man; they want to be loved and adored to the exclusion of all others, as though true love might actually exist. They want a hero they can worship until they're blue in their raw little faces. Isn't it true?" she asked rhetorically. "I, on the other hand, know that men are imperfect by their very nature. They will always lust after other women. None is a hero. A wise woman loves a man for his accomplishments and his status, and most of all for his imperfections, not in spite of them."

"It's time for Douglas to fall from grace," Cora Rae continued. "Once she determines that Douglas is not her white knight, but a man like any other, who longs to lay with every fine woman who crosses his path, he will quickly lose her affection. And she will cease to be an obstacle. Once Douglas is able to focus on me and me alone, well, the outcome should be too plain to state, don't you think? Help me undo these buttons, would you?" She turned her back to Gracie.

"Even if your plan succeeds in spoiling Abby's opinion of Douglas, how does it follow that Douglas's next logical step is to your front hall?" Gracie asked.

"You just leave that part to me," Cora Rae instructed dismissively. "Douglas will see me for who I am, once he finally has the freedom to concentrate on *me*, that is."

"Assuming I agree, how would we even manage to convince Abby that Douglas is of such dubious character?" Gracie fingers continued working the buttons of her sister's dress.

"Don't give me that tone, Gracie. It's actually a kindness to your friend. A bit of heartbreak now will save her from landing in a life where she has no place. If you think about the long term, you must acquiesce that she will be happier if it ends now. Let's wait only a few days," Cora Rae instructed, calculating. "Give me two minutes alone with him in his study, and then send Abby in to see us." Cora Rae stepped free of the dress and reached for her next choice. She seemed greatly cheered from her earlier desolation. With a new depth of confidence, she added, "I will take care of the rest."

26

CHARLESTON, SOUTH CAROLINA
1846

*A*lthough the rain had abated by lunchtime, Douglas
sent word that Abby should meet him in the Hayes
parlor, a room at the south end of the house. Now as she made
her way down the empty corridor, she pinched her cheeks one
last time for color and attempted a steadying breath. The smell
of roasted chicken and corn greeted her as she stepped into the
small room. The parlor, which seemed a cross between a study
and a petite dining room, was empty. The sideboard was laden
with food, and Abby hazarded a step closer to investigate. There
was a wicker basket full of breads, yeasty creations in divergent
shapes, some covered with seeds, others without. A tray of
cheese and dried fruits also waited, along with mason jars of
varying jams. There was a bowl of fresh fruit, and three silver
dishes covered by matching domes. Abby sniffed the air again
and guessed the shining cloches covered chicken and corn pudding, perhaps glazed ham.

"I hope I didn't go overboard," she heard Douglas say as he
walked into the room from behind her. "I was unsure of your
tastes and thought it'd be best if I provided some choice." He

was carrying a crystal pitcher full of lemonade, which he set down alongside the food. "I convinced Jasper to let me serve lunch myself. Figured it best replicated the picnic experience." He shrugged as he glanced toward the gray sky outside the window.

"All this is just for the two of us?" Abby asked, incredulous.

"If you are going to grant me the pleasure of your company, you'll have to grow accustomed to being fussed over." He walked to the square table, which had been set for two. It looked to Abby more like a gaming table than a space for dining. "So?" Douglas asked as he lifted a plate from one of the settings and approached the food. "A little of everything?"

He spoke casually, and Abby wondered how he could be so calm when his mere presence was causing her heart to pound, insistent like a heckler, demanding to be heard.

"Yes, yes, that would be lovely. Thank you." She took her seat at the table, crossing her ankles as Larissa invariably instructed.

It seemed to Abby a matter of seconds before he placed a heaping plate before her and lifted his own dish for a return to the buffet. Perhaps if she focused on the food, instead of the man, she might fasten her frayed nerves back together before he sat. She studied the chaos on her plate and saw that what she had expected to be corn pudding looked to be some sort of egg and squash cake, the likes of which she had not encountered before.

"I'm a firm believer that you have to try new foods before declaring that one is not to your liking." Douglas had apparently been watching her crinkle her forehead at the gelatinous loaf.

"I hope you haven't the same outlook on women as you do on food?" Abby asked, immediately irritated at herself for her constant inability to think before speaking. Though perhaps it was for the best that she prodded like this—what did she really know about Douglas's intentions?

He turned toward her with a serving fork in his hand, suddenly serious, "I assure you, I am hardly fickle when it comes to
matters of the heart. It seems that when I get myself set on
someone, it's rather difficult for me to aim my attention anywhere else. I've long since ceased my efforts to quit mooning
over you." He stared at her for a moment, making her shawl feel
too heavy on her shoulders. "Food, on the other hand," he turned
lightheartedly back to the credenza and speared a chicken leg,
"well, I generally just enjoy all of it." He continued loading his
plate until it was as full as the one he'd presented to Abby and
then sat opposite her at the glossy onyx table.

"Please, eat," he told her as he spread a napkin on his lap.
Abby lifted her fork and looked with trepidation at the stockpile
of food before her, trying to determine how to confront it. The
primary objective was to avoid spilling anything across her
bosom in front of Douglas. As she poked experimentally at the
squash loaf, Douglas continued leading the conversation.

"I know you are wary, that you have been disappointed in
the past. I would like to prove to you my trustworthiness, my
sincerity where you are concerned. So please, ask me anything
you'd like, and I promise honesty in my response."

She chanced a bite of the squash cake and found it surprisingly tasty, light and fluffy with a hint of garlic. She was reluctant
to ask more about his intentions toward her, lest she seem too
needy or demanding. Yet there was another way to seize the opportunity he offered.

"If I can really ask anything," she began hesitantly, "can't
you tell me about your involvement in abolition?"

"Oh," Douglas answered flatly. "Let's not do that. I've just
offered you my soul on a pallet. Wouldn't it be better if I just
continued raving about how besotted I am by you?"

"That *is* tempting," Abby smiled as she stood to fetch the

lemonade, "but if I take you at your word about your feelings toward me, then we are free to discuss other topics. Though my information is wooly, I'm fairly certain that your experience with abolition has played a large part in forming who you are."

Douglas sighed and answered quietly, "No."

Abby stood looking down at him. How could there be anything real between them if he would not talk to her about this enormously important part of his life?

"But I already know you're involved," she persisted, "so why can you not simply fill in details?"

"Please," he took the pitcher and set it down on the table before taking hold of her hand with both of his. "Understand that these are questions of life and death. I am trying to keep you far from these dealings to limit your risk. If I were truly selfless, I would say that you should quit me altogether, but I find myself unable to give you up. Can we not agree to sequester one topic without detriment to the growing bond between us? No matter what information I secrete, I will never be false. Not with you. Tell me that can be sufficient?"

"I . . . I don't know. How can I trust you when there is so much of your life you would keep hidden from me?"

"Please, Abby, do not ask me to jeopardize your safety. Let us at least try, try building something between us while leaving other things to the side. Grant me the opportunity to prove myself to you. At some point over the past months, you have taken hold of my soul, as though you are grasping it with your bare hands, at all hours, every dawn. Nothing can change that, even if I keep certain things to myself. Isn't it good enough?"

As he looked up at her, his light eyes determined, she wished it wouldn't be improper to stroke his chin, to explore the contours of his square jaw, the small dip below his bottom lip.

"Fine," she snapped as she returned to her seat, adjusting herself with a huff. "Then what else shall I ask in this little game of yours?"

"I assure you, I am not playing." They stared at each other a moment in silence.

Abby considered her options. He hardly owed her anything, wasn't beholden to her, so why should she insist that he share his every secret? As much as her own curiosity was arguing otherwise, there really was no reason Douglas had to list all the details of his illegal activities for her. She should salvage this meeting and try to turn the focus to lighter topics.

"Right then. So . . . how about this room? Why is it called the Hayes parlor?"

"Ha. I haven't any idea. Never asked." He glanced around the room as if seeing the quaint space for the first time. "Ask me another."

"Then why are we in here?"

"Where else should we be?" He smirked and leaned back in his seat, challenging her.

"Why not the dining room?"

"I felt put off by that mammoth table, didn't want to risk you sitting too far from me." His eyes flashed with mischief.

"What about Larissa?"

"What about her?" He offered a slight shrug.

"Where is she?"

"Why should I know?" He was becoming increasingly flip.

"Well shouldn't she be chaperoning us?"

"No."

"No?" Abby persisted.

"I instructed her not to join us when I sent my note." The ghost of a smile played at his lips as he rose and rounded the table toward her.

"Not to join us?" Abby's voice pitched higher, and she cursed her panic.

"Not to join us." He stood firm, looking down at her, and it seemed he was surrounded by a palpable confidence.

She felt crowded by the sudden closeness, wanted him to step back so she didn't have to tilt her head to meet his gaze. "But why?"

"You want to know why?" he asked her, reaching for her hand and pulling her to a standing position.

"Yes." She noticed her linen napkin floating toward the floor, but she was quickly distracted from it as he stepped even closer to her. She raised her eyes to meet his and saw him looking down at her mouth. She could smell him, a heady scent that was becoming familiar to her, as welcome as it was frightening.

"Why what?"

"What?" She felt incompetent to continue conversing under these circumstances, as she stood awkwardly awaiting his next action.

"What did you want to know?" he asked again, his voice shifting to a near whisper as he looked at her eyes and then her lips and then her eyes and then her lips again.

He was asking too many questions, standing too close, confusing her, his questions and his broad chest invading her space.

"Um, oh. Oh, Larissa. Why didn't you want her here?"

"So that I could do this."

With astonishing speed, his hand was on the back of her neck, and his mouth was covering hers. She thought to shove at him, like she'd have done to Matthew, but then she felt the warmth of his soft lips against hers, gentle and frantic all the same. The hand on her neck crawled into her hair as he pulled her closer, inhaling her, seeming to breathe her into himself. This wasn't like Matthew at all. Where he had pushed and demanded, harsh and unyielding, Douglas seemed to be worshiping, begging for a taste of her. He nudged at her lips with his mouth, pushing them apart and licking her bottom lip. Then his tongue was inside her mouth, exploring her, making promises with every stroke. She should stop this, shove him back and yell at him for degrading her. But this didn't feel like disrespect, it felt like sanctification. She gave in and grabbed onto his arms, the bulk of his shoulders nearly too large for her paltry hands to make purchase. She leaned into him, their chests touching, as he groaned her name into her mouth.

Her resolve was lost. She wanted to put her hands inside his waistcoat, reach beneath his shirt, and feel his bare chest, the softness of his skin against the hard muscle she was certain lay beneath. Her legs began to give out, but he wrapped his other arm around her waist, holding her up. She wanted only to keep feeling the heat of his body against her, to continue hearing his small moans as he relished her. She moved a hand to his chest and was rewarded when he whispered her name. But then he said it again, and it sounded different, strained. He ripped his mouth from hers and stepped backwards. His breath was coming in ragged bursts, his lips red and slick as he looked down at her.

"My God, I'm so sorry," he huffed.

Abby wiped the back of her hand against her own wet mouth. "You're sorry?" she asked, her voice weak as she readied to be mortified by her wanton enthusiasm.

"No, that's wrong. I am not sorry. I will be basking in the memory of this moment for days to come, the smell of you, your taste. But I am sorry if I frightened you or pushed you too far. I moved too quickly, too. . . ." He faltered.

"Frightened me?" Abby smoothed her hair with a hand, barely noticing how many strands escaped from the twist Ida had created for her earlier. She was about to say more, make a joke, when she noticed his face had turned gray.

"What is it?"

"There is something I need to tell you, before we take this any further." He dug his hands into his pockets and released a sigh of reluctance.

Her heart, which had barely begun to slow back to its normal pace, was now beating wildly again as she wondered what ghastly information he was readying to reveal about himself.

"Come sit with me," he directed, as he led her to the room's only settee, gently guiding her to sit on the green velvet. "It may be too soon for us to discuss this, but if I wait, I worry you will feel I kept this information from you for too long."

She couldn't imagine there was anything he could tell her about himself that would change what she was feeling.

"There is no gentle way to say this, but," he paused and then stated flatly, "I know about your uncle Matthew."

It was as though he had smacked her cheek with his open palm.

He couldn't know. If he knew the truth, she realized, everything would surely be over between them. "What do you mean?" Her words caught in her throat, emerging clipped and choppy even though she tried to sound casual.

Douglas coughed and looked toward the window, away from her. "I know that he, that he did things. Made you do things with him. Vile things."

Abby sat very still as she absorbed his words. She was sure he must now consider her to be filthy and soiled. Vile, that was the word he'd used. Suddenly, defensive anger took hold of her. She stood, needed to be standing to meet this.

"How do you know about it?" she asked, her voice rising.

"Why waste your time courting then, when you already know you can do just what you please?"

Douglas answered with forced calm in his voice. "Abby, please, it's not like that. You're the one who told me. You, yourself."

"I did what?" she demanded.

"After the accident with the horse," Douglas rose off the settee. "You were delirious. When I tried to help you, you were shouting at me, calling me Matthew, you said some things that made it rather obvious."

"And what?" she demanded. "You've waited all this time, reading to me and taking me to stupid parties, until you can have your turn, is that it?"

"It wasn't any of my affair, Abby," Douglas pleaded. "It wasn't my place to confront you about what I had heard. But then we started growing closer. There was no right time to tell you what I knew. I couldn't let this secret exist between us any longer. I could never judge you for it. I'm only sorry I wasn't there to stop him." Douglas looked at her with pleading eyes.

"Don't look at me," she shouted. "Don't ever look at me!" She covered her face with her hands and began to sob, still standing in the middle of the small parlor.

Undeterred, Douglas continued. "How can you tell me not to look at you when I see you everywhere I look? It is with dire admiration that I look upon you. You have risen so far above the squalor you were forced to endure. While I detest Matthew Milton, it plays little into my opinion of you that he raped you in your youth."

"Raped me?" Abby's head snapped to attention. "He never raped me," she glowered at him. "He never touched me like that. Never like that. Touched himself plenty," she nearly spat. "He used me for aesthetic purposes, grabbing bits and pieces of me and slobbering his nastiness on me. He threatened to suspend my da's allowance if I didn't stay quiet. Don't look at me, Douglas!" she yelled again. "You couldn't possibly see me as anything but disgusting." She stared at him in defiance.

"On the contrary," Douglas answered softly. "I know that you are stronger and more beautiful for all you have survived. In fact," he reached into his pocket, "I've brought you something to show you how deeply I believe in you."

Abby looked at the box in his hand and turned away. "I don't want any more of your gifts. Now you are trying to buy me? Or do you think you already own me, for your charity and care, and this is just a pity present before you have your way with me?" She looked at him accusingly.

"No," Douglas answered, "this is a gift for you to wear so that you may know my affection is always with you, surrounding you and keeping you safe, no matter what ills should befall us. A good-luck charm."

"I don't believe in luck," Abby answered quietly.

"Please," Douglas began opening the box. "Haven't I earned your trust yet? Enough to let me keep trying at least?"

He made a fair point that he'd done nothing to undermine her trust in him since the day they'd met. He had been forthcoming with her, and gentle. He'd tried repeatedly to assist her, from the incident with the horse to saving her from too many unpleasant dances at the Montrose ball. Above all, he'd hosted her in his home for half a year, treating her person with naught but respect since her arrival.

After a moment Abby asked, "So this is real then? Between you and me?"

"Yes!" Douglas exclaimed. "You are the only thing I am of sure of in this world, Abby. This," he said, as he motioned from himself to her and back, "this is genuine as bedrock."

He removed the velvet top of the box he was holding and revealed an oddly-shaped gold charm covered in diamonds so small they resembled snow winking in sunlight. In spite of herself, she stepped closer to examine it and realized the charm was a representation of a horse, caught with its legs outstretched in front and behind, as though suspended in midair.

"Truth be told," Douglas began as he removed the pendant from the box, "I had it commissioned just after the accident with Midnight. Meant it first as a gesture of apology, a reminder of the beauty of horses or something inane like that, but then I lost my nerve to give it to you. I've been carrying the thing around with me like a talisman for weeks." As he held the charm out to her, Abby saw it was affixed to a delicate gold chain, made up of unusual repeating links, resembling vines. She wanted to run her fingers over the links, twist the glittering horse in the light.

"It's grand," she nearly whispered in her regret, keeping her hands at her sides. "But I cannot accept it."

"Yes, you can," he countered. He walked behind her and placed the chain around her neck, brushing her hair to the side as he dexterously fastened the clasp. "It's been made specifically for you, so really it's incumbent upon you to accept it." He circled to the front of her, assessing the effect of the necklace. "The chain is new though. I had it switched out last week because I wanted to give you something especially strong that would surround you and symbolize my commitment. The goldsmith recommended this one. It's called a wheat chain, meant to be less vulnerable despite its slight appearance."

Abby ran the chain between her thumb and forefinger, as if to test the strength, wanting fiercely to trust Douglas's every word. "Your commitment surrounding me?" she asked.

"For as long as you'll have it."

"You mustn't tell anyone," she started, "about Matthew. Especially not my da. And you mustn't mention it to me again. Not ever."

"I will not betray you. Not on this, or anything else."

Abby looked at Douglas's piercing eyes, his straight nose, and angular chin. She saw her reflection in the dark centers of his pupils. And she believed him.

27

CHARLESTON, SOUTH CAROLINA
1846

*A*bby was battling with a bush of quince flowers in the back garden, huffing as she pulled at its stems, when she heard a greeting ring out behind her.

"Yoo hoo! Oh, no, what *are* you doing to that defenseless shrub?" Abby dropped the sprig she had been pulling at and turned with the garden shears poised between her teeth to see Gracie hovering at the entry to the garden.

She hastily removed the tool from her mouth, sorry to have been caught so inelegantly by her friend. "Gracie," Abby smiled sheepishly. "Thank goodness, come and help me. I am trying to fix a bouquet for Larissa, and I haven't any idea what I'm doing. I can't even dislodge the confounded blooms from the hedges."

"How lovely," Gracie placed the beaded purse she was holding on a stone bench beside her and approached Abby. "For what occasion?"

"No occasion. Just a gesture of thanks for all the time she has devoted to me. I have a tendency to be short with her, and I've been feeling poorly about it. I thought, a token of appreciation for all the hours, I don't know . . ." Abby trailed off as she began to recognize that something had shifted inside her since her lunch with Douglas the day before. She was feeling quite generous with her emotions, and she was suddenly embarrassed by her sentimentality.

"Well look at you," Gracie teased, her tone almost cutting, "turning into quite the genteel lady, more each day." She took the shears from Abby and deftly snipped at the flowers.

"Well while we work, we have much to discuss, don't we? I've been chomping at the bit to review the Montrose ball with you, but Mama's had me all tied up on her annual Cherries Luncheon." Gracie walked farther into the garden with a flippant shrug, dandling the blossoms on one bush then another as Abby followed. "This was the first I could get away." Gracie began clipping at small yellow flowers that Abby could not name. "How darling," she smiled hurriedly at the flowers, adding three blossoms to the bouquet, then pulling one back out and tossing it to the ground. "Mama chooses a different theme each time, though it's always based on cherries, because of the plantation's namesake."

"Gracie," Abby interrupted, concerned by Gracie's uncharacteristic bearing, her prattle and nonchalance. Reaching out for the growing jumble of flowers, she asked, "Is something disturbing you?"

"No, no," Gracie protested, looking away. "It's just, like I said, we have so much to discuss, you and I, starting with Harrison, continuing with the decor at the party. We have to review each of the ladies' dresses, and also their hair, and well, I'm so overwhelmed by all of the topics I don't know where to begin," she laughed stiffly. Abby figured she best resign herself to Gracie's blathering until the girl was ready to lift the lid on whatever was troubling her.

"Oh, by the by," Gracie turned to Abby with the shears raised between them, "I met Douglas on my way in, and he asked if you would visit him in his study. He said it was quite important and requested for you to go at once. I'm sorry I didn't mention it sooner, but all the other clutter in my mind prevented that bit from staying put."

"Oh," Abby turned toward the house and then looked back at Gracie, startled. It was unusual for Douglas to send for her like that, especially when he knew she had a visitor.

"I hope nothing is amiss. If you wouldn't mind waiting, I'll just run and see what the matter is." Abby started off in the direction of Douglas's study, dropping the bouquet carelessly beside Gracie's purse. She called over her shoulder, "I'll send Jasper with tea."

As Abby neared Douglas's study, she ran her hands over her rose-colored day dress, checking for stray bits of shrubbery that might have followed her indoors. She absentmindedly fingered the new charm around her neck as she wondered again what could be the urgency. Hopefully not a letter from Wigan bearing bad news.

As she reached the study, she heard muffled words followed by a woman's laughter. The door was partially open, and she peered tentatively inside, wondering if she should knock against the open door, or simply show herself in. Her questions were quickly forgotten as she was greeted by a display so unexpected that she struggled to make sense of what her eyes were seeing.

Douglas was standing with his back against his desk, and a woman was in his arms, her hair singing out behind her like a crimson invective. The woman, who could be none other than Cora Rae Cunningham, had her mouth pressed against Douglas's lips, and his hands were clutching her arms, as though he was unable to withdraw. As the meaning of the image before her began to crystalize, as she understood the scene to be a passionate embrace, Abby tasted crushing emptiness, and then loathing.

Suddenly, she was a torrent. "You worm!" she screamed, as he and Cora Rae broke apart and looked to her in the doorway. "You corrosive, vulgar, pretending bastard!" She couldn't look at them with their startled expressions, couldn't stand to think about what she was losing or how she had been duped.

"No, Abby," Douglas began advancing on her. She certainly wouldn't tarry to talk about any of it. Instead, she turned on her heel and ran. She barreled as fast as her feet could carry her back down the dark hallway, toward the foyer.

She heard Douglas calling from behind her, but she didn't break her stride. "Abby, Abby, come back!" He was screaming after her, but she didn't hesitate, just kept chasing the air.

She fumbled with the locks at the front door, yanked at the door, and ran straight into the Charleston evening. She felt her feet connect with the gravel drive, the scrape of pebbles sliding beneath her, then the cobblestones on Meeting Street. She held her skirts and kept running. She ran past carriages and ladies meandering homeward for their suppers, past palm trees and porches, past merchants and hope. It was as though the faster she ran, the better she could escape from her thoughts. All she heard was the pounding of her feet on the road, the sound of dirt and dust enshrouding her.

⟿

DOUGLAS RAN INTO THE HALLWAY AND GLIMPSED THE last swell of Abby's skirts disappearing from the front door. He wanted to scramble after her and explain, catch her and undo what she had seen, but he second-guessed himself and fought down his drive to go after her. Being hunted, pursued through the Charleston streets, that was not what Abby would want. How easily he had transformed into another villain in her life.

He would not exacerbate this moment by turning her into prey, tracked by a man she no longer trusted. He stepped out the door toward the drive, where not even a shadow of disturbance fluttered in the night, as though Abby had never been there at all.

"Damnation!" He cursed to himself and turned back from the door, leaving it open in desperate prayer. He tore back into his study, where he found Cora Rae waiting for him, perched on the side of his desk with a coy smile on her shimmering face.

"Good God, woman!" he shouted at her. "What is the matter with you?"

"Douglas, darling," Cora Rae rose and began to approach him.

"Have you no scruples?" Douglas demanded, and she halted at his words, her smile faltering. "To barge into my study uninvited and manhandle me like a common harlot? What were you about? What would your father say? No, don't answer. Just get out of here. Collect yourself and go." He stood against the study's open door with his arms crossed, waiting for her to leave.

"Douglas," Cora Rae nearly purred, "you can't mean that." She stalked towards him as she was speaking. "There's always been a special connection between us." She cocked her head to the side and began twirling a lock of her hair around her finger. "You can't deny you've felt it, too." She was now standing a hair's breath away from him, and she raised a hand as if to stroke his face. Douglas grabbed her wrist, hard, halting her palm midjourney.

"Don't," he seethed as he held her wrist in a vice grip. "There has never been anything between us. You had better hope, Cora Rae Cunningham, that I am able to undo the damage you have done here today." He shook his head, looking at her with revulsion. "You had better hope," he warned again. He dropped her wrist abruptly, as if he suddenly realized that he was holding something rancid.

"But Douglas," Cora Rae began, "don't you see, I did this for us. It's better she learns now that a girl like her has no future with a man of your stature. I've done everyone a favor. When I heard the click of her heels marching toward us, I had to seize this opportunity."

"You meant for her to see this farce?" Douglas demanded. "My life is not a game to be meddled with. Out!" He pointed toward the foyer and waited. He saw a flicker of genuine bewilderment cross Cora Rae's face. "Now!" he roared. Flinching, she stepped away and slowly made as if to exit the tense space, but not before turning back towards Douglas with a last coquettish glance. As she faded into the darkness of the hallway, he breathed in the silence of her departure and then wiped a hand aggressively across his mouth as if to rid himself of the memory of her, and wiped it again, unable to purify himself sufficiently for Abby. He turned and walked to the courtyard, where he planned to wait until she returned.

UNEASE, LIKE STRANGLING VINES, WRAPPED ITSELF around Douglas's limbs as he watched Jasper light the estate's outdoor torches. He had been waiting in the courtyard nearly two hours for Abby's return. The Herculean restraint he'd shown in not chasing her was dwindling fast, as the night sky seemed to grow perceptibly darker, more ominous, with his every breath.

Enough waiting. He needed to find her and explain that he had not betrayed her. He would tell her everything, that Cora Rae had appeared, uninvited, just as he'd returned home from the docks. She had been jabbering on to Douglas about meaningless drivel, when she suddenly advanced on him and pushed her unwelcome lips against his. When Abby looked into the study, Douglas had been trying to dislodge Cora Rae's mouth from his face. She had fought his physical rebuff so fervently that they were almost wrestling. He would have removed her more quickly if he hadn't been afraid of hurting her, and now he was sorry he'd tried to act the gentleman.

From Abby's perspective, Douglas and her uncle Matthew were probably equivalents now, correlative scoundrels. The only difference between them was that Douglas hadn't yet robbed her of any physical dignity, save for a few kisses. He couldn't stand the thought of her, wherever she was, detesting him because she saw what looked like deceit, fraud.

Surely she knew better than to stay out alone past nightfall. He resolved to find Demmet. They would arrange a search party to ferret her out of the darkness and bring her home. He already knew what Demett would say. "She ain't gone like it," he'd warn. "If she need some cooling off time, I don't think she'll want us wresting her back here." Well, she could cool off during the goddamn daylight hours, Douglas growled to himself as he hustled toward the stable.

───℮

NINETEEN HOURS LATER, DOUGLAS STOOD AT THE wharf, dusty and drained, staring out to the harbor in frustration as the tall stevedore beside him persisted in denials.

"I'm telling you, I ain't seen any such a lass." All the sailors were saying the same. No one matching Abby's description had been seen at the docks. He felt like strangling himself for not considering earlier the possibility that Abby might have gone to the docks directly. Of course she might have tested the idea of returning to her own family.

Douglas had been searching ceaselessly since the night before, and now he forced his eyes wider in an effort to fight the growing fatigue that came from hours of scraping the Charleston streets, and from the dawning realization he might never find her. He figured she wouldn't have had money with her to pay for passage on a ship. But, one of his own ships had set out that very morning for Liverpool, stocked with indigo and rice. His mind shot back to the day Abby met Walt and the other stevedores in the shipping office. They'd have known her, been eager even to oblige Douglas's houseguest with an accommodation. She could have claimed a family emergency, or anything really, said that Douglas sent her to join the voyage, and they would have lowered the gangplank for her with little question.

It was easy enough for a woman to blend in during the early morning bustle at the wharf, Douglas reasoned. It was not so extraordinary that few remembered seeing her, especially if she wrapped a shawl around her luminous hair and kept her soulful eyes on the ground.

"Actually, now, maybe I did see a girl like that," the long-shoreman interrupted Douglas's thoughts, the man's eyes narrowing with the effort of concentration. "I can't be certain, now, but there might have been a one, getting on the vessel with the indigo, your vessel. Had I known it to be important, I'd have paid more heed."

Douglas considered the stevedore's recollection. He was desperate for a direction in which to chase, and this was the nearest he had come to finding a lead.

He shuddered when he thought of her returning to Matthew Milton, and he prayed her rage would keep her strong. The journey across the Atlantic could last as long as two months.

Douglas had learned earlier that a second ship, a steamship, left for England that morning, bound for Bristol. If Abby was spotted near his vessel but not aboard the craft, it was equally possible that she had gotten herself aboard that steamship, as a stowaway even. If she had boarded the ship to Bristol, she would need to complete a second crossing from Bristol to Liverpool, likely by boat, as well.

He turned back to the muddled man beside him, noting for the first time that the fellow had a wooden leg.

"Tell me, which other ships are heading to England today?"

"Nothing else today, sir. It's well past noon already." The man seemed to regard Douglas with a new skepticism.

Right. A ship wouldn't begin a transatlantic journey so late in the day, of course. Desperation was making him daft.

"Well, tomorrow. What leaves tomorrow?"

The stevedore looked about the boats moored below them and then nodded to himself. "Nothing, sir. Until Friday, but then that one, there," he pointed his arm down to the far end of the wharf. "The packet ship. Just saw them working the cargo."

Fine. Splendid. He was not above traveling with the mails and cargo if it meant getting himself to Abby. Douglas recognized the ship as part of Oscar Whittaker's fleet. Surely Whittaker would wonder why a man with several ships of his own would pay good money to ride aboard someone else's craft. To prepare one of his own vessels for a journey across the Atlantic might take weeks, and Douglas did not feel the luxury of time in pursuing Abby.

If it was Wigan Abby was bound for, Douglas would be right on her heels.

28

MANCHESTER, ENGLAND
MAY 1846

The six-hour carriage ride from Liverpool had felt almost more exhausting than the several weeks spent crossing the sea. The driver repeatedly suggested taking a reprieve for the night at one of the inns they passed, but Douglas wouldn't have it. So close he was now to finding Abby that his blood was swirling, thwarting his efforts to remain composed. The driver let him off at the edge of the village, the roads being too narrow or knobby for the hansom to maneuver through. Trudging now up another hill towards the tenements, Douglas saw candlelight glowing through small windows from homes that seemed to be strewn together in a great heap, one after another, with no regard for air or movement, and he imagined workers settling down for supper after long hours in the mills. As he hurried over the paving stones, he checked the path beneath him, carefully avoiding trickles of sewage that rushed down the hills as fast as he was racing up.

Throughout his journey aboard Whittaker's overstocked ship, Douglas had repeatedly suppressed the urge to cut at something with a rigging knife, to abuse any object in striking distance as retribution for his blunders. He should have revealed himself to Abby sooner, so she'd have had more time to build trust in him before Miss Cunningham's stunt. Or he should have pushed at Cora Rae harder, with greater speed and clarity. At the very least, he should have run after Abby from the start, chased her into the street and begged her to listen. When he imagined what she must have perceived from the study doorway, with Cora Rae fastened to him like a barnacle, it was as though he was choking on air.

Douglas removed the paper from his breast pocket and checked the address again. Flat number fifty-seven. Despite his knowledge of the Miltons' limited finances, he had never imagined them in the kind of squalor he was now navigating. Finally his eyes settled on the number fifty-seven, painted in black against the door with broad, haphazard strokes. He pounded on the door, letting up slightly when he noticed its frail attachment to its hinges.

A young boy in brown trousers and faded shirtsleeves opened the door and looked at Douglas blankly.

"Well, hello, young man." Douglas smiled down at the boy, noticing that his hair was the same chestnut as Abby's. "You must be Charlie."

"Charlie," Douglas heard a woman call from within. "Charlie, who's there?"

"Ruthie Milton, is that you?" Douglas called back.

Ruth appeared behind Charlie with a handkerchief tied over her hair and a soiled rag in hand. When she saw Douglas, she started.

"Douglas Elling! My God, what's happened?" She grabbed hold of Charlie's shoulder. "Is she sick? Dead? Please God, tell me she isn't dead?"

"She isn't here then?" Douglas asked, not entirely surprised. He must have beaten her to Wigan after all.

276 | JACQUELINE FRIEDLAND

"Here?" Ruth looked confused. "No, why would she be here? She is supposed to be with you. Off in the land named after the merry King Charles. What the devil is going on?"

"Not to worry. I believe I've simply arrived before her," Douglas told Ruth, as he immediately resumed calculating in his head, running the same scenarios he'd been repeating to himself throughout his journey, trying to determine when Abby would land in Wigan. "She is in the midst of her own journey back to Wigan, I think, and I was hoping to meet her here. My ship seems to have traveled at a faster clip." Ruthie's features remained strained, and Douglas continued, "It's all been an enormous misunderstanding, I'm afraid, and I followed her here to set things right." After glancing down at his hands for a moment, Douglas added, "I suppose I should confess at the outset, I am in love with your daughter."

The furrow in Ruth's brow deepened, but she did not respond. Douglas had known Ruth before he settled in the States. In her youth, she had been a fetching woman, with her smooth skin and teasing quips. Though now she appeared muted and spent. Ruth was only nine years his senior, but her hair was graying at the temples, and the soft lines around her eyes were emphasized too drastically by dark shadows beneath them.

"Well I guess you'd better come in then." She opened the door wider and stepped aside to let him pass.

Douglas entered the flat and felt immediately too large to remain in the cramped space, with its low ceiling and clinging walls. Other than the straw pallet on the floor, the room held a small table and dining chairs, and Douglas stood awkwardly, unsure how to maneuver in this limited area. He glanced again at the table, noticing that someone had begun to lay the table with mismatched dishes for supper.

Ruth, likewise, was studying Douglas and likely forming her

own opinions based on his shining shoes and meticulously stitched coat.

"Oh heavens," Ruth pulled out a chair from the table and motioned for Douglas to sit. "What you must think of this place. You see now why Sammy wrote to you for help. We work our hardest, we do, but it just doesn't provide for more than this, with the debts and all."

"Ruth, please do not make apologies," Douglas answered as he glanced at the chair, wondering how long he would linger. "It is I who must apologize, first and foremost for arriving so close to suppertime. I was just, I didn't want to waste a moment," he finished on a heavy breath.

"Let me pour you a spot of tea," Ruth responded breezily, as though he were visiting her at an idyllic countryside cottage, as if she weren't besieged by chores to be handled before her family could settle in for the night. "You must be exhausted from your journey. Once you've been refreshed, you must start at the beginning and tell me everything. We'll make this right yet."

"No, please," Douglas stepped toward the door as Ruth bustled to the stove. "I mustn't intrude, and you've got the others returning soon, I'm sure."

"Nonsense." Ruth placed a tarnished kettle on the fire. "You think Abby's stubborn, do you? Well, I won't have you traveling so far only to be turned out without so much as a cuppa. Won't have it." She raised an eyebrow, daring him to challenge her and then opened a small cupboard to reach for something.

While Douglas sipped his tea, he confessed to Ruth. He thought to lay himself bare, as if forgiveness from Abby's mother might apply a temporary salve to his wounded soul. As the story spilled forth from his lips, unravelling like a spool of fabric, gaining momentum with each snippet he told, he could feel himself rushing to the good parts, toward the splendor of what he and Abby had begun to build together. He hurried through the details of argument and neglect, the accident with the steed, charging instead toward the *Twelfth Night*, the Montrose ball.

"My girl, at a real ball for the first time!" Ruth beamed, momentarily distracted from worry.

"Actually, it was her second," Douglas corrected with a grin. "She attended another friend's coming-out ball a few months earlier."

"Well, what a little sophisticate!" Ruth laughed. "Sending her your way sounds like it was just the thing then. She's been growing into the young lady she was meant to be."

"Well, she was," Douglas allowed regretfully, "until a few weeks ago."

When he reached the part about Cora Rae accosting him, Ruth nodded emphatically.

"No, she wouldn't like walking in on that. She'd never stand for that, my Abby. I see then." Ruth clicked her tongue and brought the empty teacup to the counter.

"She ran straight out of the house and never returned," Douglas huffed, a percussive lament still thumping in his chest. "We searched the streets of Charleston to no avail, the rooming houses, parks, everywhere. I finally thought to check the port and found that two ships bound for England sailed from Charleston shortly after she left, one of which may have included a young lady matching her description. I was aboard the very next vessel. She must have secured passage on the ship headed to Bristol. It could be two or three more weeks before she reaches us here." Douglas rubbed his hand over his weary eyes. "When I think of her spending so many more days under the impression that I was disloyal to her, I want to claw at the walls."

"You poor, foolish dear," Ruth told him, her dark eyes tilted with sympathy. "You'll stay here with us and wait until she returns. It isn't anything for us to make space."

She spoke imperiously, but as Douglas looked around the two-room flat, it was clear the Miltons could not accommodate him. From what he could tell, there were only two beds for the entire family.

"No, I couldn't," Douglas told her. When Ruth looked like she might protest, he added, "It wouldn't be proper, with Gwendolyn sleeping so nearby. I will find lodging in town."

Ruth gasped with a new idea, "I've a better plan. You'll stay with Sammy's brother. They've plenty of room there, and it's not far a'tall. You remember Matthew, don't you?"

"No, really, no!" Douglas realized he had spoken too forcefully in response to Ruth's impossible suggestion. "What I mean to say is that I wouldn't impose." Douglas was amazed that he located sufficient restraint to answer politely. "I much prefer to have my own space than bunk up with people I hardly know anymore. I would be most comfortable finding public lodging, if you could just recommend somewhere."

Ruth sighed. "If that is really how you'll be most comfortable. There is a suitable inn just by Matty and Bianca's. I do the washing there. I'll at least be able to check in on you should you be needing anything. I can send Matty and Bianca to say hello, too."

"Wonderful," Douglas answered, struggling to keep the sarcasm from his voice.

"Now, you mustn't go anywhere until my Sammy gets back and gets a good look at you," Ruth smiled. "I'm sure he'll be wanting to hear the tale of you and our Abby all over again."

DOUGLAS TIPPED THE WOOL CAP TOWARD HIS FACE TO shield his eyes from the prickling mist. As he navigated the uneven paving stones, now slick with rain, he halfheartedly cursed the damp English weather. He was heading to the Upperton Mill to await the end of Samuel's shift, as he had done for each of the last nineteen days, searching for news of Abby.

After nearly three weeks of waiting, Douglas was losing hope that Abby had chosen to return home to her parents. If he had been less desperate to find her, less frenzied, he might have considered earlier how much she detested Wigan. He had latched too easily onto the longshoreman's account of a young woman spotted near an eastbound craft, too desperate for a clue. He would not tarry much longer. If she did not appear in one week's time, he would return to Charleston and start searching anew.

And good riddance to Wigan it would be. It was no wonder Abby had complained of the place so bitterly. From the decaying homes that created a raging stink throughout the city to the pervasiveness of soot from the factories, it was astonishing anyone stayed in the place. One could hardly travel to market without being confronted by disfigured mill workers, children missing more limbs than teeth. The gentry who lived in wealth nearby were complicit, if not responsible for the harsh conditions. Douglas was disgusted by all of it.

He was particularly appalled by Matthew Milton. Matthew had rushed to see him at the inn two weeks earlier, on Douglas's second day in town. Abby's uncle had learned of Douglas's visit from Samuel and had arrived at the rooming house as a presumptive host, come to welcome the traveler to Wigan, but it was apparent within minutes that the man had another agenda.

When he had heard the rapping on the door that evening, Douglas's first thought was that Ruth or Sammy might be coming to tell him Abby had arrived.

Yanking open the door, he found neither Abby nor her parents, but an older, bulkier version of the Matthew Milton he'd known years earlier. Douglas's hands had tightened instantly to fists, ready to strike, avenge, but instead he forced a half smile onto his face.

"Matthew Milton," he spoke tightly, "I expected we might rattle into each other at some point."

Matthew seemed to take this as an invitation, handing Douglas one of two parcels he held as he walked past him into the rented suite.

"Biscuits," he said, motioning to the package. "Bianca was all in a tither that we should send you a hearty welcome, a bit dazzled she is by having a visitor from the Colonies and all."

"It's hardly called the Colonies, anymore," Douglas began, but he was cut off by Matthew's next presentation.

"I fancied this a better offering." Matthew emitted a small sound of triumph as he unwrapped a bottle of dark scotch from the other paper bundle he held. "Thought we could enjoy it together while we compared notes on business." He lowered himself into a velvet armchair, the fabric hissing beneath him.

Douglas stood above Matthew, noticing the layers of fat on his neck, the coarse, uneven hairs of his beard, the bulky gold rings on three of his fingers. He wore a dense wool coat of obvious value, which he was now unbuttoning lazily with his thick hands. Thinking about those hands on Abby's body, pushing at her, grabbing, he swallowed twice and still could not squelch the bile rising in his throat.

"Forgive me for refusing the drink," Douglas leaned against the wall, "unfortunately, the taste of acid is ripe on my tongue tonight."

"Pity," Matthew quipped carelessly. "I suppose it makes sense if I keep the scotch then." He chuckled as he laid the bottle atop the coat he had tossed onto the chair beside him.

"Still, might as well catch up. I hear you're quite a shipping man now," Matthew patted his belly.

"That's right," Douglas answered, pressing his lips together.

"I too spend much of my time on sea voyages," Matthew announced, reaching into his pocket for a cigar.

"Is that right?" Douglas asked, glancing at the bronze table clock behind Matthew and wondering how long the man intended to prolong this visit.

"Indeed," Matthew continued, holding a match to the cigar. He puffed at it twice. "You don't mind, yes?" He didn't await a response before continuing. "See years ago, when Sammy and I were each starting our shops, he seemed to equate conducting business with doing favors for friends, lending them pieces on credit and such. Of course, half those never paid up, and as you can see from the hovel they inhabit, it didn't work out well. I, on the other hand," Matthew paused for another pull on the cigar, "I figured out how to get an edge as a merchant, if you know what I'm saying." Matthew raised his eyebrows at Douglas.

"Well, we all do our best to succeed," Douglas offered.

"Even when it might cost us? Might be unpopular in certain circles?" Matthew asked, his voice taking on a new clipped quality.

"I suppose," Douglas answered impatiently. He crossed his arms against his chest, willing himself to remain composed for Abby's sake, bristling further as the pungent cigar smoke made its way across the room.

"I'm glad you see it that way," Matthew scratched his chin. "I knew that a fellow as well-off as yourself must make wise decisions," he continued, his voice dripping with false flattery. "Perhaps you'd like a stake in my next expedition," Matthew offered. "Most recently, I've been to Guinea and the Ivory Coast, collecting exotic specimens for my buyers."

At the mention of African areas known to be hotbeds of

illegal slave trafficking, Douglas's interest perked up. Just what kind of trade was Matthew involved in, exactly?

"I'm not sure I know what you mean by specimens," Douglas attempted to sound only marginally curious and began pacing casually across the faded carpet beneath him. "Are these items that you sell at your shop? Inventory for your customers?"

"Ah, yes, well I do bring uncommon pieces that fetch high prices at the shop, that's true. But I think you know what other specimens I was referencing." Matthew winked. "Come now, I couldn't have made *all* my money from selling armoires and African knickknacks, could I?"

Douglas stared silently at Matthew as he processed what the man was saying. Was this reprobate admitting, no, bragging, that he was involved in illegal slave trading? In addition to the unspeakable ways he had used his own niece, now this! Douglas's every muscle began to burn with rage. He wanted to tear into the man and pull him apart bone by bone, but instead he clenched his jaw and forced himself to remain self-possessed. He would risk too much if he let his anger take control. Matthew Milton had a bigger debt to pay than would be satisfied by injuries from fisticuffs alone. This bastard needed something profoundly more devastating than a broken nose and a bit of internal bleeding.

"This is something you just share with people? No fear I'd double-cross you and report you to the authorities? Why so confident in a person you haven't seen in years?" Douglas asked.

"Please," Matthew waved his hand dismissively. "You'd be surprised by the ubiquitous nature of the trade that continues. What would they do—perhaps slap me on the wrist. It's worth it for the profane quantities of money. The authorities simply turn a blind eye. Why forego an immense opportunity for profit? You understand."

"I see," Douglas answered slowly. "Tell me, why share this

information with me, specifically? What have I got to do with any of it?"

The fog of Douglas's rage was clearing just enough that he was beginning to realize the enormity of this opportunity, the chance to collect information from a confirmed Blackbirder and relay it to abolitionists. Learning about the illegal slave trade from someone on the inside would be invaluable to the mission. If he played his cards to the aces, he could also use the information to ruin Matthew, permanently, and let him suffer justly for all the hurt he caused.

"Ah, but you see, you do," Matthew answered with glee, standing as his excitement mounted. "As I said, I often have investors. I understand from my brother that you have quite a fleet of ships at your disposal, and funds, funds are essential to our success. It would be advantageous for me to establish a stronghold in Charleston, a gateway to the continent. I haven't any contacts in the Carolinas, and it's an opportunity fairly begging to be exploited."

Douglas agreed that Matthew must certainly not have contacts in Charleston. Otherwise he would have known that Douglas Elling was once a suspected abolitionist, the last person to whom he should be revealing himself.

"You could join me on an upcoming journey I am planning. Just a bit of investing is needed. I'm sure our costs will seem negligible compared to what you encounter regularly in Charleston. Depending on your level of commitment, I might even have you organize your own mission after that." Matthew nodded enthusiastically, apparently delighted by his own largesse.

Douglas hesitated, wishing he'd had time to prepare for this meeting. The more he learned from Matthew, the better equipped the abolitionists would be to combat these Blackbirders going forward. If he did nothing, hundreds of men and women would be snapped up from some African shore, bound for a life of slavery and disaster. There was nothing to consider or deliberate. He could not stand motionless.

"You've certainly given me something to think about," he finally told Matthew. "When, pray tell, are you planning your next excursion?"

"February, I think." Matthew's bravado faltered for just a moment before he livened back up. "I suppose you would need to devise a reason to linger in England until then. Unless you still fancy running about in search of my niece. I must say, it seems you've already taken too much trouble for a trifling scrap like Abigail. Plenty of other destitute wenches out there with physical assets to match."

"If you're interested in doing business together," Douglas uttered through clenched teeth, forcing himself to rein in the violence of his reaction to Matthew's words, "you'll not speak to me of your niece."

Matthew blinked once and then cleared his throat. "Of course," he stammered.

"We understand each other," Douglas said levelly, forcing his mind back to its calculations. "I will likely be required to return to Charleston shortly," he told Matthew, as though he was thinking aloud. "With so many months until your voyage, I believe I could return to Liverpool in time to make your departure date. Perhaps you might provide more specifics, and I could reach a definite decision."

"Lovely," Matthew's lips spread thin in a satisfied smile. "Meet me at the shop at the close of business tomorrow, and we will review the details. Come around back."

"Indeed," Douglas responded, relaxing a fraction now that he could see Matthew was readying to leave.

Matthew donned his coat and reached for the bottle of scotch.

"Leave the scotch," Douglas told him. "Every now and then I do like to have a drink by myself."

Matthew likely saw no more need for gifts after their apparent agreement. But nothing was yet finalized. As he looked from the bottle back to Douglas, Matthew seemed to reach the conclusion that the bottle must be left behind.

He nodded solemnly. "Enjoy it."

It wasn't five minutes later that Douglas sent Matthew's bottle of scotch whiskey flying into the boarding room wall, shards of his own disgust exploding all around him.

And now here he was, waiting in the slow evening drizzle to meet Sammy outside the Upperton Mill. He would ask again if Abby had returned to her parents' home today, and if not, whether they'd had any news. He knew already what the answers would be. Abby was surely going to stay as far as possible from her uncle, and so was he. Just as soon as he ensured the man's destruction.

29

STOCKBRIDGE, MASSACHUSETTS
MAY 1846

"Eleanor," Abby called across the stark schoolroom, "please come back to your seat. Mary would like to apologize for knocking into your satchel."

"But she did it on purpose, Miss," the seven-year-old pouted at Abby, her blue eyes wide with distress.

"Did not!" Mary snapped from beside Abby.

"Did too!" Eleanor shot back with a grimace.

"Come now," Abby answered, walking to Eleanor and placing her arm around the girl's delicate shoulders. "There is nothing productive about shouting back and forth. Even if Mary did knock about your things intentionally, she is ready to apologize. And you remember what we learned during our prayers on Sunday, don't you," she prodded.

Eleanor nodded contritely, as Abby crouched down to put herself on eye level with the girl and softly recounted, "Christians must always be prepared to accept an apology with gentleness and respect. Are you ready to do that?"

"Yes, Miss," Eleanor answered dutifully.

After Mary's successful apology, the girls sat side by side

again, working on their arithmetic exercises and giggling inter-
mittently. Abby returned to her desk to organize lessons for the
week, but she was interrupted again, this time, by Margaret Parsons, headmistress of the school.

"What a delight to have an arbiter as competent as you,
Abby," the matronly Miss Parsons smiled down at her. "I hope
you don't mind. I was watching from the hallway. The way you
handled Eleanor and Mary is but one of the many triumphs I've
witnessed from you since your arrival with us at Hadley."

"Thank you, Miss Parsons," Abby answered, unnerved by
the compliments.

The headmistress pulled a student chair over to Abby's desk
and continued speaking as she sat her large frame onto the
chair. "I still can't imagine our good fortune in finding an ad-
junct as competent as you." Margaret smoothed her gray skirt as
she assured Abby, "We will be so pleased to offer you a permanent position just as soon as something opens. If you ask me,"
she lowered her voice and leaned toward Abby, "I think Edna
Handler's days with us are numbered. She must be near sixty
years old, and she's first to admit that she'd be happier planting
lupines alongside her cottage than chasing children."

"Oh, Miss Handler has been lovely to me," Abby answered,
almost defensively, remembering how it had been Edna Handler
who opened the door for her the day of her arrival, ushering
her into the dining hall for tea before asking any questions. "But
you know I would jump at the chance to fill any permanent
role."

"Yes." Miss Parsons's shoulders dropped for a moment, and
Abby reflected that the woman looked to be near the same age
as the soon-to-retire Miss Handler. "I do wish you would tell us
what happened to send you here, but I understand if you are
still not ready." She looked searchingly at Abby. "You're certain

there is no one you would like us to contact?" She asked hesitantly, "Perhaps you'd let someone know where you are?"

"I told you," Abby answered tightly, struggling to remain respectful and then noticing that the chatter throughout the room had grown to a new level. "Myra, Ettie, girls, please," she reproached the room as a whole. She turned back to Miss Parsons before continuing more quietly. "I had been studying with a governess down South, when my patron's house was set ablaze by ruffians. There are none left for me to contact, as there were no survivors," Abby lied, twisting Douglas's family history to fit her purpose.

"Very well," Miss Parsons offered an exaggerated sigh, as if Abby's desire for privacy was the great tragedy of the woman's existence, "if that's the story you want to hold to." She stood and adjusted Abby's shawl on her shoulders in a tender gesture. "Incidentally," she added, "my nephew Neil will be calling for tea this afternoon. Won't you join us? I do believe he might be just the ticket to cheer you up."

"Thank you, but no. I still have to get through my preparation for tomorrow. Another time." How she wished Miss Parsons would stop trying to foist this Neil upon her, carrying on all the time about how handsome he was. Abby couldn't even bear to consider it.

"Very well. If you change your mind, we'll be in the back library past five," she spun out through the doorway, her long salt-and-pepper braid trailing behind like a separate entity.

Watching her wayward braid, Abby reflected that the woman could have been quite fetching if she simply tended a bit more to herself. The grave style reminded her so much of Larissa, who must have adopted her own austere habits during her time teaching at Hadley. Abby's heart sank at the memory of Larissa. She knew she had done her governess great disservice by disappearing without so much as a goodbye or thank you. Most likely, she would never see Larissa again and so would never be able to explain or apologize. Several times Abby had been tempted to send Larissa an explanatory letter, but then she always thought the better of it, lest her actions reveal her place of hiding. Besides, let Douglas explain it instead of her, come clean and confess his fiendishness to Larissa.

Abby felt a stinging behind her eyes. She rose to add more wood to the classroom's stove, suddenly quite chilled despite the mild April day. She would not weep. Not anymore. She shook her head in disbelief that she had actually considered Douglas an honorable man. She had opened her heart and believed all the thrilling compliments he'd bestowed upon her, as though each one had been fashioned especially for her. Every time she thought of that cob roller, she yearned to strike something. Douglas had been toying with her all along. It could not have been more than eighteen hours after his declarations of devotion that she found Cora Rae ablaze in his arms.

Abby walked to the front of the room and began erasing the equations she'd written earlier in the day. When the girls were finished figuring, they would move on to the day's spelling lesson. As chalk dust floated around her, she chided herself that she must work harder to push Douglas from her mind. She was at Hadley now, and she had a future ahead of her at this school. Thanks to Larissa's instruction and the schooling Abby had as a younger child, the headmistress had been readily impressed by Abby's academic knowledge.

Abby found a modicum of relief surrounding herself with the young girls at the school, whom she knew were free of guile or cunning. Like her brother, Charlie, they said what they felt, and their emotional displays could be trusted, relied upon to mean what they seemed to show. Here, she was respected, and she was confident that over time, her position at Hadley would begin to fulfill her entirely. She would need nothing else, she told herself, in order to feel satisfied with her life. Least of all, Douglas Elling.

30

∾

CHARLESTON, SOUTH CAROLINA
JULY 1846

Douglas pulled his mare to a halt beside the Cunninghams' porch and hastily jumped to the ground. Ever since leaving Wigan, he had the perpetual sensation that he was pushing his way through a crowd of people, as though there was constantly someone standing in his way. He bounded toward the door, his fist raised to grab the knocker, even as he was still climbing the steps of the porch.

A boy in a crisp white jacket and black trousers, a young house slave, opened the door. "Good afternoon, sir. Could I help you?"

"Yes, I'm here to see Miss Cunningham, if you please. With my apologies to her for calling without proper forenotice." Douglas cleared his throat, frustrated by the delay. He'd have preferred to barrel into the foyer and shout straight up the stairs.

"One moment, please. If you wouldn't mind just waiting here, I know they weren't expecting nobody."

"It's fine, Jonah," rang the voice of Cora Rae, as she emerged gracefully from a room adjacent to the foyer. "I will help Mr.

Elling." She did not bother to look at the slave, who glanced back at Douglas and then retreated, disappearing down a long hallway.

"Douglas," her voice seemed to rise an octave as a satisfied smile overtook her face, "what an unexpected pleasure." She continued walking closer to him.

"Don't." Douglas seethed the cold command. "I am looking for your sister."

"Well, I see you've forgotten your gentlemanly manners." She exaggerated her drawl as she continued, "I don't know how the upper class behave in Britain, but if this is representative, I don't care to find out. Don't forget you're back in Charleston now, where there are certain expectations." She glanced over her shoulder and then stepped closer to him, lowering her voice. "If you would accept my apology for behaving rashly at our last meeting, I think you might see I have more to offer than just social instruction."

"Go," Douglas demanded, "and fetch your sister," he spoke slowly, deliberately in order to control himself, "or I shall be forced to disclose to this entire household what kind of a Southern lady you really are."

"Well, I never . . ." Cora Rae gasped, stepping back as though he had shoved her.

"Get Gracie!" Douglas growled, losing the little patience he had tried to exercise.

Cora Rae blinked twice and then scurried away.

Douglas wandered over to the arched window in the foyer and stared out to the street that was just visible through the trees adorning the Cunninghams' drive. Carriages were passing, as well as people on foot, conducting the business of the day. It seemed impossible to Douglas that life could carry on for these people, all the functioning occurring habitually as always, when

Douglas's entire world had flipped. It was over four months now since he had lost Abby, and the ache was only spreading. He rubbed the heel of his hand over his eyebrows, trying to push back the worry, to focus on finding her.

At the sound of footsteps against the marble floor behind him, Douglas turned to see Gracie approaching. She was wearing a silk dress of deep blue, contrasting with her pale face and leading it to appear even whiter than usual.

"Douglas," Gracie began, "please come to the parlor. I'll have one of the house girls bring sweet tea."

"Thank you, Gracie, but I am in quite a hurry. I know it must rattle your sensibilities to entertain a visitor only in your entryway, but I would greatly appreciate it if we could speak right here, and do it quickly."

"Certainly," Gracie answered as she brushed at a stray strand of her dark hair. "Has there been any word?" she asked, her concern apparent.

"No, nothing," Douglas's answer was laced with exasperation, and he saw a look of guilt flash across Gracie's face.

"You know something," he snapped, stepping toward her. "Has she contacted you?"

"No, no, I haven't had a word from Abby. Not so much as a scribble," Gracie protested, shaking her head.

"Then why do you look as though you've been caught with your hand in the collection basket?" Douglas noticed she was wearing a silver promise ring on one of her dainty fingers, but the strained grin on her face wasn't euphoria or giddiness; it was guilt.

"I'm sure I haven't the faintest idea what you mean," Gracie argued, the pitch of her voice rising.

"Come now," Douglas warned. "If you are withholding information about Abby's whereabouts and she is hurt, even so much as a scratch, so help you God, you'll rue this day." He realized he was shaking a finger in her face.

"No, no," Gracie stammered, "I promise I haven't heard from Abby. Cross my heart and hope to die," she made an X on her chest with her finger. "It's . . ." Gracie looked over her shoulder in the direction Cora Rae had gone, "it's something else."

"Now is the time, Gracie," Douglas struggled not to shout. "Out with it."

Gracie looked around the grand vestibule before speaking.

"Rae planned it. She wanted to be caught in an embrace with you so Abby would renounce you and leave you available for the taking. I helped arrange for Abby to look through your study door at just the right moment." Gracie looked up at him helplessly, as though he could absolve her.

Douglas was aghast that Abby's friend could have been so cruel, yet another person in Abby's life who had let her down.

"Please don't look at me like I am wicked," Gracie pleaded. "Rae bullied me into it," Gracie sniffed and pulled a handkerchief from the pocket of her dress. "She threatened to steal Harrison if she couldn't have you." Tears were falling from Gracie's wide round eyes. "Had I known it would go this far, that she'd run away after she saw y'all, I never would have gone along. And now," Gracie gulped as she swiped at her eyes with the cloth, "Abby could be anywhere, and it's all my fault."

"You *should* be ashamed of your behavior, Gracie Cunningham," Douglas chided, "not only for treating your friend as a bargaining chip, but for having so little regard for yourself. If Blount is smitten with you, it should take more than someone else's manipulations to remove his affections." He gently pushed her chin up with his fingers so their eyes met. "Gracie, you must have more faith in yourself. You are a lovely young woman. Now stop wasting time with self-pity and start thinking about where

Abby might have gone. Deservedly or not, you were her closest friend in Charleston. She must have said something, anything that you would remember, that might give us a clue as to where she's got to. Think, Gracie!"

"I'm sorry," she dabbed at her eyes again, "you know Abby, she kept mostly quiet about herself, unless it was to give her opinion. Those she had aplenty. I just . . ." She seemed to be sorting through her mind for anything relevant, "I just don't know anything about where she'd have gone."

Douglas reached the conclusion that he was wasting precious time. Even if Abby would have said anything consequential to Gracie, the girl was clearly so wrapped up in her own tribulations that nothing made an impression. He could not squander any more daylight waiting for Gracie to think of something. He had to keep moving, moving until his eyes were back on Abby, until she was meeting his gaze, hearing the ceaseless plea streaming forth from his lips. He pivoted away from Gracie and charged back out the front door, calling over his shoulder as he raced away, "If anything comes to mind, send word at once."

DOUGLAS PACED THE LENGTH OF HIS STUDY, WEARING a path along the burgundy carpet. It seemed all he did these days was pace. He had been back in Charleston nearly three full days, and he was no closer to finding her than when he'd set out for Wigan months earlier. He winced as he thought of Samuel and Ruthie, so foolish to have relied upon him to shelter their daughter. They seemed to trust him still, that he would find Abby and continue to provide her appropriate refuge. He shook his head at their puzzling supply of faith in him.

"I've been everywhere, and there is just no sign of her," Douglas complained to Larissa, positioning a chair for her in his study and then dropping into the seat behind his desk. "The churches, rooming houses, the port again, it's all turned up a fat lot of nothing. Perhaps I should start traveling farther, Summerville or Georgetown, begin searching those towns." Douglas looked helplessly toward the ceiling in thought. "But what, I just pick towns and villages at random? There has to be a better way."

"Take heart," Larissa attempted to comfort Douglas as she walked past the chair he'd adjusted for her and began opening the draperies in the dark study. "If she has not returned to her family, she mustn't have gone all that far from us. She left with no money, and she's too full of pride to be begging her way through the States." Larissa's pale eyes narrowed as she seemed to parse silently through possibilities.

True, Douglas thought to himself as he watched the dust motes from the moving curtains dance in the slivers of sunlight arriving from the bared windows. Abby had run out of his house in such haste that she left with nothing. He thought wistfully about the pink dress she had been wearing when he last saw her, the color falling somewhere between a plum and an apricot. How superbly it had played off her fair complexion. Abby's appearance had been all the more radiant with the glimmering diamonds in the necklace Douglas had given her only the day before.

"The necklace!" Douglas exclaimed, nearly exploding from his seat.

Larissa looked up, surprised by his sudden exuberance. "Pardon me?" She asked, putting a hand to her own bare neck.

"The necklace I gave Abby!" he fairly shouted. "She was wearing it. She could have sold it to pay for a journey out of

Charleston!" He pounded his fist on his desk in a gesture of be-wilderment. "Why did I not think of this before? Where would she have traveled with that money?" Thoughts began racing through his mind like a vortex of revitalized hope. "It was a valuable piece. She could have gone anywhere from Columbia County to Augusta, Maine." His mind was swiftly assaulted by a deluge of possibilities. "Where could she have sold it? That's what we need to discover first. If we can figure out where she obtained the money for her travels . . ." He trailed off and then looked at Larissa expectantly. "Where do you think she might have sold the piece?"

Larissa pursed her lips, her eyes scanning back and forth as she considered the question. "There is a pawn shop on Cumber-land Street. I believe we passed by when Abby and I went to Marseille's shop for her ball gown," she proffered. "If you make haste, you might get there before he departs at the close of busi-ness."

AS DEMETT DROVE THE CARRIAGE TOWARD THE FRENCH shops downtown, Douglas pulled his watch from his coat again, flicking the cover open with an impatient tap. Every minute without her was a maelstrom, more time she would be living under false information. He felt like he was trapped under a fallen chariot, unable to breathe. He had only just begun to understand the weight of his feelings for her, had barely a moment to digest them before she disappeared, and now in her absence, his world had become airless, impossible. It amazed him that in their months apart, his feelings for her had grown only stronger as he was forced to confront all he might have lost. His fingers twitched in his anxiousness to reach the pawn shop before closing.

He returned the watch to his breast pocket and noticed the crinkling of paper. Reaching deeper, he pulled out the unopened letter from John Colby. He did not remember even picking it up, but he must have done, and placed it in his pocket in his frenzy to leave the house. Douglas had contacted Colby, his former SSLC associate, immediately after collecting sufficient information from Matthew Milton.

When he had met with Matthew in the storeroom of Milton's Furnishings & Curios the day after their initial meeting in Wigan, Matthew brought specifics to the business deal he had proposed the evening before, especially the formidable sum he sought from Douglas. Douglas had purported to agonize over the money, firing off questions, and extracting from Matthew nearly every last detail of his slaving activities. Perhaps Matthew was so candid because he knew Douglas possessed knowledge of legitimate transatlantic trading and was attempting to prove his own competency. Whatever the case, Douglas had gathered facts and particulars sufficient to thwart Matthew's upcoming trafficking expedition, and also to leave both the man's reputation and his bank account utterly devoid of worth.

After a bit of posturing at the furniture shop that day, Matthew had admitted that his last two trading voyages had been staggering failures. The first was aborted because of disastrous weather, and the second was terminated prematurely because of a decaying hull. Matthew complained that he had paid handsomely to equip both ships for their intended purposes under the assumption that he would reclaim great profit when he sold off his human cargo. After returning empty-handed from both expeditions, his funds had nearly run out. Many of Matthew's former associates were now refusing to work with him, so Douglas's arrival in Wigan was most fortuitous, Matthew explained. The upcoming voyage was his last chance to rebuild his fortune. If the journey was not a success, he would be bankrupt.

What Matthew was seeking from Douglas was a vessel swift enough to outrun the British Navy, as well as an influx of capital sufficient to fund the journey. There was also the cost of false registration papers and of course, feeding the captives. This trip would be devoted to collecting Yoruba people. The Yorubas, Matthew puffed, could be bought in the Bight of Benin for thirty dollars a piece and sold in the Caribbean for close to one thousand dollars. The potential for profit was astronomical. Given the illegal nature of the enterprise, there were dilemmas to surmount. The delay on African shores was long, as ships could not depart with their African cargo onboard until the coast was free of patrols. Many a crew ran out of foodstuffs before even raising their anchors.

Partnering with Douglas would be perfect, Matthew postulated, since a superior method for disguising a slave ship was to use that same ship to run legitimate trading voyages between slave missions.

After nearly two torturous hours, Douglas sighed loudly and agreed to help. The assistance would be contingent, Douglas added, on absolute secrecy and obviously, a large cut of the profits. Matthew eagerly agreed, desperate as he was. Douglas directed Matthew to send his remaining funds to a John Colby in Boston, Massachusetts, who would use the money toward outfitting the craft. Douglas also promised his own investment to be double Matthew's, or whatever was required to cover the remaining costs.

Colby, Douglas attested, would provide a state-of-the-art vessel, a newer, faster ship than anything Douglas had available. Since Colby was a Northerner, his involvement in slave trafficking would be more difficult to detect. Finally, Douglas assured

Matthew, Colby would surely be able to provide supplemental manpower, as well. Matthew was keen on following Douglas's every suggestion, his own accumulation of wealth apparently his foremost concern.

As Douglas sat now in the coach, holding the letter from Colby, he regretted that he had not kept abreast of the SSLC and other Underground groups after the fire. But he had at least maintained contact information for certain associates, people like Colby, whom he was certain would be receptive to the contact he initiated. Douglas flattened the crinkled envelope against his thigh and slid his finger under the flap.

Dear Douglas,

Your proposal was eagerly accepted by all involved. I suppose you knew that would happen, as the money from Milton arrived only two days after your letter. Per your suggestion, I sent much of the large sum to our common friends. I am sure they will use it wisely. Meantime, I am carrying out the rest of your vision.

Thank you for bringing this opportunity to our attention. I continue to pray that you might return to the water soon yourself. I look forward to reporting our great success with respect to the Voyager.

Fondly,

J. Colby

As the coach reached Cumberland Street, Douglas folded the letter and returned it to his pocket. Douglas would burn the letter when he returned home. This time he would be more careful. He was pleased to know that Milton's remaining funds had been donated, unbeknownst to that dim-witted muck-spout, to the American Anti-Slavery Committee.

As they finally reached the far end of Cumberland Street, Douglas bounded from the carriage before Demett could come to a full stop. Pushing open the door to the pawn shop, he was met by the heavy scent of musk and the sound of a bell tinkling above his head. The shop was larger than Douglas had expected, but tightly packed with items that clientele had seen fit to sell off for one reason or another. There was a shocking number of clocks, large and small, crowding the counters and the floor. As he stepped farther into the shop, he passed a knee-high statue of a white lion, and then a pile of small, rolled rugs. An older man looked up from where he stood reading a catalog behind the counter.

"Good evening," he called to Douglas in a French accent. "Let me know if I can assist." The man glanced at the nearest clock, likely irritated that Douglas had arrived so near closing time and then looked back to the catalog. Douglas maneuvered to the counter, where jewelry was arranged in glass display cases. Looking from one case to the next, his breath caught as he quickly grasped sight of the necklace he had purchased for Abby months before. He exhaled slowly, appreciating the luck of locating the necklace so shortly after remembering it. Looking again at the necklace, he felt a pressure on his chest as images of Abby flashed in his mind. He thought of the sway of her hips and bit down on the inside of his lip. He then glanced around at the other displayed items, snuff cases, a variety of small pistols, bracelets, and other inconsequential jewelry. Abby's necklace was clearly one of the most valuable items in the ramshackle shop, and Douglas was certain the timeworn man behind the counter would remember how it had come into his possession.

"This necklace," Douglas spoke up. "Can you tell me what happened when you purchased it?"

The man regarded Douglas for a moment before looking to see which necklace he referenced. "No, sir," he looked back up at Douglas and casually shrugged his shoulders. "I do not very well remember this lady who sell me the stallion." He shifted his body and looked back at his catalog again.

Douglas pushed a few bills across the glass countertop. "If this is the game you want to play, have at it. Just please, I'm in a grand hurry."

The clerk pocketed the bills without missing a beat. "Now that you mention it," he perked up, "I do recall the young lady who was here, *très belle*, very pretty, yes? But she was rushed, in frenzy, perhaps like you, *mon ami?*" He looked Douglas up and down before continuing. "She was sad, the lady, very sad, too. I don't know," he waved his hand dismissing his gentler side. "We agreed on the price, and then *voilà*," he clapped his hands together with a flourish, "she was gone."

"Where did she go?" Douglas demanded.

The wrinkled man made an elaborate show of furrowing his brow. "I do not know whether she mentioned anything about a destination. If perhaps I were a younger fellow, like you, it would not be such a struggle to recall, eh, *mon ami?*" He looked expectantly at Douglas.

"For crying out loud." Douglas placed another bill on the counter and suppressed the urge to grab the man by his shirt collar. "Where did she go?" he repeated firmly.

The shopkeeper took hold of the money and again placed it in his breast pocket. "I do not know for certain. So long ago. Hard to recall, yes? Only she asked about the travel north, wanting to know the best way to reach, what was it, Boston? Said she had to get back to her school, I think," he cocked his head as though struggling to remember.

Douglas watched the man's eyes narrow in concentration, and then, with a sudden and biting clarity, he knew. He knew exactly where she had gone. So many times she had spoken of Larissa's experience at a girl's boarding school, how she might be keen on a similar experience for herself. There were other schools she could have chosen, but somehow, Douglas was just certain now of where she had taken herself, could feel it in his bones. He fairly flew forth from the pawn shop, propelled by a surge of new hope as he raced to prepare his things for a journey to the Hadley School for Girls. He needed to make just one stop first.

31

STOCKBRIDGE, MASSACHUSETTS
JULY 1846

*S*unday luncheon was the only meal of the week that Abby disliked at Hadley. In the three and a half months since she arrived at the school, she had come to enjoy sitting with the girls at the long tables in the formal dining room, listening to their chatter about friends and projects. It seemed lately, she was even becoming a central part of the daily discourse, with many of the girls anxious for her opinions. But Sunday luncheon was used for instruction only, with little opportunity for conversing. There were incessant lessons about the proper moment to unfold one's napkin, which knife to use for spreading cream, and so on and so on. It was horribly boring to listen to Belinda Sharp, the school's aging watercolor instructor and resident expert on table decorum, as she droned on about tines and particular forks. So instead, Abby's mind would wander. Inevitably, her thoughts would stray back towards Charleston, tethered to the locale by yards of relentless invisible twine. Miss Sharp's words echoed Larissa's instruction so thoroughly, Abby couldn't help but be reminded of her time with her governess, and host. Still, her fixation drove her mad each time she surrendered to it.

As she stared at the volute wallpaper of the dining room, listening to Miss Sharp expound upon the direction in which a soup spoon should travel, she felt prickling behind her eyes, tears threatening. She almost slammed her own spoon back onto the table, so miffed with her inability to shore up. Wasn't she supposed to be Abigail Milton from the dregs of Wigan? She should be able to handle worse than this, this disappointment, a failed dalliance, without so much as a backward glance. But no, it seemed her brief time with Douglas had somehow turned her soft, dewy-eyed, and she couldn't abide it. She chanced another spoonful of her corn chowder, the bits of corn floating in the creamy liquid making her think of small yellow teeth, disgusting her.

When she fled Charleston in March, she imagined that a bit of distance and time would allow her attachment to Douglas to dissipate. After all, they had barely begun courting before it all went to tatters. Instead, during the months since her departure, she had become only further crestfallen. Her yearning for Douglas, for her life in Charleston, persisted like a nagging thirst. Several times throughout each day, still, something trifling would remind her of Douglas. She couldn't so much as grin without the fleeting thought that Douglas too would have been delighted by whatever had amused her.

She was fortunate to have secured a position at Hadley, and she dared not jeopardize her future by revealing her continued despair. The school's aging instructors, most of them women well past forty, seemed uninterested in idle gossip. Except for Miss Parsons, the teachers seemed willing to accept her fabricated tale of fire with few questions. But for how long would she be permitted to grieve? With each passing day, as she failed to scrub the recesses of her mind, free them from the images of that man, that woman, she feared the teachers would notice her ongoing dejection and wonder about her suitability for the school. Hadley was a greatly esteemed institution, a school with little reason to tolerate questionable faculty.

Although Miss Parsons promised that Abby was on her way to a permanent teaching position, Abby had long ago learned nothing in life was assured, not for her. Perhaps her compulsion to recall Charleston bled from the fact that at the Elling estate, she had found a place where her isolation and bitterness, her longstanding elixir of personal rage, was finally subordinated to other endeavors. But now she saw that sorrow was her only true companion, back to squeeze against her heart once more.

When she recalled how Douglas had behaved during the weeks prior to her departure, the way his eyes pursued her, regarding her as though she was his greatest epiphany, she questioned whether she misunderstood his interaction with Cora Rae. But if there was an alternate explanation for what she witnessed in the study, wouldn't he have tracked her down and explained by now? Someone with Douglas's extensive background in escape plans would likely ferret out her hiding spot with relative ease. Especially given all the times she had remarked to both Douglas and Larissa about Hadley, how she would relish the opportunity to teach at such a school, how envious she was of Larissa's experience. It would not have taken too much, if he paid heed to their conversations, to think of the place she might have gone. In light of his failure to appear, she determined over and again that Douglas simply played her for a fool.

Still, she did wonder what happened after she left. She imagined he would have checked with Gracie, and then maybe stopped at the rooming houses in central Charleston. Most likely he had given up his search quickly, distracted by his new affair with the ravishing Cora Rae. Each time Abby thought of them together, she felt a scalding pain settle into her chest, a scorching weight nearly impossible to withstand. So instead she would push the image from her mind like an undertaker pounding his shovel at mounds of dirt. How foolish of her to hope even for an instant that Douglas might come find her at Hadley. Douglas Elling had never cared for her in the manner he declared, and she would do well to cease her pointless mourning.

She sighed audibly as the soup bowls were cleared from the table and the serving girls began bringing the next course of crisp roast duckling and peas.

"Excuse me, Miss Milton, the water?" Chloe, the seven-year-old seated beside her was nudging at her with an elbow, a look of exasperation on her plump, pink face.

"Yes, Chloe? Mind we do not poke at people, now."

"I'm sorry, Miss, but you weren't hearing me the other times. I was just trying to secure your attention. Please don't be cross."

"No, I'm not cross, not with you. Pass me your glass." As she poured and watched the water slosh into Chloe's glass, Abby was mortified to realize that now even the children were noticing her foul moods, her preoccupation. Well here and now, this was the final stroke. She would have to make a change in her life at once, find something else to engage her, consume her, lest she disintegrate into a pile of angry ash, decimated by her own frail heart.

TWO HOURS AFTER THE CONCLUSION OF THE TEDIOUS luncheon, Abby sat with Margaret Parsons in the small faculty parlor, sipping iced tea and reviewing procedures for the teachers' exam. Edna Handler was retiring from her post, as Miss Parsons had expected, and Abby was the top prospect to assume the older woman's position as full class mistress for the seven- and eight-year-old girls.

"After the Board has observed you," Miss Parsons explained, "they will vote on whether to elevate you to the new post." The headmistress smiled. "Just try to be chipper and smile a bit when you do your lecture. You always excel in the subject of literature, so take confidence," Miss Parsons advised with gusto, the corners of her eyes crinkling as she smiled. "I'd like to start preparing you as soon as possible. Perhaps you want to focus on a play? Shakespeare, maybe?"

"No, no play," Abby coughed, her teacup teetering slightly in her hand as she returned it to the faded oval table between them. She could think only of Douglas and his penchant for plays. She would do something else, poetry perhaps, even arithmetic if need be. Catching herself, she continued more casually. "Perhaps you could help me choose a different genre. Plays have never been my favorite, and if I am to deliver an outstanding lecture, then I think the topic should be something I am passionate about."

"A fine point," Miss Parsons dipped her chin in agreement and pursed her pale lips for a moment of thought. "How about Poe? Everybody seems interested in that fellow. And he is so current, a clever choice for drawing notice from the trustees. Let us look into that." Miss Parsons began scribbling furiously on her writing tablet.

After a moment, Abby responded, "Thank you, Miss Parsons. I really do appreciate all you've done for me. Hopefully, I will do you proud."

"Oh nonsense, of course you will. Oh!" She looked up from her notes. "I've just had the most wonderful idea. Neil, my nephew, he's an enormous fan of Edgar Allen Poe. Let us invite him to call, and we can parse through ideas with him. Don't you think?"

Abby let out a breath as she tried to think how to turn down the suggestion of Miss Parsons's nephew, yet again. But then she thought the better of it. Perhaps this illustrious Neil Parsons was just the distraction she required. It need not be about courting, but she might benefit from the company of a person near her own age. Perhaps they could be friends, and he might even introduce her to others in the surrounding neighborhood, or from Lenox or Lee, where some of the students' families resided. Gracie came to mind, and Abby forced thoughts of the girl away. Perhaps she would meet new young women here in Stockbridge, through Neil.

"Fine, that sounds lovely," she found herself telling Miss Parsons as she absentmindedly ran her hand over the crushed velvet of the love seat beneath her. "Why don't you see if he can call in a few days. I'd like to review the Poe in our library beforehand, so I am prepared."

Miss Parsons's mouth opened in a silent O, her surprise at Abby's new willingness clear before she rearranged herself. "Wonderful. I am gladdened to see you opening yourself to new possibilities." She patted Abby's arm in a matronly gesture of approval. "I will send word to him at once."

—❦—

THREE DAYS LATER, ABBY SAT AT THE WRITING DESK IN her room at the dormitory, thumbing through the texts she had collected from the school's library, and she found herself mystified. It was grand foolishness to attempt crafting a lecture on Edgar Allen Poe. She considered his stories gruesome and disturbing, each one putting her off more than the next. The summer heat that cascaded though her narrow window was hardly sufficient to ward off the gory images of death that Poe presented. Hopefully when Miss Parsons's nephew arrived, he would offer adequate clarification on the significance of Poe's macabre meanderings.

Shaking her shoulders out, as if ridding herself of Poe's harrowing stories, she emerged from her quarters and found several of the school's older girls clustered in the hallway. They were whispering and giggling as they peered out a large picture window into the courtyard. Twelve-year-old Genevieve Pope was the first to see Abby as she approached.

"Oh, Miss Milton," Genevieve spoke too loudly, clearly intending to alert her coconspirators to Abby's presence. The other girls who had been competing for space at the window turned almost in unison to see Abby. They all quickly mumbled excuses and scurried away.

"Stella," Abby called after one girl, "come back here please." The slender girl, really on the cusp of adulthood, turned with obvious reluctance and made her way toward Abby.

"What is all the fuss about then?" Abby asked, making an effort to use her stern voice with the dark-haired girl.

"Well, if you must know," she glanced back toward the courtyard, "we were admiring Miss Parsons's nephew." Her voice had a shoving quality to it, the same as her own sister Gwen's when she was trying to convince Abby to misbehave. "They're out in the courtyard, talking," Stella continued. "He's really rather dashing. You could hardly blame us." She shrugged at Abby. "May I be excused now?" The girl appeared bored, anxious to rejoin her friends.

"Yes, yes," Abby shooed Stella with her hand, unbalanced by the girl's precociousness.

Abby stepped closer to the window and glanced outside, confident she wouldn't be seen from her location in the dark hallway. She viewed Neil Parsons in profile as he opened his mouth to laugh about something with his aunt, and the man was indeed, something to look at. He was tall and slender with dark-blonde hair cut close to his head. He was not as big or imposing as Douglas, but seemed to hold himself with an understated, masculine grace. As Abby realized she was comparing him to Douglas, she gave herself a mental cuff to the head and turned toward the kitchen, figuring she would alert the staff that it was time to prepare the tea service.

32

STOCKBRIDGE, MASSACHUSETTS
JULY 1846

After Abby decided which sandwiches and mini-tarts would round out the tea, she made her way to the Dudley Parlor, so named in honor of a family that once donated a sizeable financial gift to the school. With so many wealthy students romping through Hadley's halls, Abby found it tiresome to remember the origin of each gift to the school, a library here, a grand piano there. Yet she took note of the Dudley name because she particularly liked the petite parlor with its domestic aura. Stepping into the space allowed Abby a moment to imagine that Hadley was an authentic home, rather than simply the academy providing her respite for the moment. Although if she secured the class mistress position, then at least she would see her refuge assured for longer.

As she drew near the parlor, she heard Miss Parsons and her nephew already inside, chattering on in the easy way of family.

"Good afternoon," she announced as she met the back of Neil Parsons, who was seated in an armchair facing his aunt.

The nephew rose immediately, turning to face her and proving that he was even more impressive to behold at close range.

He appeared near her age, with fresh-looking skin and straight white teeth that showed themselves proudly as he smiled at her.

"You must be Miss Milton," his voice was smooth, confident. "Aunt Maggie, if you would please introduce us properly?" He glanced toward his aunt.

"Of course," Miss Parsons answered, an uncharacteristic buoyancy to her speech. "Mr. Neil Parsons, may I present Miss Abigail Milton, newest aide to the Hadley faculty, and hopefully soon a more permanent fixture."

"How do you do, Miss Milton." He offered a slight bow. "I'm delighted you will be joining us for tea, at last, as I've had an earful about your grace and charm already. Perhaps after I've had an opportunity to investigate these allegations, my dear Aunt Maggie can let up?" He winked at his aunt, playfulness in his voice, and Abby warmed to his straightforward manner.

She positioned herself beside Miss Parsons on the small chesterfield against the wall. As Miss Parsons explained that Abby was hoping to learn more about Edgar Allan Poe for her mock lecture, Abby wondered how a man who seemed so light and unencumbered could be interested in gruesome work like Poe's.

Neil looked from Miss Parsons back to Abby in apparent surprise.

"You're serious?" he asked. "Such morose and frightening stories? And to think, my aunt had told me you were an enlightened young lady. Well." He smiled, belying his game.

"Actually," Abby responded, "joking aside, that is precisely how I feel about his writing. I cannot grasp what pleasure a person might find in reading such chilling work, which was actually the question I was hoping you might elucidate this afternoon."

"I would be elated to provide you a lengthy inventory of reasons that Poe is an exceptional author, but I must admit, which I am loathe to do in your lovely English presence, that one of my favorite attributes of his is the fact that he is American. With so few American writers taken seriously, we must support all those in the country who deserve it." He paused as Marianne, the serving girl, entered with a tray of tea that she placed on the chestnut table. Neil nodded politely at Marianne and looked back to Abby. "Do forgive me, but as superb as I find Dickens and Pope, it's time this nation had some hefty names of our own."

Abby watched him reach out for a tomato sandwich, the fabric of his jacket pulling against the muscle of his shoulder, and she thought how admirable she found his position on American literature, a worthy cause. She would, indeed, like to have a friendship with a gentleman like him, and to meet others with whom someone so thoughtful, so introspective, spent his time.

She began imagining herself hosting animated meetings of intellectuals, a salon of sorts, where she could share concepts and companionship with like-minded individuals. Combined with her life at Hadley, the stimulation might be enough; she might yet have a suitable life, an acceptable existence. She shifted in her seat as she tried to digest this altered vision of her future. Memories of her thwarted intentions to combat Southern slavery threatened to reappear, crushing her afresh. But Abby refrained from surrendering to her thoughts, for the time being evicting them from her mind.

"I am not offended, Mr. Parsons," she ventured. "And I will try to understand what makes your Mr. Poe so special, other than his ability to frighten the packing out from under me." She found herself smiling genuinely at him, glad for his company, as Miss Parsons looked on, practically glittering. Miss Parsons opened her mouth to add something, but she was distracted by the appearance of Myra Hobson, one of the first-year students, standing in the doorway.

"Excuse me," the girl spoke out with proud authority. "I've had a note." She held up an envelope like pilfered bounty. "For Miss Milton. May I bring it? He said it's important." The girl was bouncing with excitement, clearly trussed up by her task.

Abby looked to Miss Parsons, who returned her teacup to its saucer and answered graciously. "Of course, Myra, come in."

The girl hurried over to Abby, waving the envelope about as she crossed the small room. Abby noticed Myra's eyes lingering on the tray of pastries as she handed over the message.

"Thank you, Myra," Abby said as she took the envelope. "Miss Parsons, would it be all right if Myra had a pastry, for her help with this delivery?"

"Of course, dear," Miss Parsons pushed the tray forward on the table. "Choose just one though. We mustn't spoil your supper." The girl's eyes prowled from one pastry to another, finally settling on an apricot linzer torte. As Myra trotted from the room, her prize already in her mouth, Abby edged the letter into her dress pocket. She could hardly imagine what it was about, but she knew better than to review correspondence while hosting company.

"No, you might as well open it now. Myra said it was important," Miss Parsons told her as she looked toward Neil, who was sipping his tea. "We won't mind, right, Neil?"

"Of course." He nodded agreeably. "Please."

Abby slid her fingernail under the pasty tab of the envelope before pulling out a folded paper. In a tight, deliberate scrawl, she saw words written out in a stanza, like poetry.

O Mistress mine, where are you roaming?
O, stay and hear; your true love's coming,
That can sing both high and low.
Trip no further, pretty sweeting;
Journey's end in lovers meeting . . .

Abby's breath caught as she read the verse again. She would have recognized those lines anywhere. The song sung by the clown in *Twelfth Night*. She knew it exactly! Act II, Scene 3, she was certain. Why was she holding these words now, on this pulpy card that was vibrating in her quivering hand? Her thoughts flashed to a discussion she had with Douglas once about these lines from the play he'd read to her. The day they had lunch in the Hayes parlor, he mentioned the verse again and told her that Shakespeare's fool seemed particularly wise, theorizing that a journeyer could cease traveling after meeting her true love. But it was she who was the fool, believing that he was referring to their mutual affection, that he might have been urging her to consider his home the final stop on *her* journey. Abby leaned in closer to the message, trying to decipher the meaning behind the note's arrival. The ripe smell of ink was nearly hypnotic as her mind raced to tease out explanations. Then suddenly, he was there.

She heard him clearing his throat in the doorway to the parlor. The low rumbling sound, the timber of his voice, it was unmistakable. She forced her head up and beheld him. He stood before them in his traveling clothes, improbably neat after a lengthy journey, and the sight of his windswept face knocked the air from her. She shot up from her seat, unconscious of her intention, but then stiffened, held to her place. She was crippled by confusion and looked back to the note in her hand, as if to find instruction.

Douglas's gaze roved over her, quickly assessing her, as if checking for damage. When his eyes returned to her face, there was a softness, a pleading that served to turn her own momentary relief sour, spoiling it back to anger. How dare he come here now, after all these weeks and months, looking so gratified to have found her.

It seemed a struggle for him to break his gaze from her as he turned toward Miss Parsons and Neil. "Forgive me for intruding, one of the girls showed me in. This feels highly inappropriate now, barging in as I have, but I was rather frantic to locate Miss Milton."

"Well, here I am," Abby managed to deadpan despite her shock, embarrassed in front of Neil and Miss Parsons, worried she would be called out now for the lies about her past.

Douglas continued addressing the others. "Allow me to introduce myself. Douglas Elling." He stepped deeper into the room and extended his hand toward Neil, who was now standing to greet Douglas properly. Suddenly the little room that Abby so adored seemed entirely too small. This restrictive space wasn't meant to hold a man like Douglas Elling.

"How do you do," Neil responded cautiously, and Abby noticed that Douglas was indeed significantly taller than her new friend, the crown of Neil's head lower even than Douglas's dark eyebrows. As she regarded the two men standing side by side, the optimistic musings she had entertained about a satisfying future at Hadley disintegrated like scorched parchment. For a moment, she felt only her urge to envelop Douglas, to attach her every cell to his durable body and dissolve. And then like a tidal wave, all the pain she had been struggling to extinguish over the past months came rushing at her, shouting for attention. It was there again like a fever, igniting her rage, steadying her focus, protecting her.

"What are you doing here?" she demanded, still rooted to her place, her voice hard.

She looked back at Miss Parsons and Neil, who were regarding both her and Douglas with uncertainty. Miss Parsons looked about to speak, perhaps to take charge of the interaction and rebuke Abby for her rudeness, when Douglas held up a hand.

"Please, my sincerest apologies," he was addressing Miss Parsons, smiling at her sheepishly, and Abby thought how the woman was likely powerless to resist his cerulean eyes and the subtle dimple in his cheek. Douglas glanced back at Neil, his gaze lingering on the man for a moment, a curiosity creeping into the corners of his eyes and then disappearing as quickly as it came. "I am a friend of Miss Milton's," he continued. "I've been attempting to discover her whereabouts for months. Would it be all right if I had a moment to speak with her?" His words reverberated through her veins, disorienting her, flushing her through with a sense of inebriation. She could not permit his magnetism to distort her thoughts, not again.

Miss Parsons turned from Douglas to Abby and back to Douglas again. Abby saw a look of regret pass across Miss Parsons's weathered features as she perhaps concluded that her own plans to attach Abby to her nephew were suddenly foiled. She looked toward Abby with an audible sigh, as though she had always known this moment would come.

"Come, Neil, let us walk in the garden." Miss Parsons looked at Douglas, keeping her eyes trained on him as she added, "but, Abby, you just holler if you need anything."

Neil followed Miss Parsons, but turned to Abby on his way through the door.

"All right?" he asked, apparently reluctant to leave her with Douglas, even though he himself had known her for less than an hour. She nodded at him, and he left to follow Miss Parsons. Abby turned back toward Douglas, deciding she would not offer him a seat, would not offer anything.

They regarded each other in silence for a moment, Douglas's eyes roaming repeatedly over Abby's entire person. The silence between them stretched, but Abby would not speak first, would not dispense so much as a whisper to ease whatever discomfort, whatever shame, he might be feeling. Let him bask in it, soak it up, and swell with the affliction of it.

She could see Douglas struggling against himself, emotions battling behind his eyes, manipulating his face, creating a sandstorm across his anguished features. "I don't know how to start," he finally confessed, his voice reserved now, so much quieter than when the others had been in the room. "I have been rehearsing this moment in my head for months, imagining the ways I would explain, how I could make you comprehend the depth of my commitment to you, and now that it has finally arrived, now that I stand here before you, that at long last, we are once again breathing common air, I find myself mute, an imbecile."

Abby answered curtly, "Well, whatever you've come to say, you needn't bother. You've done your gentlemanly duty now, tracking me down to offer a proper apology. But please, have off with you. My only wish now is that you will cease harassing me, so be the gentleman to which you aspire, and take your leave." She folded her arms across her chest, as though trying to hold onto her own bravado.

"Please, Abby," he stepped closer, reaching to touch her elbow, but she twisted quickly, pulling away. She would not let his touch influence her, and what right had he anyway, to place his hand upon her person.

"Just hear me out," Douglas continued, working his hand through his hair, disrupting it, dark locks charging to disorderly angles. I have been searching the world over for you. I've gone to hell and back. Well, Wigan and back. I was such a blundering idiot not to realize sooner where you'd gone, but now that I am here, please, just listen." He looked at her with pleading eyes. "If you still want me to leave after I've said my piece, I won't argue."

"Wigan?" Abby asked, surprise getting the better of her. For all the weeks since her departure, she had imagined him at the

Elling estate, sipping on brandy alongside Cora Rae, or which-
ever foolish woman would follow in Douglas's parade. Those
times that she wondered if he was searching for her, she had
found so many reasons to convince herself she was coming un-
screwed, it was difficult now to accept the meaning of his words.

"Yes, Wigan," he answered, his lip ticking up to one side
abashedly. "Just come and sit for a moment so I might enlighten
you about the torture I've suffered since that dreadful afternoon
in the study." He motioned toward the couch and raised a
pleading eyebrow.

Abby pursed her lips and considered him. She so desperately wanted cause to forgive him, a reason to topple into his
arms, but she couldn't allow it. She wanted to scratch off every
layer of her skin for considering the possibility, ever the idiot,
suffering what she deserved. Surely he was about to toss her a
bevy of lies and nonsense, but the sooner he laid out his business, the sooner she could disperse him. His sculpted jawline,
now dusted with late-day stubble, and the temptation from his
words was only augmenting her own agony. If this was the surest
way to be rid of him, so be it.

"Fine, ten minutes. No more." Abby forced herself to meet
his gaze with only challenge in her eyes as she returned to the
petite sofa. She again tried to banish the spark of hope that was
creeping into her blood, persistently returning to taunt her each
time she tried to choke it down.

Douglas sat across from her, adjusting the chair so he was
close enough to reach out to her.

"I shall only need one of those minutes, I think," Douglas
responded, "to convince you of what I want forever."

She waited, steeling herself, as he continued, "I give you my
word as an English gentleman that all I am about to say is as
true as your father's love of carving."

He could swear to her all he wanted, but it didn't mean she would believe him, no matter how searing her pain.

He sighed and began, "Gracie confessed to arranging the incident with Cora Rae. It was staged by the Cunningham girls simply for your benefit so that you would forsake me and create a space for Cora Rae."

Gracie! How dare he thrust blame at Gracie. Abby would not believe ill of Gracie simply on Douglas's word. As she stumbled to form a question, Douglas continued, "What you saw in the study was my effort to remove Miss Cunningham as she attempted to bludgeon me with her mouth. Never would I have betrayed you like that." He began reaching out toward her hand, but then pulled back. He studied her for a moment, silently imploring, beseeching, before continuing. "I would have arrived here sooner if not for my misguided intuition that you had returned to your parents in Wigan. Had I been thinking more clearly, I would have realized Wigan was the last place you'd run. The positive news is that my trip to England reunited me with your uncle Matthew."

Matthew! Was Douglas insane? After everything he knew about Abby's relationship with her uncle, why would he mention the man's name? Surely this was the last way to ingratiate himself. Perhaps she had misinterpreted the reason for his visit. Perhaps he wasn't here to make amends at all. Again Abby tried to articulate a thought, struggling between the various outrages, but Douglas held up his hand to delay her. "Thanks to our meeting, I have discovered a method to destroy every last bit of wealth and stature that man ever managed to finagle. I have realized it would be appropriate to fill you in on the details of that, as well as the other topics on which I had formerly been so tight-lipped, but not until we've sorted through the business of us. And also the news about your father, who has been promoted again."

"Promoted again?" Abby asked, her curiosity again commandeering her words.

"The foreman took ill while I was in Wigan. The owners grew impatient, and instead of awaiting the other man's recovery, they asked your father to fill the open position for the foreseeable future. Apparently loyalty is not the employers' strong suit, but it was certainly a boon to your family."

"My da is the foreman?" Abby asked, defiantly. "Of the whole Upperton Mill. You're certain?"

"From what I understand, your father will now be able to settle his remaining debts and relocate your family, move out of Wigan rather quickly. I imagine they won't miss it."

To think, her father as foreman, the good fortune her da utterly deserved. She barely had time to notice the cheer she felt for her family before Douglas asked, "If you'll permit me to return to the subject at hand?"

She nodded at him, becoming further unglued, this entire afternoon so unexpected and mystifying.

Douglas seemed steady in his concentration as he continued, "You've shown me that the best way I can pay tribute to those I love is by doing that which I believe in. From knowing you, I finally understand that perseverance is the truest test of heroism. You, Abby, have inspired me to return to the fight against slavery, to use my life for more than profit and routine. Most importantly, I am here to return to you. Not that I ever left. All this time you are the one who has been missing, but it is I who have been lost, lost without you."

He reached for Abby's hand again, and this time she did not fight him.

She surveyed his face, from his hairline to the cleft in his chin, and she wanted to believe him, so desperately she wanted to. But she couldn't. He was an expert in lies and deception, as he needed to be for his abolitionist work. She couldn't bare herself again, couldn't chance the torment, not when she was finally, finally starting to heal.

"I'm sorry, Douglas, I don't believe you," she told him as she stood, swiping her skirts into place with a gesture of finality. She needed him to withdraw at once, her resolve faltering with each passing second. "Please go."

"No, Abby, please." Douglas was standing now, too. "I worried you might feel this way, because what reason have you to trust me now, but please, I beg of you, consider the possibility that I speak the truth. What happened between us before you left, that cannot be feigned. If you will not accept my word on the matter, perhaps you could rely on the word of another." He reached into his breast pocket and pulled out an envelope. "Here," he held it out to her, "if you could just read this."

She would not let him abrade her will any further.

"No, please, just go. If you respect me as much as you say, you will leave me be, take your letter, and abide my wishes." Her voice had faltered to a near whisper, "Please . . . go."

Douglas exhaled a heavy breath as he looked down at her, conflict evident across his taut features.

"I understand that I have thrown so much at you today, and certainly I wish to respect your wishes. I will go and give you the breadth to think over what I've said, or time, or both. But I am not leaving Stockbridge. I am not giving you up." He placed the envelope down on the table. "If you would read this, I do think it would help."

When she remained silent, he added, "I will send word to the headmistress of where I am staying, and I will wait there. Indefinitely."

He reached into his pocket again and pulled out a small

box. "Also, this. It belongs with you." He placed the box next to the envelope and quietly left the room.

As he disappeared through the doorway, a fat tear rolled down Abby's cheek. She wiped furiously at her eyes, denying them their relief. She would not relent, would not yield. She would be nobody's plaything, even if it meant a lifetime of solitude. She picked up the envelope and walked toward the fireplace, but it was July, too hot for a fire. She held the envelope between her two hands, ready to tear it if burning wasn't an option, but she couldn't make herself do it. She looked back toward the table. She supposed she could at least see what he left in the box.

Removing the delicate wooden lid, her breath caught as she saw her equestrian necklace glistening up at her. Well. So he had purchased an expensive trifle for her not once, but twice now. But what of it. His purse would hardly notice the deficit, and she refused to be bought with jewels. She heard voices in the outer room and realized Miss Parsons and Neil were returning. She hastily stuffed both the letter and the necklace into the pocket of her dress. She would rid herself of them after tea, just as she must rid herself of their dispatcher altogether.

33

STOCKBRIDGE, MASSACHUSETTS

1846

bby waited until she heard the bite of the lock behind her before she let her composure slip. Leaning against her bedroom door, she shut her eyes and tried to control her breathing. She would not cry. She had made the right decision, sending Douglas away. Her behavior had been strong and self-preserving, as a girl like her needed to be.

After Douglas left, Abby had tried to resume socializing but found she was simply too shaken and distracted. She told Miss Parsons and Neil that Douglas was a friend of her former patron in South Carolina and had been anxious to ensure Abby's safety out of loyalty to his deceased friend. While Neil seemed ready to accept Abby's explanation, Miss Parsons had regarded her in silence, the corners of her mouth turning down before she shifted her broad body and resumed her post on the chesterfield. Abby had lasted only a few minutes longer before she made her excuses, explaining that the man's visit had come as a shock, dredging up painful memories of the fire she escaped in Charleston, and asking if they could resume their meeting in a few days.

And now here she was, sinking to the floor of her quarters, alone as she should be. Why had he come now, after all this time? She had finally surrendered her last hope of his innocence, of his devotion, and now, now, he appeared. Well it was too late, and she wouldn't be moved. She would not put herself at risk again for such devastation, not when he had already failed her once so completely. She had been foolish to entertain the possibility of him to begin with, and she would not be so foolish as to chance it again. She stared at the wrought-iron legs of her narrow bed, barely seeing the curved feet or the white coverlet hanging over them. Instead she saw Douglas's face, the regret and pain, the iridescent shadows under his eyes. She realized now, upon reflection, that he'd lost weight since they'd last seen each other, and she wondered for a flash if there could be any truth to his statements, his postulations of personal anguish. Well, even if he regretted the consequences of his actions, she could not rely on him anymore; he'd made sure of that.

She remembered his promise to find lodging nearby and pitched her head against the door in frustration. He should have gone, returned to Charleston. Maybe if she just read the letter he left and then sent word responding, maybe that would be sufficient, and he would go, release her from the torment of his proximity. The sooner he departed, the easier it would be to banish him from her thoughts. She reached into her skirt pocket for the envelope, still unsure she would open it. What if the words written were simply more lies, more fodder for confusion? She first pulled out the box with the necklace and set it down on the floor beside her. She reached back in, startling to find the pocket empty. Standing in a panic, she reached into her other pocket and found nothing but a hard candy she'd taken from the kitchen earlier that day. She quickly scanned the floor where she'd been sitting, seeing nothing on the crosshatched rug nor the wood planks around it. Suddenly desperate for that letter, she raced into the hallway, retracing her steps back toward the parlor.

Thankfully there was no one about to question her posture as she traversed the halls with her head bent, eyes trained on the floor. The students would be occupied with their study period for at least another quarter hour. As she walked back the way she had come, Abby saw no hint of the envelope she sought, only her own black boots against the floor. When she finally reached the Dudley Parlor, she entered the room in a gust, ready to search between cushions, in nooks and crannies on the floor. To her surprise, Miss Parsons was still present in the room, her back to Abby while she focused intently on a paper in her hand. An envelope lay on the table beside her, its mouth open in confession.

Stupefied, Abby felt herself come apart further, as though the fabric that held her together as a person was today being unlaced, strand by string, a savage ball of twine, rolling relentlessly downhill. Whatever was contained in that letter, she surely did not wish Miss Parsons to see. Now the headmistress would know for certain that Abby's tale of woe from Charleston had been nonsense, lies to serve her own purpose. She would surely lose her position at Hadley. How many more ways could Douglas Elling ruin her life?

At the sound of Abby's breath catching, Miss Parsons turned with the letter open in her hand.

She regarded Abby with a stunned expression and then looked back to the letter. Abby braced herself for whatever deluge of censure was to follow from the woman.

"I'm so sorry," Miss Parsons blurted, holding the letter out for Abby to take. Abby stepped backward, surprised. When Abby didn't take the letter, Miss Parsons turned and sat in the armchair Neil had occupied earlier. "I'm so sorry," she repeated, removing her reading glasses and placing them in her lap. "I came back to the parlor because I'd left my folio, and I noticed the letter on the floor." She folded the paper back into thirds and held it out to Abby again. "The envelope wasn't marked," she added a bit defensively.

Abby cautiously reached out for the paper as Miss Parsons handed it over. When Abby moved to pocket it again, Miss Parsons stopped her.

"You ought to read it now," she directed. "Seems to me, enough time's been wasted already." Abby saw both kindness and regret in the woman's weak smile as she left the room.

The last of her resolve evaporating at Miss Parsons's words, Abby unfolded the paper, anxious now to discover what it held. Expecting to find Douglas's small, tidy writing, she saw the page was instead covered with large, flowery cursive.

Dear Abigail,

I must be the last person from whom you ever expected to receive correspondence. Well, life has a way of surprising us, does it not? You should know, firstly, that our esteemed Mr. Elling, came barging into my home prior to his trip up north, wild in his zealousness as he demanded that I write this letter. Secondly, I suppose I should offer you apology for my assumption that you were little more than a passing fancy, like a carnival to be enjoyed but briefly, before returning to one's home wishing never to eat confections again. I can assure you that Douglas Elling has viewed you as anything but expendable.

I assume by now, you've heard about my part in the scene you witnessed before you left in such a spectacular fit. Yes, it was all my doing, my scheming, mea culpa, etc, etc. I was asked to write a letter of apology and explanation, but instead I hope you will view this letter as one of solicitation.

It will come as no surprise to you that I have chased after Douglas Elling since I was a young girl. I imagined myself in love with him. But now, as I see how your absence has affected him, I realize that I never understood what it meant to love another like that. You should see how he frets. In the few minutes I have spent in his presence since your departure, I have seen a man on the verge of complete undoing. He yells and insults, races in circles, never stopping for a moment as he hunts for you, the vein beneath his jaw pulsing out a frenzy of constant panic for your well-being. This is what I have done to the man I claimed to love, this destruction and devastation. When I see the depth of his feelings for you, I realize that what I felt for this hapless man was not love, no it was avarice and my own ambition. I hope it is not too late for me to find someone who overwhelms my entire being, the way you do Douglas.

Now please, he has been across the ocean twice in pursuit of you. So many months lost, all because I thought I'd outsmarted the charity girl from wherever-it-is. How foolish I feel now, the way I mauled him. So please, do me the favor of forgiving the man and return to Charleston, if for no other reason than reducing my shame at the debacle I set in motion. We ladies must stick together, isn't that so? Hurry up, now.

Sincerely,

Miss Cora Rae Cunningham
Charleston, South Carolina
July 1846

⁂

MISS PARSONS HAD INSISTED THAT ABBY FIND A chaperone before traveling to town, and Ms. Sharp, the watercolor instructor, was somehow chosen as her companion. Injected with a biting sense of urgency after reading Cora Rae's letter, Abby cared little about the aggravation of Miss Sharp's finicky presence, so long as she could see Douglas forthwith. She was close to erupting with agitation at the endless delays to her current purpose.

Almost a full day had elapsed after his visit to Hadley before Douglas sent notice of his address to Miss Parsons, all the while Abby nearly boiling over with impatience. When word finally arrived by courier during the following evening's supper, Abby pushed her chair back from the table only to feel Miss Parsons's firm hand on her shoulder. Decent women apparently could not go calling after supper, no matter how great their rush. So she passed a second night, suffering through her impatience. Abby's schedule for teaching the next day was such that she hadn't been able to find a break for the excursion until the late afternoon.

All the while, she had frothed in her own chagrin, smoldering with shame for her grand overreaction to the scene with Cora Rae. How much trouble she'd put everyone to, how much commotion and uproar simply because she assumed always the lowest of people. She cringed again when she thought of the worry she'd caused her parents, astounded still that Douglas traveled to Wigan searching for her. She patted her pocket for the letter to her family, a stop at the post being her next order of business.

As they stepped into the entrance hall, Miss Sharp looked appreciatively at the grand rooms flanking both sides of the vestibule and remarked on her pleasure that Abby's friend had chosen a most respectable boarding house. To their left was a dimly lit lounge filled with inviting furniture, bulging davenports, and gracious wing chairs, quiet spaces for weary travelers. The room to the right resembled a tavern, occupied by compact dining tables and a bar at the far end. As they stood awkwardly in the vestibule, Abby first surveyed the lounge area, where she saw two groups of men engaged in quiet conversation, a young couple huddled over a shared newspaper, and a lone elderly man struggling against sleep.

Miss Sharp cleared her throat. "Perhaps we should seek assistance," she prodded, pointing toward an empty desk at the back of the entryway, a bell resting atop its polished surface.

Abby stepped toward the bell but paused to survey the dining area first. The room was almost empty, save for one young man cracking walnuts at the back table.

"May I help you ladies?"

Pulling her gaze from the man with the walnuts, Abby saw a serving man behind the bar.

"Do not call back across the room, mind," Miss Sharp whispered, as she patted Abby's elbow to propel her forward, toward the slender barkeep, who was wiping the counter with a rag.

"I've come to call on one of your guests, if you please," Abby called as she hurried across the room. Reaching the bar, she added, "A Mr. Douglas Elling, from South Carolina. I believe he arrived two nights ago."

The willowy man paused his rhythmic wiping.

"Sure, yes, Mr. Elling was one of our guests, but I'm sorry, he left this morning."

"He's left?" Her words dissolved into a gasping breath.

She had missed her chance. Douglas must finally have realized she was too much trouble, the clamor of her, too much irritation. He had given up on her. She could barely think for the sudden pounding in her chest. Miss Sharp appeared beside her, pulling out one of the leather stools that had been tucked underneath the bar.

"Abigail, sit," she commanded.

Abby absently climbed onto the seat, looking back toward

the barkeep, "Did he say where he was going? Home, I presume." She put her hand to her chest, fingering the sleek charm around her neck as her mind raced. Perhaps he'd been more interested in apologizing than gaining her back. Or she had taken too long to come to the inn. And now he had gone, abandoned her at last.

The bartender filled a glass with water from a pitcher and slid it across the counter toward her. "It wasn't me who served his breakfast this morning, but my wife, let me get her."

He walked to the end of the bar and pushed open a swinging door.

"Tilly!" he shouted, his voice suddenly loud and abrasive. "Tilly, come and help a guest," he called into the recess before letting the door swing closed again.

"She'll be but a minute," he said, attempting a consoling smile before turning to stack glasses on a shelf against the back wall.

Abby tried to think if she should follow him to Charleston. But no, his departure was a clear message that he'd had enough of her negligence and madness, her reckless lunacy. So here it was that she had lost him yet again. She put her hand around the water glass, mindful not to squeeze so tightly that the glass might shatter and match her insides.

A large woman emerged in a flurry from the kitchen, her russet hair kept up in a bonnet, flour decorating her worn apron.

"What is it, Henry, I'm in the middle of six fresh loaves for dinner," she griped at her husband before noticing Abby and Miss Sharp and pasting a smile on her face.

"I'm sorry, Misses. I didn't realize guests had sat," she looked back at her husband, widening her eyes in apparent annoyance, as though he hadn't mentioned it.

Henry the barkeep seemed nonplussed, as he spoke kindly to his rotund wife. "These ladies were inquiring where Mr. Elling went after he closed his account this morning. I thought you might be able to help."

"Settled his account?" She looked toward her husband like he was a grand idiot. "He did no such thing. Said he had a man to meet in Pittsfield but would be returning before supper." She turned back toward Abby to say more, but then her attention was diverted toward the entryway. "Isn't that him walking in now?"

Abby spun so quickly in her stool she nearly toppled off. They were right, there was Douglas, striding through the front door with a satchel slung over his arm. He hadn't left town, hadn't discarded her, not yet. She was nearly paralyzed from relief. As he closed the door behind himself, he turned, walking toward the stairs, and then glanced in their direction. When he saw Abby, he froze. As realization seemed to take hold of his features, he was suddenly bounding toward her, and she was climbing off her stool, standing before him, despite the trembling in her knees.

The corners of his mouth had turned up just enough for her to hope that he was pleased to see her. He looked her over quickly from bottom to top as he'd done two days before at Hadley, his eyes now lingering for a moment on the necklace she was wearing. When their eyes met again, his smile had grown wider, and she knew that everything was right, that she was right to come here, right to hope, right to begin again.

"You read the letter," he spoke quietly as he took her hand. He laced his fingers through hers, and Abby had the sensation of something finally fitting properly into place.

EPILOGUE

⌒⌒

NIAGARA, NEW YORK
1853

I watch my two boys hollering and laughing as they kick the can across the yard, pebbles inside making a racket as the toy flies in the air. One boy is so dark he could be the stroke of midnight itself, and the other is nearly light enough to pass. They were born almost as soon as I reached New York, a month before I expected their arrival. One came racing out right after the other, both in such a hurry to touch down on free soil.

When we moored at New York Harbor, the ship's captain whispered that I was to stay put in my hiding place. During those weeks of travel, the captain had been an ally, tending to my upkeep and making certain he was the only sailor who knew I was aboard. Still, I was fretting inside the wardrobe, worrying he wouldn't come back, questioning if this journey had been my greatest mistake. The captain returned for me just as he'd promised, after the pier had gone quiet, and he handed me a new dress, thick brown wool for wintertime, and a paper to keep in the pocket. He told me I was now Sally Mae Lyons. If anyone stopped me, I was to say I was searching for domestic work after the widow who employed me passed. I ain't never had my own surname before, but the paper in my pocket said that my circumstances were changing.

The pains began just after we left the docks, lighting me up as I walked behind the captain in the cold night. It felt like my body was taking its revenge on me, twisting my insides and squeezing. Maybe if I hadn't stuffed myself into the wardrobe all those weeks at sea, laying stiff and contorted across the bottom day after day, maybe I would have labored easier. But we had luck with us even through the pain, my babies and me. The house where we were meant to rest wasn't far, and there was a white lady waiting for us there with wrinkled skin and kind hands. She put away her surprise at my condition and just took up her task like she was waiting for it. She brought Jeremiah into the world by the light of one candle in her cellar and then held my hand tight when she told me there was still work to do. Next came Ezekiel, white as the cotton I had run from, screaming at double the volume of his older brother, howling out a battle cry, making sure God knew he had arrived, knew that he was free.

Thelma told me before I left that traveling would be work, and that's every bit the truth, especially when you got two mewling babies and a flow of bleeding that won't cease. We were out of doors again the next afternoon, traveling west before my milk even came in, but there was no time to waste, not if we wanted to outrun the catchers. The white lady and I, we wrapped up those wailing babies, and she helped me lift my weary body into the back of a white man's covered wagon. We just had to keep running, running, all the time, the babies and me. By the time we reached Ulster County, I thought that all the blood had done run out of me, but it kept right on seeping, turning my gray blanket all to brown.

The boys were wailing like banshees, and that quiet white man, he just kept looking ahead, driving the horses onward all the time. I thought about all the babies I'd seen nursing at Cherry Lane, wet nurses with the pickaninnies day after day, always one or another flimsy babe to their bosom, and I couldn't figure what I was doing wrong. Finally, near Albany, my boys was starved enough to cooperate, affixing themselves to my breast in tandem, content like they had found the answer to everything. All the while, I was peeking out and watching the dusty road behind us, looking, looking all the time. My head was swirling with the dizziness of fear, with the weight of exhaustion.

I was bleeding too much, but there weren't nothing I could do, except to keep on hugging my babies, telling them over and again that they was free. I kissed each one on his downy head before I closed my eyes for the last time. Then I took my final gasp, the air rushing out and away, as if it were behind me already, forever in the past, like all the ugliness of slave life. In that last moment, I was still holding Jeremiah tight to my breast and Ezekiel asleep against my belly.

The man driving the wagon, he had to carry my body into the forest, covering me with just shrub and twigs before getting back on the road. But that righteous white man, he swaddled up my babies and laid them back inside the carriage. He kept on with the journey and brought them boys all the way to Rochester, the city where we were supposed to have our next respite. There was a white lady and her three brothers, Quaker people, waiting in Rochester, and they knew what to do with boys like mine.

The Society of Friends brought my boys across the lake to St. Catherines, Ontario, where an entire village awaited, teeming with refugees. The community was built by former slaves, escapees, who had crossed to Canada and would live out their lives under the sparkling banner of freedom. St. Catherines received

my children, wrapped them boys up with the security of same-
ness, found them a nurse of their own, a home.

The boys live now in a sturdy cabin occupied by two families
of colored folk. One of the women in the house ran all the way
from Georgia when she was just about seventeen, like me. She's
been living in St. Catherines long enough now that she married
and has three girls of her own, but she still had room in her
heart for my boys. I see her now, a stern woman, but kind too,
sitting on the stoop, trimming green beans as she watches the
boys run after their makeshift toy. They, my hearty, beautiful
boys, can laugh as they kick that can about, glad simply to be
finished with their lessons for the day. Even with this other family, my boys are still brothers, still free.

The boys started calling that other woman "Mama" soon after
they learned to talk. When I see that portly lady loving them up,
making sure they keep their ears clean, that they wipe the
crumbs from their chins, it brings me a joy I wouldn't have expected. A white pastor comes to see them each month, talks to
them about God and their purpose on this earth.

I pray for my friends, for Dicky, Thelma, and Abel. I hope
one day the Underground will find them, even though I know
that they are too frightened, too old, too unlikely. I pray too for
my boys and what they will do as men. I wonder how they will
react when they come across suffering, because surely people
suffer, even in Canada, even when they're free. I like to imagine
the boys will hear my voice inside their heads. I'll be telling
them go on, boys, go on and walk toward it, go on and trouble
the water. Don't you wait on God to do it for you. You got to
trouble that water, trouble it until there's ripples, until there's
waves. My sons are the Lyons brothers from St. Catherines, and
I hope that mankind will hear them roar.

ACKNOWLEDGMENTS

Trouble the Water is the result of over ten years of research, writing, imagining, and re-imagining. I would like to express my gratitude to the many people who supported me throughout this complex process and helped propel me toward the finish line.

I am deeply grateful to Brooke Warner, Lauren Wise, Crystal Patriarche, and everyone at SparkPress for believing in my manuscript and turning my story into a real book. They also connected with me with the fabulous Caitlin Hamilton Summie, Rick Summie, and Libby Jordan, publicity gurus who have helped spread the word about my book in more ways than I could have imagined.

Special thanks goes to my instructors and friends from Sarah Lawrence whose guidance on this project was consistently insightful, sensitive, encouraging and invaluable. In particular, Myla Goldberg, Brian Morton, Porochista Khakpour, Victoria Redel, and Suzanne Hoover were mentors of the first order. To my classmates, Mira Singer, Regina Mullen, Jacob Ritari, Moses Utomi and Renee Nebens, your feedback continues to play on a loop in my head, and I thank you for your time and generosity.

I would also like to thank those friends of mine who have inspired me with their successes as authors and who have, most graciously, consistently cheered me on in my own endeavors: Julie Buxbaum, Courtney Sheinmel, Amy Blumenfeld, Jonathan Tropper, Laura Dave, Charles Taylor, and Bethany Ball.

A heartfelt thank you goes to my dear friends, family, and beta readers, Aliya Sahai, Robyn Pecarsky, Jenna Myers, Amy

Tunick, Abby Schiffman, Sheila Friedland, Allison Friedland, Julie Mosow, Abby Dorsey, and Eileen Rosner.

Thank you to Seymour Zager for encouraging me and continuing to find the humor in everything, always. My sister I thank for listening and supporting me in more ways than I can count, and for helping me to appreciate the staying power of a line well-said. Thank you to my father who has for forty years happily corrected my grammar. I extend the deepest gratitude possible to my mother who has always known how to push me—just so. She inspires me daily with her kindness, her commitment to self-discipline, her accomplishments, and her tolerance for my incessant chatter. An enormous thank you goes to my loving children for their patience when my writing took time away from them and rooting for me from the bottoms of their hearts. Finally, to Jason, thank you for helping me find more hours in the day, for standing by my side, always, and for believing in this story from the very beginning.

ABOUT THE AUTHOR

credit: Rebecca Weiss Photography

JACQUELINE FRIEDLAND holds a BA from the University of Pennsylvania and a JD from NYU Law School. She practiced as an attorney in New York before returning to school to receive her MFA from Sarah Lawrence College. She lives in New York with her husband, four children, and a tiny dog. This is her first novel.

SELECTED TITLES FROM SPARKPRESS

SparkPress is an independent boutique publisher delivering high-quality, entertaining, and engaging content that enhances readers' lives, with a special focus on female-driven work.
Visit us at www.gosparkpress.com

Hidden, Kelli Clare, $16.95, 978-1-943006-52-6. Desperate after discovering her family murdered, a small-town art teacher runs to England with a handsome stranger in search of safety and answers in this suspenseful, sexy tale of treachery and obsession—perfect for fans of Sandra Brown and Ruth Ware.

The Opposite of Never, Kathy Mehuron, $16.95, 978-1-943006-50-2. Devastated by the loss of their spouses, Georgia and Kenny think that the best times of their lives are long over until they find each other; meanwhile Kenny's teenage stepdaughter, Zelda, and Georgia's friend's son, Spencer, fall in love at first sight—only to fall prey to and suffer opiate addiction together

Girl with a Gun, Kari Bovee, $16.95, 978-1-943006-60-1. When a series of crimes take place soon after fifteen-year-old Annie Oakley joins Buffalo Bill's Wild West Show, including the mysterious death of her Indian assistant, Annie fears someone is out to get her. With the help of a sassy, blue-blooded reporter, Annie sets out to solve the crimes that threaten her good name.

A Dangerous Woman from Nowhere, Kris Radish, $16.95, 978-1-943006-26-7. When her husband is kidnapped by ruthless gold miners, frontier woman Briar Logan is forced to accept the help of an emotionally damaged young man and a famous female horse trainer. On her quest to save her husband, she discovers that adventures of the heart are almost as dangerous as tracking down lawless killers.

The Year of Necessary Lies, Kris Radish. $17, 978-1-94071-651-0. A great-granddaughter discovers her ancestor's secrets—inspirational forays into forbidden love and the Florida Everglades at the turn of the last century.

About SparkPress

SparkPress is an independent, hybrid imprint focused on merging the best of the traditional publishing model with new and innovative strategies. We deliver high-quality, entertaining, and engaging content that enhances readers' lives. We are proud to bring to market a list of *New York Times* best-selling, award-winning, and debut authors who represent a wide array of genres, as well as our established, industry-wide reputation for creative, results-driven success in working with authors. SparkPress, a BookSparks imprint, is a division of SparkPoint Studio LLC.

Learn more at GoSparkPress.com

CPSIA information can be obtained
at www.ICGtesting.com
Printed in the USA
LVHW030023270221
680068LV00001B/3

9 781943 006540